PRAISE FOR
REGARD FOR THE DEAD

"If you love books with a lot of twists and turns, this is the book for you. Tim Savage's book is a must-read for all mystery and detective readers!"

—**J. R. Sharp**, Award-Winning Author of *Feeding the Enemy* and *Breaking from the Enemy*

"*Regard for the Dead* begins innocently enough with typical mystery story scenes, then, with a surprising twist, morphs into the macabre, building an unexpected thesis on death. Timothy Savage builds his characters as likeable, normal kids next door, then thrusts them into dealing with the bizarrely abnormal. Or is it our modern society that is ultimately abnormal? Savage shows that it doesn't always take a superhero to solve a mystery. It's a fun, fast, enjoyable read."

—**Brandon Currence**, Author of *Looking for the Seams*

"Timothy M. Savage brilliantly weaves a supernatural thriller onto the gritty streets of the City of Brotherly Love. *Regard For The Dead* resurrects ancient myth, mixes [in] the ordinary, and with a thought-provoking cast of characters lands the reader on a plane of extraordinary."

—**Mary K. Savarese**, Author of *Tigers Love Bubble Baths & Obsession Perfume (who knew!)*

Regard for the Dead

by Timothy M. Savage

ISBN 978-1-64663-504-7

Published by

 köehlerbooks ™

3705 Shore Drive
Virginia Beach, VA 23455
800-435-4811
www.koehlerbooks.com

REGARD
FOR THE
DEAD

TIMOTHY M. SAVAGE

VIRGINIA BEACH
CAPE CHARLES

1

Monday, May 28
10:36 p.m.

A tall, athletic young man descended the steel staircase from West Philadelphia's elevated Sixtieth Street transit station into a warm spring night, his feet pounding on the stair treads in a galloping rhythm. Dressed in a maroon *St. Joseph University Hawks* track suit and high-end basketball shoes, he sported a finger-thick, gold chain necklace and a diamond stud in each ear. Reaching the sidewalk, he sauntered west along Market Street. A dozen steps down the block, he was brought up short when a low voice rumbled from a deep shadow, "Yo! Jerome! Where do you think you're going?" The young man stopped under one of the few functioning streetlamps on the block when the voice said, "Don't you walk away from me."

"Hey man," Jerome said, spinning around to face the concealed voice. "I'm just in a hurry to get to my Grandma's." His eyes darting from side to side, he searched the blackness of the doorways along the sidewalk, looking for the source of the voice.

"Really? That's great. Be sure to say hi for me, too." The timber of the voice then dropped and demanded, "The time's come. Where's my money?"

"I haven't got it right now, Riggs." The young man stuffed a hand into the pocket of his pants and extracted a small fold of cash. "This is all I got, and I was going to give it to Grandma to pay the light bill."

The voice chuffed. "Huh. Save it for her because that's not gonna do it."

"I'll be able to pay soon. I'm up for the draft. I swear. They say I'm going to go in the first round. I'll probably get a signing bonus."

"You don't seem to understand. I want payment tonight."

"Why?" Jerome asked, wiping a nervous sweat from his brow.

"Because I know some important people are looking for you, and when they find you, there may not be anything left for me."

"Huh? What did I do?" Jerome pleaded.

"Some folks don't like being disrespected in public."

Pointing a finger at his own chest, the young man said, "I didn't do nothing!"

"I kinda feel sorry for you, but not really. I need payment. Now."

"I, well, um," he stammered.

"I'm not going to be the loser in this deal. Give me the chain and rocks. Maybe I can get something for them."

"Come on, man. What are you doing to me? I'll pay you. I promise."

"The diamonds, fool. Hand them over," the concealed voice demanded.

Visibly shaken, Jerome unclasped the heavy gold chain from his neck and removed the diamond studs from his earlobes. "If I bring you cash, can I get these back?" he said, holding them out toward the shadowed source of the voice.

"Just set them down right there. I don't care what happens to your gear. You should've tried a pawn shop if you wanted it back."

Stooping down to set the jewelry on the sidewalk Jerome said, "Here. It's yours. And if anybody asks, tell them I didn't do anything."

"That's none of my business, but you might want to watch your back."

2

Bright sunlight streamed through the soaring masts and endless rigging of the tall ship *Moshulu*, permanently moored at Penn's Landing on the Philadelphia waterfront. It glared off the varnished wood, brass, and white-painted topsides, causing the man ascending the gangway to reflexively shield his eyes. Squinting hard, he paused at the top of the steps and scanned the umbrella-shaded tables distributed around the deck of the century-old ship converted to a restaurant.

The waitress, circulating among the scattered patrons, called out to the new arrival, "Sit wherever you like."

Looking around, he asked, "the bar?" The waitress smiled and pointed the way. "Thanks," he replied and crossed the deck into the deep shade of the bar's awning. Turning to face the entrance, he eased back onto a stool, wiped the perspiration from his forehead with the back of his hand, and resumed observing the gangway and tables.

At the backbar, hunched over a sink full of lemon-smelling soap suds, the muscular red-haired bartender said, "I'll be right with you, sir."

The man replied, "Take your time," and then after a moment of hesitation, snapped around to look more carefully at the bartender.

Raising a finger and pointing at the bartender, the man asked, "Don't I know you?"

The bartender kept his attention on the sink when the man's eyes widened and voice boomed, "Kevin Patrick Maloney!"

Kevin cracked a slight grin when the man said, "How long has it been?"

Without looking up, the bartender replied in a casual tone, "Dunno. Ten or eleven years? Probably that night in eighth grade when your old man caught me with a beer and told me to get the hell out."

The man cracked a wide smile and slapped both hands on the bar top, "I can't believe it's you!"

Finally looking up, the bartender wiped a hand on the tail of his Hawaiian-print uniform shirt and extended it across the bar. "How are you, Mark?"

"Living the dream," he said, gripping Kevin's hand. "What about you?"

"I'm good," Kevin replied, a half grin stretching across his freckled face. Releasing the grip, he returned to drying a cocktail shaker with a towel.

"You know," Mark said as he clapped his hands together, "I always knew I'd find you in a bar one day, but I didn't expect you to be on that side of the wood."

Setting the shaker aside, Kevin shrugged, pulled a pitcher from the sink and toweled it dry. Mark continued, "Where have you been hiding out for the past decade? You just disappeared, and now I find you over-serving people at a Penn's Landing tourist attraction. It's like the *Twilight Zone!*"

"It's a long story," Kevin said.

"I got time. Especially for one of my old school chums."

Kevin's eyes drifted across to the distant Jersey side of the Delaware River. "We moved in kind of a hurry after my brother Michael's accident," he said softly. Looking back at Mark, Kevin said, "My mom was heartbroken after he died, and then dad got a job offer in Virginia Beach." Kevin dropped his gaze to the sink again. "It happened so fast I didn't get to tell anybody. I guess I never thought about how hard it was for the folks we left behind."

"That was a tough time. I'm sorry it went down like that," Mark said.

Kevin was quiet for a moment, then looked up and gestured toward the beer taps with his bar towel, saying, "On me?"

"Yeah, sure. Since you're buying."

While Kevin filled a glass, Mark swiveled around to watch the waitress chatting with customers and clearing tables. She wore a tailored flower-print shirt and khaki shorts that showed off her trim lines. Her hair was pulled off to one side and a fresh hibiscus flower was tucked neatly behind her right ear. Then, startled by the clunk of a heavy glass on the bar behind him, he spun around and returned his attention to Kevin.

Mark tilted his head toward the waitress and said, "What's her story?"

"That's Daisy, and I have no idea. I really need this job, so I'm keeping my curiosity in check."

"Say no more my friend!" Hoisting the beer to eye level, Mark said, "Here's to self-restraint and sobriety!" After a long drink, Mark said, "Ah, that tastes good." Setting the glass down, Mark asked, "So, what brought you back to Philly?"

"Family, I guess," Kevin shrugged while wiping down the bar with his towel. "Mom decided to move back after dad passed. My older brother, Brian, never left."

"I didn't know about your dad." Mark softened his voice. "I'm so sorry. He was one of the good guys."

Kevin nodded and then twisted the towel between his hands. "Thanks."

Mark asked in a brighter voice, "How's your brother? Wasn't he on the Llanerch volunteer squad? He had the red pickup truck with the lights on top and big tires."

Kevin smiled, "Yep. He was always doing something to that jalopy."

"Those were the days," Mark said.

"He's a city firefighter with a daughter and an ex-wife," Kevin said and then added, "In fact, we're sharing an apartment now."

"I was going to ask where you're staying," Mark responded.

"How about your family?" Kevin asked. "Your old man still covering sports for the paper?"

"He's retired. I took over his column after graduating from Penn State."

"Good for both of you! Third generation newspaper man. That's cool."

"It worked out well. I'm not sure why, but the editor still keeps up Dad's press credentials. It's probably for the free tickets. Dad always had the connection on the tickets."

"Nothing wrong with that, especially at the prices they charge these days. How's your mom?"

"Same as ever."

"Is she still volunteering in the school lunchroom?" Kevin asked.

"She'd be lost if she couldn't go in every day. It keeps her young." Mark took another swallow of beer, then asked, "So, how long have you been working here?"

"Not long. I needed money, and it was the first place that offered me a job." Kevin grinned, "The manager said I wouldn't last a full pay period, so I kinda took it as a personal challenge."

The waitress approached the bar and unloaded her tray of empty glasses. She said to Kevin, "Two lights." While Kevin poured the beer, she turned to Mark and asked, "Who are you?"

"Hello, the name's Mark Francini." He extended a hand, but the waitress ignored it. "I'm an old pal of Kevin's."

"I should've known," the waitress sneered.

"What? Why?" Mark stammered.

Immediately after Kevin placed the beer glasses on her tray, she walked away without another word. Kevin said in a hushed voice as they watched her walk away, "Since I'm not expected to last another week, she doesn't feel like she has to be nice to me, and now that includes you, too." Then Kevin said to her back in a louder voice, "Isn't that right, Daisy?"

Daisy continued walking and extended a middle finger behind her back where only Kevin and Mark could see.

"Wow, making friends everywhere I go!" Mark laughed as his eyes locked on a man taking a seat across the deck. "Listen, I'm gonna go talk to that guy who just sat down, but I'll be back to chat some more."

Kevin flipped his bar towel over his shoulder and glanced at the figure slouching low behind a newspaper. "Is he some kind of secret sports informant or something? Because he's doing a bad job of hiding in plain sight."

"Yeah, something like that. He might have something on a kid my dad discovered a few years ago. I told him to meet me here because this is mostly a tourist crowd and nobody would recognize him," Mark commented while looking around. "And until you showed up, nobody here knew me either."

Mark picked up his beer, crossed the deck and sat down across the table from the man behind the newspaper. The conversation was quiet, with the two men leaning in over the table and speaking in hushed tones. As Daisy approached the table, Mark held up one finger and pointed to his beer. Before Daisy could finish another circuit around the occupied tables, the informant disappeared into the men's room. When he came back out, he descended the gangway and merged with the pedestrians strolling between the historic ships along Penn's Landing.

Mark tipped back the remains of his beer and let his gaze wander up into the rigging of the sailing ship's four masts and forest of yardarms. When Daisy returned and set a fresh beer on the table, she asked, "Done with that glass?"

Mark snapped his attention back to deck level and said, "Yes, please, and I'd like to ask you a question, if I may?"

"Sure, but only one. And nothing about a date. I don't date men I meet in bars."

"Fair enough. My wife doesn't let me date women I meet in bars either," Mark joked, but Daisy only forced a smile. "I really want to know where you're from, but since I only get one question, I better make it about my buddy Kevin over there."

"Quick on your feet, aren't you? How do you know Kevin?"

"We went to grade school together," Mark said.

"Is that so? An actual school? With teachers and everything?"

"St. Denis. In Havertown. It's not called that anymore . . ."

"Huh. Really?" she interrupted. "Judging by his math skills, I figured he was a kindergarten dropout."

Mark laughed and continued with his query, "So what was he doing previously, and how long has he been here?"

"That's two questions. I guess you can't count either."

"Easy now," Mark protested. Pausing, he drummed his fingers on the table before saying, "How about you tell me what he was doing before he showed up here."

"Cat herder," she replied.

"Come on, I'm serious," Mark stammered.

"Really, I have no idea, but it probably involved a lot of drinking since he seems to know his way around a bar."

Mark rolled his eyes and said, "I guess I chose poorly."

"That's okay, I'll give you a break. The last bartender, O'Neil, quit after he got his first paycheck. Kevin showed up the next day. We get paid biweekly, and tomorrow is payday."

"You are a wealth of information and insight." Mark grinned while handing her a twenty- dollar bill from his wallet. "Keep the change."

Mark took his fresh beer back to the bar and sat on a stool opposite Kevin. Kevin asked, "Yo, is this story going to make you famous from coast to coast?"

Mark shrugged, "No, but if I dig into it a little more, it might get a little play on the sports networks and other gossip outlets. Mr.

Anonymous said a local basketball player my dad used to cover is skipping out on his college team appointments. Maybe he's banking on this year's NBA draft." Mark jotted a few notes on a pair of bar napkins. He stuffed the first one in his pocket and handed the second to Kevin. "Look, I gotta head back to the office, but that's how you can find me. By the way, if you're free, my wife and I are having a little family cookout Sunday afternoon. You should come by for our big announcement."

Kevin looked at the napkin and smiled. "Is that really your address?"

"Yep."

"I'd love to see the old place, but I'm working."

"So quit after you get paid tomorrow."

"Who told you I get paid tomorrow? Oh, never mind." Kevin said, shaking his head, "Daisy can't keep anything to herself."

"Tell me," Mark said, "if this place has such a hard time keeping bartenders, how long has she been here?"

"Dunno, but long enough that they made her the boss."

3

Kevin cruised his white Jeep Wrangler up Darby Road into the busy neighborhood of Havertown, a bedroom community nine miles west of Philadelphia. Turning west on Colfax Road, Kevin coasted downhill into the Paddock Farms neighborhood. Built in the 1950s boom times, the narrow streets were lined with identical red-brick houses, each with a centered front door and four symmetrically placed windows. A right turn took him up Ashwood Drive toward his destination. Near the north end, the house at 2644 was indistinguishable from the rest, except for neat green trim and an unusual asphalt driveway shared with the house next door.

Kevin idled by the house, searching for parking. Vehicles filled the driveway and the street. Unable to find a space, he continued around the next corner where he tucked the jeep between a driveway and a fire hydrant. After a short pause to straighten his shirt and smooth his wind-blown hair, he tucked a bottle of wine under his arm and walked back to the house.

On the front step, Kevin looked through the screen door. The heavy wood door was open to the unoccupied living room. At the base of the stairs, lying atop a blanket-covered animal carrier, a thick tabby cat stared back at him. "Cat people," Kevin mumbled to himself just as the sounds of cheering and clapping attracted his attention. Kevin reversed direction and walked back to the driveway, then turned left toward the back yard.

A group of people on the elevated wooden deck crowded around a petite blonde woman. The men in the group hung back, exchanging comments and grins while the women in the middle hugged and giggled. Kevin arrived at the bottom step just as an older man looked his way from the merriment. He was nearly bald, with deep lines in his tanned face. The unlit stump of a cigar jutted from the corner of his mouth.

"Is that you, Maloney?" came the voice as rough as gravel.

"Hello Mr. Francini. It's good to see you," Kevin replied.

"Mark said you might come. I didn't believe him, but here you are, and just in time." Kevin ascended the four steps to the deck where the elder Francini put his arm behind him and guided him forward toward a group of older women. "Hey Betty, guess who it is? It's Marky's old pal, Baloney Maloney!"

A short woman with white hair in a curly perm broke away and stutter-stepped her way to Kevin. "Mario! Why do you have to call him that? Sometimes I can't believe what comes out of your mouth." The woman took Kevin's hands and pulled him closer. "Kevin, my dear, you haven't changed a bit! Well, except for the muscles," Mark's mother said as she squeezed him in a hug so firm it made Kevin gasp.

"It very nice to see you, Mrs. Francini,"

"We'll have to have you over for dinner sometime so we can catch up," Mario said.

"That would be great." Kevin replied.

"Have you met our beautiful daughter-in-law, Jessica?" Betty asked as she dragged Kevin by the hand toward the center of the crowd. "Jessica, I have someone here I want you to meet!"

Mark was standing behind Jessica and side-stepped around her to intercept his enthusiastic mother. "Thanks, Ma. I'll take over,"

Mark said to his mother before turning to Kevin. "I was afraid you wouldn't make it." They shook hands and Kevin offered the bottle of wine. Mark took the bottle and set it on a nearby table loaded with food. "You didn't quit your job, did you?"

"No. We have two bartenders on the weekend. Daisy said I could come in late as long as I promised to stay until the next pay day."

"Well, you just missed the big announcement, so I better get you caught up."

Tapping Jessica on the shoulder, Mark introduced them. "Jess, this is my friend I told you about." She smiled and they made an awkward attempt at shaking hands in the crowd.

Jessica said, "It's so nice to meet you."

"We just announced that Jess is pregnant," Mark continued. "Due in December!"

"That's great. Congratulations!" Kevin said. "You too, Mark. Your kid is going to have it made. Fantastic parents, all this family, and this beautiful house to grow up in."

"Thank you," Jessica gushed. "Did you know the family who lived here, too?"

"I guess Mark didn't tell you?" Kevin asked, glancing at Mark.

"Tell me what?"

"This is . . . was my house," Kevin gestured toward the house with a thumb.

Jessica glanced over at Mark with a half-dismayed look. "He only told me it belonged to a family he knew from school."

Just then she was distracted by Betty tapping on her shoulder, and Mark quickly led Kevin away from the crowd of women toward a large tub filled with beverages.

"Thanks for making me look bad," Mark grinned.

"That's what happens when you bring home strays," Kevin replied. Mark laughed and pulled two beers from the ice and offered one to Kevin.

"No thanks," he said. "I gotta work after this. Speaking of work, any news on your missing basketball player?"

"It got more interesting today. I'm going on a little field trip tomorrow if you want to ride along. Hopefully, I'll hit pay dirt."

"Nah, I'd just be in the way."

"No, no. We can catch up. It'll be great."

While they discussed Mark's project, a stout man with a short-buzzed haircut stepped in behind them. He placed a thick hand on Mark's shoulder. "Congratulations, Mark. How about giving me that beer if your friend isn't going to drink it."

"Thanks, Skip. Drink up." Mark handed the beer to him and then introduced Kevin. The two strangers shook hands. "Skip is Jessica's very protective big brother."

Without missing a beat, Skip slipped his arm around Kevin's shoulder and pulled him aside and asked in a loud voice, "So when did you become acquainted with the scoundrel who violated my sister?"

"First grade."

"Wait a minute!" Mark interjected. Becoming very serious, he asked, "What do you mean violated your sister?"

Skip and Kevin began laughing, and Skip said, "You just got done telling everybody how she's pregnant and all. It was you, right?"

"I did it and I'm damn proud of it," Mark declared, breaking into a smile. Reaching into the tub and pulling out another beer, he declared, "Now that you guys have collectively laughed at me, I will wait on other, more agreeable guests," and walked toward an older couple standing by themselves.

"He's a good guy, even if he did compromise my sister's virtue," Skip joked. "Maybe a little sensitive, but all around okay." Kevin nodded in agreement. Skip released Kevin's shoulder and leaned against the deck rail. "So what's your life story in twenty words or less?"

"St. Denis with Mark. First to eighth grade. Moved to Virginia Beach when my dad got transferred. Just moved back . . . "

"Stop right there," Skip interrupted. "That's twenty." Then in a quiet voice, "You didn't mention the service. Marine, right?"

"Navy Corpsman, until last month."

"That's like a medic with the Devil Dogs, right?"

Kevin nodded, and Skip continued. Squinting at Kevin, he said in a hushed voice, "Not old enough for the late unpleasantness in Iraq. Afghanistan right?"

"Camp Pendleton with six months in Helmand. How did you figure all that out?"

"You look like a California Hollywood Marine," Skip pronounced. "With the Reef sandals, fancy sunglasses in your pocket, and the San Diego surfer-dude shirt."

Kevin rolled his eyes at the remark. Skip held up his hand. "Now cut me some slack, buddy, I was at Al Asad and Bagram with an A-10 squadron. Now, I'm a crew chief on Guard C-130s. Been over and back more times than I can count with bonus stops at Kandahar and Camp Leatherneck. I've seen a thousand guys just like you on my bird." Skip leaned his head toward Kevin's ear. "I get it. You're trying to lay low. Don't have to say a word, 'cause I get tired of the looks and endless questions about the wars, too."

Kevin stepped back a little and examined the man before him. "Yeah, I see it now." Kevin said with a grin. "Senior NCO. Master Sergeant. Right?"

Skip touched his finger to the tip of his nose, and then took another pull from his beer. "Got a job lined up? I'm happy to see about openings at the helicopter plant out in Coatsville."

"I'm going to get on with the fire service, and in the meantime, I'm tending bar down at the Bongo Deck restaurant on the *Moshulu*."

"Sounds like a good plan for a man of action like yourself." Shaking Kevin's hand, Skip said, "Good luck and if you need anything, just call. Mark's got my number."

"Thanks," Kevin replied as Mark returned to the tub of beverages.

"Are you done with Kevin, or are you going to harass him like you do me?" Mark asked.

"Kevin's a good guy," Skip said, gesturing toward Kevin with his beer bottle. "Me and him are simpatico. Me and you, on the other hand, are in-laws."

4

"**C**ome on little brother, you don't want to be late for the exam."
Kevin opened his eyes to the shadows and dim daylight of his brother's Center City basement apartment. Groaning, he pushed himself to an upright position on the sagging couch where he'd been sleeping. "I'm up," he murmured.

"Good thing 'cause the bucket of ice water was coming next."

"No need for that." Kevin yawned as he fumbled for the lamp next to the couch. The switch made a squeaking click as it rotated, and a split second later the room was cast in yellow light. Kevin squinted his eyes at the hulking form of his brother close behind him and mumbled, "Would you really douse me in ice water?"

"Dad did it to me. I'd do it for you," Brian said, now clearly visible standing behind the couch. Brian was dressed in a pair of tartan plaid boxers and gray T-shirt, holding an empty bucket. Kevin stretched and yawned again while Brian turned to the kitchenette and began manipulating a coffee maker.

Kevin asked, "Did it really help you on the civil service exam, like dad claimed?"

"You were too young to understand, but I was pretty hung over. Dad's *Ernest Shackleton Therapy* cleared my head in a hurry. I would've slept the day away if he hadn't done it." After some clinking of crockery in the dark kitchenette, Brian turned around and held out a steaming mug. "Drink this. It's good firehouse coffee. Guaranteed to keep you jittery for twelve hours." Kevin took the mug as Brian said, "Those are some nice lines on your face from my very corduroy couch."

"Yeah, thanks. I've been working on it for hours," Kevin replied, rubbing his face with his free hand.

"Still wearing yesterday's clothes is also a nice touch. This has all the makings of a good story. Is it suitable for sharing?"

Kevin braced his elbows on his knees, held the mug with two hands and let the steam run up his face. He inhaled the strong smell of coffee and took a tentative sip, followed by a full swallow before answering Brian. "It's not all that interesting."

"You talk. I'll let you know when it's boring," Brian directed.

"Remember that guy I told you about from the old neighborhood?"

"You mean Skid Mark?" Brian snickered.

"That's him. He asked me if I would help find some missing college basketball player named Jerome Lawrence."

"Really? That kid's supposed to be a big deal at St. Joseph's. Hometown hero and all that," Brian remarked.

Kevin took another drink before continuing his story. "This is all hush-hush stuff I guess, so don't tell anybody at the firehouse. Jerome was supposed to be going to team meetings and physical therapy appointments, even though school is out, but he hasn't showed up in a week. Anyway, I agreed to go on what Mark called a stake-out of his grandmother's house. I thought we would be in a car, just taking turns watching for him. Turns out, we're walking around his grandmother's block, talking to everybody in West Philly until two in the morning."

"That's pretty bold," Brian laughed. "Did you find Jerome?"

"Nope, but we found some people who knew him."

"I'll bet you found some real characters, too."

"You can say that again," Kevin said. "One shadowy dude claimed Jerome still owed him money, and then a couple of other guys said they saw him the previous night." Kevin swallowed more coffee before continuing. "According to them, Jerome was wandering down the street like he was lost and shied away from anybody who tried to talk to him. They also said he was wearing rags that didn't fit and no shoes."

"I guess Jerome isn't really missing," Brian observed. "It sounds more like he doesn't want to be found."

"Well, that's kinda what I thought. Maybe he went on a bender or got mixed up in something. Whatever it is," Kevin shrugged, "Mark wants to dig deeper."

Brian scratched at his day-old beard and took a sip of his own coffee. "People don't change that much for no reason."

"That's what we said." Letting out a yawn, Kevin continued, "I have this evening off, so we're going back again today. Maybe we'll have better luck."

"Maybe. But in the meantime, take a shower and get your brain in gear. You need to score well on this test. Veteran status doesn't carry the weight it used to."

Brian turned on the light in the kitchenette and began rummaging in a cabinet while Kevin shuffled toward the bathroom. Brian called over his shoulder, "I'll have some good brain food for you when you get done cleaning up."

Kevin paused at the door to the bathroom and turned to Brian. "It's not enough that you sound just like Dad, but now you're doing Mom quotes, too?"

5

Mark and Kevin exited the Southeastern Pennsylvania Transit Authority's Market-Frankford train at the Sixtieth Street Station in West Philadelphia. They descended the southwest steps of the elevated steel and glass platform and exited the station on the corner of Market and Sixtieth Streets. A steady flow of passengers moved through the entrances. There were some conversations between travelers, but the majority silently ignored each other as evening vehicle traffic passed with occasional honks and squealing brakes.

The street level businesses were barricaded behind metal shutters that were locked down for the night, except for one small convenience store. The lights were on and a neon sign flashed *OPEN*. Between the dark store fronts, the steps of boarded-over doorways were occupied by idle men in groups of twos and threes chatting with each other and the occasional passers-by. Before long, all of them were watching the two out-of-place men newly arrived on the corner.

"Welcome to the neighborhood," Kevin said.

"Let's see if we can make some friends," Mark declared, pulling a couple of photos of Jerome Lawrence from his back pocket. He handed one to Kevin, along with a small flashlight. "The flashlights were a good idea," he complimented Kevin.

"Like the boy Scouts say," Kevin replied, "be prepared." After surveying the surroundings, he asked, "Where do we start?"

"Let's try the high traffic areas here at the platform, then maybe east and west along Market and North and South on Sixtieth."

"Got it," Kevin replied.

The two men split up and began by showing the photo to people descending the stairways from the train platform. "Can you help find this missing man?" Kevin asked over and over. Most of them just shook their heads or replied with a quick "No."

Across the street, Mark got similar responses.

After a while, Mark walked over to Kevin. "We aren't making any headway here. I think we need to go for the folks who aren't moving. These people are reflexively ignoring us because they have somewhere to go."

"Agreed. We could be handing out dollar bills and they would still say no. We did better with the folks on their front porches and the kids on the corners."

Mark led the way east on Market Street. They attracted sideways glances and pointing fingers, but Mark appeared not to notice. Instead, he adopted a charming smile and began quizzing everyone they met. Some people they questioned appeared suspicious of the two, wanting to know why they were looking for Jerome. Mark naturally explained that he was a reporter for the paper, and Jerome was part of a story he was writing.

The change of direction brought more discussions, but no more information than before. By the time Mark and Kevin crossed the street and worked west, the sun was below the horizon and darkness was falling.

The search led them back across Sixtieth Street and farther west on Market Street. A handful of people suggested they might have seen the face in the picture, but none of them offered anything concrete. After covering three more blocks with even less success, the pair reversed course again and walked back to the center of their search area.

The full moon was becoming visible over the buildings. Its light washed the neighborhood in pale white, interrupted by deep shadows. Turning right at the intersection where they started, Mark and Kevin walked a block south on the west side of Sixtieth. There they encountered an old man sitting in the doorway of a boarded-up discount store. The dim illumination revealed a bent aluminum cane lying across his lap and a foot wrapped in dirty bandages.

Mark grimaced and looked away from the old man. "What is that stench? Rotten meat?" Mark asked Kevin in a whisper.

"Something like that," Kevin replied in a steady voice as he approached the old man and stooped down to his eye level. "Pardon me, sir, we are trying to locate someone. I was wondering if you could help us?"

"I'll tell you what I know if you fellas got a cigarette."

"I'm afraid neither of us smoke, but if you have any information that can help us, we'll get you some smokes. What kind do you like?"

"When I was a young man, I liked the Camels. They used to give us those. Nowadays, I just take what I can get."

"Do you live around here?"

"Here, there." He gestured all around with a gnarled hand. Kevin followed where he pointed with his eyes. "I know what goes on here. This neighborhood is full of all kinds a people and I know most of them."

"What's your name?" Kevin asked the man.

"They call me Mister Willy."

"Mister Willy, my name is Kevin, and I really need to know where I can find this young man. Do you know him?" Kevin held the photo out for the old man to examine. Mr. Willy took it in his left hand and held it at arm's length. "Here, let me put some light on it so you can see it better." Kevin turned on his flashlight and pointed the beam at the face in the photo.

Mister Willy's eyes widened, and he drew in a rasping breath and said, "I know this one." Mark and Kevin glanced at each other as Mister Willy continued. "His Grandma lives over that way there. His momma took off and nobody knows where she went. But this boy was something! I seen him every day going to school from the time he was old enough to walk until he was big. Bigger than me."

Mark whispered behind Kevin, "This is good."

Mister Willy took a few labored breaths and then continued. "Most of them children were skipping school and running with gangs. Naw, no not this one. Some time back I didn't see him come by no more. I didn't know what happened to him; maybe he took off after his momma or he grew up and went away." Mister Willy stopped and loudly coughed several times before catching his breath. "Didn't see him for long time, until yesterday. He come up the street. But he didn't look right. Like he was a baby again."

"What do you mean?" Kevin asked.

"His face was all round. Child-like. He was missing the diamond in his ear, and he didn't have much hair. Just like a baby. I tried talking to him, but he didn't do nothing but grunt and try to get away from me. He ran across the street, but then just stood there looking at me. He kind of backed around the corner by that doorway there, like he was hiding. Then I didn't see him no more. Just gone. I dunno where he went." Mister Willy was quite animated while he told the story, but became winded and tired after a few minutes. When another coughing fit subsided, he repeated his initial request, "Sure you boys don't got any cigarettes?"

"Tell you what Mister Willy, we'll go get you some smokes. While we are doing that, can we call somebody for you? That bandage on your foot doesn't look too good."

"I won't go to no hospital again. It don't hurt me none, except when I walk on it too long."

Kevin turned to Mark and pointed down the street to the flashing neon sign. "Let's go get a pack for this gentleman." Kevin stood up and said to Mister Willy, "We'll be back in a minute."

Walking back the direction they came, he said to Mark, "I want to get something for his foot while we're there. That wound is probably festering under that mess. Something tells me this shop doesn't take plastic. How much cash have you got?"

"I've got a ten," Mark answered.

"If I forgo lunch, I can put in another five."

"That's generous of you, but that doesn't buy much these days," Mark observed.

"Well, let's see what we can get."

At the shop near the platform, the cashier gave them a nearly finished roll of packing tape and they bought a pack of Camels, a butane lighter, two bottles of water, a Hershey bar and two faded 76ers T-shirts from the window display.

Returning to Mister Willy's doorway, they found him holding a yellow cat in his lap and stroking its back. When the cat saw Kevin and Mark, it bolted across the street and ran half the way down the block, where it disappeared into a dark shadow.

"Alright, Mister Willy. We got a pack of Camels and some stuff to make a new bandage. Can we do that?"

"You going to let me have the whole pack if I let you look at my foot?"

"Since neither of us smoke, I don't think that will be a problem," Mark chuckled.

"I want to lay you back so I can take a quick look." Kevin reclined Mister Willy as far as he could and said, "Just relax." Kevin laid the back of his hand on Mister Willy's forehead for a moment. "What's your birthday?" he asked while timing the pulse in Mister Willy's wrist.

"December 12, 1943. Why'd you want to know that?" he replied.

"Just finding out how old you are and making sure you're oriented," Kevin answered. Then turning to Mark, Kevin said, "I need some light on his foot." Mark clicked on his flashlight and Kevin pointed to where he wanted illumination. "Mister Willy, do you know what day of the week it is?" Kevin quizzed while he wrapped his hand in the plastic shopping bag like a mitten before pulling up the pant leg to expose the affected foot.

"It's Tuesday. I know because the garbage truck's been around."

"That's right," Kevin said while removing the filthy wraps from around the foot. "Now tell me how you feel. What's your number-one health problem?"

"I been better. I can't walk too far 'cause I get dizzy and tired."

Kevin continued to remove bandages and when he got to the bottom, there was a gauze pad that was saturated with yellow ooze. "Mister Willy, I'm going to wash this foot off and put on some clean dressings, but you need to go to the hospital and get this looked at by a doctor. It's infected and you're probably running a fever."

"I don't wanna go back. They're gonna take my Camels and lock me away," the old man pleaded. Kevin shook his head. He picked up the pack of cigarettes and held them in front of Mister Willy. Kevin looked into his eyes, but Mister Willy's eyes followed the cigarettes.

"You are going to lose this foot if you don't go. After you finish the smokes, promise me you will go to the hospital."

"Okay, I'll go, but not until I'm done with the Camels."

Mark ripped the T-shirts into strips while Kevin washed the wound. Kevin then wrapped the wound and secured the dressing with the plastic tape.

"When was the last time you ate?" Kevin asked. Mister Willy shook his head. "Been a little bit, huh?" Kevin said and held up the chocolate and a bottle of water. "I want you to eat this. And then drink all the water." He opened the candy bar and water bottle and set them next to the bent cane. Mister Willy snatched them up and nibbled on the chocolate and sipped at the water. When he was halfway done with the bar, and water, Kevin gave him the pack of cigarettes and lighter. "Remember your promise."

"I'll do it."

"That cat seems to like you," Kevin observed.

"He's my new friend. I call him Morris, like the cat on TV, except for the kink in his tail. He's been staying with me at night."

"I don't think Morris cares for me, but I'm not a cat person anyway," Kevin joked.

"One more thing, Mister Willy," Mark added, "don't feed any chocolate to the cat. It's poison to them."

"I didn't know that. Thank you, fellas. Since you been so good to me, I'm gonna help you a little more. That boy Jerome is right over by that door. Just like last night." Kevin and Mark's eyes followed Mister Willy's crooked finger and saw a large figure crouched in the shadows cast by a medical office building. Even from a distance, his face looked pale and puffy. He was dressed in a dark, hooded coat and torn trousers. His feet were bare and dirty. His hands were stuffed into the pockets of the coat.

"Thanks, Mister Willy," Kevin said as they stood up. "Be well." Turning to Mark, he commanded, "Let's move."

Walking away from the dark doorway, Mark said, "That guy definitely resembles Jerome. We'll know for sure when he stands up. It's hard to hide when you are six foot seven."

"I don't feel like a foot race tonight, so let's work our way over there in a casual, indirect fashion," Kevin suggested. "If he doesn't want to be found, he might get skittish and bolt."

"He's barefoot, how fast can he run?" Mark asked.

"Depends on why he's hiding," Kevin said.

"Good point," Mark acknowledged.

"Let's go a little ways back toward the train station before we cross. Maybe just watch him for a little bit."

The two men walked north without looking back toward the man in the shadow. They stopped when they came to the end of the block. Kevin glanced back and said, "I can see his head just jutting out into the moonlight; he's looking back the other way."

"Let's get across the street," Mark said, leading the way and stopping behind a corner.

Kevin eased around the corner and said, "Still there. If he keys in to our movements, he'll probably take off as soon as he sees us closing in. We'll move slow but be ready for a chase."

"Okay, I'm ready to run," Mark grimaced, "but you do understand I just report on sports. I don't actually do them."

"You don't say!" Kevin teased. "I'll lead the way, and you catch up when you can." Kevin emerged inch by inch into view, but their quarry did not react. Kevin shuffled forward, remaining close to the wall. Mark followed Kevin's lead, taking a long time to close the half block to the dark figure. When Kevin was at the corner of the medical office building, the man rose to his full height, tensed and ready to run.

"That's him," Mark confirmed in a whisper.

Advancing a few steps closer, Kevin addressed the figure in a calm voice, "Jerome. Jerome." The face offered no recognition of the name and his eyes began to dart from Kevin to the street. On Kevin's next step closer, the man flinched. "Go!" Kevin whispered, and then sprinted toward his target. Kevin caught the man's wrist but couldn't get a grip before the giant bounded away down the street. Kevin stumbled, regained his balance, and gave pursuit. The man ran south to the next corner before jinking right onto Chestnut Street. Near the far end of the block, he ducked into a dark alley on the north side of the street. The man was faster than Kevin despite his bare feet, but Kevin closed the gap when the man crashed into something in the darkness.

Kevin followed the giant between the buildings, dodging around toppled trash cans and a discarded couch before emerging into a clear area almost within reach of Jerome. A tall fence shrouded in weeds and sapling trees stood between them and the next lot. With massive strides, Jerome powered up to the barrier and easily vaulted over the top. Kevin followed, but fell behind again when confronted with the fence. He leaped halfway up and scrabbled over the top of the rough, rusty chain-link. Dropping back to the ground on the other side, he paused and looked around. His shirt and pants were torn from rolling over the top of the fence. He patted himself under the torn clothes and then fished the flashlight from his pocket.

The flashlight's beam revealed knee-high, scrubby weeds growing between a half-dozen rows of rusting cars and trampled plant stems betraying Jerome's path. Kevin took two steps forward, but then paused at the sound of Mark impacting the fence. "Come on slowpoke," Kevin whispered. The fence rattled and creaked for a few more seconds, until Mark flopped onto the ground. He grunted as he pushed himself back to his feet. "I'm here," Mark panted, "but I'm not ever doing that again."

"Ditto. When you've caught your breath, get your light and follow me."

"Sure," Mark puffed. Bent at the waist with his hands on his knees, Mark slowly took several deep breaths and let out a long exhale. "Let's go."

Kevin moved down the path of broken stalks and flattened weeds, slowly playing his flashlight from side to side until he stopped and held up his hand. He swept the area ahead and to the left with his light again. "There," Kevin whispered. "Some kind of animal looking back at us. See the bright yellow eyes shining between the two white cars?"

"Yeah. Probably an alley cat," Mark agreed, hurrying to catch up. "Keep going."

Kevin led them another dozen steps farther into the dark, their lights casting shadows against the walls of the surrounding buildings. Somewhere off to the right, something crunched on loose gravel. Mark swept his light over the area and caught another glimpse of reflective eyes looking back at them.

"Another cat?" Mark asked.

Kevin pointed his light at the same area. Lowering his voice, Kevin said, "Our guy is over there, too. See the shadow on the cars?" From his position to Mark's right, Kevin's light revealed a shadow in the shape of a hooded human head and shoulders. The shadow's hood moved, twisting back and forth. With each movement the eyes glinted in the beams of light.

Kevin crept forward, cutting between rows of dead cars while Mark circled left and closed at a wider angle.

"Jerome, we're here to help you. We just want to talk," pleaded Kevin, but the shadow continued to creep away toward the back wall at the east end of the lot. Mark and Kevin converged slowly, picking their way through the cars, weeds, and trash. When there was nowhere left to go, the hooded figure hunched down and disappeared behind a car ten feet in front of Kevin and Mark. Kevin called out "Go!" and they quickly converged on the spot, but there was no one there.

"What the hell? Kevin blurted. Standing at the spot they last saw the shadow, he pointed his light at the ground and said, "No Jerome, and all we got left is a pile of his ratty clothes."

"What's going on here?" Mark asked with a slight quiver in his voice.

"I don't know but disappearing like that is a pretty good trick."

"I'd call it downright spooky," Mark replied.

"Don't be so dramatic." Kevin said as he directed his flashlight beam over the wall and fencing. "There's got to be an explanation."

Mark aimed his light at the ground between the car and the wall. "Kevin, I don't see where he could've gone." Returning his beam to where Jerome was last seen, Mark said, "Look, the clothes pile is moving."

Kevin picked up a broken car antenna and used it to lift a layer off the pile. Peeling back a discarded coat revealed a cat, its eyes glowing in the beam of Mark's flashlight. As Mark inched forward, it leaped out of the pile toward him with a screech. Mark flinched, causing him to drop his flashlight and stumble backwards while the cat disappeared into the darkness.

"That looked like the same cat we saw with Mister Willy!" Kevin declared.

"If you say so. I'm afraid I didn't get a good look at it," Mark groaned, while picking up his flashlight.

Kevin began searching for the cat under the cars in the immediate area but stopped after working down one row. "We're going to have to come back when it's light if we hope to find any answers here."

"There are too many places to hide," Mark agreed.

"This is getting out of hand," Kevin sighed. "Why are we doing this again?"

6

Wednesday, June 6
2:53 p.m.

Kevin leaned against the Bongo Deck bar with his back toward the empty seating area. Daisy sat on a bar stool and watched as he rubbed the palm of his right hand with a bar towel. The skin was pale and peeling. She asked, "Is that hand okay? Did you wreck your bicycle coming to work?"

"No, no. It's nothing. I got something on it the other night. It dried up the skin. See?" Kevin said, turning around with his hand held out.

Daisy wrinkled her nose. "Is it contagious?"

"I don't think so. My brother said it could be a chemical exposure."

"Does it hurt?"

"No. If enough skin comes off it might, but for now I don't feel a thing."

"Good, so there is no reason you can't get back to work stocking the bar," Daisy scolded.

"No ma'am. Thanks for your compassion and concern," Kevin replied with a smile.

He unloaded several liquor boxes and put the contents in cabinets under the bar. When the boxes were empty, he walked them to the dumpster in the northwest corner of the parking area. Climbing the gangway up to the Bongo Deck, Kevin was greeted by Mark, who was sitting on a stool at the end of the bar.

"Yo, Kevin!"

"Well, if isn't Mark the bounty hunter. Meeting another secret informant today?"

"Actually, I came to see you."

"How thoughtful," Kevin replied as he washed his hands at the sink behind the bar.

"It seems I don't have your phone number, and nobody was answering the phone at your brother's place. Any chance I could get your cell number?" Mark inquired.

"You could," Kevin replied with a laugh, "if I had a cell phone."

"Really? You don't have a cell phone? Everybody has a cell phone," Mark insisted.

"Not me," Kevin declared.

"Why not?"

"Do you know how much money an entry-level bartender makes?" Kevin asked.

Mark laughed, "You got a point there. I guess if you aren't going to give me a phone number, you better give me a beer," he joked while pointing at the taps.

Kevin poured a beer and placed it on a napkin. "So how about that guy Jerome, huh?"

Mark took a long drink of beer before answering. "That chase was crazy, but you were great! Where did you get those moves? I've never seen anything like that—except on TV."

"If you did something besides watch TV, you could have run him down, too."

"You're right," Mark agreed. "I could use a little more exercise and a few less of these," Mark hoisted the beer in a toast, "but you were awesome." He took another sip before continuing. "When do you want to go again? We need to get a better look at the vacant lot and maybe figure out where he went."

"The way he slipped away was pretty slick. I'm sure we missed something while we were stumbling around in the dark. Yeah, we can go look again. Make it the Sixtieth Street station at six thirty tomorrow morning." Kevin suggested.

"Why so early?" Mark questioned with a sour look.

"We'll have good low angle light, and plenty of time before work," Kevin said, his index finger tapping the bar.

"Fair enough. I need to get closure so I can print something."

"I don't know what we are going to find, but I'm betting it won't be closure."

"You're probably right," Mark agreed. Then he gestured toward Kevin's right hand. "What is up with the hand? Some kind of over-use injury?"

"Funny," Kevin scoffed. "I think it happened when I got hold of your buddy Jerome. Maybe some kind of chemical on his clothes that made my skin react."

"Maybe I should start a list?"

"What for?" Kevin asked.

"You know, for future reference. This story seems to have a lot of weird elements."

"Like the reflective eyes?" Kevin asked.

"Yeah, things like that. I didn't think human eyes did that."

"Not like animals," Kevin said. "The reflection must have been the cat, but they sure had a human quality to their movement."

"I'll add that to the list, too."

"Alright. Tomorrow at six thirty?" Kevin confirmed.

"I'll be there. I'll check with Jerome's grandmother to see if she's spotted him again."

"Maybe we'll find Mister Willy again," Kevin speculated. "He seems to have a handle on Jerome, but then again, I hope he's in the hospital looking after his foot."

"We'll find out tomorrow."

7

Thursday, June 7
6:39 a.m.

M ark and Kevin walked south on Sixtieth Street, retracing the chase from two nights before. All along the street, sounds of voices and cooking could be heard through the open windows of the row houses. A few people were emerging into the cool air. "This street looks a lot different in the light of day," Mark observed as the sun climbed over the buildings and into the scattered clouds of the morning sky.

"Sure does," agreed Kevin. Scanning the surroundings as they continued down the block, he remarked, "No sign of Mister Willy."

"That's too bad. Maybe we'll find him later."

After turning right on Chestnut, they paused at the Liberty Bible Church, a large gray building wedged in between the row houses. "This is it. In here," Kevin said and led the way into the alley on the east side of the church. Arriving in an open space behind the church, Kevin surveyed the area where they had climbed over the fence. "This is a rusty mess. I'm surprised anybody could make it over."

"I thought that the other night," Mark lamented.

"We need to check the perimeter of the lot," Kevin directed. "There has to be an open gate or gap. Maybe where the fence meets a wall or turns a corner."

"It's going to have to be done from the inside. The fence cuts off of this group of houses," Mark said, pointing to the back yards to the east. "I doubt somebody cooking breakfast wants to see us out their kitchen window."

"Good enough. I'll go over the top and check inside. You go around the block and look at the outside where you can get a view."

Kevin sized up the fence as Mark walked to the left along the fence and out through an alley that ran from the back of the church to Millick Street.

Scaling the fence in daylight, Kevin avoided the sharp metal and thorny plants previously concealed by darkness. He dropped to the other side and scanned the junkyard. It was roughly rectangular with seven rows of junked cars, each having eight to ten hulks. An aisle about an arm-span wide separated the rows. Knee deep weeds covered all the space not occupied by cars. Kevin examined the fence in the southwest corner and then turned north toward Ludlow Street. The fence was rusty but intact. Most of the west perimeter was overgrown with weeds and trees just like the section behind the church. Dodging around debris and a stack of shipping pallets he converged with Mark standing outside the fence on the north side, bordering Ludlow Street.

"I didn't see any easy ways in or out," reported Kevin.

"Same here," agreed Mark. "This north section is new fence. It runs down to those buildings on the east side and stops at their back wall."

"Jerome probably led us in here knowing he could easily get in and out but we couldn't. Very clever," Kevin concluded. "I think we better take another look at the spot where he ditched us, just to be sure."

Mark eyed the fence. "If there's no easy way in or out, then I guess I'm doing the belly flop again," he said with dread in his voice.

"Not necessarily," Kevin reassured him. Looking around the junkyard, Kevin gestured to the stack of pallets leaning against the inside of the fence. "We can use those to make a more dignified entry."

Kevin walked back to the pallets and selected a few that seemed to be in good shape. He leaned one against the inside of the fence. "Stand back, I'm going to chuck these over for a make-shift ladder." Kevin hefted a couple pallets up and over the top. "Stand them up next to the corner post. You can use them like a ladder."

Mark arranged the pallets and then climbed up. He swung his legs over and dropped to the ground. "Okay, what's next?" he asked.

"We go back to where we came in the first time." Kevin led the way through the dew-covered weeds around the west perimeter. When they arrived at the back of the church, Kevin looked along the path they had just walked. "Look at the weeds and saplings. The sun angle reveals where they are knocked down." Kevin spread his hand over the trail of trampled plants. "See that?"

"Got it," Mark commented. Kevin gestured to the other track leading away from where they stood.

"See this?" Kevin asked.

"That must be Jerome's path from the other night, eh? That's cool, Kevin. Where did you learn that?"

"Scouts." Kevin answered quickly as he started searching along Jerome's path.

"Was that the same Scouts we were in together, in third grade? Because I don't remember anything like tracking in my Cub Scout book," Mark commented. "About the only thing I learned was how to tie a Windsor neck-tie knot."

"I'm surprised you learned that much," Kevin chuckled. There were five rows of cars between them and the east wall of the junkyard. They walked along the trail in the weeds until it split. "You go the same way you did the other night," Kevin said. "Call out if you find anything unusual." They pressed forward between the junked cars, eyes on the ground.

"Would you consider a bowling trophy from 1986 a noteworthy find?" Mark asked, holding up a broken piece of engraved wood.

"No more so than a hub cap from an old Chevy," Kevin replied as he frisbee-tossed the old piece of metal in Mark's direction. Mark flinched when the hub cap clanked off the side of a faded green Ford Maverick. Approaching the east wall, they examined the area where Jerome disappeared. "There's nothing here," Kevin commented.

"Where's all of Jerome's clothes the cat was hiding under?" Mark asked. "They should still be here."

"Unless he came back, they have to be around somewhere. Keep looking," Kevin said casually as he walked off toward the southeast corner. Mark stepped forward to the exact spot where they saw Jerome before he disappeared. He turned around and surveyed the paths he and Kevin had traveled. Mark scratched his chin and squatted down for a lower angle perspective.

"I don't get it, Kevin. There's no way out." Standing up again, Mark asked, "Where did he go?"

"I think the answer to your question is over here," Kevin said, pointing at the ground on the other side of a rusted blue Chevy step-side truck.

Mark walked over to Kevin and asked, "What is it?"

"You tell me."

"Is it him?" Mark asked as he surveyed the soiled feet protruding from a stand of weeds.

"I think we'll leave the final determination to the professionals, but judging by the size of those dogs, I'd say it is." Kevin crouched down next to the feet and examined the remains. "You better call the police and tell them there's a body and there may be some kind of hazmat, too. Judging by the shrunken skin, whatever I got on my hand is probably all over him."

"Okay." Mark replied, retrieving his phone from a pocket.

Kevin pulled back the weeds for a better look. "His entire body is dried up," he observed.

Mark grimaced at the sight of the disfigured body and said in a weak voice, "This is not how I expected Jerome's story to end."

Kevin replied, "I seriously doubt this is the end of the story."

• • •

The sun didn't travel a whisker across the sky before police officers arrived on Ludlow Street. First was a white patrol car, with the Philadelphia Police shield over diagonal blue and gold stripes on the door. Kevin and Mark stood inside the fence next to a chained and padlocked gate, waving to the officers.

The first officer out of the car walked to the outside of the locked gate. "Bring the cutters," he instructed the second officer, who was just emerging from the car. "Please stand over there and place your hands on the fence where we can see them," the first officer instructed Kevin and Mark. They did as they were told while the second officer retrieved long-handled bolt cutters from the trunk and proceeded to cut the padlock. He removed the chain and pushed on the gate, but the hinges were frozen with rust and wouldn't budge. Then both officers leaned into the gate, but still couldn't make it move.

"Sir, would it help if we pull from the inside?" Kevin asked.

"I guess we'll be here all day if you don't," the first officer relented. "Come on."

With Kevin and Mark pulling from the inside and officers pushing from the outside, the gate finally gave way with a piercing squeal. Mark breathed a sigh of relief, "I was beginning to think I'd have to climb out."

"I really don't need to see that again," laughed Kevin.

"You called it in?" the first officer asked, looking at Kevin.

"I made the call," Mark offered as they walked out to the sidewalk and moving where the first officer pointed along the fence.

"I'm Officer Parker. I'm going to pat you down one at a time and Officer Ingles there is going to be watching, so don't do anything you're not told to do. You understand what I'm saying?" Kevin and Mark nodded in reply. "Now, don't either of you move unless I tell you."

"Got it," Kevin replied.

"Face the fence please," Officer Ingles said to Mark and placed his hand on his back, pressing slightly between the shoulder blades.

"Well, this is a first for me," Mark commented as he and Kevin turned to lean against the fence and spread their arms and legs.

Standing behind Kevin, the first officer asked, "What's your name?"

"Kevin."

"Okay, Kevin, do you have anything you want to tell me about before I start? Weapons or contraband? Anything sharp that might stick me?"

"I got a wallet and a pocketknife."

"I'm going to remove them from your pockets," Officer Parker said as he patted down Kevin, and then fished the wallet and knife from his pockets. He tossed them to the ground out of arm's reach and said, "Okay, your turn." The two officers changed places silently, and Ingles pressed his hand lightly on Kevin's back. Parker then spoke to Mark, "Same thing for you. Anything I should know about?"

"Just my phone and wallet."

Officer Parker repeated the search and extracted Mark's phone and wallet. When he was finished, he collected Kevin's wallet and knife and examined their ID cards. "Kevin Patrick Maloney. You go by Kevin or Pat?"

"Kevin."

"California, eh? You're a long way from home. What brings you to Philly?"

"I grew up here. Just moved back."

"Is that so? I had an uncle in California. He was a piece of work. Anyway, you got a local address and phone number?" Parker asked while he jotted notes in a small notebook. Kevin gave him the information for his brother's apartment, and the Bongo Deck. Parker then looked at Mark. "You related to Mario?"

"He's my old man. You know him?"

Parker replied, "Yeah. Used to do lots of stadium duty," as he handed back the wallets, knife, and phone.

"Okay, Mr. Francini. You two don't exactly fit the demographics of this neighborhood. What's going on?" the officer asked in a matter-of-fact tone.

"Kevin and I were trying to locate a guy named Jerome Lawrence, and we think we found him. Over there."

"Why were you looking for him?"

"Like my dad, I'm a reporter for the paper, and a few days ago I got a tip that St. Joseph's University star basketball player wasn't showing up for his physical therapy appointments. That player turned out to be Jerome. His grandmother lives a couple streets over, so I decided to ask around and maybe get a scoop on the story. Two nights back, we found a person who we thought was Jerome. We tried to talk to him, but he bolted. Then he gave us the slip when he jumped the fence into this junkyard. We came this morning to see if we could find out where he went. As it turns out, he's probably still here."

Officer Parker listened intently to the story, then asked Kevin. "Okay. Would you like to explain how you came to be inside the fence today and where you found the deceased?" Kevin continued the story, describing their path around the outside and pointed to where they crossed the fence on the pallets. "You two sit tight for a minute while I consult with my partner," Parker said as he and Ingles stepped toward the car. Kevin watched him and Officer Ingles exchange a few inaudible words. Parker nodded his head and spoke into his radio microphone, requesting a homicide detective and crime scene technicians.

"A'right pal, let's see what you found," Parker said.

Kevin and Mark led the officers to the southeast corner of the junkyard, where the body was obscured by the high grass and derelict cars. Officer Parker looked back at the street, and up at the surrounding buildings. "Only a couple of boarded up windows overlooking the lot. It's no wonder nobody saw it."

"What do you make of the shriveled look of the body?" Kevin asked Parker. "Could he have been exposed to something?"

"No idea. I'll leave that to the experts."

Parker led the way back to the gate and indicated that Mark and Kevin should wait by the police car. A moment later, two more officers arrived in a van with the same shield and stripes markings.

The additional officers checked in with Parker and began taping off the area. After a long delay two detectives in an unmarked car arrived, closely followed by a sport utility vehicle marked *Crime Scene Investigator*. The detectives huddled with Parker and Ingles and then walked into the junkyard. A second van marked *Medical Examiner* arrived, choking the narrow side street with city vehicles.

Officer Ingles turned and addressed Kevin and Mark, "You two stay put. The detective will probably want to talk to you."

"We'll be right here," Kevin nodded, and he and Mark leaned against the car. They watched the slow-moving activity around them.

"I wonder how long they are going to keep us." Mark said.

"I haven't got a clue," Kevin replied. "But I'm sure there will be more questions before the day is over."

"I'm going to have to submit a story at some point." Mark lamented. "What in the heck am I going to write? This is not normal stuff for a sports reporter."

It wasn't long before people began gathering from the surrounding buildings, attracted by the police cars. The street slowly filled with chatter from clusters of spectators. They were focused on the police and ignored Kevin and Mark standing near the trunk of the cruiser. After a while, two young men with dreadlocks and dressed in similar basketball jerseys and sagging trousers strolled past Kevin and Mark. They leaned against the front of the police car and watched the proceedings. Kevin elbowed Mark and silently gestured toward them. Mark nodded his head and they watched in silence.

The technicians took photos and examined the body. After a short discussion with the detective and uniformed officers, the body was zipped into a black bag and lifted onto a gurney. Four people were required to carry the body and gurney across the lot to the gate. From the size of the bag on the gurney, it was obvious the body was very tall.

The two young men at the other end of the police car glanced at each other. "Damn, is that him?" one asked the other.

"He had it coming. That shiver clown won't be coppin' feels around here no more," he scoffed while watching the technicians load the body in the van. When the doors to the van were closed, they walked off.

"Did you catch that?" Mark whispered to Kevin.

"Yeah. Those two seemed to know the score," he replied.

"Can we get out of here?" Mark commented quietly. "It's coming up on ten o'clock. My feet are killing me, and I need to find some breakfast."

"Sounds like a good idea," Kevin agreed just as Officer Ingles walked in their direction.

"The detectives are pretty busy, so they'll get back to you. You're free to go," Igles said.

"Thanks," Kevin replied with a wave, and headed in the direction of Sixtieth Street.

"Do you think we need to tell the police what we heard?" Mark asked.

"I suspect we'll get a chance to talk real soon."

8

Thursday, June 7
10:33 a.m.

Mark and Kevin exited the underground portion of the Market-Frankfort train line at the corner of Eighth and Market Streets in Philadelphia's Center City. "I hope you don't mind *The King*. It's the closest thing to my cubicle," Mark gestured across Market Street to the building that housed the newspaper's offices.

"If it's on your tab, Burger King is fine with me," Kevin replied, following him into the restaurant located next to the station stairway. The two men placed orders at the counter, collected their food, and sat at a table by the street window.

"That was something, wasn't it?" Mark asked.

"Yeah, it was. Never done anything like that before," Kevin agreed.

"I wonder how long it will be 'til the police are dragging us in for questioning?" Mark asked.

"I don't think it will be more than a day or two," Kevin replied before redirecting the question. "Got a good lawyer?"

"You don't think it will come to that, do you?" Mark asked.

"If it does, I won't hesitate to blame it all on you," Kevin stated with a straight face.

"Thanks buddy," Mark replied with a smirk. "So, what do you think about Jerome?"

"The whole thing is fishy," Kevin declared. "I mean, what do we really know? The runner vanishes in front of two witnesses, then a body is found nearby thirty-six hours later." Mark nodded in agreement while Kevin took a sip of orange juice. "The easy conclusion is the body and the runner are the same person."

"Indeed. Especially since they are similar in appearance," Mark agreed.

"Right, but the timing doesn't fit," Kevin asserted. "It takes more than a day for the the grass and weeds to grow that high. The corpse was four or five days old at least. It should be bloated or stink to high heaven, but it wasn't. There weren't even any flies."

"Which makes it unlikely that the person we found was the runner," Mark conceded. "But judging by the look on your face, there is more to it, right?"

"Yeah, it's the runner's feet," Kevin said in a softer tone. "They were not the feet of someone who was happily wearing thousand-dollar basketball shoes a week ago."

"What makes you say that?"

"Only a person who has well-calloused feet, or couldn't feel pain, can run like that over city streets and through a junkyard."

"So, the runner is some homeless guy who never wears shoes and happens to be really tall and looks a lot like Jerome?" Mark asked in disbelief. "I don't buy it."

"Now that you say it, I don't either," Kevin concluded.

"What about the pain part?" Mark offered.

"He could have been on drugs or something."

"Okay," Mark exhaled. "Let's try again. We got this big guy hopped up on drugs, who runs away and dies in a junkyard, only to be found a couple days later dried up like a raisin."

"Yes, but I didn't see any blood," Kevin stated flatly.

"What?" Mark asked.

"His feet should've been all chewed up, but they weren't. Drugs or adrenaline mask the pain, but they don't stop bleeding. There should have been a blood trail or footprints."

"You're right," Mark sighed.

"And the feet on the body would show the wear and tear, too."

"Yeah, but they were just shriveled up like he'd been plucked out of the bathtub," Mark said before letting his head sag into his hands like a deflated balloon. He sat there with his head down for an uncomfortably long time until Kevin spoke up.

"How about those two guys leaning on the cop car? I'm wondering what they know."

"They seemed a little surprised, so I doubt they were directly involved."

"Yeah, but they weren't shocked either. It sounded like there was some common knowledge about Jerome going around the neighborhood."

"Yes, it did," Mark agreed. "I don't know what they meant by calling him a *shiver clown*, but from the context, I think Jerome was persona non grata."

"I've never heard that little term of endearment before either, but it looks like somebody was fed up and went for a permanent solution."

"A really permanent solution," Mark sighed.

"On a slightly different tack, can you turn this into a newspaper story?" Kevin asked.

"It won't make sense, it doesn't have an ending, and the editor will probably fire me, but I can write a story," Mark lamented. "I could suggest the body is Jerome, but not say a word about how he got there until we get the medical examiner's report."

"Good idea. Look, I need to get home and take a nap before work. Let me know if you find out anything new," Kevin said as he cleared the trash from the table.

"You bet," Mark said in a resigned voice.

"It's been fun, and thanks for breakfast."

Mark's eyebrow shot up and he chuckled. "You got a weird idea of fun, pal. But really, thank you. I'd still be knocking on doors without your help."

9

Monday, June 11
11:52 a.m.

Daisy sat on a bar stool reading a newspaper while Kevin set up for opening. "Looks like it's going to be a slow week," she announced from her perch. "The forecast is calling for cool and overcast."

"You're probably right, but tourists can be full of surprises," Kevin countered, as a breeze swirled through the bar, scattering a stack of napkins.

"Speaking of surprises, here's your friend's article on Jerome Lawrence. It doesn't mention a cause of death. Was he holding back?"

"No, not really," Kevin said as he collected the stray napkins. "Whatever the cause, it wasn't obvious to us. I'm sure the medical examiner will release more information soon. Frankly, I was a little surprised they could get an ID so quick. The body wasn't exactly in perfect condition."

"The article said he was identified by family."

"Must have been his grandmother. His father was never in the picture, and his mother is long gone." Kevin walked around behind Daisy and looked at the photo that accompanied the article. It was the same photo Kevin and Mark had used in West Philly. "He could've made it big," Kevin lamented.

"The Lord has a plan for all of us. Even lost souls like you," Daisy declared.

"Thanks, but why do you care?" Kevin said with a smirk.

"You've lasted almost a month. I guess you're growing on me," she said as she folded up the newspaper. At the same moment, a man and a woman walked up the gangway to the Bongo Deck. They paused at the entrance and swept the empty deck with their eyes. Turning at the sound of footfalls on the gangway, Daisy faced the new arrivals.

The man was dark haired, average height with a thick build. He wore a sport coat over an open-collared shirt. Bushy black and gray chest hair and a heavy gold chain were visible at the neck of his shirt. The woman was the same height as the man and wore a gray jacket over her blouse that matched her slacks. Obviously younger than her partner and physically fit, she wore her dark blonde hair pulled back in a neat ponytail. Her light brown eyes seemed to take in every detail.

"Not tourists," Daisy whispered just loud enough for Kevin to hear. She stood up from her seat and smiled as the two approached, while Kevin took a slight step back. "I'm Daisy. Welcome to the Bongo Deck."

"Pardon the interruption. We're looking for Kevin Maloney." The man's baritone voice resonated in the space but lacked inflection.

"Sure, who might you be?" Daisy asked with a smile.

"Detective Powers. This is Detective Johnston," as they each handed Daisy a business card.

Daisy studied the cards in detail and then looked back at the two visitors. "Nice to meet you. I'm the manager of the Bongo Deck, and this gentleman is my bartender, Kevin." Daisy handed the business cards over to Kevin, who took them in his left hand while simultaneously slipping his right hand in his trouser pocket. "Kevin, have you run afoul of the law and failed to inform me?" Daisy asked in a bright voice.

"It appears I have," Kevin replied playfully.

The two detectives looked at each other before Powers resumed the conversation, "We're tying up some loose ends regarding Jerome Lawrence. Would you mind answering a few questions?"

"Happy to help." Kevin gestured to the bar stools and said, "Make yourselves comfortable. Can I get you a refreshment?" The two shook their heads and remained on their feet. Daisy retreated to the kitchen stairway and disappeared from sight.

After a pause, the previously silent Johnston asked, "How long did you know Jerome Lawrence?"

"I never met the man. In fact, I never even heard of him until Mark asked me to help track him down a week ago," Kevin replied.

"You mean Mark Francini?" she clarified.

"Yeah. Sorry, I just assumed you've already been to see him."

"Why did Mr. Francini want to find him?" Johnston followed up, her voice subtly lower.

"He's a sportswriter, and he was trying to run down a hot tip. Did he tell you about that?"

"He mentioned it," Johnston affirmed while looking directly in Kevin's eyes.

Kevin shifted on his feet but didn't avert his eyes. "Um, I'm not an expert on college basketball, so I may have the details mixed up, but I guess Jerome played for St. Joseph's. I understand he was about to skip out on the rest of his education to enter the NBA draft. Mark thought if he could get the scoop, he'd be the first to publish the details. I've heard being first is important to reporters. Anyway, he was still the first to come out with the the story, just not like he thought."

"How do you know Mr. Francini?" Powers asked.

"I've known Mark since first grade, but I lived out of state for a while. He and I only recently reconnected." Powers made some notes, and Johnston picked up the questioning.

"Tell us about your attempts to find Jerome."

"Sure," Kevin nodded. "The first time we walked around the area where his grandmother lives. Everybody there knew who he was but weren't able to help much. The next time, we worked around the Sixtieth Street station, showing a photo and asking for information. We weren't having much success, but then we got lucky with an old guy called Mister Willy. He knew all about him, had even seen him walking the street, dressed in shabby clothes, and no shoes. We happened to be talking to Mister Willy when Jerome plopped down right across the street. That was when we tried to talk to him, and he bolted. We followed him into the junkyard on Ludlow but lost him in the dark. The next time we went looking, we found the body. That was Jerome, right?"

"The deceased has been positively identified," Powers stated flatly.

"How about the cause of death? That poor kid looked more like a strip of beef jerky than a person."

"The cause has not yet been determined," Powers answered and then resumed questioning. "I'm a little curious. Most people are rattled the first time they come across a corpse. The patrol officers said you were pretty matter of fact about it. This isn't a first for you, is it?"

"No, it's not." Kevin's voice trailed off, but his eyes met Johnston's, who was watching him attentively.

"You served as a corpsman in the Navy," Powers stated.

Kevin's eyes flicked back to Powers. "Yes," Kevin answered stiffly. "Checked me out?"

"We do our homework before an interview, Mr. Maloney," Powers said and then turned to Johnston, "Got enough?" She nodded and Powers continued. "Is this the best place to find you if we have more questions?"

"I will be right here."

"Thank you for your time," Powers said as the two detectives turned to the gangway. Before descending, Johnston half turned and looked at Kevin once more with a softer expression.

"If you think of something else we should know—anything—please call the number on the card," she said. Kevin gave a left-handed half salute with the business card in between his fingers but remained quiet. He watched the two walk down the gangway before he let out a big breath. Daisy immediately reappeared from the stairway.

"Were you listening in?" Kevin asked.

"Yes." Daisy said bluntly as she resumed her seat. "I hope this doesn't complicate getting on with the fire service," Daisy commented.

"I can't say for sure, but I don't think so."

"That's good, because the sooner you get a job, the less I have police snooping around. It's bad for business."

10

Wednesday, June 13
12:03 p.m.

Low clouds scudded across the Delaware River, and wind swirled under the Bongo Deck's awning, rippling the canvas and rattling the frame. Daisy was standing behind the bar, pouring a soda from the fountain, when she looked up to see Mark step off the gangway, hair tousled and sport coat flapping in the breeze. "You again," she sighed. "Does your wife know how much time you spend in bars?"

"She knows the score, so it's fine."

"You keep telling yourself that, sugar."

"Where's the barkeep?" Mark changed the subject.

"He's late. Did you keep him out until all hours of the morning chasing vagrants again?"

Mark opened his eyes wide and pointed a finger at himself. "Me?"

Daisy gave him a glaring look as she went about opening the bar for the day.

"Not this time. I accept no responsibility or blame for your employee's tardiness."

"You sound just like a politician. Maybe you should run for office," Daisy suggested before she went to the far end of the bar. Mark didn't respond, other than to shake his head and crack a smile.

For a long time, they both sat at the bar, trying to read a section the newspaper, but the swirls of wind across the ship kept folding the pages. When Kevin finally came up the gangway, Daisy threw a bar towel at him, followed by a nasty scowl.

"I'm sorry I'm late. The SEPTA train was delayed." Kevin walked behind the bar and washed his hands in the sink.

"Why were you on a SEPTA train?" Mark asked in a surprised voice. "You only live a few blocks from here. Did somebody steal your bike or something?"

"I went to check on Mister Willy, but he was nowhere to be found. One of the shop keepers said he was around yesterday, still limping, and with the yellow cat trailing him around." Kevin reported. "I hope he's at the hospital. That infection could kill him."

"I never figured you'd care that much," Mark said.

"Shows how little you know," Daisy chimed in from her end of the bar. "Kevin's probably a very caring and compassionate individual."

"Uh, thank you?" Kevin said to Daisy. Turning to Mark, he said, "What in the wide world of sports brought you back today?"

"Mrs. Lawrence called me about an hour ago. She said she saw Jerome's ghost this morning, walking down her street."

"I don't think she saw a ghost. My money says there's somebody who resembles her grandson, and he's as solid as you and me," Kevin replied.

"That's what I told her, but there's more. I have the medical examiner's unofficial findings."

"And?" Kevin asked.

"He died on or about June first. Shot once in the hand and again in the neck."

"I can't say that I'm surprised," Kevin said.

"My contact in city hall said the police are treating it as a homicide, maybe gang related," Mark stated.

"And whoever pulled the trigger probably dumped the body in the junkyard," Kevin concluded.

"Could this be a case of mistaken identity? Maybe the shooter was after this look-alike guy but found Jerome instead?" Mark theorized.

"That's as plausible as anything else," Kevin agreed. "But I think it has more to do with the shiver clown thing we heard the Bobbsey Twins talking about. They seemed pretty sure Jerome was the target."

"I think you're right. I'll look into it," Mark agreed. "No matter what, this story is a long way from finished."

11

B rian stepped down through the front door into the little basement apartment. He dropped a duffle bag by the doorway before extracting a bottle of beer from the refrigerator. He popped off the cap and sank into the near end of the couch. At the other end, Kevin looked up from the TV news broadcast and said, "Good morning, bro, looks like you had a long shift with that big fire."

"The fire was just another abandoned building, but a dismembered senior citizen on the elevated section of the SEPTA tracks was a little out of the ordinary."

"I only caught a little bit on the news. That was Engine 57, too?"

"Yeah, and a crazy story. Nobody knew about the guy on the tracks. It was a cat lover that saw Tigger stuck up on a girder and called it in."

"Stupid cats." Kevin grumbled.

"We had to bring in some equipment to get up to the inaccessible part of the track. Blocked off Market Street traffic for a couple of hours. When we finally got up there to get the cat, we found the remains of some poor guy who'd been hit by the train." Brian stopped to sip from the beer before continuing. "Of course, the cat didn't want to come down. It was a mean cat, too. Hissing and what not. It tried to scratch Shelby's face, and he finally just wrapped it up in his coat so it wouldn't bite him."

"It wasn't yellow, was it? With a kink in the tail?"

"If you mean a light orange color with stripes, then yeah, I guess so. I didn't really see the tail because it got away before the animal control folks showed up. It was fighting mad and didn't want to be handled."

"Did you see the old guy?"

"We all did. It wasn't your typical recovery operation, you know? Parts were all over the place. On top of that, I think the old fella was half mummified before he died."

"What do you mean mummified?"

"It kinda looked like all the liquid was sucked outta his body."

"That's how Jerome looked, too." Kevin was quiet for a moment, staring nowhere in particular. "Did he have a big bandage or wound on his foot?"

"Yeah, he did. Well, what was left of it."

"Could have been Mister Willy." Kevin said in quieting voice. "Poor old guy. I wonder how he got to Sixty Third?"

"Rode the train like any normal person?"

"He lived on the street, so I doubt he had any money. If he did, he wasn't spending it on a train ride."

"What's this Mister Willy to you?" Brian asked.

"He's the guy who helped me and Mark find Jerome. He had a cat that followed him around everywhere. It hissed and ran away every time someone else got near it. I looked at his foot and put a new dressing on it and told him to get to a hospital, or he was going to lose it. I was out at the Sixtieth Street station yesterday to see if he was okay."

"He lost his foot alright, but I guess it doesn't matter now."

"Poor old guy. All he wanted was a pack of Camels," Kevin said in a soft tone. Brian tipped back the rest of his beer and stood up from the couch.

"I'm going to hit the hay. I'm off all day tomorrow if you want to do something."

"Yeah, but I gotta work."

"No problem. I was thinking we could go fishing for a couple hours and then I'll drop you off in plenty of time."

"I haven't been fishing since Dad was alive. He and I went out on a head boat a couple times from Virginia Beach." Kevin nodded his head for a moment and then said, "That sounds great."

12

M ark sat at a window table in the Burger King, drinking a cup of coffee and leafing through the sports pages of several newspapers. As he folded up one paper and began leafing through the next, the door opened and Kevin entered, followed shortly by Brian, who held the door for an elderly lady going out. Mark looked up as they approached the table and said, "Miss me so much you had to come for breakfast?"

"Not exactly," Kevin snickered in reply.

Mark smiled in recognition of Kevin's brother as they sat down. "And you brought company." Mark and Brian shook hands as he said, "Brian, it's been a long time. Good to see you."

"It has been a while," Brian replied.

"Did you hear about the guy on the SEPTA track?" Kevin asked in a rising voice.

"The way you said that makes it sounds like the beginning of an off-color joke, but I know it's not a joke because I'm in the news business."

"So you saw it on TV like the rest of Philadelphia?" Brian asked.

"Yes."

"That was Mister Willy, and probably the cat," Kevin declared.

"I didn't hear about the cat. What's with the cat?" Mark asked.

"I thought you just said you were in the news business," Kevin teased.

"I am, but a cat on railroad tracks isn't my department," Mark responded.

"They rescued a cat," Kevin directed a thumb toward his brother, "but it ran away before animal control got there."

"I guess cats really do have nine lives. It's too bad Mister Willy didn't have a few more to spare," Mark said, as he turned his gaze to the people walking by outside the window. After a moment he refocused on Kevin and Brian. "Poor guy. I doubt anybody is going to claim his remains, I wonder what happens to Mister Willy now?"

Brian described the process in a monotone voice that came across as more of a rumble. "The medical examiner's office will hold on to the remains for three months or until someone claims them. They may also do an examination to determine cause of death."

"How long will that take?" Kevin asked.

"They pretty much move at the speed of government, so unless the courts or the police ask for expedited service, I wouldn't expect them to unzip the bag before next month."

"Maybe the cops will ID him before then and find the next of kin." Mark suggested.

"Maybe, but he's pretty low priority unless they suspect a crime."

"Well, I guess we wait for some kind of resolution. Thanks for the insight, Brian, but you aren't exactly a ray of sunshine," Mark teased. "We can work on that, if you want."

"As I said, speed of government."

"Kinda like waiting for the city to post scores for the civil service exam," Kevin commented. "I'm going to have to find a real job before long."

"Might as well start looking now. They'll call you as soon as you start doing something else," Brian joked as he stood up from the table. "Okay, little brother. Let's grab a biscuit and go see if we can catch some fish before you go to work."

"That sounds like more fun than going to my cube and reviewing the baseball disabled list," Mark lamented.

"Yeah, it does, doesn't it?" Brian asked with a grin.

"Good to see you again, Brian. Remember to catch and release!" Mark said, remaining in his seat, rubbing his temples as he watched the brothers leave. After a lengthy stare out the window, he offered one of his newspapers to another patron and exited to the street.

13

The new summer sun glared off the wood deck of the old sailing ship as Kevin went about the business of preparing for the day. He squinted against the light and sweat glistened on his face. His shirt was damp already, even though he'd just started working.

"Tomorrow is supposed to be a little cooler," Daisy reported as she emerged from the restaurant stairway.

"I know you're trying to be optimistic, but it isn't working." Kevin wiped a bar towel across his brow between words.

"Make sure everything is ready, and then we'll hide in the AC until we see somebody."

"You are a hell of a boss," Kevin remarked.

With their tasks completed, they walked down to the air-conditioned restaurant where they took up a place near a window that overlooked the Bongo Deck gangway.

While chatting with Daisy and some of the kitchen staff, Kevin watched a vehicle park near the bottom of the Bongo Deck gangway. Mark got out and climbed the steps. "It's just Mark, I'll go take care of him. Stay here and chill."

"Don't mind if I do," Daisy replied casually.

At the top of the gangway steps, Kevin greeted Mark. "Long time, amigo."

"Almost two weeks," Mark replied.

"Where have you been hiding?"

"Jess and I took a few days off. Took a little trip out to Ohio to see the Pro Football Hall of Fame."

"How was that?" Kevin asked.

"More my pop's style, but we had a good time." Settling onto a stool at the shaded end of the bar, Mark said, "Mr. Bartender, how about a cold beer?"

Kevin nodded at Mark's request and filled a glass from the tap. "What brings you around? Got another secret meeting or did you just miss me?" Kevin asked, setting the glass on the bar with a thunk.

"I got a little info that I thought you might find interesting."

"Oh yeah? The last round of *interesting* got me a funny skin rash and a visit from the law enforcement community. What's this one good for?"

"Nothing so dramatic as that. It's really a follow up."

"Alright, hit me," Kevin said.

"According to a coworker's contact, Mister Willy, also known as William Howard Woods, had three hands."

"As in fifteen fingers?"

"Yes. The medical examiner pulled an extra hand from the body bag."

"No kidding! So where did the extra hand come from, or how did it get in the bag? Whose is it?"

"Slow down there, Buckaroo. The hand was pretty damaged, but it was big. Very big. Like Jerome Lawrence basketball player big."

"Holy crap! Do you think when the firefighters were cleaning up, they just put all the parts in a bag without counting?" Kevin paused, took a breath and then said, "That's a strange thing to find on the train tracks."

"I should say so. Strange enough to bring the detectives around again."

"I suspect you're right." Kevin scratched his chin. "Maybe it was the barefoot Jerome look-alike? Could he be involved?"

"That is the obvious choice, but how did his hand get mixed in with the remains of Mister Willy? And where's the rest of him?" Mark asked before taking a sip of his beer. "This is going to launch an investigation at the medical examiner's office, and fire department, too."

"What a mess. This whole thing gets weirder all the time." Kevin paused in silence before saying, "What if the hand is actually Jerome's."

"I seriously doubt somebody stole the hand off a dead body in the medical examiner's office and put it on the railroad tracks, conveniently located such that the fire department would find it when they rescue a cat and simultaneously find Mister Willy," Mark rejected.

"I guess they'll be doing some more testing, huh?" Kevin added.

Mark held up his beer in a toast, "Here's to more tests leading to more questions!"

14

Kevin sat at the little kitchen table opposite his mother in her small South Philadelphia apartment. A television on the far side of the room was making noise in the background. Mrs. Maloney was petite with a full head of permed silver hair. Her wardrobe consisted of a housecoat over a dressing gown and slippers. A pair of purple-framed reading glasses were perpetually perched on the end of her nose. As she scooped instant coffee into a mug of hot water and stirred it slowly, she said, "Honey, are you sure I can't make something for you? You're looking a little thin. Maybe we can fatten you up a bit."

"That's okay, Mom. I get plenty to eat with Brian's firehouse cooking, and they feed me at work, too."

"Well, you can stop in anytime, and I'll fix you a good meal. I worry about you boys. That's my job, you know," she declared before sipping from her mug.

"And I appreciate it, too," Kevin replied. His gaze drifted from his mother to his right hand. It had color again, but it was still peeling like a sunburn. He folded his hands together and said, "I do have a question for you. A kind of serious thing."

"I'm here for you no matter what. That is my job, too."

"I know. I know." Kevin looked up from his hand and glanced at the TV. The program's host was introducing a new topic for discussion among the women clustered around a fancy table. After watching for a moment, Kevin turned to his mother. "It's about when people pass away. And the ways people prepare for it. And react. You know?"

Mrs. Maloney exhaled, and a half grin curved her lips, "Honey, I know we've had our share of tragedy, what with your brother Michael's accident and your father passing, but don't worry. I'm not going anywhere any time soon. Before the cancer took your father, we did all the planning for the both of us. The details are worked out. Brian has a folder with all the papers and a key to the safety deposit box. You don't have to worry about a thing."

"That's good mom. I was wondering about that, but that's not it."

"Oh," she said. "Is there somebody else you're worried about?"

"Well, yeah. I guess so. There was this old guy I met when I was helping Mark Francini research a story. You remember Mark, right?"

Mrs. Maloney nodded, "Sure I do."

Kevin paused to look out the window of the little third floor apartment. Clouds drifted by, occasionally dimming the bright sunlight. Looking back to his mother, Kevin said, "He went by the name Mister Willy. He wasn't important to anybody, as far as I could tell, and I think he lived on the street out near Cobbs Creek. You see, it's just that he shouldn't be dead, but he is, and the way it all happened keeps playing over and over in my mind."

"I'm not sure I understand. Are you alright?" she asked. She gestured to the TV with her coffee cup. "Those old hens keep talking about this Trauma Disorder. You're not having bad dreams about the war, are you?"

"It's called PTSD mom, and I'm fine. Really. It is just the way Mister Willy got killed. The circumstances were so unusual, and I can't seem to let it go."

"Listen, honey, sometimes our feelings don't seem to match the situation. Like when your father passed. I was heartbroken and sad, but after all the cancer treatments and the inevitability of losing him, I felt the weight of the world lifted from my shoulders. It was very confusing to be happy and sad all at once. What helped me most was talking about it. You gotta let all the emotions out. Don't keep them bottled up inside. I found that I could be all torn up about something, but as soon as I said the words to somebody, it didn't seem so serious anymore."

"I guess I can see what you're saying."

"I want you to know I'm here for you, but sometimes you need the help of somebody trained in these things."

"Mom, I don't really want to go talk to some VA shrink," Kevin groaned.

"I was actually thinking your Uncle Matthew would be a good one to talk to about this."

"I didn't think of him. I guess I just thought of him as the relative who showed up for holiday dinners. He was the bringer of fancy boxed candies and funny kids' jokes."

"He's done a lot of grief counseling. He used to be the archbishop's go-to priest for that kind of thing."

"He seemed ancient when I was a kid, how old is he now?"

"Oh, come on now. He's eighty. That's not so old."

"Sorry," Kevin chuckled. "The last time I saw him was Easter dinner in eighth grade before we moved. Is he still teaching at the seminary?"

"I don't think he will ever leave St. Charles. He loves it there," she said, getting up from the table. She shuffled over to the counter and collected a pencil and a small black notebook from a drawer. Flipping through the pages, she finally put her finger on a name and copied the information onto a scrap of paper. Handing it to Kevin, she said, "Uncle Matthew would love to hear from you."

15

Kevin steered the open-top jeep into the driveway of St. Charles Seminary. He coasted to a stop at the security booth, where he leaned across the empty passenger seat toward the guard and said, "I have an appointment with Father O'Conner." The guard nodded his head and raised the gate to let Kevin drive onto the property. The complex of soaring towers and columned granite buildings occupied a ridge fronting Wynnewood Road. The grounds swept down a gentle hill across acres of manicured lawn to Lancaster Avenue. The perimeter was ringed with an iron fence and perfectly trimmed, impenetrable shrubbery. Kevin drove through the beautiful grounds, breathing in the scent of flowers and fresh-cut grass. Turning around the west end of the main complex, he parallel parked along the curb near the door of the faculty offices. He made his way through the doors and into the heart of the building.

In contrast to the exterior of the building, Father Matthew O'Conner's office wasn't an expansive space. There was just enough room for a desk, file cabinet, two chairs, and dark wood, floor-to-ceiling shelves. The shelves were filled with a cluttered collection of books. Stuffed into the empty spaces were magazines and other reading materials. A crucifix hung above the door. The only light came from the half-shaded window and a desk lamp. Father Matthew O'Conner was sitting motionless in the desk chair facing the window when Kevin knocked on the frame of the open door.

"Come," the old priest's voice rumbled, as his stationary limbs came to life and pivoted the chair toward the door. He was dressed in a black cassock with a Roman collar. His head was mostly bald except for a thin fringe of gray hair around the sides and back, and his skin sagged at the cheeks and chin.

On seeing Kevin, his eyes widened, and a smile turned up the corners of his drooping mouth. "Come in here, young man," the priest said.

When Kevin stepped into the office, his uncle slowly pushed himself up out of the chair. He was half a head taller than Kevin, despite a hunch in his back, and his clothes hung loosely from boney shoulders. Stepping around the desk, he extended his wrinkled hands and wrapped Kevin in a hug.

"I thought you might not recognize me," Kevin offered.

"Well, I haven't seen you in ages, but nobody else comes to see me unless they are wearing one of these," he said, pointed to his collar. "And even a half-blind old man like me can clearly see you are not." They both chuckled. The priest returned to his chair and gestured to the other chair. Kevin sat and looked around at the office. Once they were both seated, the old man continued, "Your mother says you've moved back into the city. Are you settling in well after the Navy showed you the world?"

"I'm not sure about seeing the world, but everything's alright. I'm staying with Brian for now—until I land a good job and can get a place of my own."

"What kind of work are you seeking?"

"I just took the civil service exam, and I hope to get on with the fire department. For now, I'm working at the Bongo Deck on the *Moshulu*, down on Penn's Landing."

"Very good. Remind me, the *Moshulu* is a four-masted sailing ship, yes?" Kevin nodded in response. "Did you know *Moshulu* is a Seneca word that roughly translates to *one who fears nothing*?"

"I didn't," Kevin admitted.

"Is Commodore Dewey's flagship still there? That's a fine piece of history."

"The *U.S.S. Olympia* is still there."

"Maybe we'll go see it one day before it dissolves into its most elemental state and disappears into the Delaware River." The priest then squinted at Kevin and said, "How is your mother getting along? She is always in my prayers."

"I think being close to family helps. Brian or I go over to see her as often as we can and sometimes take her to Mass. Her spirit seems brighter than when I last saw her in Virginia."

"That's good. She is a strong woman, and much has been asked of her," Matthew observed. He looked into Kevin's eyes. "So, how are you in here?" he asked, lightly tapping a fist to his own chest. "I sense you have something you want to talk about. Some ghosts in the machine as it were." Kevin wriggled a little in his chair and turned his head down for a moment before speaking.

"I do." Kevin paused again and fingered the peeling skin on his right hand. "I don't know why it keeps bugging me. It's not like when my brother died, or the Marines I was with in Afghanistan. It is not at all intellectual. Maybe more primal?"

The priest perked up at Kevin's words. "Alright," he said, voice softening. "Take me back to the beginning, to a point when your mind was still free of this matter and then lead me through the circumstances."

"An old schoolmate of mine asked me to help him find somebody." Kevin then continued to relay the facts of the story of Jerome and Mister Willy, concluding with the medical examiner's discovery of the odd hand.

Father Matthew leaned back in his chair and squinted at the crucifix over Kevin's shoulder for a moment before saying, "That is an interesting narrative."

"It doesn't make sense to me because they shouldn't be dead," Kevin replied. "Especially Mister Willy. He needed medical attention but wasn't in immediate risk of dying. When I went looking for him, he was gone. Come to find out he was run over by a SEPTA train. He died alone, chasing a cat that somehow didn't get hurt. And the third hand! How does that figure in? It keeps rolling around in my mind, and I can't explain it away."

"The hand aside, it seems you are bothered by the thought of dying alone," Matt suggested. Kevin nodded his head as Matt continued, "That's common in most cultures. We are built for community living. What your reaction tells me is that you are connected with humanity. It is why you became a corpsman instead of a commando." Kevin managed a weak smile at the statement before the priest continued, "You can rest easy on that count. As for the rest of the story, I like a good puzzle, and you have brought me a fine example! It's rather like Sir Arthur Conan Doyle, isn't it?"

"I am afraid I don't know him." Kevin admitted.

"Modern education is such a confused mess," the old priest lamented as he sat forward in his chair and leaned on the desk. "You have heard of Sherlock Holmes, haven't you?"

"I saw the movie with Robert Downey Jr. a couple years ago," Kevin replied sheepishly.

"Well, Sir Arthur Conan Doyle wrote many, many Sherlock stories, and they came in book form before motion pictures ever existed." The priest pointed to the bookcase behind Kevin's left shoulder. "Near the bottom. Little, with green library binding." Kevin turned to follow the direction and began combing the titles. He pulled a small, flat book off the shelf and held it up for the old man to see. "That's the one. Take it with you, some homework, eh?"

"Okay. So what do I do now?"

"I will help you. Together we'll gather facts and work toward a satisfactory conclusion that allows you to settle your mind. The circumstances of these deaths may be much more practical than they appear."

"What if I can't get past it?"

"Well, then you are in the right place for that, too. Perhaps I should see about enrolling you in the seminary."

"I'm glad you think so highly of me, but no thanks."

"No matter. We'll work on this together in a logical manner, and it will lead us where it may," he said, rocking back in his chair. "Very few problems of this world cannot be mastered by persistent thought and analysis. After that, there is prayer."

"Okay." Kevin sighed and rubbed his right hand across his brow.

"I may have missed a clue in your story. Show me your hand," the priest said, his face brightening again. He took Kevin's right hand in his own and examined the dry, peeling skin. "What is the matter with your hand?"

"I don't know. I noticed it the day after we chased Jerome—or his twin. I think it's from something that was on him. It only happened where I made skin-to-skin contact."

"It's important to our puzzle, and we must gather all the factual information available to us," Father Matthew declared. He picked up the phone on the desk and pushed a button. "Do we have any portable blackboards around that will fit in my office?" He listened to the voice on the phone for a moment. "Are there any classrooms not in use?" After another moment of listening, he said "Reserve it for the semester in my name. Thank you," and replaced the phone in its cradle. Heaving himself up from his chair, he said, "Follow me."

Kevin followed the priest down the hall to an elevator. He pressed the call button and after a brief wait, the car could be heard squeaking and the light in the call button extinguished. The door to the elevator car opened, and they stepped in. Turning to Kevin, he said, "Now we shall descend to the bowels of St. Charles, and there we will find answers."

Father Matthew led the way down a dim hallway to a closed door. "This should work," he said as he turned the knob. The door swung smoothly, revealing a space closer to a closet than a classroom. The only indication it was ever used for teaching was the chalkboard that spanned one wall, otherwise it was occupied by stacks of folding chairs and collapsible tables. Three small windows at ground level let in beams of dusty summer light. Kevin walked across the room and looked up through one of them. The sun was still climbing to the top of its arc, and the sky was pale blue with summer haze. A stiff wind rocked the trees.

"So, what's the plan? Why do we need a bat cave?" Kevin asked, turning back to his uncle.

"The human brain is a complex organ that is seldom used to full effect," Uncle Matthew explained as he flipped on the overhead fluorescent lights. The white light washed out the beams of sun and filled in the shadows. He stepped toward the chalkboard and looked directly at Kevin. "Here, in this dedicated environment, we will harness as much of the mind's power as possible by using different elements of your memory."

With one eyebrow cocked slightly higher than the other, Kevin asked "So how does it work?"

"First, we select a new location to store all of your memories and thoughts on the subject at hand." The priest took a stick of white chalk from his pocket and dropped it on the ledge at the bottom of the chalkboard. "Next, we are going to clean up that space by organizing all the parts. After we are finished here today, you will be able to come back to retrieve, modify, or store anything you like."

"I'm not sure exactly how this is going to help, but let's go."

"Good. I like your enthusiasm. I will give you an example of how this works. I want you to take a good look around the room. Take a photo in your mind of what you see here. The tables, the chairs, the windows. Now look this way, at the chalkboard. Look at it in detail." Kevin looked around the room and turned to the front. He walked a little closer to the chalkboard.

"When you think you have it all, close your eyes, and recall the details of the room. Can you see them?" Matt asked.

"I'm with you so far." Kevin said, eyes pressed shut.

"Good. How many erasers are on the ledge of the chalkboard?"

"Two."

"Excellent. You are using the visual part of your memory. Eventually we will excite all the other senses and reinforce those memories. Now, I'm going to write what we know so far on this board, along with anything else we think is useful. We will organize it by time and relationships, building a structure to frame our details. This uses our ability to sequence and associate ideas. When we are done today, you can take a snapshot in your mind to mull over at any time, okay?"

"Sure. I think I get it."

"Let's begin with a timeline. How far back can we place factual events?"

"Like when Mark and I went to find Jerome?"

"We can go back much farther than that. Do you know when Jerome was born? His mother or grandmother's birth dates?"

"I don't know but I get it. Big, big picture," Kevin's voice rose with enthusiasm. "I don't have exact dates, but Jerome Lawrence was nineteen. Mark said that's the minimum age for the NBA draft."

"Good," said the priest as he drew a bold line across the top of the board. He made a mark near the left side and wrote *Jerome Lawrence?* under it. He made another mark to the left and wrote *Mother?* under it. He made a similar set of marks for *Father, Grandfathers* and *Grandmothers.* "We'll fill in the details as they come to us," he said, tapping the timeline with his finger. "Complete information removes doubt about our conclusions," he declared, looking directly into Kevin's eyes. "Now, what day did you start looking for Mr. Lawrence?"

"I went to Mark's house on June third. That was a Sunday. We went the following day, so it was on the fourth. We went again on Tuesday the fifth. That was the night we found Mister Willy and Jerome." The priest made more ticks on the timeline and added labels. After another few minutes, the timeline was as complete as could be made from memory.

"Look at the timeline," Matthew instructed. "Remember it. We will change it again, but this is our start." Kevin looked carefully at the events of the several weeks. The priest moved to the side and began writing names on the board in loose columns. He drew lines connecting the known relations, forming a map of interactions based on the story.

Kevin looked at the diagram, his eyes widening as he spoke, "Is it me, or is everybody connected except Jerome and the cat?"

"That is very good! You are already developing new avenues of investigation."

"They both connect to Mister Willy, but not to each other. The night of the chase, the cat appeared when Jerome disappeared, and vice versa."

"This is an insight. Hopefully the first of many. Eventually we will try to explain it all with a unified hypothesis."

"I'm kinda getting it. It's like fill in the blanks." Kevin said.

"For example, the cat reacted negatively to you and Mark but was comfortable with Mister Willy. We know animals often react to scents of other animals. Do either of you have a pet?"

"Mark has a cat."

"The yellow cat might have smelled it on Mark's clothes and reacted to it by running away," Father Matthew offered.

"I don't know much about cats, but it seems reasonable," Kevin agreed.

"Yes, it does, but it may be completely wrong. We don't have enough information to make a sound conclusion. So, for now, we stick to collection. Conclusions will come later." Kevin nodded. "If you need to revise our work here, just call me. We will meet again soon, but you may come back at any time," Father Matthew said, touching the gray fringe on his head with his finger. "Eventually, you will be at peace with what happened and won't need to come back at all."

16

Mark strolled up the gangway to the deck of the ship. He paused and looked around at the empty tables and chairs under the Bongo Deck awning before walking over to the bar, where Kevin was focused on a small green book. As Mark approached Kevin snapped it shut and tucked it under the bar.

"Whatcha reading?" Mark inquired.

"Just something my uncle gave me," Kevin shrugged.

"Where is everybody?" Mark asked.

"Too hot or too windy," Kevin said. "Beer?"

"That might be the best offer I get all day."

"Coming right up. Seeing as it is hot as hell, and you are the first customer of the day, it's on the house," Kevin said with a smile.

"Why, thank you very much," Mark grinned.

Kevin held a glass under the tap and pulled the lever forward. A stream of foamy gold liquid streamed into the glass until it overflowed. Mark grimaced when Kevin handed him the glass half filled with foam.

"I think your keg needs changing."

"I'm waiting until I have more customers."

"So I get the dregs?" Mark questioned.

"What do you want? You aren't paying for it."

"While this may be true, I still want to get my free's worth." Mark attempted a sip but stopped when his nose submerged in the suds. After wiping off the foam, he set the glass on a coaster and said, "So, I got some more information you might like to hear."

"What's that?"

"The medical examiner sent out specimens from the third hand."

Kevin's eye's widened. "Did they get an ID?"

"Nope. And what's more, they couldn't get a useable DNA sample."

"Did they repeat the test?"

"My guy says they did it twice, and on the second time it was hand carried to the lab by the supervisor." Mark tipped up the beer glass and managed a sip of the beer before he wiped away more foam from his nose. "What do you think of that?"

"I'm not sure I like where this is going."

"I know what you mean," Mark said, abandoning the beer after another attempted drink and wipe. "Incidentally, the lab reported the sample only had thirty-eight chromosomes instead of the expected forty-six. Despite its similarity to Jerome's massive paw, they couldn't genetically prove it was a human hand, let alone identify who it belonged to."

"Interesting, but I'm still betting the lab screwed up," Kevin concluded. Looking out at the white capped waves on the Delaware River, he asked, "I wonder what creature in the animal kingdom has thirty-eight chromosomes?"

"Do I look like a geneticist?"

"No, not really. You look more like a guy who is afraid of some suds," Kevin joked. "But really, I'd like to know because I've got a hunch about this, and it involves a certain cat."

"Well, tell you what partner. Since my employer was kind enough to replace my flip-phone with a new smart phone, I'll bet we can find out." Mark made a showy gesture of pulling the new gadget from his pocket, pressed a button and then typed a question into the search bar of the browser. "According to this list of animals by number of chromosomes, your options are pig, rattlesnake, marten, raccoon, and cat." Mark made an equally showy gesture of returning the phone to his pocket. "Bet you wish you had one."

"Okay, Skid Mark," Kevin laughed. "Are we in third grade again?"

"Easy with the old nicknames there, buddy, but I will admit your hunch was pretty good."

"Yeah, well, this mystery seems to have cat written all over it."

"I don't know what you have against cats, but I'll bet there is an explanation for it," Mark said.

"Let's hear it."

"Before my Granny Dotty died a few years back, she was in this nursing home out in West Chester. You remember Dotty?" Mark paused.

"Sure I do. She was a stitch."

"Anyway, the home had a couple of cats that roamed around the place to keep the residents company. Now, Granny didn't have any use for cats, so she shooed them away whenever one came near her. We all knew this, so for a laugh we would bring one of the cats into her room. She would throw stuff at us until we took it out or it got away on its own. Consequently, the cats were never near her room. They just scooted on by, so they didn't get hit with something. Well," Mark continued, "one day, the head nurse called my mom to tell her it was almost time, and she better get up to the home right away. I remember we all drove out there, and darn if there wasn't a cat quietly sitting on the windowsill in her room. Dad asked the nurse about it, and she said it wouldn't leave, and that cats are somehow attracted to people who are dying. The nurse said nobody knew why for sure, but some researcher theorized that dying people give off some chemical that attracts the cats. I guess this is common stuff in nursing homes."

"So what happened to your Granny?"

"She died in her sleep that night. The nurse swore the cats just know when it's time."

"You're saying the cat was hanging around because it knew what was coming." Kevin summarized. Mark shrugged in response, and then Kevin remarked, "Yeah, that doesn't make this any less creepy."

"Just what I heard," Mark said.

17

Friday, June 29
7:07 a.m.

Brian and Kevin sat on the couch watching an early morning TV news program. The woman on the screen was describing the next story to follow the commercial break. "That's gonna be your guy on the SEPTA tracks," Brian remarked while nudging Kevin.

"I wonder what's new about a homeless guy who's been dead for two weeks."

"No idea but stay tuned, and we'll find out." Brian stood up from the couch and stepped away to the small kitchen. "Want anything while I'm going?"

"No, thanks."

Before the commercials finished, Brian was back in his seat with a bowl of cereal. On the screen, a handsome, deep-voiced man was describing the circumstances that kept SEPTA from releasing the surveillance video of the accident at the Sixtieth Street station. The screen then switched to a grainy, washed out, black-and-white view of the outside of the train station. In the corner of the field of view, a man shuffled by. It was little more than a flicker of movement, but Kevin watched it intently.

"That's Mister Willy," Kevin observed. The video switched to a view of the platform. A white speck flitted across the screen to the edge of the platform, followed a moment later by a limping man. The man crossed to the edge of the platform where he stopped and sat down. He then lowered himself onto the tracks and disappeared from view.

"I can't believe he was chasing that stupid cat!" Kevin burst out.

The reporter then explained that a train arrived about five minutes later and that investigators believe it collided with the man on the tracks.

"That's a pretty crummy way to go," Brian mumbled through a mouthful of corn flakes.

"Yeah, it is." Kevin replied with a descending voice, looking down at his healing right hand.

"You're okay, right?" Brian asked his brother.

"It just sucks. I mean, dying alone like that. It's crazy. Try to get a cat off the tracks, and then get hit by a freaking train! And then lying there, feeling life drain out of you while that stupid cat watches you die."

"Not the way I want to meet my maker," Brian declared.

"Me, neither," Kevin mumbled as he turned to his brother. He drew in a deep breath, held it, and then finally exhaled with force. "I never told anybody this. There was this guy in my platoon, Lance Corporal Okobi. His real name was Abiola, but everybody called him Abi. He was first generation American, you know? His old man came to America in the 1980s to get away from some kind of African civil war." Brian put down his bowl of cereal and faced his brother, as Kevin paused a second before continuing.

"All the guys told him protecting the corpsman was the most important job he could do, so he asked to be my battle buddy, and from then on, he followed me everywhere. I couldn't even go to the head by myself! Anyway, most of the guys would tell me stuff like 'If I get my junk blown off, just let me die.' But not Abi." Kevin paused and glanced away from his brother for a moment before continuing his story. "The night we were waiting for our flight to Kandahar, the whole unit was spread out in an airplane hangar at March Air Force Base. Most of the guys were stretched out on the floor sleeping, but not me and Abi. We were talking and he says to me, 'It's an honor to be your battle buddy.' I told him he was full of it, but then he tells me he would make sure I was safe to help the rest of the guys. He said he would give his life for me, but he made me swear that if it came to that, I wouldn't let him die alone. And if he did die, I'd never leave his body unattended."

"That's quite the request," Brian acknowledged.

"Yeah." Kevin glanced around the room before settling his gaze on the TV. "Abi said bad things happened to the souls of dead people if they're left alone. I had never heard that before, but I figured it was some Africa thing. You know, like hyenas eating the bodies or something. Anyway, I assured him he was going to be fine."

"He didn't get killed, did he?"

"No, but he did get wounded. While we were trying to evac this guy who triggered an IED, Abi got shot in the ass."

"Really?"

"Yep. I looked at the wound and said to him 'You're a one frickin' lucky Marine.' The bullet went in and out his left butt cheek and then in and out the right. Four neat little bullet holes."

"When we finally got them on a helicopter, I told him he had to hold the hand of the other Marine until they got to Camp Bastion. As long as he did that, they both would live, and no one would be alone." Kevin paused for a moment, took a deep breath and then said, "I haven't seen Abi since."

"Do you know what he's doing now?"

"He told me once he was going to a Mortuary Science school in Cincinnati after he got out." Kevin shrugged, "I guess he was really serious about never leaving the dead alone."

"I suspect that when the time comes, nobody wants to be alone," Brian said.

18

"What's new, amigo?" Mark greeted Kevin from his usual table in the Burger King.

Taking a chair, Kevin carefully laid out his breakfast before he answered, "I want to find the cat, and the look-alike, or whatever it is."

"Why? What are you looking for? The story is over, leave it to the police. They'll tag a guy for Jerome's murder, and it'll be done."

"Sure, Jerome's story has an ending but there are still questions about Mister Willy that need answers."

"Like what?" Mark asked.

"The third hand for one. Whose is it?" Kevin took a slow breath before continuing. "I understand it isn't sports news anymore, so there's no angle for you, but I can't let this thing go. The public doesn't care about a random homeless guy, and the police are going to close the case because they don't have time to investigate stuff just because it's weird."

"That's right. The cops will find Jerome's killer and Mister Willy will be written off as an accident."

"But that's where this whole thing goes astray. I kept telling myself the same thing, but there is more. Jerome died because he was on the wrong end of a gun. It's tragic, and wrong, but the conclusion will make sense. Mister Willy isn't so straightforward, and it all revolves around the cat and the Jerome look-alike."

"I don't disagree, but what are you going to do?"

"I'm not sure, but I have to at least try. Are you in?" Kevin asked. Sipping from his cup of orange juice, he looked Mark in the eye.

Mark sighed and looked down at his tray of empty wrappers and coffee cup before saying, "Even if you find something else, there's no guarantee it brings closure. Sometimes there's no explaining why bad stuff happens." Mark then looked around and nodded his head, "Dang it! It doesn't make sense, but since I got you into this, I guess I have to help you get out."

"That's very thoughtful of you."

"I think so," Mark scoffed. "So, what's next?"

Kevin cracked a little smile. "Gracias, amigo. I think we are going back to the neighborhood in West Philly. The cat will lead us to something."

"Do you really think you're going to find one cat in the middle of a major metropolitan area?" Mark asked.

"Won't know until we try!" Kevin said in a peppy voice.

"Okay, fine. We'll go tomorrow morning, but remember I said it first: this is screwed up."

"Thanks. I'm sure it will be worth it."

"Hang in there. We've only covered four blocks." They continued walking and searching. On the west side of the street, Kevin queried a young man descending the front steps of a row house.

"Yo. Can you help us find this cat?"

The young man stopped and glanced at the paper Kevin held out. "I don't know about that cat." Stroking the whispy goatee on his chin, he continued, "Did you try the crazy Cat Queen? She gets all the cats up in the house with her. Hundreds of 'em."

"Where can we find the Cat Queen?" Kevin asked and waved Mark over from the other side of the street. He trotted over to listen in.

"She's up on Dewey Street. Middle of the block."

"How do I get to Dewey Street?" Kevin asked.

"You really don't belong here, do you?" the man said. Kevin shrugged and the man continued, "Just go left up there at the intersection. You see it? Then go half a block down that street, Dewey goes right. She's on the right side, with vines and trees growin' up the walls."

"Thanks, my friend. You're a lifesaver."

The young man nodded his head and mumbled, "Cat people," to himself as Kevin and Mark walked away.

The two continued north, following the instructions to Dewey Street.

"Looks like the place," Kevin said, gesturing up the street.

Mark slapped Kevin's back and said, "As advertised. Good find, amigo."

The sun now made it to ground level, slanting to the west side of the street. The shadows were growing shorter by the minute. Cars were parked bumper to bumper on the east side of the street, leaving just enough room for the one-way traffic to pass. Row houses filled the block without break. Each house was two stories tall with a little front porch, and a miniature front yard. At the center of the block was a house that matched the description they'd been given. Ivy and weeds dominated the little patch of earth between the porch and the sidewalk. Accumulated garbage was strewn about the porch, the paint peeled from the woodwork, and cracks had spread across several windows.

"Number nineteen South Dewey Street is definitely not going to win yard of the month," Mark muttered under his breath.

Kevin looked across the street at the tattered, red-trimmed house opposite. There were stacks of random construction materials on the ground and a rusty lawn mower on the porch. "This looks neat by comparison, at least there is organized junk." Kevin then added in a soft voice, "They have a cat, too."

Mark spun around to see a white and black cat sitting on a pile of lumber scraps. It was watching them. "It's probably the lookout for the Cat Queen," Mark said and turned back to Number 19. "If this place is occupied by a hundred cats, it is going to stink to high heaven," Mark cringed. "Feel free to lead the way."

Kevin paused to take a deep breath, before walking up the uneven concrete walkway. "Hang back and keep a long view of the situation," Kevin directed, and then climbed the steps to the porch. Mark stood at the front of the lot on the sidewalk, made a thumbs up gesture, and smiled. Kevin turned to the door and knocked. Immediately, several cats appeared in the windows.

"There are cats peeking at us already," Mark reported.

"Great. We must be in the right place." Bumping and scraping sounds were audible from outside the door. A loud meow was followed by the rattle of the locks and click of the door latch.

An old woman's voice came from behind the door. "Stay back. Stay *back*. We have visitors. I don't know who it is. Stay back." Kevin looked back at Mark and made a funny grimacing face. Mark shrugged his shoulders and smiled a toothy grin. The door opened a crack and a strong smell of ammonia and feces issued from behind the door. Kevin wrinkled his nose and held his breath. "Can I hep you young man?"

"Uh, good morning. I hope so." Kevin turned his head and glanced back at Mark and took a deep breath. "We are looking for a cat that might be sick. It got away from animal control in this area."

Kevin held the picture up for the eyes peeking out from behind the door. "It looks like this, and it has a little kink in its tail, too."

"I know one like that, but the stripes are all wrong in your picture."

"This isn't the exact cat we are looking for. It just resembles it." Kevin remarked. "When was the last time you saw it?"

"Oh, I think he was here last night. He comes and goes through the back door. Willy comes to check on me and make sure we are doing alright."

Kevin's eyes got big. He glanced back at Mark in confirmation and took another breath. Turning back to the door, Kevin asked, "Did you say the cat's name is Willy?"

"That's right." The eyes peeking out from behind the door were intense. "Last night he come as a cat, but a couple nights before he was my cousin William. That's how I know to call him Willy." Kevin's jaw slacked at the statement. The voice questioned, "What do you want with him? He ain't sick. That cat has the soul of my dear William, and he comes to look after me." Suddenly turning sharp, "I won't tell you nothing more. Now, leave me alone!" The door closed abruptly, followed by the sound of the locks and latches snapping into place. Kevin stood silently, as the scrape and shuffle retreated from the door.

"Well, that was something." Mark commented from the sidewalk.

"I am not sure what just happened, but I am pretty sure we found where the yellow cat hangs out when it isn't playing on the train tracks."

"I think you're right," Mark seconded. "And you know, we are only a block and a half from the junkyard."

"Interesting," Kevin said as he stepped down from the porch.

"I wonder what the back alley looks like?" Mark asked.

"Let's circle around and see what we can find."

Mark led the way north toward the end of the block. Turning to Kevin he asked, "what do you make of the Willy connection?"

"I'd bet she saw that cat with Mister Willy. In her mind, wherever the cat is, Mister Willy can't be far away."

They arrived back on Market Street and turned right, walking east under the elevated SEPTA train tracks to Sixty-First Street. They turned right again and walked south down the block. A large, two-story building gave way to duplex houses separated by more narrow alleys. Looking down the alleys, they could see the backs of the row houses on Dewey Street.

"Next one and we should be looking right at the back of the Cat Queen's place." Kevin observed.

"Here we are." Mark stopped walking and looked down the narrow gap between the houses. Garbage cans and refuse filled most of the alley separating the duplex houses. The back of a white house was visible at the far end. "It looks like there is a cross alley and a little space between this side and the other. Plenty of room for cats to frolic."

While Kevin and Mark stood on the sidewalk discussing the alley, the front door of the duplex opened. A woman dressed in a pair of bright green sweatpants and a black Jimi Hendrix T-shirt stepped onto the porch. Her hair was wrapped in a towel, and she carried a toothbrush in her hand. She called out "What are you lookin' at?" Both men turned and looked up.

"Good morning," Mark replied. "We are trying to locate a particular cat that got away from animal control near here. It might be sick. It looks like this," he said holding up the paper. "Have you seen it?"

"Are you kidding me? I can't see that from here, I don't have my contacts in. Come up closer." Mark carried the paper up the porch steps. She studied it for a moment. "I seen a cat like that. Mean sucker, probably on account of a broken tail. Sneaks through here going back to see Miss Woods. Did you try to talk to Miss Woods?"

"We did, but she wasn't very helpful. When was the last time you saw the cat?"

"The other night it went running back. I haven't seen it since." Kevin and Mark looked at each other, and then back to the woman.

"That's great. By any chance do you know an older man in the area who goes by the name Willy?"

"Mister Willy came by here and went up my alley last night. Moving fast, too."

"Are you sure it was Mister Willy, and not someone who resembled him?" Mark asked.

"Shoot. He's been around here since I was a child. It was him alright. His color was a little off—kinda pale—and he must have got his foot fixed or something. He was almost running, and I've never seen Mister Willy hustle anywhere my whole life."

"Would you be willing to call me if you see the cat or Mister Willy again? It is important that we find them because they both might be sick."

"Like rabies or something?"

"We don't really know yet, but we need to find out."

"If I see them, I call you?"

"That's right, and we'll come out. Any time of day." Mark wrote his cell number on the sheet of paper and handed it to her.

"Do you mind if we take a look?" Kevin asked, gesturing to the back alley.

"Go ahead. Knock yourself out."

"Thanks," Kevin replied. Mark came down front the porch and the two men started into the alley.

Kevin pushed ahead into the shadows. When he got to the end of the alley, it opened into the cross alley that divided the houses on the east and west side of the block. He looked back just in time to see Mark moving a garbage can. As he began dragging it, a yellow cat sprang from a recess behind it. It bound down the alley toward Kevin, who immediately stepped into the alley, arms stretched wide in anticipation of catching it. It then reversed course toward Mark who dropped the garbage can out of surprise and inadvertently created a barrier.

Trapped, the cat's crooked tail went up and the fur on its back stood up. It hissed and bared its teeth as Kevin slowly closed in from the end of the alley. "That's it! Get something to put over it!"

"Like what? All I got here is trash."

"A blanket, or box. Hell, dump out the garbage can and drop that over it."

Mark dumped out the contents of a garbage can on the ground. He carried it with the open end forward, ready to trap the cat under it. On the other side, Kevin picked up a broken broom handle and a cardboard box. Slowly they converged toward the center of the alley. "Easy . . . easy," Mark said.

The cat backed against the wall and continued to hiss at the two approaching men. Mark lowered the can close to the ground and near the wall to prevent the cat from escaping underneath. Kevin followed his lead, crouching with his box. As they brought the can and box closer together the cat leapt up and sprang off Kevin's back, clawing into his shirt and skin as it made its escape. Mark dropped the garbage can and lunged for the cat, getting a hand on its tail but then losing his grip after he crashed into Kevin's leg.

"Damn it!" Kevin cursed as he spun around trying to make a pursuit. The cat made it to the end of the alley before either man could get untangled. It turned left out of sight as soon as it made the cross alley. Kevin scrambled to his feet but arrived too late. He came to a stop and said, "It's gone. It probably knows every hiding place on the block. We'll never find it."

"Forget the cat," Mark surrendered. "We need to get you cleaned up."

"What? Did I step in something?" Kevin asked, turning to face Mark.

"No. I'm talking about the mess on your back."

"Did it get me?" Kevin asked, craning his neck to look over his shoulder.

"You're bleeding like crazy from the claw marks," Mark replied, looking at the rips in Kevin's shirt and rivulets of blood originating at each puncture.

"Must be really sharp claws, because I don't feel anything."

"Come on tough guy. Let's see if my new girlfriend has something to patch you up. Mark stepped up to the porch of the red duplex and knocked on the door. The same woman answered, but this time without the towel and toothbrush. "You boys find anything in the alley? You made enough noise to raise the dead."

"We found the cat, and it's as mean as you claimed," Mark replied. "I'm going to clean up the garbage I dumped out trying to catch it, but first, do you have anything to clean up my friend's back?" Mark put his hand on Kevin's shoulders and turned him to display the bloody shirt.

"My, oh my, look at what that cat did to you! You sit down there on the top step and take off your shirt. I got something for that. What's your name, sugar?"

"Kevin, and that's Mark."

"Mark, you get busy cleaning up the mess you made. I'll be right back." She disappeared into the house. Mark looked around the corner into the alley and groaned.

"Stupid cat. Now I'm picking up somebody else's garbage!"

"I would gladly trade places," Kevin replied.

Mark huffed and walked back to the scene of the confrontation. He righted the trash cans and collected the bagged garbage. The loose refuse he left and dragged the can back into place. Returning to the front step, Mark said, "Looks better than when we arrived."

Just then the woman returned to the porch with a large first aid kit. She opened it and snapped on a pair of nitrile gloves.

"Do you get a lot of wounded on your front porch, ma'am?" Kevin asked.

"What makes you say that?" she asked as she began working to clean up the blood.

"It's not the first time you put on a pair of gloves, and your kit is a lot more comprehensive than most."

"Observant, aren't you?" she said flatly. "It looks like you got four little punctures in the skin. The rest are scratches. If that cat's got something, you better get checked, too," she declared.

"May I ask your name?"

"Penelope Holmes, but everybody calls me Nel," she said as she fashioned four little wound dressings and taped them onto Kevin's back. "I'm a nurse at Presbyterian Hospital."

"I should have guessed."

"But you didn't." When she finished, she handed Kevin a clean white T-shirt with a faded image of Michael Jordan on the front.

"Thanks for fixing me up. My partner is a coward when it comes to blood," Kevin said.

Nel smiled and then turned to Mark, "You boys know something more than you're saying. So, tell me now, what's wrong with Mister Willy. For real."

Kevin and Mark looked at each other. Finally, Mark said, "You don't really want to know."

Nel crossed her arms, tilted her head and said, "Out with it."

"He is supposed to be dead," Kevin blurted.

"Hit by a SEPTA train," Mark added.

"Two weeks back? That was Mister Willy?" she asked. Mark nodded. Nel looked up, extended her hands upwards and exclaimed toward the morning sky, "Oh, Lord help us. This is some kinda serious business!"

20

K evin slowly paced the basement classroom while recounting the events of the previous Saturday morning. Uncle Matthew leaned against the chalkboard and listened intently. When Kevin finished, he stood still, crossed his arms over his chest, and stared at the notes from the previous visit. Neither man spoke for a long time. Finally, Kevin shifted on his feet, dropped his hands to his hips and said, "Now what?"

"Let's fill in the timeline," the priest said. He pointed to the blank space on the chalkboard. "Mark from the train accident to surprising the yellow cat in the alley." He picked up a piece of chalk and handed it to Kevin.

Kevin marked out the events on the timeline, then switched to the new people on the relationship diagram. He added the Cat Queen and Nel, then drew some new lines.

"This doesn't make sense anymore," Kevin observed. "Almost everything is connected. There are no obvious inclusions or exclusions."

"You are correct. We need to adjust the diagram for time."

"Yeah, I get it." Kevin erased the new people and lines. "We have two events." He stepped farther down the board and made new diagrams. "One for Jerome and one for Mister Willy."

The priest grinned. "Now we have a common element."

Kevin circled the word cat on both diagrams and said, "How about that?"

"Good work. Now let's talk it out." The priest walked toward the back of the room, unfolded a chair from the cart, and sat down.

"Okay" Kevin said, turning to face Father Matthew.

"When did Jerome die?" Matthew asked.

Kevin walked over to the timeline and put his finger on the board. "This is when we found him, but the medical examiner said he'd been dead since June first."

"And who saw the person who looked like Jerome after that date?"

"His grandmother, Mister Willy, Mark, me, and a few others we met on the street."

"That is a pretty good sample of reliable witnesses, but we can be fairly certain it wasn't Jerome because his body was in the junkyard. Now, did any of those people also see the yellow cat?"

"I don't know about Jerome's grandmother, but I know Mister Willy, and Mark and I saw it," Kevin said.

"Were the cat and Jerome ever seen together?"

"I don't think so," Kevin shrugged.

"That could be a significant connection."

"If they are never together, how can they be connected?" Kevin asked.

The old priest shifted in his seat and looked again at Kevin. "Think of them as two sides of the same coin."

"I get it. We can make an indirect conclusion about the relationship." Kevin paused and then added, "If there is a relationship."

"Perhaps we can devise a test later, but for now we'll collect more information. Another common element is the fact that there are two look-alikes. When did Mister Willy suffer his demise, and who has seen someone who looks like him since?"

"So far, we know of Nel and the Cat Queen."

"Nel is probably a good witness, but I'm not sure about the Cat Queen," Matthew stated.

"Maybe Nel can help us find more witnesses," Kevin surmised.

"That's possible, but I wouldn't suggest trying to catch the cat again."

"You can say that again. The scratches still aren't healed."

"How do you mean?" Matthew asked.

"When they aren't bleeding, they kind of ooze. Scabs don't really form over the wounds. It's like there is some local anticoagulant that keeps them open. I've already ruined one work shirt. My boss isn't happy about that."

"Another medical oddity to add to the peeling skin where you touched Jerome."

"I guess we need a list of stuff like that, too."

"Excellent idea," the priest said. Kevin's chalk squeaked as he wrote a column of facts on the left side of the board.

1. Dry skin after direct contact.
2. Cat scratches that won't heal.
3. The chimera can run fast on tender feet over gravel, broken glass, and trash without bleeding or slowing down.
4. Skin is pale.
5. He hides in recesses or shadows. Stalking or hiding?

The priest stopped him after the last observation. "Two things I am curious about."

Kevin paused and turned to face the priest. "What's that?"

"First, your choice of words to describe the appearance of Jerome and Mister Willy. You wrote *chimera*."

"That just came to me. It was a word I learned in school. It's a Greek mythological creature with a bunch of animal parts, but it can also be a thing people wish to see that isn't actually there or is impossible."

"I am impressed. Maybe your education wasn't as bad as I thought. Clearly Jerome's grandmother and the Cat Queen wanted to see these people, even though it seems impossible, given the timeline we have established."

"I didn't get that far, but you're right."

"Very well, now tell me about the chimera's actions."

"It is common behavior among animals and humans alike. Cover your six, don't stand out, keep a good field of view in front. Be ready to run but hold very still. It works for hiding and stalking."

"Cover your six?"

"Sorry, protect your backside, you know, where you aren't actively looking."

"I think I see what you mean. Maybe it is both—stalking and hiding." The priest stood up from his chair and walked up next to his nephew and said, "It strikes me as a cat-like behavior."

"Thinking back, you're right," Kevin grunted.

"Anything else?" Matthew asked.

"Not off the top of my head."

"Excellent. Let's move on to some information I found, and maybe we'll gain a small amount of historical perspective." The old priest stepped toward the door. "Shall we return to my office for a bit of refreshment while we discuss church history?"

"Sounds good," Kevin agreed, as he clapped chalk dust from his fingers.

Entering the office, Kevin sat across from his uncle in the cramped space. The window shade was drawn, and the room was lit only by the desk lamp. The old priest poured hot tea from an electric kettle into a cup. He added a little sugar and cream before he placed the cup and a box of cookies on the desk.

Kevin commented, "Mom always said you loved your sweets."

"It's my Achilles' heel, but I don't think it's done me much harm," the priest said, patting his belly. He took a cookie in one hand and the cup of tea in the other. "I've been making some inquiries about our phenomenon and haven't had much success. There aren't many threads to pull on this ball of twine, but I did come across some interesting historical church interactions with cats."

"I'm all ears."

"Good. How are you on historical popes?"

"I won't win *Jeopardy* with that category," Kevin grimaced.

"No matter. Do you have any knowledge of Gregory IX?"

"Afraid not."

"I had to stretch my recollection a little, too," Father Matthew said between bites. "Sadly, he is best known for outlawing cats in Europe during the Middle Ages."

"I had no idea cats were ever illegal."

"If you only relied on modern sources, that might be your conclusion. But that isn't an accurate description of what he did. He actually issued a Papal Bull intended to eliminate threats to Christianity." The priest took sip of tea before continuing. "Our dear Gregory didn't actually ban cats, but that is how it was taken when it filtered down to the level of the illiterate masses. Black cats, in particular, became a symbolic threat."

"So, what was the actual threat?" Kevin asked.

"Cults that were thought to be satanic in nature." The priest retrieved an old book from the shelf next to his desk and opened it to a marked page. He pointed to an illustration of a half man, half cat creature standing before a group of prostrate people.

"What's known of this particular ritual involved a pale, emaciated man that kissed the initiates and thereby removed all their Christian memory. The leader," he pointed to the standing figure, "was thought to be Satan himself. There were also various ritualistic orgies and other activities involving black cats in particular."

"Sounds like modern performance art. What year was this?"

"The Papal Bull was delivered to King Henry of Germany in 1233. The King was tasked with the elimination of this cult. He and his clergy were unable to find any cult members, despite threatening the citizenry with torture, so they went for the cats. Before long, cats—especially black cats—were no longer welcome in Europe until the end of the 19th Century."

"Did it work? Did the cult disappear?"

"From our modern perspective, it's hard to gauge the effect on the cult, but for sure, if there are no cats, it's hard to have cat rituals."

"So, what is it to us? I doubt we have any cat rituals going on here. I mean, barring the performance art and all."

"It's not yet clear, but maybe there is a connection to our circumstances." Pointing at the book, the priest continued, "There are very few things in this world that are actually new. The illustration could represent the same thing as our mysterious happenings."

"Are you saying some pale guy in West Philly is killing people with a kiss?" Kevin looked up at the old priest. "I think we're getting way ahead of ourselves."

"That's not quite what I mean. Try this as an analogy," the priest offered. "Our ancestors created some concept of dragons in mythology, probably from the discovery of fossilized bones of dinosaurs."

"Yeah, I've heard that theory before."

"Like the dragons, the artist who created this illustration conceptualized a creature or an event he'd never seen, based on what few descriptions he had available to him."

"But a half cat, half man creature roaming the city in the twenty-first century? It sounds nuts," Kevin concluded.

"I agree, but I'd like you to think about it for a bit. Think of it as creative problem solving, like our chalkboard in the basement. Let your mind wander. Consider every idea, no matter how fanciful it may seem. Write them down if you need to.

"Okay. I will give it some thought. Heck, it will probably keep me up all night."

"We'll talk about it some more next time."

21

Kevin was standing behind the bar drying glasses when Mark took a seat opposite him. "What's new, pussy cat?" Mark asked.

"If only you knew how loaded that question is," Kevin replied, as he set down the last glass and flipped his towel over his shoulder.

"How's the back?" Mark asked.

"It took three days and a couple of ruined shirts to really stop oozing, but it's alright now." Gesturing to the taps, Kevin asked, "Want a beer?"

"Since you offered," Mark grinned. "You know, this place is starting to grow on me. It will be a real shame if you ever get a job somewhere else."

"Yes, a real shame." Kevin poured a beer and placed it on a napkin in front of Mark. "I have some news for you," Kevin said in a hushed voice.

"I have something for you, too," Mark said, mimicking Kevin.

"Great. You better go first."

"Gladly." Mark took a long drink and exhaled in satisfaction before saying, "Nel called me this morning."

"Did she see the cat or the Mister Willy look-alike?"

"Both. She said the cat has come and gone several times since our visit. Then last night she saw our Mister Willy guy going into the alley. She hasn't seen either come out since."

"Did she see them together, by any chance?"

"I don't know. She did ask when we might come back out to her place. I think she's a little freaked out."

"We can go out tomorrow morning."

"I'll call her this evening, and then meet you at the Sixtieth Street station at eight." Mark took another drink of beer and looked at Kevin. "What have you got?"

"I hope you brought your open mind because this is going to be a little bit out there."

"Everything about this is *out there*, but not to worry, I'm a news professional—objective and receptive," Mark bragged.

"Do you remember what you said when we couldn't figure out how the guy got away?" Kevin asked.

"You mean from the empty lot? Where we found the cat under the pile of clothes, and a dead body? Yeah, I remember. I said it was spooky."

"Would you be willing to make it black magic?"

"I was mostly kidding, but I take it you aren't."

"No, I'm not," Kevin deadpanned.

"So, where is this coming from? I don't see you going off on a tangent like this on your own."

"I told my Uncle Matthew about our adventures, and he's doing some Sherlock Holmes stuff."

"The priest Uncle Matthew?"

"Yeah, him."

"He's still around? He's got to be at least a hundred by now."

"He's not that old, and he still teaches at St. Charles. More important, he's doing some research. It didn't seem relevant at first, because of some information I couldn't get straight, but now it kinda makes sense."

"Okay, lay it on me," Mark replied. Kevin took a breath and

looked around the deck before continuing.

"The cat and the look-alike guy could be the same entity, and we aren't the first to encounter this thing."

Mark's expression was frozen for a long moment before asking, "How do you know?"

"Ever heard of Pope Gregory IX?"

"Come on. Do you think I paid attention in Sister Julie's class?"

"Good point," Kevin laughed. "Anyway, he ran the show during the 1200s and sent the Germans on a hunt for a man-cat satanic cult." Mark cocked his head at the description. "The inquisitors were cleared to burn people at the stake and started a general panic about black cats. In fact, cats of all colors weren't welcome in Europe until the late 1800s."

"Is that where the *bad luck* thing came from?"

"Possibly. Uncle Matt showed me an old book with drawings and some descriptions that kinda go along with what we've found."

Mark shook his head. "Son of a gun. I try to get a scoop on an NBA draft story and I get satanic cats."

"Sorry about your luck," Kevin said.

"So, what's next?" Mark asked.

"We go see what Nel has to say, and hope she tells us something that makes us look like we have over-active imaginations."

22

Wednesday, July 4
8:17 a.m.

The streets of West Philadelphia were wet from pre-dawn rain showers, and rays of yellow sun slanted between gaps in the lingering clouds. Kevin and Mark descended from the Sixtieth Street Station and started west on Market Street, walking around puddles as they went. At the next intersection, they turned the corner on to South Sixty-First Street. No vehicle traffic or other pedestrians were on the quiet side streets and only an occasional stray sound could be heard from the many open windows. Reaching 16 South Sixty-First Street, they came to a stop and scanned the street and side alley before climbing the concrete steps to the front porch. Kevin raised a closed hand as he approached the door, but before he could knock, it swung away, and his knuckles only met air. Nel stood in the dark opening, dressed in shorts and a Black Keys concert T-shirt. She wore oversized round-frame glasses and her hair was covered by a red bandana. Planting a hand on her hip, she hissed, "Why are you two always prowling around so early in the morning?" Kevin and Mark exchanged glances, but neither man spoke. She waved them into the small foyer, and then continued, "Why can't you do your business at normal-people hours? And on a holiday!"

Crossing the threshold, Mark offered, "I hear you. Blame his work schedule, and thanks for keeping an eye out."

"Usually, it pays to know what is going on in your neighborhood," Nel replied in a lower grumbling voice, "but I'm not so sure about this."

"You said on the phone that you saw the cat coming and going, and you saw Mister Willy, too," Mark restated.

"That's right. He came up the alley and went right in Miss Wood's back door," she explained, "and neither one has come out since."

Kevin entered the conversation by asking, "Did you see Mister Willy and the cat together? You know, at the same time?"

"No, it was one or the other," Nel replied. Then after a pause, "That's kinda funny, isn't it. They were together all the time before."

"When did you last see Mister Willy?" Kevin asked.

"Just after sunset the night before last, and he ain't come back out."

"Do you think he's still in there? It's been over a day." Mark asked.

"Probably, but I think you are going to have to go over there to find out," she declared.

Kevin and Mark looked at each other again. "I guess that's what we'll do. Thanks, Nel. Keep that first aid kit handy," Kevin remarked, leading the way out the door.

Mark followed Kevin out to the street where they stopped, facing each other. Kevin said, "I got a feeling this isn't going to be like our last visit."

"Yeah, I got that tingle, too. So how do you think we should do this?" Mark asked.

"Okay, we have a front and back door. Maybe two people inside, along with a bunch of cats. Maybe we have a cat that is really mean," Kevin described before a slight pause. "We know for sure it is going to stink to high heaven."

"Do we split up and cover front and back?"

"I don't think so. I think we should go to the back door together." Kevin fidgeted a little and continued. "The back is where the action is, so let's concentrate there."

"Alright, just like trick-or-treat, right?" Mark said.

Kevin groaned, "Just like that, except it's Independence Day," and led the way around into the alley. They maneuvered between the trash cans and puddles to reach the back door of the Cat Queen's house. Trash, mostly cat food cans and restaurant take-out containers, littered the area. Kevin climbed the back steps and turned to look back. He spotted Nel, looking down from a second-floor window. He gave her a curt wave before asking Mark, "Are you ready?"

Mark stood at the bottom of the back steps and nodded to the house. "Can a person ever be ready for something like this?"

"You're not scared, are you?" Kevin asked.

"No, not me, not scared. Maybe a little nervous about how this might turn out."

"It'll be fine," Kevin said, then made a fist and knocked on the door. He waited a moment and then knocked again.

"No cats looking back at us this time," Mark observed.

"That's strange," Kevin replied before trying again. Rapping harder this time, the door creaked opened a hand width. Kevin pushed lightly on the door, and it opened wide. Kevin repeatedly called out, "Anybody home?" until he recoiled from a stench issuing from the doorway. "Oh, good lord. There is something dead in there," Kevin said, turning away and gasping for air.

"Are you okay?" Mark asked.

"Yeah," Kevin replied as he pulled his shirt collar up over his mouth and nose and then looked back to the door. "Hello? Miss Wood?" he called into the house. There was not a sound to be heard. "Come on," Kevin said, waving Mark forward.

Both men's eyes started watering as they moved into the house, stepping over trash piles and litter boxes filled with cat feces. Kevin turned to Mark and gestured to the door, "Prop the door so it won't close and open some windows if you can. Between the trapped heat and stink, we could suffocate in here."

"No kidding." Mark stopped and tried to push open a window next to the door. "Painted shut." He followed Kevin further into the house. "I can't believe anything could survive in here."

They moved into the largest room on the ground level. On the floor, near the front door, was a pile of yellow flower print cloth. Stepping closer, they could make out the emaciated hands and feet of an old woman jutting out from a thread-bare dress and apron. The skin was dried and shrunken like a raisin. Kevin said, "I think we've found the Cat Queen."

"Oh man," Mark groaned.

"Get the front door open," Kevin directed Mark, who was standing behind him with his hands over his mouth and nose.

"She looks just like Jerome did," Mark observed as he unlatched four different deadbolts and a chain.

Kevin bent down for a closer look. "Yeah, she does."

Mark managed to get the front door and a big window open. "Let's step out and get a breath before we look around more. I'm feeling a little dizzy."

"Yeah, me too," agreed Kevin. They moved to the front porch and sat down on the steps. Kevin took a few deep slow breaths, looked up at the heavy gray sky and asked, "Where are all the cats?"

Mark panted next to him, "Probably took off when the food ran out."

Kevin shook his head and said, "That's feline loyalty for you. At least they didn't start eating the corpse."

"I could've gone the rest of my life without that image," Mark sighed.

"I heard they start with the face."

"Stop already!" Mark whined. Retrieving his phone from his pocket, he held it up and asked, "Shall I call it in?"

"Why don't you call Nel first. Let her know where we are," Kevin recommended. Mark recalled the number from the phone's memory, initiated the call, then held it to his ear.

"She's not answering," Mark reported after several seconds.

"Okay. Call the police and then go tell Nel the situation. I'll look around the house some more. If there is anything interesting, I will have a few minutes to find it before we get kicked out."

"Got it." Mark dialed 911 and then led the way back into the house and went directly to the back door. Kevin walked slowly, scanning with his eyes while covering his mouth and nose with his shirt. Ahead of him, Mark shouted to Nel but didn't get a response. Kevin ignored the sounds from the back of the house and headed up the trash strewn staircase to the second floor. He paused at the top of the stairs and listened to the sound of random raindrops on the roof before quickly surveying the two rooms at the top of the stairs. Finding only more refuse, he turned back. At the top of the stairs, Kevin heard Nel calling him from the back door, panic in her voice.

"Hey! Where are you?"

"Upstairs. I'm coming down."

"Miss Wood came out the back door. Mark went after her," Nel gasped from the back door.

"What?" Kevin replied. He came bounding down the steps with a confused look on his face. "Can't be. She's in here," he called back.

"She just pushed me out the way! Mark is chasing her!" Nel repeated in a panicked cry. Kevin made his way to the back of the house and emerged into the fresh air. The random raindrops had become a shower, and Nel stood at the bottom of the steps with her hands over her head, palms up, trying shield her face.

"She's in here." Kevin tried to explain while gesturing toward the door. Nel stood still, shaking her head.

"No, no," Nel replied.

Kevin paused for a long moment, then moved down to Nel at the bottom of the back steps. He gently reached for her right hand and examined it closely. The skin was pale white and beginning to peel back like scales.

"What is it?" Nel asked.

"Did your hands make skin to skin contact?"

"Yes," Nel confirmed as a tear formed in the corner of her eye.

"Does it hurt? Kevin asked.

"No," Nel shook her head. "Who was that? I don't understand."

"I'm not sure anybody does," Kevin exhaled.

The sound of sirens could be heard approaching from the direction of the morning sun. They were accompanied by low wails and frequent horn blasts. "Only Engine 57 is close enough to get here so quickly," Kevin commented. He and Nel sat on the back steps, their hair damp from the rain.

"We see them all the time at the ER," Nel said in a choked-up voice as she examined the palms of her hands. The skin was shriveled as if it had been submerged in water for a long time.

"That's my brother's company."

"What's his name? I probably know him."

"Brian."

"He got a last name? Since I don't know yours, neither."

"Maloney."

"Might as well be Smith or Jones then. Half the guys in the fire department are named Maloney," Nel observed, her voice becoming lighter.

"Funny. He says that all the time, too," Kevin said with a laugh in his voice.

"Scar on the back of his right hand, like this." Nel traced a line diagonally across her right hand with her left index finger.

"That's him," Kevin confirmed. "The peeling skin thing lasts for a few weeks." Kevin held up his hand to show her his pale right palm. "I got the same thing when I touched Jerome, or his look-alike, or whatever the hell it is." They sat in silence listening to the sirens for a moment until Kevin asked, "Do you always remember people's scars?"

The answer was interrupted by Mark, who was walking back up the alley. "Disappeared into an abandoned building," he panted. "I didn't think following it in there was a good idea."

"Smart." Kevin said. "The trucks will be here any moment. We should probably meet them out front."

"After you," Mark offered.

They went in the back door, Kevin leading the way, followed by Nel and Mark. "It must have been hiding from us as we walked through to the front door."

"Upstairs maybe. There isn't anywhere to hide down here," Mark replied.

"My Lord!" Nel cried out as she entered the house for the first time. "I had no idea." She slowly followed Kevin over and around the piles of cat food cans, paper sacks, pizza boxes, and other trash until they came to the front room. Rounding the corner into the living room, she gasped, covering her mouth with her hand at the sight of the shriveled corpse. "Poor dear. Poor dear!" She said as new tears came to her eyes. "I think she broke her hip. See the leg jutting out?"

"Probably," Kevin agreed.

"She must have been in terrible pain. Oh! Just lying there, waiting to die. Oh, Lord." Mark came up behind Nel, and gently guided her forward to the front door. The three of them stood under the narrow front porch as the rain started coming down harder. "I never seen somebody dead like that," she said. "They look more alive when they get to the ER."

A fire engine came to a stop in front of the little row house, completely blocking the street. Three firefighters in full turn-out gear immediately dismounted from the truck and approached the house. The first firefighter called up to the front porch, "Strange meeting you here."

"Hey Brian, sorry to get you guys out here in the rain for this," Kevin replied.

Brian then turned to Nel, "Hey Nurse Nel, you okay?"

"I'm a little freaked out right now," she replied in a quiet, quivering voice.

"We got it from here, you just relax." Looking back to his brother, Brian said, "What have you got?"

"It looks like this shut-in lady broke her hip and died on the floor," Kevin said.

"And?" Brian added.

"What do you mean?'" Kevin replied. Brian and Kevin looked each other in the eye, and Brian cocked his head toward Mark and Nel.

"Is this related, you know, like the others?" Brian asked.

"Yeah. I think so. She's desiccated like the others," Kevin replied, and then asked, "What? No police this morning?"

"They will be along shortly, and I'm sure they will have questions for you."

"They will. Can you send them around the block to number sixteen? We'll wait there, out of your way."

"Sure thing," Brian replied.

"Might want to wear your mask in there. It stinks to high heaven," Mark advised as they moved out of the way of the firefighters.

23

K evin entered the dark faculty hallway at St. Charles from the
blazing light of the late morning sun. When the door clanged
shut behind him, he came to a stop. The space was dim and
cool. The only source of illumination was the window at the stairwell
end of the corridor and the handful of open office doors. After his
eyes adjusted, Kevin resumed walking, his hands in his pockets and
bare skin prickling at the chilled air. He hesitated opposite Father
Matthew's open door. Framed in the doorway, the priest sat with
his back to the window, presenting only a silhouette, his features
obscured in shadow.

"Hello again," the priest's voice rumbled. Without a word,
Kevin took a reluctant step through the doorway into the window's
luminance. The soft and diffused light from the north-facing pane
revealed the characteristics of the younger man's expression.

"You've had another encounter with the mysterious," Uncle
Matthew observed. Kevin froze in place. "It shows on your face,"
Matthew continued.

"I guess you might call it that," Kevin responded, "but the
mysterious is getting a little predictable."

"That's good. It means we are learning something about the game. It has a pattern," the priest said, rising from his chair and pointing the way out of the office.

They moved at the pace of the old man's shuffle toward the elevator. "Come, tell me about your experience, and we will update our chalkboard in the basement."

Rumbling to a stop, the elevator chimed, and its doors opened to the deserted hallway in the basement of the building. The pair emerged and made their way to the classroom in silence. Upon entering, Father Matthew softly closed the door and gestured toward the chairs. Kevin made his way to a chair but didn't sit. Instead, he looked to one of the windows and began recounting the details of the latest encounter with the cat and the imposter. He talked about the appearance of the imposter and the condition of the Cat Queen's body. He concluded with Mark's pursuit and the arrival of the fire department. The priest listened intently, with no changes to the expression on his face or his posture. "That is quite a morning," he said.

"You can say that again," Kevin sighed.

"It does seem consistent with your other two encounters. I think we can rule out any coincidence or accidents. I'm afraid there's something going on that is directed by forces we don't yet understand."

"You sound a lot like Sherlock Holmes," Kevin remarked.

"Good, you've been reading. But perhaps Van Helsing is more appropriate," the priest commented as he approached the chalkboard.

"Who's Van Helsing?" Kevin asked. "Isn't that a movie?"

"Another deficiency in your literary education, I'm afraid," Father Matthew groaned. "We will address that another time. For today, we will focus on what our unfortunate individuals have in common."

"Besides the fact that they're all dead?" Kevin asked.

"Indeed. This is a very complicated puzzle." Matthew stepped to the chalkboard and took up a piece of chalk from the ledge. "Let's advance our reasoning with the usual reporter's questions: who, what, where, when, and how?" The priest wrote the names of the three victims on the board in a column headed with *who*. Then he created a grid with the questions across the top. "Now fill it in with factual information."

"I'm with you. Another way to organize our information." Kevin stepped to the board and began filling in the streets where each person was found in the *where* column. After completing the list, he looked at Father Matthew and said, "I think this column might work better with a map." The old priest remained silent and nodded. In the *how* column, he recorded the apparent cause of death. In the *when* column he wrote the approximate date of death. When he got to the *what* column, he paused. "They died, but what else happened to these people?" Kevin stepped back from the board and sat down on a chair. He let out a heavy sigh and looked out the window.

"It's difficult to answer because we don't know much about the process," the priest offered. "Maybe we'll learn more later."

Kevin stood up from his chair and wandered around the room in silence. His uncle followed the movement with his eyes but said nothing. Kevin let out another great sigh.

"They were all found within a couple blocks of each other. They were all unmarried or unconnected. They died alone. Their bodies were all desiccated." Kevin paused for a moment and walked back to the timeline on the chalkboard. He picked up a piece of chalk and added the cat lady on July first followed by a question mark. He then stood looking at the board, chalk poised to write, when he started tapping the chalk against the board with increasing rapidity. After a moment he stopped, spun around and faced his uncle.

"Tell me, my boy!" the old man nearly shouted.

"I think we can predict the timing of the next event," Kevin said with conviction. "There were about three weeks between when Jerome went missing and Mr. Willy was hit by the train. About three weeks after that, Miss Wood dies after falling in her house."

"Indeed. So, in three weeks, we might expect another desiccated corpse."

"I think so, and probably within the roaming area of a mean yellow cat." Kevin then followed with another question. "Which brings us back to the cat and the chimera."

"Yes. That relationship must be understood before a resolution can be secured," Matthew concluded.

"Yeah, and that is going to require getting personal with this thing," Kevin stated, "and that's when people get hurt." He looked at his uncle and said, "I know we aren't the first people in the whole world to encounter this thing—or something like it. Somebody out there knows more about it. We need to find who."

"I am already making inquiries," Matthew replied.

24

Kevin sat on the couch eating a bowl of cereal and watching the morning news. The woman on the TV was describing a row-house fire in West Philly that had only been contained after doing severe damage to two of the neighboring units. She reported there were possibly two fatalities in one of the units. A cat had also been rescued from the burning building. The screen switched to a nighttime video of the firefighters pouring water on the fire from hose teams on the ground and a ladder extended over the building. It then switched to a wet, bedraggled yellow cat being carried by a firefighter. It was motionless and looked nearly dead, but the reporter's voice-over said the cat was being transported to the Animal Care and Control Team facility. Kevin quietly swore under his breath. "Well, I'll be damned!"

He got up from the couch when an advertisement interrupted the news. Placing his bowl in the kitchen sink, Kevin began to rummage through the refrigerator. Just as he selected a container of orange juice, Brian stepped in the front door. He dropped his duty bag just inside threshold with a thump. "G'mornin', little brother."

"You look like you had a full night," Kevin observed. "Breakfast?"

"No thanks," Brian waived, "but if you get me a brew, I've got some interesting news for you."

"What's up?" Kevin asked as he found several beers at the back of the bottom shelf.

"I think you have another case."

"Then it *was* the yellow cat. The news showed it. Was there another one?"

"If you mean another corpse, yes," Brian replied as he accepted a bottle of beer.

"Any details?" Kevin asked as Brian twisted off the cap and took a long drink.

"Ah, I needed that. okay. First off, there was the cat. It tore the crap out of Skinny's coat before he whacked it gently on the head with a wrecking bar. He handed it off, but I think Animal Control let it get away."

"They didn't mention that part on the news. Wouldn't that about kill a cat, and who's Skinny?" Kevin asked.

"The news people never get the whole story. Anyway, Skinny's our chauffeur, and the scratches on his hands were still oozing at the end of the shift. Just like your back did. I'm pretty sure that ain't no normal cat." Brian took another drink of his beer and dropped onto the couch. "The other part was a little more on the wild side. We found a body that was badly burned near the source of the fire— pretty typical—but the one we found in the next unit was reduced to ash, like it was cremated."

"I take it that isn't normal."

"Nope. This fire wasn't hot enough to do that, and definitely not in the second unit where we found the ashes. If you will pardon the pun, I think it was bone dry before the fire, and it lit off like an old newspaper. I don't think anybody else knew what they were looking at, but the medical examiner's report will probably show I'm right."

"Not what I was expecting, but I think it gives us another data point," Kevin said.

Brian squinted his eyes at Kevin. "You have a graph or something?"

"Uncle Matthew and I are kinda keeping a record of these encounters."

"Care to elaborate?" Brian enquired.

"After the Cat Queen died, I went to visit Matthew again, and we pieced together some information." Kevin walked to the couch and sat down next to his brother. "We observed that Jerome, Mr. Willy, and the Cat Queen were each about three weeks apart. If the MO, or whatever it might be, is consistent, we expected the next one would be this week."

"Looks like you might be right."

"I hate being right about people dying," Kevin trailed off.

"People die every day, little brother," Brian reminded him. "Not to change the subject, but don't you think the police need to get involved in this before it gets out of hand?"

"I'm not sure what to tell them. Except for Jerome, I can't point to a crime, or even a possible crime."

"Yeah, now that you mention it. But still, it might be worth talking to a detective about it. That way when these shenanigans go public, you aren't going to be suspect number one."

"I don't see how they could make me the lead suspect," Kevin said.

"You found two of the four bodies. That might draw a little attention," Brian observed.

"I hate to break it to you, but you've been there, too," Kevin replied. "But I think I see what you mean. I will make an appointment to talk to my homicide detective buddies. Maybe they will want to take the lead on this after I explain the situation."

"The cops are probably too busy to follow up, but you should give it a try."

25

Kevin walked up the old sailing ship's gangway dressed in the usual employee tropical shirt and khaki shorts. A coyote-brown backpack hung over his left shoulder. When he started across the deck toward the bar, Daisy dropped the towel she'd been using to wipe tables and met him halfway. She crossed her arms over her chest as she and Kevin came face to face.

Daisy shifted her weight from foot to foot and said in a low voice, "Your detective friends are here to see you again." Kevin leaned right to look past Daisy. His eye twitched slightly. Daisy dropped her hands to her hips and asked, "Is there any chance you won't be able to work your shift?"

Straightening up and looking her in the eye, Kevin said, "I was expecting them sooner or later."

"Uh huh. So, there won't be a problem?"

"No problem," Kevin replied. Daisy turned back to her table and Kevin crossed over to shake hands with the detectives. "Thanks for coming. I didn't expect to see you so quickly." Kevin gestured across the river and said with a grin, "You picked a beautiful day to get out of the office. Eighty-two degrees, sunny, and a clear view of the battleship *New Jersey* across the way."

Detective Johnston returned a slight smile, but Powers said in an abrupt voice, "We don't get many calls stringing together four deaths."

"I thought it might be important." Kevin walked behind the bar, dropped his pack, and washed his hands in the sink. Tossing a menu on the bar, he asked, "Can I interest you in a beverage or something from the kitchen? On the house?"

"Ice water," Detective Johnston replied.

"Make that two," Powers chimed in.

Kevin plucked a couple of clean glasses from behind the bar, added ice and filled them from the fountain. He placed a beverage napkin and a glass in front of each of the detectives.

Powers picked up the glass and simultaneously drank and wiped his forehead with the napkin. While Kevin was filling another glass with ice, Powers set the glass on the bar and asked, "So, what do you think is going on here? What's your theory?"

"Just so you understand, I'm not trying to do your job, or play Sherlock Holmes," Kevin said.

"Okay" Powers said with a nod before Kevin resumed.

"I think there are some similarities that look fishy," Kevin said while pouring himself a Coke. "First, there is location. All four of the bodies were found within a few blocks. Next, all four were in a similar physical condition."

"The body found in the fire hasn't been examined yet," Powers interrupted. "How do you know about its condition?"

"I wasn't on the SEPTA tracks either," Kevin agreed. "A guy I know was present at both scenes. He described them to me."

"What's his name?" Johnston asked, clicking a ballpoint pen and opening a small notebook.

Kevin paused and then said, "I don't want him to get in trouble."

"Don't worry about that. What's the name?" Powers asked.

"Brian Maloney."

"Your brother, right?" Johnston said, looking up from the notebook.

"Yeah."

"Go on with your story," Powers instructed.

"Other than the fire victim's status," Kevin said, "the rest of the deceased were unmarried, or essentially alone in the world, and there was three weeks between each one. That can't be chance," Kevin concluded. Johnston finished taking notes on what he said and began flipping backwards in her notebook.

"Not exactly three weeks, but close," she said with a slight lift in her voice.

Powers asked, "You got witnesses or a weapon? What else you got?"

Kevin didn't immediately resume, but glanced at Daisy, who was now standing at the end of the bar, observing the conversation. She grinned at him, and Kevin responded by shrugging his shoulders.

"A couple things. First, there are . . . ghosts," Kevin started again.

"You're kidding, right?" Powers growled.

"Ghost maybe isn't the right word," Kevin said.

"Then what are we talking about?"

Kevin paused to take a drink and hesitated another moment before continuing. "This is my best guess. Each time, there's somebody that looks very similar to the dead person wandering around the neighborhood after the person died. The ghost, the look-alike, chimera, whatever you prefer, never says anything, and never shows up again after the next body is discovered."

"Why do you say the person looks similar?" Johnston asked.

"Jerome's grandmother said the ghost was just like him but looked younger, and he didn't have the same hair. It was like it was shaved off and had only grown back just a little. Also, probably more important, he wasn't wearing diamond ear studs. She said Jerome always wore them."

"Did anybody else see this guy?" Powers asked.

"Yeah. Mark, me, and several others we interviewed. I thought the description was dead on."

"Nobody has seen this person since then?"

"Not that we could find."

"What about William Wood? Who saw him?"

"We talked to a neighbor who knew the real guy all her life. She described the ghost as looking healthier than she'd seen him in years. He was moving better, too, but he never said a word. Completely out of character for a non-stop talker."

"What's the neighbor's name?" Johnston asked.

"Penelope Holmes. She lives on Sixty-First Street."

"Was there a look-alike for Miss Wood?"

Kevin took another drink from his Coke, and then leaned forward on the bar with his right hand extended palm forward. "See that pale area on my hand? After I grabbed Jerome's arm, or rather the ghost's, the skin there just dried up and started peeling off. Nel has the same thing from colliding with Miss Wood's ghost. I don't know what it is. It doesn't hurt or have any other symptoms. It's like the ghost sucks the moisture right out of the skin." Kevin pulled his hand back.

"Have you seen a doctor?" Johnston asked.

"No. Like I said, it doesn't hurt or do anything else. Mine is mostly healed, but it takes a while." Johnston made a small humph sound as she made more notes in her notebook.

"This is interesting information, and you have clearly given it some thought," Powers observed.

"Yeah, but none of it really makes sense."

"I agree," Powers nodded.

"And what about the third hand they found on the SEPTA tracks?" Kevin asked.

"How do you know about that?" Powers replied defensively.

"Mark has a guy in city hall who knows a guy."

Powers rolled his eyes and said, "Of course he does. Look, we will look into it when we get a chance, but I have to be straight with you, the medical examiner hasn't found anything to indicate foul play, Jerome excepted, and you haven't got anything that suggests criminal activity, either."

"Do you agree there could be a pattern? A connection?" Kevin asked.

"We get what you're saying, but a ghost story isn't going to get much attention from the department or the prosecutor," Johnston added in a softer tone of voice that contrasted sharply with Powers.

"That's what my brother said. You have plenty of real criminals to chase down. Well, thanks for hearing me out."

"Look, we will take whatever information comes up, but don't make this into a huge deal. Trying to make connections between everybody that dies under odd circumstances in Philadelphia isn't good for your sanity," Powers offered.

"I hear you, and you're probably right."

Looking right into Kevin's eyes, Johnston said, "Detectives can get into this kind of crazy loop, too. So, try to keep it at arm's length, alright?"

"Arm's length," Kevin replied. The two detectives turned to leave when Kevin blurted, "Before you go, I wondered about something Mark and I heard about Jerome."

Powers and Johnston stopped and turned to Kevin. "What? You holding something back?" Powers asked.

"No, no. I just thought of it. We overheard two guys talking at the junkyard, and they referred to Jerome as a *shiver clown*. What the heck does that mean?" Kevin asked.

"It's a street name for a particular type of perv. You don't really wanna know the rest," Powers said as he resumed his turn to the gangway. Johnston looked Kevin in the eye and shrugged before following Powers to the entrance.

When they disappeared down the gangway, Kevin looked at Daisy and said, "I guess that's it for Inspector Maloney."

"Maybe, but not for Detective Johnston. She's got a thing for you," Daisy chuckled.

"Get out of town," Kevin said.

"I was watching her make eyes at you. Trust me. I'm never wrong about these things," Daisy declared.

26

B rian stood at the kitchen counter whisking a bowl of eggs when Kevin came in the door. Brian asked, "Just in time. Want an omelet?" as he poured the eggs in a skillet.

Squinting at the bright lights, Kevin replied in a tired voice, "Sure."

"Why are you up? You know it's nearly two in the morning."

"It's never too early for breakfast," Brian advised. "What's got you down? Tough night?"

"Naw, it was just another weeknight in the summer, except for the visit from the homicide investigators." Brian nodded in understanding as Kevin walked to the kitchen sink. He filled a glass with water and then said, "My pals, Powers and Johnston, came to see me about the tip I called in. They agreed with most of my conclusions, but since there doesn't seem to be a crime, they won't waste any time on it."

"I think I mentioned that," Brian said as he worked a spatula in the skillet in rhythm with the bubble and pop of the cooking eggs. "Give me a plate."

Kevin retrieved two plates from a stack of mismatches in the cabinet while Brian added other ingredients to the skillet. "You did, but I was hoping they'd pick up the ball and run with it. They won't, and then they told me to leave it alone because it will drive me crazy."

Brian turned to face Kevin and said, "If I didn't already know so much about this thing, I'd think you were crazy. Hell, some of the guys at the house think we—you and me—are going off the deep end."

"Listen, about that. I don't want you to get dragged down by this."

"I'll be just fine," Brian declared as he flipped the contents of the skillet. Then gesturing toward Kevin with his spatula, he said, "But you still need a job, and a reputation as a crazy man won't help." He slid the first omelet out of the skillet onto the plate. Brian then poured the remaining egg mixture in the skillet and began working the spatula again. "Oh, by the way, there is a message on the machine for you. It isn't a job, but you will want to hear it."

"Who is it from?"

"It's Mom. Just go listen to it," Brian said as he worked in the kitchen. Kevin walked into Brian's bedroom where an answering machine sat on a small table. Kevin pressed a button on the top.

"Kevin, it's your mother. I got a call from some boy named Abby or something. He said he knew you from the Marines. I didn't understand what he meant, since you were in the Navy, but if you know him, he would like you to call him at area code six one four, eight eight five, five oh three six. Call me anytime boys." The machine beeped and was silent again. Kevin grinned and returned to the kitchen.

"Well, how about that?" Brian asked.

"A true blast from the past! I hope he's okay. I wonder what made him look for me in Philly? Nobody knows I'm here. *I* didn't even know I was coming here."

"Hey, Watson, did you consider he looked for Mom?"

"Yeah, you're right." Kevin picked up the plate and began cutting the omelet into chunks with the edge of a fork. "We probably talked about where Mom lived sometime after Dad died."

"So, this is good news, huh?" Brian asked.

"Hell, yeah." Kevin laughed before scooping up a fork full of eggs.

27

Kevin coasted his bike to a stop alongside the ship's gangway and locked it up under the steps. He trotted up to the deck of the *Moshulu* and dropped his backpack behind the bar. Whistling quietly as he set about preparing to open for the day, Daisy walked up the steps from the kitchen and asked, "Why so chippy, Skippy?"

"I got a phone call from a buddy of mine," Kevin said in a bright voice.

"What's so special about this buddy of yours that it puts you in a better mood than a day of working with me?" Daisy asked. Kevin looked up with a grin on his face.

"You're pretty fun, Daisy, but you don't have anything on this guy. He was my battle buddy. Like a wing man, you know? Anyway, the last time I saw him he had a couple bullet holes and was getting carried to a helicopter."

"So he was dying and now you know what happened to him and that's why you're so happy. Right?" Daisy questioned.

"No, no. He was wounded alright, but he wasn't going to die. We were so busy I lost track of him after he med-evaced back to San

Diego. Man, I can't wait to see him again. You see we went everywhere together for something like ten months straight. His job was to keep me alive, so I could keep my Marines alive. Man, I can't wait to give him a punch in the shoulder."

"I really don't get men sometimes. Last time you saw him he was full of bullet holes, and all you want to do is punch him?"

"Yeah, it's great, isn't it?" Kevin laughed out loud and was interrupted by Mark crossing the deck from the gangway.

"What's got you giggling like a schoolgirl?" Mark asked.

"A buddy of mine is coming to town. I haven't seen him in a year and a half. You'll have to meet him," Kevin replied.

"Very nice, but before we get to that, I have some interesting news for you."

"Yeah?"

"Yeah, but you will have to pour me a beer to find out what it is."

"Always a catch with this one," Kevin said to Daisy as he filled a glass.

Daisy looked at Mark and said, "Which is kinda weird, since I don't think he's much of a catch."

"Love you, too," Mark grumbled as he took the beer glass offered by Kevin.

"Easy now, you two," Kevin said. "We can all get along. So, what's the big news?"

"It seems somebody wants you." Mark took a long swallow of beer before continuing. "I got a call from our lady-friend in West Philly about job openings at her hospital."

"Nel? Really?"

"Know anybody else out that way who would be slightly interested in your well-being?"

Kevin shrugged. "What did she say? Any details?"

"She gave me the personnel office info and a web page address where you can apply for work." Mark handed Kevin a sheet of paper with some handwritten notes on it.

"The hospital needs patient transporters, phlebotomists, and an OR tech."

"You aren't trained to do any of that stuff, are you?" Daisy asked.

"Yeah, Kevin, inquiring minds want to know, are you qualified to do any of that stuff?" Mark added.

"Yeah, probably. I've never worked in an operating room, but I've seen it done. Patient transport and drawing blood is a piece of cake." Kevin shrugged toward Daisy. "I doubt it pays as much as this."

"Yeah, like this pays so well." Daisy replied. "With tips, a good bartender might make some okay money. Your tips, on the other hand, don't even clear minimum wage." Mark and Kevin both laughed.

"That is not entirely inaccurate," Kevin agreed.

"Then I think you should visit the personnel office right away," Mark recommended.

"Yes, you should," Daisy chimed in. "I can find another crap bartender."

"Are you really calling me a crap bartender?" Kevin asked.

"Oops, did I say that out loud?"

28

Kevin wandered up and down the baggage claim area at Philadelphia International Airport for the fifth time, looking at the posters, signs, and employees. He alternately examined the surroundings and the people emerging from the various passageways. None of the people seemed to satisfy him, so he continued to search the surroundings. Finally, after fidgeting for several more minutes, he spotted someone of interest. He looked right at a tall, slender Black man carrying a backpack in his hand. The man didn't see him, so Kevin called out. "Abi!" The man's head came up, and he scanned the flow of people ahead of him.

"There you are!" Abi called back. Coming together, Abi dropped his pack and wrapped Kevin in a strong hug. Pounding on Kevin's back, he said, "Man, it's good to see you!"

"Likewise! A year and a half is a long time, brother," Kevin said picking up the backpack. "Do you have any more luggage?"

"No, I travel light and fast."

"Once a Marine, always a Marine."

"Semper Fi, Doc," Abi replied with a grin.

"Come on, let's get out of here. I want to show you around Philly." Kevin led the way through the exit doors. They crossed the busy flow of traffic picking up passengers curbside then climbed a flight of stairs to the next level of the parking garage. Kevin led the way to the open-top jeep and lifted the backpack into the back seat.

"I see you still got the all-terrain party transport," Abi observed.

"Yeah, it isn't doing much all-terrain, unless you count potholes, and definitely no party anymore. I'm a responsible citizen now."

"Right, I'm sure you are," Abi said as he climbed into the passenger seat. Kevin dropped heavily in the driver's seat.

"Abi, I am so glad to see you, man."

"Everything is okay, right?" Abi asked.

"Yeah. Everything's fine. The people here don't get the warrior-culture thing, so I don't really talk to anybody about it. But I'm fine. There is some other stuff I want to tell you about, and maybe you can help me make some sense of it, but I am fine. Better than that. I'm great."

"Okay, Doc. But remember that I am here to make sure you stay combat effective."

"Abi, that isn't your job anymore. The gunny won't come looking for you if something bad happens to me."

"I'll always look after you because we are friends. You have important things to do, and I will make sure that you are around to do them. No more arguments. Now, take me to get one of these beef-cheese sandwiches you talk so much about." Kevin shook his head, laughing as he cranked over the engine of the jeep.

"Cheese steak. They are called cheese steak sandwiches."

Kevin drove the jeep out of the garage and maneuvered onto Interstate 95. The highway rose up the approaches to the Girard Point Bridge. From high above the Schuylkill River, downtown Philadelphia was spread before them.

"How do you find your way around such a big city?" Abi yelled over the wind noise of the jeep at highway speed.

"It isn't hard. The roads are all laid out in a big grid. It isn't the streets that require navigation, it's the people. They can be kinda rude." Kevin smiled again. "But once you get to know them, they will treat you very well. That's why they call it the *City of Brotherly Love.*"

29

Kevin maneuvered the jeep into the Penn's Landing parking lot. He and Abi climbed out of the vehicle, and Abi pointed to the old sailing ship. "That's where you work?"

"Yep, well, kinda. I just got a job at a hospital, but I'm still here until next week," Kevin replied, leading the way toward the gangway.

"That's outstanding, Doc."

"Yeah, I hope so. It's steady work, and I might be able to roll into a better job." The two climbed the gangway to the main deck, where they were met by Daisy.

"You miss work so much you had to come back? Didn't anybody ever tell you never hang around your job when you're not on the clock?" Daisy remarked.

"I wanted you to meet Abi and show you he is a real person. Abi, this is Daisy." Daisy extended a hand to Abi and looked him up and down. Abi took the offered hand to shake it, but she held on to his hand.

"Indeed, you *are* a real man," she cooed while rubbing her other hand on his muscular forearm, "much more so than this freckled Irish runt."

"It is very nice to meet you, Miss Daisy," Abi replied.

"Just Daisy, Abi. I think we can be friends right away." She led him across the deck to a table in the shade. Kevin followed, and they all sat down.

"Don't get any ideas," Kevin said turning to Abi. "She is a sucker for tall, handsome men, but she's like a dog chasing a car. Once she stops one, she doesn't know what to do with it." Abi laughed and squeezed her hand.

"I am a fan of attractive women such as yourself. Maybe we can get together in the future, but for now I'm here to see my battle buddy."

"Suit yourself. In the meantime, would you like a cool drink? Kevin is buying," Daisy declared.

"Since you have a nice tropical theme here, maybe you can make a Mai Tai?"

"I can't, but Freddie over there might be able to swing it." Daisy pointed toward the bar where a tall well-muscled man was filling out some paperwork on a clipboard.

"My replacement?" Kevin asked. "That didn't take long."

"Bartenders are a dime a dozen," Daisy grinned. She turned to the bar and called to Freddie. "Can you make a Mai Tai?"

"A little old school, but, yes, ma'am."

"Thank you." She turned back to the table. "He's very polite, too."

"Great," Kevin laughed. "So, you won't miss me at all."

"No, not really." Daisy looked at Abi, "Need something to eat?"

"No, thank you. Kevin took me to Geno's for a wiz sandwich. I don't understand why, but tomorrow, he said we are going to Pat's, across the street."

"I think you mean a steak with cheese wiz, and I see why you are going to Pat's tomorrow." Daisy stared at Kevin with a serious look on her face as he erupted in uncontrollable laughter. Gesturing toward Abi, she said, "Did he really order a wiz sandwich from the man who has a *Speak English* sign in the window?"

"I did not, Miss Daisy. He wouldn't let me order," Abi interjected.

"Oh, thank the Lord. They would have eaten you alive, kicked you out of line, and banned you for life," Daisy said, and walked away. Kevin and Abi both continued to laugh about Daisy's reaction.

"Fantastic, Doc. You always find such interesting people!"

"Daisy is an interesting lady—very interesting," Kevin chuckled and then asked, "So, what are you doing now? Are you in school like you planned?"

"After separating from the Corps in April, I moved back to Ohio. I'm starting school in Cincinnati at the end of the month."

"Good for you. What are you going to study?"

"I'm going into the family business. You know the one I told you about, the one from the old country."

"Really? Wasn't your grandfather a witch doctor or something? Where do you go to school for that?" Kevin asked.

"No, no. He was an undertaker." Abi rolled his eyes at Kevin, and chuckled. "He was the man who collected the deceased in the village. He made sure everybody was dead, buried, and stayed that way."

"Yeah, but you told me some drunk stories about witch-doctor stuff, too. Where does that come in?"

"You remember those stories? I underestimated you."

"You are my friend. I listen to everything you say, as if my own mother was telling it to me."

"Your mother told you *not* to join the Navy, and yet you did!"

"I listened to her. I just didn't do what she wanted me to do."

Abi laughed at the reply, "I see how it is. But really, I am going to Mortuary School on my GI Bill money."

"That's good, steady work there. Good for you."

After another moment, Daisy reappeared at the table with a glass filled with an orange liquid, topped with a miniature green and pink umbrella. "If it isn't any good, please tell me, so I can school Freddie." She placed a napkin on the table with the drink and followed with a glass of Coca-Cola for Kevin. Kevin looked up at Daisy. "Thank you, Daisy."

"You are welcome," she said, looking at Abi. "So, are you going to tell Abi about your dead people adventures?"

"I might."

"I think you should. Maybe he can figure out what is wrong with you."

Abi picked up the umbrella-adorned glass and held it out at eye level. "Devil Dogs!" he said in a firm voice. Kevin repeated it and touched his glass to Abi's. Abi took a sip of the drink and smiled his approval.

"It's good?" she asked.

"Yes, it is very good. Freddie did well," Abi said, taking another sip of the drink. He then turned to Kevin. "You must tell me about the dead people. They are my future!"

Daisy looked at Abi and laughed.

"Thanks Daisy. I'll take it from here."

"Just trying to be a conversation starter," Daisy said over her shoulder as she walked away.

Kevin turned to Abi. "I really do want to tell you about it, but not here. We'll talk at the apartment, with my brother. He's seen them, too."

"This is your older brother, the fireman?" Abi asked.

"Yeah, him."

"Okay. We'll talk about old friends and good times until then," Abi declared.

Kevin held up his glass and said, "Here's to old friends and good times!"

Abi responded by touching glasses again. "I can drink to that."

30

Kevin and Abi reclined on opposite ends of the well-worn couch, watching the late TV news. A woman on the screen was describing the latest Philadelphia police investigations. "Your local news has about as much killing and destruction as a Marine Corps after-action report." Abi observed.

"It's not that bad. I think there were only three hundred and twenty-some murders last year," Kevin commented.

"Not quite one a day. You'll have to work on that if you want the high score," Abi replied. He shifted in his seat, looking directly at Kevin. "Since we're talking about it, are you ready to tell me about your dead people?"

"I guess so. It's weird stuff. If it was anybody but you, I'd just keep my mouth shut."

"Death is a natural part of life, and the passage can be good or bad. We've seen plenty of the bad kind. Which is this?"

"It's not good, I'm sure of that, but it isn't bad, like snipers and landmines, either. It's more suspicious-bad." Kevin got up from the couch and stepped to the kitchen. "You want anything while I am up?"

Abi followed him with his eyes, "Nah, I'm good, and you're avoiding the topic."

"No, I'm not." Kevin opened the freezer. "Are you sure you don't want something? There's some ice cream in here."

"You didn't offer that. You know I'm all about the frozen dairy delight."

"Yeah, I figured," Kevin scoffed and started scooping ice cream into bowls.

"Go back to the beginning, when you were not bothered by this," Abi suggested.

"Funny, that's what my uncle said, too." Kevin replied. "Okay, from the top. So, I was working at the bar, and Mark, this sports reporter I know, shows up one day. We start talking, and he tells me about some kid named Jerome. He's a big-time college basketball player from West Philly who just drops off the face of the planet. Mark gets this idea that we can find him and get this big news story. Well, it didn't turn out anything like he expected."

"What did Mark expect?" Abi asked.

"Mark guessed Jerome was lying low to avoid the press because he was now eligible for the NBA draft."

"Okay, that's a reasonable place to start," said Abi.

"So, we ride out to this neighborhood and start asking around. Much to my surprise, we find a couple of guys who saw him since he went missing. They said he acted strange, was dressed in shabby clothes, and was missing all his gold and diamonds and stuff," Kevin said as he carried the bowls back to the couch and handed one to Abi.

Abi ate a spoonful and said, "I wasn't expecting coffee ice cream. Good choice."

"We aim to please," Kevin said, before taking a bite of his own and sitting down again. Resuming his story, Kevin said, "Then, on our second trip, we come across this old guy sitting in a doorway. He goes by Mister Willy, and he's got this yellow cat with a busted tail that follows him around. Trying to get in good with him, we buy him a pack of smokes, and he points out where we can find the kid. It turns out he's right across the street, and sure enough, the kid's got no shoes and is dressed in rags. We try to work our way toward him, but he keys in on us, and I can tell he's going to run. I get a good look at him as we approach, and the descriptions are right on. No ear studs, it looks like his head was just shaved, and he's pale as me." Kevin took another bite of ice cream and looked at Abi, who looked right back with no expression. "You following me?" Kevin asked.

"Yes, very well. This is an interesting story. Continue."

"So, just as I reach for his wrist, he bolts. He's something like six foot seven, maybe two hundred and forty pounds of muscle. Even with no shoes, running over concrete sprinkled with broken glass, he leaves me in the dust. I follow him for several blocks into a junkyard and, in the confusion of getting over the fence, I lose sight of him. A minute later, when Mark finally belly-flops over the fence, we break out flashlights and start tracking him through the trash and weeds. Eventually, the trail leads to a corner of the lot, where we see eyes glinting back at us, so we move to box him in. When we get there, he's gone, and there's this yellow cat under a pile of old rags."

"Interesting."

"Yeah, and I'd swear it was the same cat we'd just seen with Mister Willy," Kevin said.

"When you grabbed for Jerome's wrist, did you touch his skin?" Abi asked in a serious tone of voice.

"Yeah, that was weird, too. On my hand where I grabbed him, the skin just dried up. It didn't hurt or anything, it started peeling off. I figured there was some kind of hazmat on me or something."

Abi nodded slowly, shoveling out more ice cream, and said, "Are you ready for some African mythology?"

"It might as well be now," Kevin agreed.

"My mother told me about this at the first funeral I attended when I was a little kid," Abi said. "It was handed down from my great-grandfather. It starts with a cat that stalks people near a village. Like cats everywhere, it's shy and a little bit lazy. It just waits for somebody to go out in the jungle alone, then it pounces."

"Sounds about right for predatory animals," observed Kevin.

"So, the next part is where it starts to sound similar to your experience," Abi said. "In the legend, a person who falls victim to the jungle cat wanders back into the village as a ghost."

"The cat made them into a ghost?" Kevin asked.

"My great-grandfather claimed the cat stole the life spirit and left the empty shell of the person. *Ghost* is the word my mother used. I'm sure there is a more accurate term in her native language."

"Like when we were in Helmand and the translator always claimed something was an idea that didn't translate well," Kevin said.

"Exactly," Abi agreed before he continued, "in the village, if the ghost got close, people would push it away. Wherever they touched the ghost, the skin died."

"What a coincidence," Kevin said looking at his hands. "So, how did they get rid of the cat and these ghosts?"

"I don't think they had a way to chase them off. The ghost would be seen around the village until somebody else died. Then the ghost would be replaced with the ghost of the next victim. The key was to make sure there were no new victims. Then the cat and ghost would leave."

"It reminds me of a Brothers Grimm fairy tale, except it teaches the lesson of why you should never go into the jungle alone."

"Actually," Abi said, "My mother told me this story so I would understand why the dead and dying must be attended at all times."

"Yeah, don't feed the cats or before you know it you will be up to your eyes in ghosts. How old were you when you first heard this story?"

"I wasn't in school yet, so maybe four or five."

"Well, that explains your enthusiasm for the battle-buddy system."

"It is important to me," Abi admitted while he finished his ice cream, carefully capturing every last bit with his spoon. When the bowl was empty, he carried it to the kitchen sink and then returned to the couch. "That story is part of the reason I am going to mortuary school. I want to make sure people end up where they are supposed to go."

"It's surprisingly similar to Jerome's story."

"You know, with all the people who die alone in big cities, if one of these cats got loose here, it could make a lot of ghosts."

"You got that right," Kevin agreed. "What happened to the bodies in the African story?"

"I am not sure what you mean. My mother's telling of the story didn't include bodies. I always assumed the ghosts were the bodies, minus the soul."

"Mark and I have bodies to go along with our ghosts," Kevin declared. "Each one of the ghosts was a duplicate of a dead body. Given our experience with the Cat Queen, I'm pretty sure the ghost and the dead body are separate entities."

"How many of these ghosts have you seen?"

"I have personally seen three. All in the same neighborhood, within a few weeks of each other. My brother Brian suspects there was a fourth, but the body was destroyed in a fire. The firefighters on the scene caught the cat, but it escaped after tearing apart a firefighter."

"First thing in the morning I will call my parents," Abi said. "Maybe we can find out how the bodies and ghosts fit together."

31

Kevin, Brian, and Abi occupied a table in the back of the busy Burger King, quietly eating breakfast when Mark walked in the door. Brian spotted him first. "About darn time," he scoffed in a loud voice. "These media types are all the same—driving by after all the hard work is done, getting just enough video to file a story, only to get it all wrong."

"Firemen! All sirens and lights and bragging about their hoses!" Mark called back, as Brian stood up from the table and extended a hand. "Good to see you again." They shook hands, grinning ear to ear, then Mark slid into a chair next to Brian.

Kevin introduced Mark and Abi. "Nice to meet you," Abi said. "So you're the guy who stirred up all this trouble?"

"Guilty," Mark laughed. "As you know, Kevin and I go way back, but you know things I don't. We'll have to compare notes sometime. He's very secretive and doesn't like to share."

"I believe you're right," Abi confirmed.

"Yeah, yeah, enough of the Kevin fan club," Brian said. "Let's get to the Twilight Zone stuff."

"Fine idea," Kevin chimed in. "Just to fill everybody in, Abi is from a distinguished line of Nigerian undertakers and witch doctors. Consequently, he has access to some insights not normally available to three average Joes like us. For example, just this morning, after a call with his parents, he was able shine a light into our little dark alley of mystery."

Abi rolled his eyes and said, "I told you last night there are no witch doctors. You must have witches in need of care before you can have doctors to care for them."

"Hah, that's what you say," Kevin snickered. "Besides, it's the information that's important. Abi, would you care to explain?"

"Yes, but there are no witch doctors. Just undertakers."

"Okay, no witch doctors for now, but please proceed," Mark jumped in.

"In the belief of my parents' generation, and before, there was a jungle cat that came around the village and made ghosts of the people who recently died. Some people said it was the cat that killed them, others said the cat was just an opportunistic scavenger. Either way, when the cat started stalking on the edge of the village, a ghost followed soon after."

"Well, that sounds familiar." Mark said. "Do the ghosts do anything?"

"The ghost wanders around looking for another body to occupy. If the ghost is touched by a living person, it tries to move in, but gets rejected by the spirit in the body. The flesh dies where the contact was made. It's rejected by the living and the dead."

"That seems to follow our experience, too," Mark commented. "So, what happens in the long run here? Is it something bad? It seems to me that we are just swapping out souls, and eventually everybody will get a turn."

"I don't know. My parents are certain that the spirit may not go to the afterlife until the body of the deceased is underground. That is why it is so important to always attend to the dead, so the cat or ghost may not steal the body as a vessel. In my parents' tradition, the body was buried as soon as possible. This kept the jungle cat away and made a safe passage to the afterlife. That's where my ancestors came in. They were the tribal version of the undertaker."

"So, getting the body buried wasn't about preventing the spread of disease and eliminating the smell of rotting flesh?" Brian asked.

"The tradition is much older than the modern understanding of disease," Kevin explained.

"Yeah, but anybody can understand the smell of the dead," Brian replied.

Abi jumped back into the discussion, "That's true, but in Africa, a dead body doesn't last long. It is consumed by animals and insects very quickly, starting with the big scavengers. It is not like the lady you found inside her house. My parents said it is important to the family of the deceased to have the body washed, prepared for burial, and attended constantly until it is buried. This keeps the vessel intact and ensures the spirit can go to the afterlife. If not, the cat might seize it, make the person into a ghost, and then it will be wandering around until it can find another way to the afterlife."

"I can see how having the ghost of your mother-in-law wandering around your backyard might lessen the old mojo a bit," Mark quipped. "So how do we break this chain of wandering ghosts, if that is what we have here?"

"I don't know." Abi replied. "In the jungle, the cat will go elsewhere if there's no prey. In my parent's village, ghosts haven't been seen in a very long time. No one alive has seen one because the undertakers do a good job. In this big city, lots of people die every day, and some will be unattended and could easily fall victim to a jungle cat or ghosts."

"But there is another question. Are the ghost and bodies one entity or separate? Abi's folks didn't have any insight there. Not too helpful, I know," Kevin commented looking around the table. "But at least we have some theory of what is happening. Maybe. If you can believe African lore."

"It beats my explanation, and it's got more details than the Dark-Age-cat-cult thing," Brian said. "Maybe Uncle Matt can do something with this. He is pretty well versed in world religions and death stuff."

"That's our next stop," Kevin agreed. "Abi and I are going to see him today."

32

Kevin drove the jeep through the front gate of the seminary campus and maneuvered around the buildings. "This place is huge!" Abi observed as they drove in a long arc behind the main complex.

Kevin laughed in agreement as they turned down another lane. "My uncle's been teaching here for a million years, so he probably knows every little nook and cranny."

Finding a parking space near the entrance of the faculty building, Kevin swung the jeep in between the lines and shut off the engine. Kevin said, "He'll be pleased as punch to meet you. He's a really friendly guy." They dismounted the vehicle and began walking toward the building when the priest emerged from a doorway into the daylight.

"Hello, boys!" he called out with a grin on his face. "It is very nice of you to come out today." Kevin was enfolded into a friendly embrace by his uncle.

"Father Matthew O'Conner, this is my good friend, Abi Okobi," Kevin introduced the two.

"It's very nice to meet you, sir." Abi offered his hand, and they shook like long lost friends.

"Likewise, Abi." The priest gestured toward the open lawn between the buildings. "Let's walk while we talk. I am in need of fresh air and my bones are not protesting so much today." The old man led off with the younger men flanking him. After a dozen steps, he resumed the conversation, "Kevin tells me you are from Ohio."

"Yes, sir. Columbus."

"I once went to Columbus, a long time ago. The bishop sent me to give a lecture at the Pontifical College Josephinum. It was outside the city, surrounded by woods, and near a small river. Does that sound familiar?"

"It isn't far from my parents' home. I went there to play soccer from time to time."

"Very good, then at least we have trod the same path before, for a few moments anyway," he puffed.

"I was just a kid, sir. I didn't really know what the place was until later."

"No matter. Kevin tells me you are going to mortuary school, yes?"

"The profession is a tradition in my family," Abi replied. "Many generations of my family prepared the dead of their village."

"It is a noble service," the old man said. He walked in silence for a while, his breath becoming more labored. Then he said, "Remarkable. First a Marine, and then a future mortician." The old cleric looked from Abi to Kevin and back. "Both of you might have made fine priests."

"I don't think celibacy is in the cards for either one of us," Kevin said.

"Ah, the ladies' men." The priest smiled and continued, "No matter. There is a place for every willing soul to make a contribution in God's kingdom." The three paused at a bench under a large tree. The old man sat down, and the young men joined him. "Abi, tell me what your parents said. Let's start with the normal burial ritual."

"My mother and father grew up in remote Nigerian villages. They came to the US as college students. It was my mother's side that dealt with the deceased and directed other families on how to proceed. The usual method included collecting the body and cleaning it with water. It was then wrapped in cloth and carried feet first in a meandering procession to the burial ground. The random route was to confuse the spirit, so that it couldn't find its way back too quickly. A pit was dug, and the body was laid in it and covered. The grave was marked with an object of value to the deceased, followed by a mourning period."

"Good," the old man said. "Preparing a body for burial is a common practice around the world, and nearly every faith has special ritual for the dead. They usually include washing. Most also include some kind of special attire or clothing. There is also perfume or oil. Did they describe that as part of their practice?" The old priest asked.

"I don't think it was part of the ritual, but my mother said herbs or flowers were sometimes used with the water."

"I see. So how do we get to the cat part of the story?" he asked. Abi then began to describe the jungle cat appearing in the village, followed shortly after by the appearance of a ghost after a death.

"What conditions would precipitate a visit from the jungle cat?" Father Matt asked. "I suspect it happens when the proper burial mechanism breaks down because there are too many bodies to bury."

"That is probably correct. If disease, war, or some natural disaster causes many people to die unexpectedly there could be problems. When the death rate is normal, then all the bodies can be accounted for and buried."

"No unattended bodies means no place for the cat to prey," Kevin chimed in.

"How do we know the spirit of the person is removed by the cat?" the priest asked.

"That is just the traditional belief. I don't think there would be any way to know for sure," Abi offered. "Again, I can ask my parents to see if they have more information."

The priest looked at Kevin and said, "Are you getting all this? There will be many follow-up questions for Abi's parents."

"Yes, sir. I think so," Kevin nodded.

"Is it your understanding that the cat and the ghost are separate entities, where one creates the other?"

"I think so," Abi answered.

"Are the cat and ghost ever seen together?"

"I don't know for certain, but I don't think so. The cat comes into the village, a ghost appears, and the cat is not seen at the same time as the ghost. Maybe the ghost is at night and the cat is during the day."

"Another nice bit of information to have," the priest observed. "I hope you will not irritate your parents with all this questioning."

"I don't think so. They like talking about the old country."

"That's good," the old priest said. "I think we are making some headway in finding answers. This is very helpful." Father Matt slowly pushed himself to his feet, and when he caught his breath again, he said, "We can be reasonably sure that this phenomenon is not new. That means someone is knowledgable on the topic, and I'll find them. This fits much better than the Papal Bull and extermination of cats across Europe, but that's not to say they aren't both connected." He turned to look at the two younger men. "Enough business. How about you drive me to that Italian ice place down on Fifty-Ninth? Rita makes a pretty good treat for a day like today."

"You know it is a chain of stores called Rita's, right?" Kevin asked.

"Yes, of course I know that. It just happens there is also a young lady who works in the store named Rita."

Kevin turned to Abi, "Don't worry, they sell another form of ice cream. It's how I knew you two would get along." Abi and Father Matt laughed.

33

The late afternoon sun, reflected by buildings across the street, made irregular polygons of light and darkness across the drab basement apartment. On the couch, Brian dozed under a green Philadelphia Eagles blanket. At the clicking of the lock and turn of the doorknob, his eyes opened a crack and tracked Kevin and Abi entering. Catching sight of Brian's eye movement, Kevin said, "Sorry, didn't mean to wake you."

"Don't worry about it. I was just resting my eyes. I should get up," Brian said as he stretched his arms and yawned. "Did you have an informative visit with Uncle Matthew?"

"You could say that," Kevin replied. "We got some more homework. He asked a lot of questions we couldn't answer. Then he wanted to get some Italian ice."

"Did you go see his girlfriend, Rita?"

"Yep. Imagine my surprise at finding a girl behind the counter actually named Rita!" Brian and Abi both chuckled.

"So, what kind of stuff did he want to know?" Brian asked, swinging his feet to the floor and dragging himself upright.

"He was mostly looking for confirmation of things we've already seen," Kevin explained. He reached into his pocket and pulled out a napkin from Rita's. Kevin looked over the notes written on it and then said, "After another phone call, we learned Abi's ancestors passed down the story of the jungle cat. According to Abi's folks, it came around the village at times of more frequent deaths. Usually during an outbreak of some disease, but there was also a story of a flood that attracted the cat. During the civil war in the 1980s, when Abi's folks left the country, there were rumors of haunted villages in remote areas."

"I guess that makes sense, more prey for the cat," Brian said.

"Nobody they knew had personally seen a cat or ghost, so this is all second-hand information," Abi added. "They didn't know if the bodies were desiccated, or if they were any different from what you found."

"The easy part," Kevin said, "was confirmation that the cat and ghost weren't seen at the same time."

Brian stood up, rubbed his eyes and said, "Well that's something, but I take it there is a hard part?"

"There is. Uncle Matthew wanted to know more about the ghost getting to the afterlife by using a fresh body as a vessel."

Brian nodded, "Hmm, that is a little harder to answer. It isn't exactly black and white."

Kevin looked at Abi. "Want to take a stab at explaining the extra part?"

Abi nodded once and said, "My father just had to toss another idea into the mix to make it even more complicated." Abi cleared his throat and then continued the explanation, "Since he's a professor, he gave us a little more academic view about the village culture. He said it is believed that the spirit of the individual is a permanent force. It never ceases to exist. That is why it is thought that the ghost is the spirit seeking passage to the afterlife."

"That isn't unusual, is it?" Brian asked. "Don't Christians, Muslims, and Hindus all assign some kind of permanence to the soul?"

Abi paused a moment, and then continued, "Yes. The human is assumed to be just a temporary form in the journey of the soul. It comes from somewhere to be here and is going somewhere after."

"That makes sense." Brian stood up and glanced out the street level window. "The exception is the people out there who claim there is nothing after this life. We are a one-shot deal. Nothing before, and nothing after."

"Exactly. Most faith systems assume that the spirit, or soul, or life force, if there is one, endures past death. It goes to Heaven, Hell, Purgatory, the underworld, or becomes something else, like in reincarnation." Abi caught his breath and then continued, "The opposite is no soul, no spirit, no gods, and no place after this."

Brian raised his hand and snapped his fingers. "Boom, boom. Out go the lights."

"Is that a reference? Because, it sounded rehearsed," Kevin asked.

"A song, way before your time," Brian chuckled.

"Anyway," Abi said after pausing. "Now, thanks to never-ending professorial reasoning, we have something else to consider."

Brian looked from the window to Abi and Kevin, "Sounds serious."

"Yeah, it is," Kevin said. "What if our understanding of the soul is incomplete? What if there is a third option we never considered?" Brian's eyes opened wide as Abi began again.

"Assume the spirit, or soul, is indeed on a journey," Abi said, "like a person going from one place to another. What happens if there is a roadside bandit that preys on them when they are vulnerable?"

"You mean like getting mugged?" Brian asked.

"Yes. Suppose God, or nature, or whoever makes spirits, sends them on a journey, and along the way some are destroyed."

"That wasn't exactly covered in catechism," Brian remarked as he walked to the kitchen and began filling the coffee maker. "Okay. I gotta think about this for a second." Brian scooped coffee into the top of the machine. "Anybody else want a cup of joe?"

Abi responded, "I'll join you."

Brian switched on the coffee maker and collected two cups before turning to Abi and Kevin. "Let me talk this out," Brian said. "God sends souls down to animate humans. The humans live their lives and then die. Then there are two ways to go. Up to Heaven or down to Hell, with maybe another little temporary detour some place in between, depending on what kind of life they lived. If the person is a Hindu, maybe the soul comes back again as a butterfly or cow, or something like that. Either way, the soul keeps going somewhere." Kevin and Abi nodded, and Brian turned to watch the black liquid drip into the carafe. "That's the conventional teaching." When it was half full, he poured coffee in the two cups and put it back under the coffee maker. Brian handed one to Abi and resumed his summation. "What you are suggesting is a mugger, who is not God, not the devil, but just a thing preying on souls, like a pick-pocket lifting wallets from tourists. He steals the wallet, or soul, uses the important stuff for a bus ticket, or bottle of cheap booze or some dope. He chucks the wallet and then moves on to the next victim. All that's left in the wallet is an expired library card and baby pictures." Brian paused and sipped his coffee before continuing. "In the case of our victims, the soul is all used up, doesn't go to Heaven or Hell, and this cat goes about its business looking for another hit."

"Yeah, that's a good way to put it," Abi said, looking up at the window.

"And that doesn't really get all of it," Kevin added. "Abi's dad pointed out that if there is a third way, there could be four or five, and on and on. It is a religious and philosophical quagmire!"

Abi mumbled, "Yes, yes," staring intently over Kevin's shoulder.

"What are you looking at?" Kevin asked, turning to follow his gaze, but Abi remained silent, slowly stepping forward.

"I saw a glimpse of something up there, too." Brian said.

Abi took a long drink of his coffee. Finishing the cup, he said, "Did I see a cat looking in the window?"

Kevin led the way to the door, followed closely by Abi and Brian, saying, "What color was it?"

"White with orangey stripes," Abi replied.

"Come on!" Kevin hissed as he pounded up the steps and then paused at the top, just below the level of the sidewalk. Raising his eyes above ground level like a periscope, he searched in every direction. His body motions slow and smooth, he gestured for Abi and Brian to follow and resumed climbing the steps. He turned right after emerging from the stair well and Abi immediately matched Kevin's actions, and split directions. They drew farther apart, staying in the long shadows cast by the adjacent buildings. The street was empty of people. Cars were parked bumper to bumper along the near side, and traffic was sporadic. Brian padded up the steps in his stocking feet and poked his head out above ground. Kevin held his finger up to his lips. Brian nodded and remained stationary.

Standing at opposite ends of the building's facade, Kevin and Abi scanned the street. When Kevin made eye contact with Abi, he extended his index and middle fingers. First, he pointed to his own eyes and then jabbed them toward the parked cars. The two men eased down to their hands and knees and scanned under the cars.

Brian dropped back down a couple steps and whispered, "Be right back," and then disappeared down the steps. After a few moments, Brian came up the steps with a large aluminum flashlight.

"Genius," Abi whispered.

"Look for the eyes to reflect back," Kevin instructed.

Brian turned on the light and from the edge of stairwell directed the beam under the nearest cars. The first two cars revealed nothing, but under the third, Brian caught a flicker of movement in the beam. "That silver wagon!" Brian hissed. Kevin and Abi immediately moved to their respective ends of the car. "Near the front," Brian further instructed. Kevin and Abi lay on their bellies, putting their heads sideways on the ground.

"I see something," Kevin called. "Closer to you."

"I see it. It's a cat alright. I can see the tail moving," Abi confirmed.

"Brian, get the light over here," Kevin said in a quiet and calm voice. "I want to see what color it is."

Brian tumbled out of the stairwell and nearly fell on Abi as he flopped to the ground. The metal flashlight slipped from Brian's hand and clinked on the pavement. The cat flinched at the sound.

"Sorry," Brian whispered, as he retrieved the flashlight and dropped it into Abi's hand.

"There!" Abi exclaimed as he played the beam over the cat, showing the retroreflective qualities of its eyes and the white of its bared teeth. The cat hissed at Abi and backed away from him. Kevin quietly wriggled half under the car toward the cat, now spotlighted from the other side. "Look like the right cat?" Abi asked.

"I can't see the tail, but it's for sure the right color," Kevin confirmed.

Brian pushed himself upright. "Hold on Kevin! Let me get something to wrap it up."

"If you can get it to back my way just a bit, I can get its body and not have to mess with the teeth." The cat was frozen in place, beyond reach of either man.

Brian tramped down the steps and returned quickly with the green blanket from the couch. "If we can subdue it long enough to get it balled up, you might not get torn to pieces."

"I'm going to shift around to the side. Be ready to catch it when it bolts." Kevin directed. He repositioned to the street side of the car and belly crawled headfirst under the car, inching a little closer. Just as he reached for the cat, a minivan screeched to a stop, just short of Kevin's legs extending from under the car. In that instant, the cat made a break toward Abi, scratching his hand on the way by.

The minivan driver leaned out the window and yelled, "What are you doin'! Get outta the street!"

"We're trying to rescue a cat here!" Brian yelled back.

"Well, your cat took off over there. So, get outta the street before ya get hurt!"

Kevin scrambled out from under the car and straightened his shirt.

"Thanks for your help, and you have a nice day, too!" Brian yelled back as the driver pulled away, and then added, "Damn, that was close."

"I almost had it," Kevin said.

"I meant you almost got your legs run over! That would have sucked just a little bit there, boyo."

"Yeah, that too," Kevin agreed, glancing over his shoulder at the street.

"Was that your cat?" Abi asked, rubbing the scratch on his hand.

Kevin pointed to the scratch. "We'll know for sure if your hand doesn't start scabbing over like it should. Let's see if we can spot it again," Kevin directed Abi.

"How the hell did it know to look for us here? It's not like it can look us up in the white pages," Brian suggested.

"I don't know, but I think the better question is why? Is it stalking us?" Kevin asked as he started down the street. Abi crossed the street and moved down the opposite sidewalk, shining the flashlight into the dark shadows created by the sinking sun. Brian stood at the top of the steps, with the blanket tucked under his arm.

"I can't believe it, hunted by a frigging house cat!" Brian spat as he watched Kevin and Abi check potential hiding places along the street.

Kevin and Abi worked a block east before returning the way they came, and then turning successively north and south. "There's no sign of it," Abi said.

"If that is our cat, it will be back." Kevin observed. "Let's knock off. It knows we are looking for it. We'll do better if we change up our strategy."

They returned to the apartment and stood outside the stairwell. Kevin looked up at the walls of the surrounding buildings. He examined the basement windows and looked back up at the utility poles and across the street.

"Are you thinking about persistent surveillance?" Abi asked.

"We need something like that." Kevin said as he led the way back down the stairs. "If that scratch is still oozing tomorrow, we'll know it's the right cat, and a game camera might catch it in action."

34

Abi rolled over on the couch, squinting at the morning light filtering into the apartment. He rubbed his eyes with his fingers and then patted the patchwork of bandages stuck to the back of his hand. "Here goes nothing," he said and pulled at one side of a tan plastic strip. A tiny expanding globule of deep red blood built on top of the scratch. "That cat is bad news," he grumbled as he put the bandage back over the wound.

On the floor behind the couch, the nylon of a sleeping bag rustled against an air mattress. Abi rolled onto his back and called in a hushed voice. "Kevin." There was no response. "Kevin!" he called a little louder.

"What?" came a cotton-mouthed voice.

"Are you awake?"

"Why do you always ask if I'm awake? If I'm talking to you, I'm awake."

"Right now, that's true, but when I hear you profess your undying love for Miss Hayes, I suspect you're talking in your sleep," Abi mocked.

"Whatever. Who told you about Miss Hayes?"

"You told me in your sleep. Who is this mysterious woman? Can I meet her?" Abi inquired.

"Doesn't matter, and no, you can't meet her. Why did you wake me up? I don't have to take you to the airport for hours."

"The scratch, it still bleeds."

"Well, that answers the million-dollar question, doesn't it?"

"I think you should cover the windows. That cat is probably getting the goods on you," Abi said.

Kevin sat up from the floor poking his head over the back of the couch. He looked at the little windows. "I'll fix that cat," he yawned. "If we cover the windows, it will be harder to predict its movements. We've got to have some kind of bait to keep it coming around."

"Ah, that's the brilliant tactical mind I know. Especially the part where you use yourself as honey for the flies."

"Eff you. I'm getting up," Kevin responded. He rolled off the air mattress, stood up, and disappeared into the bathroom. The light came on and the door closed. Abi rolled over and buried his head under the pillow. He was asleep again in a twitch.

35

"**A**re you really trying to catch the cat?" Brian queried.

"Yes, I am." Kevin stood in the center of the apartment looking out the windows, empty boxes and packaging at his feet. "I doubt I can lay hands on it again, but hopefully these game cameras will pick it up," Kevin replied.

"Pictures are close enough for me. I'm not thrilled about caging a broken-tailed, anti-coagulant feline in my humble abode."

"I don't think it will get that far. Come on and give me a hand. I have a couple good places to put the cameras, but we need to meet the neighbors for this to work."

Kevin and Brian climbed the steps carrying the cameras and crossed to the opposite side of the street. "One goes over there for a broad view of the block," Kevin suggested. "If the other is at the base of the utility pole it will give a low cross angle, and a little closer view in front of our windows."

"Looks good. Any chance the neighbors will mind us taking pictures of them?"

"Not if we're saving animals from extinction," Kevin quipped.

Brian grinned and followed Kevin to the door of the most suitable building for mounting the camera. Kevin knocked and waited for an answer.

"You could try the doorbell," Brian said.

"Thanks, wise guy," Kevin replied, pushing the button twice. A double chime echoed from somewhere behind the door. Shortly after the sound faded away, the door opened a crack. A single bloodshot eye was visible in the darkness behind the door.

"Yo. What do you want?" the deep voice inquired from the dark.

"Hey, I'm your neighbor, Kevin, and this is my brother, Brian. We live right over there, in the basement apartment."

"So, what?"

"We're trying to help Brian's daughter with her science fair project, and we need to get some pictures of urban songbirds."

"Huh."

"Anyway, we'd like to put this game camera up on your wall. It automatically takes pictures of animals as they go by. It will let Brian's daughter count how many birds live in our part of the city."

"That sounds pretty dumb to me, but I had a kid in school, and I had to do some stupid stuff, too." The door closed for a moment and opened fully, revealing an unshaven, middle-aged man in a white tank-top undershirt and boxer shorts. "Where you wanna put it?"

"I was thinking we can put about so high," Kevin gestured with his hand over his head, "zip tied around the downspout over on the corner."

"That's all you wanna do? Go ahead. I don't see how that can hurt anything."

"Thank you, sir," Brian chimed in.

"No problem. Your kid live over there with you guys?"

"No. She's with her mom. We split up a few months back," Brian added.

"Yeah, I understand 'bout that." The man scratched his chin and looked at Kevin. "So how does this thing work?"

"It has a motion sensor and a little camera in it. When it sees an animal, it snaps a shot and saves the image as a file on a little memory card. When we got all the pictures we need, we'll come back and get it," Kevin described.

"Right. Okay. You guys have fun with the birds." The man turned and closed the door again.

"Let's get this thing up and working," Kevin said. Fifteen minutes later, the cameras were in place and recording images. "All we need now is time and some results."

36

Mark gathered his cup of coffee and zig-zagged through the workday crowd to his usual table in the Eighth Street Burger King's front window. He removed a laptop computer from his shoulder bag, placed it on the table and switched it on. After getting comfortable in a chair, he sipped his coffee and looked around the restaurant. He was watching a loud-mouthed old man harass the manager when Kevin slipped into the seat opposite him.

"Good morning, amigo," Kevin greeted him.

"You know, if you weren't such a cheapskate, you could own one of these machines yourself," Mark said, gesturing to the computer between them. "Then I wouldn't have to meet you at Burger King at such an obscene hour."

"A little touchy today," Kevin observed, "and yes, I could, but you have one and you were coming here anyway. So, why duplicate our efforts?"

Mark groaned and took another drink of his coffee. "It's too early in the morning for your brand of logic. Just show me what you got."

Kevin slipped two SD flash memory cards from an envelope and handed them over. Mark examined them and inserted one into a slot in the side of the computer. On the screen, a menu came up asking if the images should be copied onto the computer. Mark selected *yes* and a progress bar began moving across the bottom of the screen. "This is going to take a bit," Mark advised.

"I'm not in a hurry. Are you?" Kevin asked.

"No, not really. How's the job at the hospital going?"

"The first week was all training, so I haven't really started doing my job."

"What exactly are you going to do?"

"Patient transport within the hospital."

"Sounds like more fun than a barrel of monkeys," Mark said with a grin.

"It's not, but it's a foot in the door."

"Just a foot in the door?" Mark asked.

"Yeah. There are a lot of jobs in the hospital that I can move into at some later time, but it is easier to get them from inside the system."

"How's the pay?"

"A little better base rate, but no tips," Kevin shrugged. "I'm hoping to break even." The computer made a digital ding sound.

"Okay! Let's see what this gizmo captured." Mark turned the computer so both of them could see the screen. Mark began clicking through the grainy pictures taken from the high wide view of the street. There were photos of birds and people. A couple of rats appeared in the frames, eyes glowing with reflected light, but no cat. "Looks like nothing on this one."

"One down, one to go." Mark ejected the card and inserted the other in the slot. He clicked the import button, and then sat back with his coffee cup. "What happens if we don't find anything?"

"I'll put the cards back in the cameras and try again."

"Finding one cat in a big city seems impossible to me."

"No more impossible than a cat finding a particular human in a big city, and that's already happened," Kevin disagreed. "Surveillance is a long, slow process. We just have to be patient."

"I suppose so," relented Mark.

"I'm going to get some chow. Want anything?" Mark waved his hand in a no signal, so Kevin walked to the counter. When he returned to the table, Mark had an image isolated on the screen.

"Check out this photo."

"Something interesting?" Kevin slipped back into his seat and turned the computer. On the screen was a pre-dawn image of Brian with his pants halfway down, mooning the camera. "Hah!" Kevin exclaimed. "That is what I call a smart-ass." Both men laughed, as Mark resumed clicking through the images.

"I don't see any cats in here."

"It's just our first try."

"Should I save these files?" Mark asked.

"If you don't mind. We might want to come back and compare pictures."

"Okay." Mark ejected the card and handed it back to Kevin. "We'll try again."

37

Monday, August 13
12:39 a.m.

Kevin's eyes shot open at the sound of pounding on the exterior door of the apartment. "I'm coming. Hold your horses!" he called out and rolled off the couch. Staggering once, he found his footing and stood erect. Kevin looked around the dark room. Blue and red lights pulsed through the ground level windows. "What the hell is going on out there?" he asked himself. Rubbing his eyes and finally moving in a coordinated fashion, he pulled on a T-shirt and adjusted his USMC green running shorts before making his way to the door. Opening it a crack revealed a uniformed police officer standing at the top step. The officer's face was relaxed in expression, but his right hand rested on the butt of a holstered pistol. The sleeve of his shirt was marked with the stripes of a sergeant. Kevin let the door creak fully open. "What's going on out here, officer?"

"There was an incident a few doors down." The officer gestured with his free hand toward the far end of the block. Kevin stepped out the door and shuffled up to street level.

"Yeah? What can I do for you?" Kevin asked.

"Do you know any of your neighbors?"

"Not really," Kevin shrugged. "I know the lady upstairs, and I met the guy across the street the other day. It's my brother's place. I'm just temporary. Why? What happened?"

"What's your name?"

"Kevin Maloney." Kevin squinted, scanning the front the officer's uniform. "Nice to meet you. What's your name sergeant?"

"Archer. How about your brother?"

"Brian is working. He's a firefighter over at Engine 57."

"Afraid I don't know him. So, you don't know a Mr. Powers, do you?"

"No. What happened to him?"

"Well, that's what I'm trying to figure out then, isn't it?"

"Sorry, didn't mean it like that. I've been zonked out since I got home from work."

"Okay. If you hear or see anything about Mr. Powers, give us a call." Archer handed Kevin a card and touched the bill of his hat in a sort of salute. "Good night, Mr. Maloney."

Once the officer was walking away, Kevin slipped on a pair of flip-flops and climbed the steps to the sidewalk. He watched Archer cross the street and pound on another door. When the officer was engaged in another conversation, Kevin strolled west down the block. At the yellow taped boundary of the scene, he watched police technicians collect evidence and take photos.

He looked up and down the street, and then surveyed the field of view of his game cameras. "Missed it," he commented to himself. Finally, Kevin reversed course for the steps of the apartment, saying, "Brian and Mark are going to love this."

38

K evin looked out the ground-level window at the morning street scene. Cars passed and pedestrians were strolling where the police and city vehicles had been a few hours before. He showered, dressed, and collected his wallet, keys, and the memory card envelope. Outside, he strolled west, surveying the block and surroundings in detail until he came to the center of the previous night's activities. When there was a break in the traffic, he crossed the street and made his way back to the cameras. He exchanged the memory cards with a second set and then reactivated the cameras. After examining the fields of view, he slightly adjusted one of the cameras. "Better," he said, and then walked east. At the end of the block, Kevin turned north to Burger King.

When Mark stepped into the restaurant, he spotted Kevin at the window table, reading a newspaper. Mark approached him and said, "I didn't expect to see you this morning."

"I had an interesting night and thought you might like to know about it," Kevin replied.

"Let me get some coffee and a sandwich," Mark said, and made his way to the counter. He returned with several items on a tray.

Sitting across from Kevin, he mixed some sugar and creamer into a coffee cup and took a sip. "Okay. Talk."

"I think we had an incident near the apartment," Kevin said while holding out the memory cards.

"Really?" Mark said and reached into his shoulder bag to extract the computer. After Mark switched it on, he looked at Kevin again and said, "Go on."

"I doubt we have any photos because the cameras are pointed the wrong way," Kevin said, "but it's worth a look."

Mark took the first memory card and inserted it into the slot on the side of the computer. Kevin resumed, "The cops showed up sometime after midnight. I got a knock on the door by a uniform cop asking if I knew a Mr. Powers."

"Who's he?"

"No idea, but I guess he lived near me and Brian. I think he took a header from the top floor of a building at the west end of the block."

"Hmmm. That doesn't sound like a cat scenario, but maybe it's like the incident on the train tracks."

"Yeah, that's what I was thinking."

When the grid of miniature thumbnail images showed up on the computer, Mark rotated the computer so both men could see the screen and started clicking through them. Most of the shots were just people walking by. None of them were remarkable, so he kept clicking. The images got progressively darker where the camera recorded nightfall.

"Stop. Go back." Kevin said. Mark slowly clicked through the images in reverse order. "There. What's up with those eyes?" The image was a person looking in the general direction of the camera, but not directly at it. "That's crazy. People reflect a little light from a camera flash, but the don't have the eyeshine like animals." Both men leaned toward the screen and examined the image in detail.

"That face isn't right either." Mark said. "It's like the moon-face we saw on the Jerome look-alike."

"You are dead on. That might be the look-alike guy that runs with the cat," Kevin said. "Can you see what he's wearing?"

"Looks like a dark sweatshirt and maybe tuxedo pants?" Mark pointed at the stripe down the trouser leg. "The finish of the fabric is different."

"Yeah maybe. Those might be slippers. There isn't any color in these images. Just dark and light, but this guy should stand out in a crowd in those pants."

Mark clicked through more images until they found an image of a police officer.

"That's Archer, the guy who woke me up," Kevin said.

"Looks like your typical Philly cop. Okay. I'll save these and then take a peek at the other card." When the computer finished saving the files, Mark ejected the first card and inserted the second. While it was loading, he sat back and ate some of his breakfast. After another sip of coffee he said, "Got the creeps yet? This thing is getting close."

"Yeah. But we know it's out there," Kevin said. "That's half the battle in overcoming fear." The second set of images revealed nothing unusual. "I suspect we need to go through the previous images and see if this moon-faced guy shows up."

"We weren't looking for people before. Just cats," said Mark.

"That was a big mistake on our part," Kevin commented.

"But one we can correct. I will start looking at the old files tonight. There might be something there."

39

Kevin walked toward the employee's side entrance of Presbyterian Hospital with a dozen other workers converging from the street. Approaching the door, he came face to face with a disheveled woman clutching a purse under her arm. Kevin sidestepped to go around her, but she matched his step and remained between him and the door. He came to an abrupt stop and focused on her face. "Aren't you one of the detectives who came to the *Moshulu*?" he asked.

"Yes. Detective Johnston, and I need to speak with you," she said as she pulled stray hair out of her face.

"Happy to help, if you can make it fast. I have about three minutes until I have to clock in. It's a new job, and I'm still on double-secret probation."

With her free hand, she grasped his wrist and pulled him out of the loose stream of people. Kevin followed without resistance, saying, "You're the second police officer to come looking for me today. What's going on?"

Johnston looked down, shuffled her feet, and then raised her eyes to meet his. "My partner died last night under unusual circumstances.

You probably didn't know it, but he lived just down the block from you and your brother."

"That was your partner? I didn't make the connection. The same Powers I met at the *Moshulu*?"

Johnston nodded her head in confirmation.

"I'm so sorry," Kevin said. After a pause, he asked, "Besides living on the same street, what brings me into it?"

"In addition to being busted up from the third-floor fall, his body was all shriveled up like a raisin."

"Really?" Kevin scratched his chin and then added, "That's not good."

"No, it's not, but it's not a surprise to you, is it?"

"What do you mean?"

"Give me a little credit. The guy across the street told Sergeant Archer about you and your brother putting up game cameras. Something about endangered birds in the city?"

"So, we're doing a little surveillance of our front door. Is that a problem?"

"You guys suspected something, so you were keeping tabs on the neighborhood." Kevin looked away from Johnston for a moment, and then back at her again when she asked, "Am I right?"

"Yes. So, what do you want from me?" Kevin held out his empty hands.

"Look, sailor boy. My partner is dead, and I'm tired from being up all night. A little less attitude and a little more cooperation would be nice."

"Okay. Look, we got one shot of a guy that could be connected somehow."

"How do you know? What makes him stand out from all the others walking past your door?" she asked in a tired voice.

"It's kind of a long story, but basically, the ghosts, or apparitions, or whatever they are, look like grown up babies. Kind of a moon face with pale skin, and the eyes reflect light like an animal."

"Like a cat?"

"Yes."

"Is there anything specific about this guy that might help identify him?"

"He was wearing tuxedo pants and slippers."

"I want your pictures," Johnston demanded.

"Is this you or the police asking?" Kevin asked.

Her voice softened slightly. "Me. I'm asking. This is about a guy I worked with for two years. He was my mentor." Taking a breath, she exhaled, "I want to get to the bottom of it."

"You aren't supposed to be working on this, are you?"

"No. If my supervisor knew, he'd have me sent to psych."

Kevin remained silent for a moment, scratching his head. "Okay, since this isn't official yet, we'll share what we've got, but only if you can help us when we need it. Fair?"

"I don't know about that. What kind of information are you looking for, and why?"

"Don't know yet. Detective Powers is just one piece of the puzzle. If we work on this together, we might get to the end a lot sooner."

"Fine. If I can help, I will, but I can't make any promises. The pictures?" Kevin removed the folded envelope containing two flash memory cards from his backpack and handed them to Johnston. Tucking them into her purse, she said, "We need to keep the lines open. You still got my number?"

"Actually, no. I was hoping to steer clear of law enforcement," he said.

She pulled a police business card and pen from her purse. Johnston wrote a number on the back and handed Kevin the card. Kevin took the card and looked at it.

"I have to run, Detective D. Johnston." Kevin pocketed the card and strode off to the hospital entrance.

Johnston watched him go and then, after a moment of hesitation, called after him, "I'll be in touch."

40

K evin emerged from the hospital side entrance into the warm summer night. The brightest of stars were starting to show through the glare of the city lights. Looking up into the dark sky as he rounded a corner, he collided with a woman walking the other direction.

"Damn, sorry about that," Kevin blurted.

"It's alright," the woman replied, as she massaged her forehead where she'd bumped into Kevin's chin.

"I hope it doesn't leave a mark," Kevin said before he recognized Johnston. "It's you again. What brings you back so soon?"

Still holding her forehead, she said, "I brought you some high-capacity cards for your cameras. Yours are crap." With her free hand, she fished a small package from her purse and handed it to Kevin. "This will get you another day between card changes and let you use the camera's highest resolution. I looked through your images. They are all grainy and you're probably missing images because the cards are filling up." Johnston pushed her disheveled hair back into place and straightened up before saying, "I can help you with your surveillance, if you'll let me. Maybe we can find a better setup for the cameras."

"Yeah, sure." Kevin agreed, examining the new memory cards. "Gathering intel wasn't exactly part of my training. What have you got in mind?"

"Tell you what . . . I haven't got anywhere to be right now, so why don't you walk me through what you've got."

"You want to come back to the apartment and snoop around? Like now?" Kevin asked with a suspicious expression as he slipped the cards into his backpack.

"Look. I want to get to the end of this journey. Probably more than you do. It's personal now."

"What about official police department business?"

"Don't worry about that. The boss told me to take a few days off, on account of losing my partner."

"Alright. I'm game. I was going to catch the train home, unless you have wheels."

"The boss really wants me to stay home, so he took the keys to the department car, too."

"Then the train it is," Kevin said. "Come on."

The two walked south on Thirty-Eighth Street to Market Street and made their way east toward the Thirty-Fourth Street Station. "There's a Chinese place here on the next block that stays open late. You hungry?" Kevin suggested.

"I'm not hungry, but if you want to get something, go ahead," Johnston replied.

"Excellent, I'm starved. You grab a table out front, and I'll go in and order."

Kevin headed to the door and turned back to ask Johnston if she wanted something to drink. She shook her head no, and he continued inside. After a few minutes, Kevin returned to the tables grouped outside the door of the Han Dynasty Restaurant. "I got you a bottle of water. That's what you were drinking down at the *Moshulu*."

"Nice of you to remember," she remarked.

"It's a bartender thing. Gets you more tips if you remember what people are drinking."

"I'm sure it does," Johnston agreed. She fidgeted with the bottle cap for a while before finally opening it and taking a sip.

"You okay?" Kevin asked, after watching her hesitation.

"Look, you've been involved in the thing from the get-go," Johnston said and then paused to watch a couple cars go by before continuing. "I don't know what's going on. I can't get my mind around it, but I'm certain there's something fishy."

Kevin nodded his head as he shoveled down chicken and rice. "You're crossing over from the world of tangible facts into what my uncle would call an encounter with the mysterious."

"What is that supposed to mean?" she asked.

He sucked on the straw of his drink and then explained, "You know, stuff that doesn't fit within our understanding of how the world works."

Johnston nodded at the words. "Okay. What does it take to understand it? You know what I mean?"

"I get what you're asking, but I'm not sure myself. With help from my brother Brian, Mark, Uncle Matthew, and now you, we'll figure it out." Kevin stopped talking and began shoveling in food again.

Johnston watched him eat for a long time, and then looked out at the street and let out a sigh. Turning back to Kevin, she asked, "Do you always eat so fast?"

"Eat when you can because you never know when you'll get your next meal."

"Sounds like something my father would say."

"My kind of guy," Kevin replied between bites.

"Okay, I know about Brian and Mark. Who's your uncle?" she questioned.

Kevin looked up from his take-out container. "He's a priest." Kevin took a long sip from his drink and piled in another mouthful of food.

"Look, I'm not the religious type," Johnston said. "I deal in hard facts, not faith. How's a priest going to help?"

"He's probably the smartest guy in town. He teaches Latin, Greek, and bunch of other stuff at the seminary. He's also the archbishop's go-to guy on death and dying. If there is anyone equipped to unravel the mysterious, it's him," Kevin said matter-of-factly and resumed eating.

"I guess I need to meet him."

"You like Italian ice?" Kevin asked.

"Sure, who doesn't?"

Kevin grinned and said, "I don't have to work Sunday, I'll take you out to meet him then."

"Since I'm not working either, I guess that will be just dandy. You aren't taking me to mass or something?"

"Nope. Just taking Uncle Matthew for an afternoon visit with his girlfriend Rita," Kevin said. "You can ask him about anything as long as you are willing to answer a few of his questions." Kevin stuffed in the last couple spoonfuls of rice and took a long drink before sitting back and exhaling.

"I guess you're done?" Johnston asked after a long silence.

Kevin nodded and promptly stood up from the table, collected the debris from his dinner and dropped it in a trash can. He turned to Johnston, who was still seated. "Are you coming?"

"Yeah. Right behind you."

Kevin and Detective Johnston walked the remaining two blocks to the Thirty-Fourth Street Station and descended the steps to the underground platform. They passed through the turnstiles and waited for the next train to arrive. Kevin turned to the detective and asked, "Since you seem to know everything about me, how about a little game of fill-in-the-blanks about you, seeing as how we're kind of in this thing together now."

"Not much to tell. Been on the force since after college. I rode around in a patrol car until I made it into homicide. Been looking at dead people for almost three years."

"Yeah, that's the elevator ride version of a life story if I ever heard one."

"Like I said, not much to tell."

"Bull. Let's start at day one. Where were you born?"

"Okinawa."

"Yeah. No story there," Kevin scoffed. "What about your first name? It's not on your card."

"It's just Johnston," she said. "It's easier that way."

"Easier than what? Dee? Donna? Dianna? Darcy? What?" Kevin pestered.

"Look, my first name isn't a good cop name, so the only person who uses it is my mom."

"Well, that's pretty silly, but I'll let it slide for now," Kevin relented before changing subjects. "So, how did you come to be born on Okinawa of all places?"

"Dad was a grunt Marine. Mom was a schoolteacher on the base. Pretty typical."

"Swaddled in the big green blanket, huh? Where are your parents now?"

"Mom's got a little place down the shore. Took early retirement after Dad's vehicle got blown up in Iraq," Johnston said, a shadow of sadness crossing her face. "Came back to Dover in a million little pieces."

"Oh crap. I'm sorry."

"It was years ago. It's ancient history as far as I'm concerned."

"If you don't mind me asking, what unit was he in?"

"He was a company gunny, First Battalion, Second Marines."

"I know some of those guys. We rotated in behind them in Afghanistan."

Johnston looked down the tracks in the direction of the approaching train. "You're one of the few people I've met who knows enough to give a damn about Marines."

Kevin looked down the tunnel, too. A point of light was growing more intense in the darkness. "Those bastards stirred it up in Helmand, leading the way for us."

"Well, I guess you and me running into each other was supposed to happen. Seems mysterious, huh," Johnston commented as the whoosh of air and noise ahead of the train engulfed the platform.

"Funny, but I think it's more of a coincidence," Kevin disagreed, but his voice was drowned out by the squealing of brakes as the train came to a stop in front of them. The doors opened and the sound of a human voice crackled unintelligibly over the speakers inside the train. "This is us." Kevin said, and they stepped into the carriage.

41

Kevin and Johnston exited the train at the Eleventh Street station and climbed the steps to street level. Emerging into the semi-darkness of the city at night, Kevin looked around. "This is a beautiful evening. Even in the city." Kevin looked at Johnston and said, "We've got about six blocks. You okay?"

"Keep going. This is nothing," she said.

"Yes ma'am," Kevin replied, and kept walking south. Stores were closed up for the night, but the streets were still busy with people coming and going from restaurants and clubs. "So where did you go to college?" he asked.

"Back to filling in the blanks, are we?"

"Passing the time," Kevin said casually, "and filling in the blanks."

"Do you really want to know?"

"You said it before. I'm probably the only person around who gives a damn."

After a long pause, Johnston said, "Penn State."

"What was your major?"

"Crime, Law, and Justice."

"Did you always want to be a cop?"

"When I was in grade school, I wanted to be one of the Three Tenors."

"Opera singer? Really?"

"Yep, then I found out that not only am I not a tenor, but I can't sing."

"Aw come on, everybody can sing a little."

"No really. I'm so bad the music teacher told me to just mouth the words!"

Kevin burst out in laughter. "That's some kind of career planning." He laughed some more, and Johnston's stony face cracked a smile.

"How about you, tough guy." Johnston returned. "Did you always want to join the Navy?"

"No, I wanted to be a milkman."

"I never hear that one. Especially since there aren't milkmen anymore."

"Yeah, well, that's why I joined the Navy. Since I couldn't get what I wanted, I went with the next best thing."

How's that?"

"Instead of delivery stops, there's a girl in every port."

"So, you think you're some kind of ladies' man," Johnston laughed.

"I'm serious. Chicago, San Diego, Twentynine Palms, Pearl . . ." Kevin listed locations with a straight face. Johnston grabbed Kevin by the arm and stopped walking. She looked him right in the eye with a dead-pan expression.

"Hah! Got you." Kevin laughed even louder. Johnston cracked a smile again.

"You're still a sick pup."

"Four years with infantry Marines will do that."

"Yeah, it will," Johnston said in a fading voice.

"Sorry," Kevin immediately blurted out.

"Forget it," she said as they resumed walking.

Soon they turned on to Spruce Street. Johnston stopped, her eyes glazing over when Powers' apartment building came into view. Kevin stopped next to her and said, "Are you still good? You're getting into some heavy stuff on no sleep."

"Yeah. We're here to look at your camera locations. That's all," Johnston said in a quiet voice.

"Okay, but if you need to step away, it's alright with me."

"Show me what you got," she said, her voice growing stronger.

Kevin walked up the block to the apartment across the street from Brian's. He pointed out the locations of the cameras. "The camera on the utility pole covers the low angle, pointed along the sidewalk. This one here gives a broader view of the front of our building. It caught the sharp-dressed man."

"You have this well covered, but have you been looking in the street behind your place?" Johnston asked.

"No. Not really. We've been concentrating here," Kevin said. "But I see your point. Any stalker worth a damn would be working the alley side too."

"Powers never used the front entrance of the building. If he got mixed up with this guy, it was back there."

"I guess that's why we never saw him in the neighborhood. Brian doesn't have parking back there, so we never go that way."

"You really need coverage in the back, too. How about relocating the low camera?"

"Yeah. Sounds good." Kevin crossed the street and kneeled down next to where the camera was secured. Johnston followed him across. He pulled a small knife from his pocket and cut the camera loose. "We're going to need a couple more zip ties. I'll grab them from inside." Kevin dropped down the outside steps and unlocked the door. "Come on in."

Kevin crossed to the bedroom. Johnston stood in the doorway at the bottom of the stairs, surveying the living room. "Not exactly big, is it?"

"No. Not really," Kevin shrugged. "It's got about as much space as the barracks, but with two fewer guys. So, if you disregard the rent, it's a slight improvement." After a minute, Kevin returned from the bedroom with four three-foot zip ties and a roll of green camouflage tape.

"How did your brother end up in this shoe box?"

"Divorce. After all the lawyers and child support, he's got about two bucks left at the end of the month. A guy he knows got him a deal." Kevin held up the ties and tape. "Shall we?"

"Yeah, let's see what we can find."

"After you," Kevin said and pointed up the stairs.

Johnston led the way and Kevin locked up. Back on the street, Johnston walked east to Ninth Street. "Where do you park your jeep?" she asked.

"I leave it at my mom's place most of the time," Kevin replied. "How do you know I drive a jeep?"

Johnston looked at Kevin and cocked an eyebrow.

"Right, you're a cop who does her homework." They turned right on Ninth Street and walked the short distance to Cypress Street. On Cypress they walked a few steps before stopping in a shadow. There were walls, fences, and garages. Infrequent security lights gave weak illumination to the area. Garbage cans were tucked into every nook, and cars were squeezed into the available parking spaces. "If I were a cat, where would I travel?" Kevin asked.

Johnston turned to face Kevin, "Why are you looking for a cat again?"

"I'll fill you in later," Kevin assured her.

"I'm sure you will. I'm not familiar with feline behavior, so I'm relying on your expertise for this one."

"Really?"

"I was allergic to furry animals as a kid."

"Did you have any pets?" Kevin asked.

"I had a guppy."

"So, we're covered if we need to know how a fish swims."

"Funny," Johnston replied.

Kevin said, "Look for anyplace a person might stay out of view."

Johnston surveyed left and right as she slowly walked west on Cypress Street. "Powers' place is toward the other end of the block. We'll want to angle the camera that way."

"The camera has a fixed focus, about thirty to forty feet in front of it. Anything farther will be blurry." Kevin looked up at the tops of the fences and walls and kept shaking his head. After walking past a couple more houses, he came to a stop at a vine-covered wall and metal light pole. "Here we go."

"Looks good." Johnston said, catching up to where Kevin stood. "The garage across the way and this wall form a choke point for anybody walking through here."

"The vines give the camera good concealment," Kevin said, pushing aside leaves to expose the light pole. "Yep, this will work. Here, hold this." He handed the tape and zip ties to Johnston and fitted the camera into a suitable gap at arm height. "Give me a zip tie."

Johnston handed one to him and he cinched it around the pole and top of the camera. He took another tie and did the same thing around the bottom. "Give me about two feet of tape." Johnston tore off a length, and Kevin placed it over the corners of the camera.

"What's that for? Aren't the zip ties enough?"

"The tape brakes up the square shape. It blends in with the leaves."

"Smart."

"It was in the camera manual. More tape, please."

"At least you're honest," she said as she tore off another strip of tape. "Thanks for not playing it off like it was obvious."

"I'm not afraid to read the instructions. There. That will work. I'll take another look in the morning to make sure it's well hidden." Kevin finished smoothing back the leaves so it looked undisturbed. "Okay. Let's finish going around the block and see if there is anything else we missed."

Johnston led the way down the street, carefully examining every recess and shadow. "I wish I had my flashlight," she said while yawning and rubbing her eyes.

"Take your time. We're in no hurry. Just a typical night, looking for bad guys." Kevin said in a smooth, reassuring voice.

"You've told yourself that before."

"Yeah, a few times. But here I don't have to worry about IEDs and snipers. So really this is just a walk in the park," Kevin replied. "But I'd still like to have my weapon and Abi covering my six."

Kevin and Johnston walked the remaining half block without finding anything unusual. Behind the last building, Johnston pointed to a back door. "That's his place."

Kevin nodded, "That's a little too close close to home."

Turning right on Tenth Street and then rounding the corner onto Spruce, Johnston sniffed and rubbed moisture from her eyes before asking, "What's Abi?"

"Are you alright? And *who* is the word you are looking for."

"I'm fine. So who's Abi?"

"My battle buddy," Kevin said. "Abi is short for Abiola. It's an African name. He's this wiry kid with the absolute soul of a warrior. I think it runs in his blood," Kevin smiled. "He stuck to me like glue. Probably saved my life a thousand times before he got sent home with a Purple Heart."

"Did he make it?"

"Yeah, it wasn't too serious. He's going to mortuary science school now." Kevin was quiet for a moment before regaining his voice. "Okay, enough about me for one night. Let's get back to the apartment. I gotta get off my feet." They walked back to the east end of the block and descended the steps to the apartment. After opening the door, Kevin directed Johnston to the couch and turned on the TV with the sound muted. "I got butter pecan ice cream, tap water, and beer. What's your pleasure? I'm going with the ice cream," he declared.

"A beer sounds good," Johnston replied. Kevin pulled out a bottle, popped the cap, and handed it to her. Then he returned to the kitchen.

"So, tell me about the cat," Johnston requested.

"I said I'd fill you in, didn't I?" he observed as he scooped ice cream into a bowl.

Johnston took a long pull from the beer bottle, leaned her head back on the couch, closed her eyes and then exhaled, "You did."

Kevin returned to the couch and sat at the opposite end. "Mark and I first encountered the cat when we were looking for Jerome, the basketball player kid. Remember him?"

Johnston opened her eyes and looked sideways at Kevin. "You said something about a cat with the old man, Mister Willy, but what I heard was pretty farfetched."

"It is—or was." Kevin paused long enough to eat a spoonful of ice cream. "At the very least, I'm pretty sure the cat and the ghost are connected."

"So the perpetrator has a cat, and the cat is part of his MO?"

"I'm going out on a limb, but I think the cat is the perpetrator."

"Yep, that's quite a limb," she said as she rolled her eyes.

"Hang in there with me," Kevin begged. "What if the cat causes fatal accidents?"

"Are you kidding me? I never heard of a house cat documented as the cause of death."

"Me neither. But if a cat runs in front of a train, and somebody tries to save it. Boom. They get a free ride to the morgue."

"What about the cat?" Johnston asked after another drink of her beer.

"It's a cat. It jumps off the track and watches. That's what cats do."

"Okay, I could see that as an accidental death," Johnston conceded.

"And what about tripping an old lady, causing her to break a hip."

"Possible, I guess. Old folks are susceptible to devastating falls."

"How about a cat knocking over a candle?"

"Okay, I see where you're going. Cat-caused accidents. I can't arrest a cat and charge it with a crime. And what about Powers?"

"I don't know anything about how he died, except I suspect he fell from the third floor. Is there something else?"

"The medical examiner will settle it," Johnston said with finality.

"But will they check for yellow cat hairs?"

"Is that really what you think? The same cat is involved in each of these deaths?"

"Yes, and I have the scratches to prove it. Each time it cozied up to its next victim, and not long ago we saw it here on this street."

"How did a cat find its way from West Philly all the way over here?" Johnston yawned while gesturing in a wide arc with her beer bottle.

"I don't know. Walked, or maybe it rode the train. But you hear all these stories of animals traveling long distances to find their way home. So, it must be possible."

"Oh, you're giving me a headache," Johnston droned. "Cats killing people. And I suppose it makes them into ghosts, too."

"Yes."

"Great. Look, I'm exhausted and going home." Johnston pushed herself off the couch and said, "We can talk more about this later." She took a wobbly step forward, and then raised her hand to her head. Kevin stood up and placed a steadying hand on her shoulder.

"Why don't you sit down and close your eyes for a minute. When you're ready I'll call a cab," Kevin suggested, guiding her back to the couch.

"I'll be okay in a few minutes. I shoulda skipped the beer. I've always been a light-weight."

"Not your fault. Stress and half a beer will do that," Kevin reassured her. Within a few moments of sinking into the couch, Johnston was sound asleep.

42

T he first glow of morning was edging up from the east horizon when Brian turned his red Jeep Cherokee from Ninth Street onto Spruce. He idled along the street, looking for a parking place. As he rolled past his apartment, he said, "What the hell?" A dark figure was crouched by the dimly lit window. Another six cars down the street, Brian jerked his vehicle into a vacant spot. He switched off the engine and gathered his gym bag from the passenger seat.

"Time to make a new friend," Brian whispered to himself as he exited the car. He softly pushed the driver's door closed until it clicked and then wrapped his left arm in his gym bag like a shield. In a slight hunch, he padded from the car toward the front of his apartment, staying in the shadows of the neighboring buildings. Creeping footstep by footstep, he maneuvered around the building's front steps. Peeking around the handrail, he assessed the shadow figure. It was dressed in dark clothes and its feet were bare. The shoulders and nearly bald head were oriented away from Brian, and its full attention was on the window.

Brian drew closer, until he was only a body length away. He inhaled deeply and brought his protected arm forward and balled his right hand into a fist. The shadow's head jerked around at the sound of the breath and saw Brian spring forward. They collided as the shadow tried to get to its feet. Brian shoved it hard with his padded arm, forcing it down the steps toward the below ground entryway to the apartment. It crashed to a stop against the landing, where it remained completely motionless.

"Well, that went better than I expected," Brian said as he drew back to the apartment window. Knocking on the glass he hissed "Kevin!" When there was no immediate response, he rapped harder. Finally, there was movement visible on the couch, illuminated by the flickering light of the TV.

"What's going on out there?" came a woman's voice.

"Of course, this is the night he gets his game on!" Brian said to himself. "Get Kevin!" he called to the woman standing in the living room. After another moment, Kevin's face appeared close to the pane of glass.

"What the hell's going on?" Kevin asked.

"I think I got your guy out here. He's on the landing. Might be knocked out."

"Okay. Don't touch him. We'll call for help and sneak a peek from down here."

"Be careful. That door chain isn't real strong," Brian said from outside the window.

Inside the apartment, Kevin went to the kitchen and grabbed Brian's large aluminum flashlight from a drawer. Johnston flipped open her cell phone and called 911. When a voice came on, she said, "This is Detective Johnston. Badge two seven four five. I need backup and an ambulance at 904 Spruce. No sirens or lights please." She listened for moment, and then said "I'm going to leave this line open and set down the phone. okay?" She then set the phone on the kitchen counter.

"Kill the TV," Kevin said.

When she switched it off, the room fell into a near black darkness. After a few moments she spoke again. "Can you see?"

"Enough to find the front door."

"Good," she said. Johnston placed her left hand on Kevin's shoulder and with her right withdrew her compact revolver from an ankle holster. "I'm going to keep a hand on your shoulder and follow you to the door. That way I will always know where you are. Don't turn on the light until I tell you. Got it?"

"Got it," Kevin replied. With the flashlight in his right hand, he moved to the door. He patted in from the doorframe until he found the deadbolt.

"I'm going to open the door a crack. Ready?" Kevin asked.

"Go easy," she answered as she raised the weapon to a defensive posture. Kevin slowly turned the deadbolt, and when it made a slight click, he moved his hand to the doorknob.

"Here we go." The door opened just enough to allow outside air to flow in. "You smell that?" Kevin whispered.

"Yeah, he stinks bad. Keep going. I can't see him yet," Johnston directed. Kevin had his shoulder braced against the door and inched back. "Stop. Now hold the light over the top of the door and get ready to switch it on."

Kevin positioned the flashlight with his finger on the rubber button. "Ready?" he breathed.

"Ready," Johnston replied.

Kevin counted down, "switching on in three, two, one." The flashlight clicked and the landing was slashed with a bright white beam. Johnston stepped closer to the door on the inside, and Brian inched up to the top of the steps on the outside.

Brian called from outside, "I can't really tell, but it doesn't look like he's breathing."

Inside, Johnston moved closer, pistol locked on the lump at the bottom of the stairs. "Open all the way to the chain," she said, and Kevin backed away another half step. With the door open wider, Johnston looked at the face. "I'm not sure, but I don't think he's moving at all. Can we get more light?"

"Okay," Kevin said. "I'm going to turn on the outside entry light," Kevin announced before flicking the switch. The landing was flooded with a pale-yellow light that revealed more of the motionless figure on the bricks. "I'm going to go get zip ties and gloves. We'll hog-tie him while he's knocked out."

"Go," Johnston directed.

Kevin switched off the flashlight and slipped past Johnston, disappearing into the bedroom. After a short time, he came back to the door, wearing purple medical exam gloves and holding a half dozen ties and a pool cue stick.

"What's that for?" Johnston asked.

"I'm going to see if he's responsive from in here, before we try to restrain him."

"Good call," she said.

Kevin crouched down on the floor and inched forward to the door. He extended the cue stick out the door and poked the figure in the shoulder. Nothing happened. Kevin pushed on a leg, and again there was no response. Kevin pulled it back in and set it aside.

"Was that my pool cue? Why are you using my cue?" Brian called from outside.

"Brian, heads up. I'm going to close the door and remove the chain."

"Sure. Might as well put the rest of my meager belongings in jeopardy, while you are at it," was the response from outside. Kevin moved around Johnston, avoiding her line of sight out the door. He closed the door and removed the chain, then opened it again smoothly. "So far so good?"

"Still no movement," Johnston observed.

"I'll start with the legs." Kevin dropped to the ground and Johnston stepped sideways, keeping her revolver trained on the figure from above. Kevin pushed the long zip tie under the legs. He reached over and pulled up the end of the tie and closed the loop. Then he pulled the loop tight.

From above, Brian said, "I think it's going to take both of you to get him turned over to secure the hands."

"Yeah. How about I tie them in front and run the tie through a belt loop on his pants," Kevin said. "We'll save it for the folks with actual cuffs."

"Sounds good," Johnston agreed.

Kevin put one tie around the near wrist and then tucked it through a belt loop. He then pulled the other hand from under the body and placed it in position to secure it. "If he were just stunned, he'd be awake now," Kevin observed as he finished securing the second hand and snugging up both ties. Looking up to the top of the steps and the intensifying glow of the sky behind Brian, Kevin observed, "The sun will be up soon. By the way, why are you home early?"

"Appointment with the lawyer this morning."

"Well, it's a good thing you came along," Kevin said, and then turned to Johnston, "you okay?"

"Yeah. I'm fine," she replied. "Who is this guy, and what was he doing?"

Brian answered, "I saw him peeking in the window when I came home, so I snuck up from behind. When he tried to bolt, I encouraged him to take the steps," he explained. "Is this your cat guy?"

Kevin looked over the unmoving form. "I think so. All the things we've seen before are here. Moon face, pale skin, and he resembles the last victim," Kevin reported.

"Who is this guy supposed to look like?" Brian asked.

"My guess is Detective Powers," Kevin said.

Detective Johnston inched closer without letting down her guard. "I guess it resembles him, but the face isn't right," she said.

"Look closer. The shape of the eyes and nose are right. It's just everything is puffy. We saw the same thing with Jerome," Kevin said.

"Yeah. I see it," Johnston admitted with a sigh.

"Hey Brian, by the way, this is Detective Johnston."

"Nice to meet you," Brian responded with a brief wave of his hand.

"Same," Johnston said.

A police car came to a stop just past the front door. Two officers stepped out and walked over to where Brian was standing. The first asked, "Where is Detective Johnston?"

Brian responded, "She's down in the doorway keeping the creep under the gun."

The officer directed Brian back from the scene. "Why don't you have a seat right there on the front steps and we'll take over."

"All yours, but be careful, and please wear gloves. There is something on him that will mess up your skin." Brian stepped back, and Kevin climbed the steps to join his brother.

Johnston called up from the door of the apartment, "Get him cuffed. I'm going to step back for a moment and hang up the phone."

"Yes ma'am," the officer replied.

43

Emergency vehicles blocked Spruce Street for the second time in a week. Brian and Kevin sat on the front steps of their building, watching the activity around them. Brian pointed out the faces appearing in the doors and windows of their neighbors and remarked, "It's kinda fun being on the receiving end of all this attention."

"Oh, brother," Kevin replied as they watched the three-person ambulance crew wheel a gurney from the street to the top of the steps. "What a way to start a day."

Detective Johnston stood back in the apartment doorway, while four uniformed officers secured the unmoving lump at the bottom of the stairs. When they finished exchanging the zip ties for cuffs, they motioned for the waiting ambulance crew.

"Hey, Maloney, what did you do to this guy?" a gray-haired medic called out to Brian as he unloaded the medical equipment strapped to the gurney.

"Top of the day, Jimmy. I didn't do nothing except give him some directions." The crew chuckled and then directed their attention to removing the motionless figure. "Hey, don't touch his skin," Brian added. "There is something on him. He's like human hazmat."

"Yeah, he smells like it, too," one of the officers confirmed.

"I don't think there is any hurry on this one. There's no vital signs and he hasn't moved since we got here," reported the police officer at the bottom of the steps.

"Thanks, Mack," Jimmy said, and then turned to the other medics, "Okay you two, let's slide the backboard under him and see if we can get him in position to transfer." The backboard was removed from the gurney and laid on the steps near the lifeless figure. The ambulance crew then slowly lifted and guided the limp body on to the board. Jimmy then carefully strapped the body in place, with the head immobilized in an orange brace. "Alright, I don't think he's going anywhere now. Let's get him out of here."

The ambulance crew, with the help of two police officers, lifted the backboard and carried it up to the gurney. They laid the whole package on the gurney and put two more straps on top to hold it all in place. While cinching down the upper strap, one of the police officers blurted, "His eyes just popped open!"

Brian, watching from his position on the steps said, "I think I saw his leg twitch, too."

Jimmy pulled out a penlight and shone it over the face of the body. The eyes were open and searching side to side. "You aren't dead yet, buddy. Just stay calm," Jimmy said, but the body on the backboard began to squirm in the restraints. "Hey, hey. It's okay," he reassured, but just as fast as it started moving, the eyes closed, and the body went limp again. "This one's special. Let's get him to the rig."

The crew rolled the gurney out into the street and spun it around to go into the ambulance. They lifted and pushed the gurney into the ambulance. "Check his vitals again, and get oxygen and the monitors on him," Jimmy directed.

Jimmy stepped onto the sidewalk and waved a police officer over. "Yo! We're going to back out of here the wrong way. Would you be so kind as to clear the way and hold up any traffic on Ninth?"

"You got it," he replied with a head nod. Jimmy returned his attention to the back of the ambulance just as a commotion broke out inside. Banging and grunts were coming from the back.

"Hey, take it easy in there!" Jimmy shouted, just as one of the crew tumbled out of the rear door.

"He just started going crazy!" the medic said as he dropped to the ground and put a hand up to his face. Jimmy reached down to steady him for a moment before turning his attention to the inside of the ambulance. "Hang in there, Tony. Glenn, are you okay?" Jimmy called. There was a muffled response from the front of the compartment. Jimmy climbed in, and immediately poked his head back out. "Maloney, I need a hand!"

Brian jumped off the stoop and raced over saying, "I'm here."

"I don't know what the hell just happened, but Glenn got the crap scratched out of his face, and the guy is gone!"

Watching the exchange, Kevin called out a moment too late, "Get out and close the doors! Don't let it get away!" Just as Brian and Jimmy looked up, a yellow cat streaked out the doors and into the street. It paused between cars long enough to display its distorted tail and then disappeared from view. "Too late! Damn it!" Kevin swore.

The sky was almost full light, and the sun was beginning to cast the first long shadows of the day as Brian and Jimmy bandaged the bleeding crew in the back of the ambulance. "These wounds might require some doctoring." Jimmy commented.

"I hate to be the bearer of bad news," Brian said, "but these aren't regular scratches. There is some anti-clotting stuff on that cat, and these are going to take a while to heal up."

"Well, isn't that grand." Glenn replied, holding a bandage on his hand while Jimmy taped a pad on his head.

"We'll go get it checked out. On the bright side, you guys might get a few days of paid leave out of it," Jimmy reassured him.

Detective Johnston walked up to the back of the ambulance. "You guys up to telling me about what happened?"

Tony spoke up from under the large gauze dressing over his left eye. "The guy started squirming again while Glenn was checking vitals, and the next thing I know there is only empty clothes on the backboard, and a frickin' cat is attacking my face. I knocked it away, and it went for Glenn. Glenn had his hands full and couldn't do much, so the cat scratched him up really good. Then when Jimmy came up, it froze for a second, and then took off."

The patrol officer looked stunned. "You tellin' me the guy we just loaded up morphed into a cat?"

"Yeah. It's freaking unbelievable, but that's what it seems like to me, unless you see our guy somewhere." Tony replied.

"I felt him slide right out from under my stethoscope," Glenn mumbled from under the tape and bandages. Detective Johnston exchanged a look with Brian but didn't say anything.

"Okay, you guys, let's get this show on the road," Jimmy encouraged. He and Brian stepped out of the ambulance and closed the back doors.

"I'll call you later to see how the boys are doing. Maybe we should kinda keep this on the down-low for a while until it's clear what happened?" Brian said to Jimmy. Jimmy nodded his head, walked to the driver's door of the ambulance and climbed in. Everybody cleared away and the ambulance backed to Ninth Street, where it turned and drove off.

Johnston directed the patrol officers to route traffic around the street and tape off the sidewalk. Kevin and Brian watched from the front steps as the officers set to work.

Johnston turned back to the brothers, "There's going to be investigators here in a minute and your neighbors are going to be asking a lot of questions, too."

"Yeah, they are," Brian replied as he stood up. "I think I'll catch a shower while we're waiting, if that's alright with you." Johnston nodded as he passed on the way to the down the steps.

Kevin looked up at Johnston, "You conked out hard last night. Do you feel okay?"

"I'm fine," she shrugged. "Most rest I've had in a couple of days." They remained silent for a while, staring out into the street. Finally, Johnston looked at Kevin and said, "But a cup of coffee wouldn't hurt."

"Ask and you shall receive," Kevin said, standing up and leading the way into the apartment. Entering the kitchen, he found Brian had already put on a full pot of coffee. "Brian likes a cup or three of liquid sunshine," Kevin commented while Johnston dropped heavily onto the couch. Neither one spoke until Kevin poured coffee into a *Kiss Me—I'm a Firefighter* mug and asked if she wanted anything in it.

"No. Black is right for today," Johnston replied.

"I think we're really up to our necks, and frankly, I'm not sure how it ends," Kevin said while handing her the mug and then sinking into the other end of the couch.

"I think the best thing we can do is cool it for a day," Johnston said, staring into the dark liquid. "We need to get a little distance and perspective. I'll say something to the officers outside."

"You're right," Kevin agreed. "It's just like after a firefight. We're both tired and feeling the effects of the adrenalin let-down."

They sat quietly while Johnston sipped from the mug. "Strong stuff," she commented, "but good."

"Brian's firehouse blend."

The quiet continued for a while, until Johnston spoke up. "Did you get in a lot of firefights?"

"Filling in blanks?" Kevin asked.

"I guess so."

"More than our fair share, but mostly it was the IEDs," Kevin said in a softening voice. "Lost some good guys."

Johnston looked down at the floor, and then back to Kevin. "When the investigators get done here, I'm going to head home and get cleaned up. Then I have to explain this to my boss."

"Sounds like fun. Let me know if I can help."

"Probably not, but you should get the memory cards from the cameras. That was quite a show."

"You can say that again."

Johnston sat on the couch long enough to finish her coffee, and then walked to the kitchen and placed the cup in the sink. She collected her purse and looked at Kevin. "I'm going back up to wait on the steps, are we still on to see your uncle on Sunday?"

"By all means, yes."

"What time do you want me here?"

"I'll come get you, if you like?"

"It will be easier if I just come here. What time?"

"Two o'clock work for you?"

"Sure. See you at two," Johnston said as she let herself out.

After the door closed behind Johnston, Kevin went to the door of the bedroom and called to his brother, "Hey, you decent? I need to call Mark."

"Yeah, come in."

Kevin opened the door and entered the little bedroom. He punched in a number on the phone and after a short pause said, "It's Kevin. I know it's early, but you are never going to believe what happened here this morning." Kevin listened for a moment and continued. "We're okay, but we've got to meet and download the camera cards." Kevin listened again and responded, "Yeah, Brian and I will bring them out to the house tonight." There was a short pause. "Okay, see you then." Kevin hung up the phone and turned to Brian. "I assume you didn't have a hot date or anything tonight."

Brian grinned and shook his head, "No, but I'm anxious to hear about yours."

44

The jeep growled along the wide West Philadelphia street, heading northwest through mixed neighborhoods of residential and commercial buildings. Kevin shifted gears and hummed to himself as he drove. The top was folded back and the windows rolled down, allowing the wind to ruffle everything inside the vehicle. Johnston sat in the passenger seat with one hand holding her hair back out of her squinting eyes.

"Gotta love this weather. Sunny and mild. Not a cloud to be seen anywhere!" Kevin observed from behind a pair of Ray-Ban aviator sunglasses.

"It's nice," Johnston replied with a reserved smile.

"You know, Southern California is like this every day."

"Is that so?" she questioned. "I've never been."

As they rolled to a stop at a traffic light, Kevin pointed to the glove box. "There's an extra ball cap if you get tired of the hair thing."

"I'm okay," Johnston replied.

"It will keep the sunburn off your nose, too," he said with a laugh and touched the tip of her nose.

"I'm fine," she said, swatting away his finger.

"Have it your way." Kevin smiled and continued, "You know what I really like about driving topless? The smells, you know? You can smell everything. The grass, the dust and dirt, the people, and even the trash."

"All smell drive, I get it," Johnston replied, and Kevin grinned.

They pulled away from the stop and cruised another dozen blocks up the street before stopping again for another traffic light. A group of teenagers was waiting at the corner. One of the older boys called out to Johnston "Hey girl, you look fine!"

"Thank you," she replied politely to the teen. Then she added, "You're not too bad yourself," which sent several boys in the group into a fit of laughter and finger pointing.

A second teen said, "You should ditch oldie locks and come with us. We can show you a real good time." Then hitching his pants up by the crotch, added, "Anything you want."

"I'm sure you can, but you'd be surprised by what I got right here," she said, slapping her hand on Kevin's thigh.

"Damn, girl!" the first teen blurted just as Kevin eased out the clutch and started pulling away from the corner and the group of laughing kids. Kevin laughed and Johnston smirked as strands of hair blew across her face again.

"Glad to see you have such a rapport with the general public," Kevin teased.

"Is it like this everywhere you drive? People talking to you?" Johnston asked, her hand still on Kevin's leg.

"Only if the top's down and there's a pretty girl in the passenger seat." Kevin grinned at Johnston and raised his voice over the increasing wind noise as the vehicle accelerated. "Pedestrians don't usually talk to me when I'm alone."

"Do you get a lot of pretty girls riding with you?"

Shrugging, Kevin said, "So, I gotta tell you a little more about my uncle."

Johnston returned Kevin's glance and asked, "Changing subjects on me?"

"Not much to tell. I've never been all that lucky in love. Besides, you know the old military joke. If Uncle Sam wanted me to have a girlfriend he would have issued me one. But seriously, I do feel like I need to warn you about Uncle Matthew."

"Right, okay," Johnston relented, withdrawing her hand from Kevin's leg.

"He's probably a little crazy. At least he seems that way to me. But he knows what he's talking about, and he remembers everything you say."

"I'll keep that in mind," she acknowledged.

"Have you ever been out to St. Charles?" Kevin asked.

"Nope."

"You'll like it. Everybody does. It's a very peaceful retreat from the insanity of the city."

Kevin turned the jeep into the entrance. They idled up the driveway and Johnston looked up with wide eyes.

"You weren't kidding. Beautiful," Johnston agreed. The security guard raised the barricade across the driveway and the jeep rolled through into a parking place. Kevin shut off the engine and sat still for a moment, watching Johnston turning every which way to see the surroundings. "Maybe a little overbearing, but I do like it."

"You seem a little edgy today. Are you okay with this?" Kevin asked.

"There was a cop shot and killed in North Philly last night. My old precinct. I didn't really know him, but it kinda set me off. One more pin prick, you know?" Johnston replied.

"I didn't see the news this morning. I'm sorry," Kevin said. "Look, we can skip this if you want."

"No, no. I need to work our case. The only way out of it is to go through it."

"I know how you feel. Okay, let's go see what Uncle Matthew has to say about our latest encounter with the mysterious."

45

The old priest shuffled into the dim room and patted the wall several times before his fingers touched the light switch and pushed it up. A row of fluorescent tube lights flickered and buzzed before finally filling the space with harsh white light. Father Matthew stepped slowly into the center of the classroom, followed by Kevin and Johnston.

Turning to face the blackboard, Kevin said, "I see you added some details since my last visit."

Father Matthew nodded in agreement, "Indeed, I've been following the reports in the paper and on the news. It is all public information and not hard to come by. It fills in the gaps nicely, wouldn't you say Miss Johnston?"

"It does look impressive, but I think Kevin was warned about going all Sherlock Holmes on this."

"Yes," Kevin agreed, "but in our defense, this started as a coping exercise, not a detective's intelligence center."

"That may be, but you definitely crossed into my world," she said surveying the details. Looking at Father Matthew and pointing to the right side of the blackboard she said, "I'm not quite sure what all the groupings do."

"Very good," he responded. "They lend an idea of the relationships of the people, whether they are spatial, chronological, genetic, familial, and so on. Some have more than one type, as you can see."

"I guess it is just a different way of mapping these things out."

"We are seeking connections and repetition. Very few things in this world are truly random or isolated," Father Matthew declared. "Now why don't you sit down and tell me about your most recent encounter."

Johnston sat lightly on a cool metal chair, but Kevin remained standing. He looked out the window and recited the events of the past several days, beginning with the policeman knocking on the apartment door. He then followed with finding a photo of the individual in question on the game camera. Johnston listened carefully, interrupting when she didn't agree or had another detail to add to Kevin's description. Occasionally, the priest would hold up a finger for Kevin to pause, then get up and make a notation on the blackboard.

After Kevin completed the account, he added a description of the latest photos taken by the game camera. The photos included a blurry frame of Brian looking down the stairway, but most of the photos were the side of a Philadelphia Fire Department ambulance.

"When your visitor was on the landing, he was unconscious?" Matthew asked.

Johnston spoke up, "I got a good close look at him. He wasn't just out. He wasn't moving—no breathing, nothing. He looked and acted dead."

"And he began to move exactly when?" Father Matthew asked.

Kevin jumped in, "As soon as the guys got him up out of the stairwell Brian and I both saw a leg twitch, and Officer Murphy said he saw the eyes open."

"Fine. Now when exactly did he go limp again?"

"Maybe ten seconds later."

"What time of day was it? Do we know that? You said it was nearly dawn."

"I'm afraid I don't know. I wasn't looking at my watch," Kevin said.

Johnston reached into her purse. "Hold on, I can get close. I made a call to 911 and hung up when everybody arrived. It might be off by four or five minutes." Johnston scrolled through the call log on her phone. "Here it is. I placed the call at ten after six and hung up nine minutes later. So, six nineteen."

"Very good. I can work the rest of it out later." Father Matthew wrote the relevant figures on the black board. "I think we might need some new groupings. How many people have been scratched by the cat and who has seen the actual transformation between human and cat?"

"Scratches include me, Mark, Abi, Glenn, Tony, and Skinny."

Father Matthew wrote the names on the board.

"I know Glenn and Tony from the ambulance, but who is Skinny?" Johnston asked.

"He's a chauffeur for Engine 57. He made the mistake of picking up the half-dead cat from the scene of the fire," Kevin clarified. "Glenn and Tony are the only two people I know who have witnessed the transformation, but I don't know if they really saw anything. It happened remarkably fast."

"Do we think they are reliable observers of the facts?" Father Matthew asked.

"What we know was reported from the scene immediately after it happened. It's about as good as we could hope for from a witness," Johnston opined.

Father Matthew finished creating the new column on the board. "Is there anything else of immediate concern?" the priest asked, looking at Kevin and Johnston. "No? Then let's look over the facts we have collected and see if anything stands out."

They sat in silence for a while before Kevin spoke up. "We need to expand our list of confirmed characteristics of the visitor."

Father Matthew walked back to the board and said, "To include what?"

"It can appear as a yellow cat or as a person," Kevin said. Then he added, "The human resembles the last person to encounter the cat at or around the time of death." Matt scrawled the new information as fast as Kevin spoke. "Scratches delivered by the cat are really slow to heal."

Father Matthew stopped writing and stepped back from the board. "Anything else?"

Johnston nodded at the accumulation and chimed in. "How about the fact that it can be knocked out? If you want to control, capture, or kill it, you need to know about vulnerability." Father Matthew added it to the board and turned back to Kevin and Johnston.

"That's a serious point," Kevin agreed. "What exactly did Brian do to immobilize it?"

"Precisely. Was it a bonk to the head, or Brian pushing on a weak spot?" Johnston asked. Then she offered another question, "Has anybody directly witnessed the presence of the cat or visitor around the time of death of the victims?"

Father Matthew then added, "And how did the cat get from Sixtieth street to Ninth street?"

"Brian asked the same thing, but we don't know the answer," Kevin said. "Could be there is more than one. Maybe we need a list of the things we don't know."

"And what is this thing's function? I mean, why is this thing on the planet?" Johnston asked, a quiver of exasperation escaping her otherwise steady voice.

"Very well. Things we don't know yet." The priest started the list and then commented, "But not to worry, we've made tremendous gains already." There was a quiet pause for a moment, then Father Matthew spoke up again after he finished writing. "With this last question, Miss Johnston has caught up with our conundrum." Father Matthew placed his stick of chalk on the ledge and swiped the chalk dust from his fingers. "Now, I think we should take a break," the priest said and then gestured toward the door. "The abstract is time consuming and often best left to simmer for a while."

Kevin looked at Johnston and chuckled, "Rita's?"

46

Brian and Kevin slouched on opposite ends of the couch, their eyes focused on the old TV. The announcer on the screen was talking about week two of the NFL preseason and the coming matchup between the Eagles and Patriots. Between them was a large bowl of tortilla chips and another containing yellow liquid cheese. In a slow, continuous repetition, Brian took a chip, dipped it in the cheese and then popped it into his mouth. After about a dozen chips, he drank a swallow of beer. When the TV announcer's image was replaced by commercials, his eyes rolled to Kevin. He asked, "How are you and the lady detective getting along, I mean, beyond chasing this multi-species intertransformationist?"

"Multi-species what?"

"Intertransformationist."

Kevin squinted his eyes. "Did you make that up? Because I doubt that's a real word."

"I did, but it sounds good, don't it?"

"Maybe," Kevin chuckled.

On the TV, the commercials gave way to the football field, and a line of players stretched from one sideline to the other. On a whistle, they ran in unison toward the other team. The brothers sat in silence as the football was kicked to the far end zone of the field where a player caught the ball and dropped to one knee.

When the game was interrupted by another commercial break, Brian turned to Kevin again. "Now, back to you and Johnston. Is this gonna be something?" Brian asked again.

"I don't think so," Kevin replied.

"What does that mean?"

Kevin shrugged his shoulders.

"It's a yes or no question," Brian said. "She hung out with you all day yesterday and the whole night before," Brian declared, his voice rising in pitch. Then he patted the cushions they were sitting on. "She slept right here on this very couch, and you even got to see her back-up piece." Brian pointed his index finger and cocked his thumb while making a clicking sound. "No one ever sees a lady's piece unless there's, you know, something."

"Nothing happened. She just lost her partner, and she wants to find answers. I'm just the guy that has some information."

"I don't buy it. There's more than that."

"I disagree. She's what the Marines would call a *hard charger*. She's all about her job, you know? I didn't even know her first name is Della until Uncle Matthew coaxed it out of her, but if it makes you feel better, my boss Daisy is on your side. She said she could sense something when Johnston and Powers came down to the *Moshulu*."

"Yeah, there you go, trust a woman's intuition," Brian declared.

"Did you really just say that, considering what you're going through?"

"I did. Women have very reliable intuition—except when it's wrong or involves money."

Kevin laughed, "Is that your vast experience talking?"

"No, it's a thing Skinny says."

"And he's the authority on women? The fireman who has been married and divorced how many times?"

"Three, but that's not the point."

"I know what you are getting at. Maybe something could happen. We seem to click. She's easy on the eyes and clearly pretty smart." Kevin shrugged, "Look, I'm going to just lay low for a little bit. She's in a tough spot and dating is the last thing on her mind."

"I think you're scared to make a move with an older woman."

"She's not that much older."

"But you're still scared," Brian laughed.

Kevin shrugged. "I'm more scared of this multi-species intertransformationist."

"Yeah, about that. You gotta do something about the peeping tomcat. We can't have that thing creeping around the neighborhood and pushing people from third floor windows."

"Why me? I didn't ask for this. It's your problem, if it's anybody's. After all, you're the sworn public servant who rescues cats from trees."

"Cats. Not intertransformationist creatures," Brian replied.

"You think it pushes people out windows?" Kevin asked.

"I don't think it was an accident."

"You're probably right," Kevin agreed. "It might hang out as a cat, waiting to push an unsuspecting victim from a high place, but then it might also lead them into dangerous situations. That matches up better with the video of Mr. Willy chasing the cat toward the train tracks."

"This is messed up, brother," Brian said. "Do you hear the conversation we are having?"

Kevin nodded his head and then said, "Yeah, I know, but this isn't just about some cat. For one, it is not a cat. At least not the kind of cat we know." Kevin took a handful of chips and munched on them in silence for a few moments. "We don't know what it is. We don't know how it works, and we don't know it's vulnerabilities."

"So, you're saying we don't know jack. We don't even know how many there are or even what to call it!" Brian exclaimed.

"You gave it a name, but I guess we gotta catch it to find out the rest," Kevin said in a quiet voice.

"How? We don't know how to do that either."

"I'm not sure, but we'll find a way."

47

Kevin, Brian, and Mark sat at the front window table, ignoring the morning breakfast crowd streaming in and out of the restaurant. The game camera photos flashed on Mark's computer in a slow rhythm, showing the same features over and over again. Mark said, "I don't see a cat or a creep in any of these. Am I missing something?"

"I think our quarry has moved on," Kevin replied.

"It probably got spooked and decided to vamoose," Brian agreed.

"How do we find it again?" Mark asked before taking a sip of his coffee.

They sat in silence until Brian shrugged his shoulders and said, "I got nothing."

"I'm drawing a blank, too," Mark seconded. Then Mark looked at Kevin and asked, "How do Marines find bad guys hiding in the jungle?"

Kevin sat in silence for a long time and scratched his chin before muttering, "They read something Chinese."

"Okay, you lost me there," Mark said.

"Sun-Tzu's *Art of War* or the *Thirty-Six Stratagems*, and if that doesn't work, they go to von Clausewitz."

"Never heard of them," Mark responded.

"I guess that fancy Penn State education didn't include classic literature," Brian chuckled.

"And you know all about it, Mr. Smarty Pants?"

"No, but at least I heard of the *Art of War*," Brian replied with a laugh.

Kevin grinned at them, and then returned to the subject at hand. "We're learning about our adversary, but if it has weaknesses, we have to find them faster than it finds ours. Right now, I think we're losing the battle."

"How so?" Mark asked.

"It knows where we live, but we don't know where it lives. What does it eat? How often does it take a dump? It knows how to lure people into killing themselves, but we don't even know if it can be killed."

"I see what you are saying," Mark said. "The cat knows what it's doing, and we're just reacting. We have to flip it over. Kinda like a football game where one team knows the other team's playbook and can anticipate the next move."

"Yeah, you're on the right track," Kevin agreed. "We have to get ahead of it."

"I don't know about you, but that sounds impossible," Brian observed.

Kevin took a sip of his beverage and responded. "It's not impossible, but it's not easy either. I think we need to hit the streets in places it might operate. If we can get the regular guy on the street to tell us where it's been, we can pinpoint the search. Once we reduce the search area, it will start reacting to us."

"Force it to make a mistake," Brian chimed in with a smile.

"We are talking about the entire Philly metro area, right?" Mark asked.

"Like I said, it won't be easy," Kevin reiterated.

Brian stretched out his arms and yawned while saying, "How about Johnston? She'll want in on this conversation."

"I'll fill her in next time I see her," Kevin agreed.

"I'm sure you will," Brian laughed.

"Why do you have to go there? It's not like that."

"Sure thing, bro."

"Well, my good fellows, I have a day job that requires my attention," Mark said, packing up his computer and bundling up his food wrappers. "But I must admit, reviewing stats for the MLB teams with no hope of the pennant race doesn't hold a candle to this excitement."

"Brian and I will come up with something and let you know what's next," Kevin assured him.

"As a matter of fact, I'm formulating a plan right now," Brian added.

"Yeah?" Mark asked.

"I'm planning to take a nap," Brian announced.

"Genius," Kevin said.

48

Wednesday, August 22
10:12 a.m.

Kevin took a seat in front of Father Matthew's desk. "It's different coming here during business hours," he said.

"How so?" the priest asked.

"For one thing, there are cars in the parking lot and seminarians in the halls."

"True," Father Matthew nodded as he spoke and then gestured to his own ear with a crooked index finger, "and there are many more ears to hear. I'm not sure we are ready to share our story with the wider world, so we must be careful what we say in the office."

Kevin lowered his voice, "I've been thinking. We've got to get ahead of the cat." Father Matthew nodded in agreement, and Kevin continued, "We're reacting to its moves. We need to take a chance and get on the offense."

"We are thinking alike," the old man said with a nod. "But before we discuss that, I must inquire about the well-being of Detective Johnston. When we met, she seemed unsettled. Much like you were on your first visit."

"She told me as much. First the loss of her partner, then the death of an officer from her old precinct has her feeling off balance.

The medical examiner hasn't released Detective Powers' body yet, so I hope the funeral for Officer Walker will give her a place to grieve."

"Hmm. Yes. Your intuition is very good. Are you sure the Lord hasn't been calling you to the priesthood? Have you been listening?"

"I have enough on my plate. I really just want to be done with this cat."

"Indeed," the priest said. After a long silence, he leaned forward, waving Kevin in closer. In a voice just over a whisper, he said, "We need bait."

"But we don't know what it eats, or where to find it. We don't even know its name."

"Do not be discouraged," Matthew's voice continued in a low whisper. Kevin leaned in a little more. "We know it preys on weakness. With the right arrangement, we don't need to find it. It will come to us."

"Yes, what do you have in mind?"

"I'll get to that in a moment," the priest said. "First I want to review a few items with you."

"Like what?" Kevin asked.

"Mister Willy."

"What about him?"

"The cat was attracted to him?"

"It hung around him when we weren't nearby. When Mark and I got close the cat took off."

"I suspect Willy thought of it as a companion, yes?"

"Yeah. That's true," Kevin agreed.

"And tell me about Willy's health. At least what you knew anyway."

"He wasn't in good shape. He had some serious chronic health issues."

"Do you think the cat could sense that, too?" the priest asked.

"I suppose if a cat has the ability to change species, it could also distinguish between a healthy and unhealthy person," Kevin said. "What are you thinking?"

"You said Willy had infected wounds but wasn't getting treatment."

"He did." Kevin answered. "He'd have lost his foot soon if he didn't get some kind of care."

"Or he'd die from the infection."

"Probably within a couple weeks." Kevin paused for a few moments, and then said, "If I could smell the festering wound, the cat could too. Do you think the whole train platform thing happened because the cat got impatient for him to die?"

"I think the cat could be better described as *hungry*," the priest said.

The two of them sat in silence, while Kevin looked at his feet. When his head came up, he looked out the window and said, "Hungry? Yeah, I guess that's it. I mean, we don't know if it eats anything, but it is constantly moving. It has to replace that energy somehow." Kevin paused again. "We're back to Abi's father's premise that this thing feeds on souls."

"I think we are."

"Like a vulture on roadkill," Kevin murmured and then fell silent again, eyes looking ahead but not focused. Kevin asked, "Can't we just set out a can of tuna and a saucer of milk?"

"Troubling problems sometimes require equally troubling answers."

"I was afraid of that," Kevin sighed. "So, what is your proposal?"

"We will create a scenario similar to Mister Willy. A volunteer will pose as a homeless person until the cat comes calling. Then we spring a trap."

"I suspect that if the cat can detect life-threatening vulnerability, it can tell if somebody is faking, too."

"Then we'll need to enlist somebody who really is at risk," Father Matthew declared.

"I gotta say, I'm not enthusiastic about this plan. It's a good way to get hurt, or worse." Kevin added, "I want to think about this for a while. Maybe we can come up with something else before resorting to live human bait."

"It will be a waste of time," Matthew asserted. "You know it as well as I do."

"Who is going to be the bait? I don't happen to know a sick homeless guy who is willing to participate in a life-or-death experiment."

"I will bait the trap," Matthew said in his quietest voice.

"No, I don't think that is a good idea," Kevin objected. "Besides, you are way too healthy. It won't be fooled."

"Hmm. I am an old man, and not nearly so healthy as I appear. My medicine cabinet can attest to that."

"Uncle Matthew, you can't do it. I need your brains backing up the brawn. Besides, my mom would kill me if she found out I let you go out there as bait." Kevin looked around the room and then back to his uncle. "We can find somebody else. This city is full of people on death's door. Besides, we might get lucky and find the cat in some alley, befriending another guy like Willy."

"Then you will have to hit the streets."

"We got lucky before," Kevin sighed. "Maybe we can get lucky again."

49

Friday, August 24
7:08 p.m.

The sun dipped below the tops of the city buildings, blanketing the streets in shadow. The humid air was still, and the day's accumulated heat radiated from the pavement. Vehicles growled along Spruce Street, with occasional brake squeaks and honks punctuating the low background note of engines. Kevin, Mark, Brian, and Johnston walked east from the apartment to the corner of Spruce and Ninth. Pausing on the street corner, Kevin described the evening's objective.

"The Marines might call this an *area denial operation*. If we can make it hard to earn a living around here, the cat will move on. Hopefully, moving downhill toward the river, where we can squeeze its area down to nothing and catch it. Tonight, we're going block by block to identify obvious hiding places and find anybody who might have seen it. We'll hand out flyers and get the folks to call in any sightings. We may get lucky with some information about its location and direction of movement." From his backpack, he passed around yellow reflective vests and clipboards with information flyers.

"So, what's the play?" Mark asked, "Because I doubt we're going to get any help saying we're trying to find an inter-species creature that's part human and part cat."

"We're doing an urban animal study for Penn State, and we need to find this cat because his tracker came off."

Mark examined the flyer and commented, "Sounds like a good story. The logo makes it look really official."

"But how about my home phone number on the flyer! I'm not so cool with that," Brian objected.

"Sorry, what else was I supposed to put on the flyer?" Kevin offered.

"It's a little on the unethical side, but most of the people we encounter won't know anything," Johnston said in a flat voice. "As we get away from high traffic areas, I think we'll get better results. Remember to lead with the picture on the flyer and don't forget to mention the broken tail. It will get you past people's natural suspicions."

"Sounds like a scam to abduct children," Mark observed. Then, in a breathless voice he said, "Hey little girl, have you seen my kinky tail pussy cat?"

"Like I said," Johnston replied.

"Alright, let's get going," Kevin encouraged. "Brian and Mark go up to Tenth and then go south to Lombard and circle back on Ninth. We'll go down to Eighth. Cover all the alleys, doorways, and behind the dumpsters. Don't forget to shine your flashlight into every dark corner. If we don't meet on Ninth, the first back to the apartment will call the other's cell phone."

The two search parties split up and started toward their respective streets. Kevin and Johnston walked east between the tall buildings of the Pennsylvania Hospital. The foot traffic was light and there weren't many places for a cat to hide along Spruce Street. When they turned the corner, the street passed between two green spaces. To the right was the hospital complex and passageways between the various buildings. To the left was a grassy area with a paved loop path.

"This area has some good hiding places." Johnston observed.

"Let's try the loop first," Kevin said while pointing to the grassy area. "Then we'll come back to the hospital." They crossed the street and saw several people with small dogs. "I'll go left. You go right, and we'll meet back here."

Kevin approached the first person he came to, holding up the flier in front of himself like a shield. "Pardon me. We're trying to locate a feral cat. It's part of a study. It's easily distinguished by a kink in its tail. Have you seen it?" The older woman held a small quivering chihuahua on a gold chain leash that yipped at Kevin's approach. She told the dog to be quiet and looked at the photo for a moment.

"There aren't many cats around here. If Zsa Zsa saw one, I'd still be chasing her. Sorry, I can't help you," she said. Kevin thanked her and moved on. Farther up the walk there was another woman sitting on a bench. She was watching a medium size dog, trailing its leash, sniffing around the grassy area. At Kevin's approach she snapped her fingers and the dog returned directly to her. It sat down at her feet and panted.

"Hi, I'm hoping you can help me," Kevin declared, offering a flyer. The dog followed Kevin's movements with alert eyes.

"I've never heard of this study. I usually know about these things."

"Uh, we're tracking feral cats with radio collars. This one is particularly active. That is until it shook loose from the collar."

"Interesting," she sniffed. "I saw a similar cat around here a week ago, but I haven't seen it recently."

"This one has a hitch in its tail," Kevin offered

"I didn't really see the tail."

"Did you notice anything peculiar about its behavior, by any chance?"

"No, it just seemed to pass through late in the evening. We don't see cats around here much. This area is mostly dogs, so they tend to stay away."

"I appreciate your time," Kevin said. "Please call that number if you think of anything else. It will really help if we can find Morris."

"Morris. That's funny," the woman smiled.

Kevin and Johnston converged on the far side of the loop and walked south. "Anything?" Kevin asked.

"One sighting. A beagle chased a light-color cat a week ago."

"Okay, we're just getting started."

"I did come up with something else we can use," Johnston offered.

"What's that?"

"We need to zero in on the street people in the area. They seem to be our indirect target anyway. The locals will know about them just as much as a stray cat," she said.

"Genius. I guess that's why you get the big money."

"It's part of the job."

On the way back to Eigth street, Kevin suggest Johnston call Mark with the recommendation.

"I already did."

"Damn, you're good," Kevin exclaimed.

"Just the tip of the iceberg, sailor," Johnston grinned. "By the way, you gave a nice little briefing back there. Good job taking charge."

"Just like the Navy. Show a little initiative, and they make you the boss," Kevin shrugged.

"I'm impressed. You can think on your feet, and you really care."

"I guess so," he said, after a pause he continued, "but I'm still not sure why. Most people would just let this cat thing go."

"You aren't most people," Johnston said. "It's what I like about you."

50

Mark and Brian made their way south on Tenth Street. The few people they encountered acknowledged them but kept walking. They searched the alleys along the street but didn't find any sign of the cat. Returning from an alley, Mark's phone began making an ascending ping noise. He pulled it from his pocket, touched a button, and held it to his ear. "Yo," he said, then listened in silence for a moment. "Will do," Mark said and put the phone back in his pocket. He then called to Brian, who had wandered to the other side of the street. "Della says we need to inquire about street people in the area, too."

"Really?" Brian gasped in disbelief.

"Yeah, it actually makes sense. That's how we found the cat in the first place."

"Okay. Roll the bums, too, but I wouldn't go around calling Johnston by her first name if I were you, and definitely don't say I told you about it," Brian chuckled.

"She's that touchy?" Mark asked.

"She is, and she's got a gun."

"Okay, okay, enough said," Mark agreed.

Walking south to Clinton Street, they encountered more pedestrians. Brian approached two young men waiting on the corner. Holding out a flyer, he said, "Pardon me, we're trying to locate this cat. Have you seen it?"

"Oh, I can't help you," said the closer of the two. The man flipped his long blonde hair with his hand and proclaimed, "I'm an animal lover. Keeping pets is cruel. Who am I to deny an animal its rights?"

Brian winced and then tried again. "It's a stray cat. It has a kink in its tail. Have you seen it?"

"Ignore him, he got started early tonight," the other man said. "I've seen it. It's a very rude cat. I offered it some dolphin-safe tuna and hormone-free milk, but it wasn't interested. Then when I tried to pick it up, it scratched me." The man extended his hand, palm down and fingers spread wide. With his other hand, he pointed to a group of parallel scratches.

"It got you good. Did it hurt?" Brian asked while looking closer at the scratch.

"Not so much, but it wouldn't stop bleeding for days."

"Do you normally bleed easily?"

"No, I thought it might be the supplements my holistic advisor recommended."

"Could be," Brian offered, "but that sounds like the right cat. When did you see it last?"

"It hasn't been around here for a while," the second man said.

The blond man returned to the conversation after wandering a few steps away and then coming back. "I saw it yesterday. It came to see me at the ACME grocery store. I think it's a very loving cat. I would adopt it, but I can't deny it the freedom to be itself."

"What's that? We didn't go to the ACME yesterday." The second man stepped closer to Brian and whispered, "He's on a lot of medication. Sometimes he loses track of time. We were at the ACME the day before yesterday. I'm not sure what he's talking about. I didn't see the kitty."

"We'll get down that way soon. Is that the ACME on Fifth?"

"Yes," he said. Brian nodded and started to walk off.

"I hope you find your pussy!" the blonde man said with a giggle.

"Thanks, me too," Brian said with a wink. He stepped across the curb and jogged to catch up with Mark on the far side. Drawing alongside Mark, Brian said, "I got some good information from those two."

"Really? I though they were trying to hook up with one of Philly's finest hose handlers," Mark observed.

"I'll leave that to the guys on the calendar."

"So, what did they know?" Mark inquired.

"They had some interactions with our cat. The one guy is probably very sick, and the cat was checking him out. The other guy tried to feed it and got scratched for his trouble."

"Was it a bleeder?"

"He said it took days to stop," Brian said.

"How long since they saw it last?"

"The feeder said a while ago. The other guy said he saw it the day before yesterday at the ACME on Fifth."

"Nice! That's a solid lead."

"Yep. He wasn't a very good witness, but maybe we can refocus our search further east."

51

The sun was fully down, but the night was still warm. The street echoed with the sound of air conditioners rattling in window frames and on rooftops. Kevin and Johnston walked west in the semi-darkness of Lombard Street, aiming their flashlights into shadowed corners and alleys. "I think we've run the course of tonight's search," Kevin surmised while wiping perspiration from his forehead. "We haven't seen anybody in two blocks."

"Hang in there. We could still find something on the way back," Johnston said while examining the details of the street. Ahead, the shape of two men with reflective bands could be seen coming toward them. "I think we can hold up at the corner and wait for Larry and Curly."

"I see them," Kevin seconded. "I hope they did better than us." Then after a moment's thought, he asked, "Which one is which, and does that make me Moe?"

"Wouldn't you like to know," laughed Johnston.

The shadows of the men paused at the bottom of a stoop and engaged a person sitting there. After a brief exchange, they continued to where Kevin and Johnston were waiting under a streetlamp.

Emerging into the light, Mark declared, "I think we got some good news."

"Definitely a solid lead," chimed in Brian.

"Good, let's head back to the apartment to sort it out," Kevin replied. The four spread out on both sides of Ninth Street and walked north. A few people sat on their front steps, but nobody had information about the cat. When they arrived at the intersection of Clinton and Ninth, Mark and Brian stopped under some trees near the Pennsylvania Hospital's old front facade.

"What have you guys got?" Kevin called across the street.

"Hang tight," Brian replied before deviating off the street. Mark followed and soon they were crouched down next to a man sitting on a bench. Next to him was a tattered half-full garbage bag. "Hello friend, I was wondering if you could help me with something?"

"I ain't got nothing for ya," was the response.

"We're just looking for a missing cat. Maybe you've seen it?" Mark added.

"Ain't got no cat, don't want no cat."

"Okay, sorry to bother you," Brian said, backing away from the man.

"Only cat I know about was down by Starr Park."

"What color was it?" Mark asked, approaching the man again.

"It had some orange stripes and a busted tail, and it was real friendly with Hector. Right before he died."

"What happen to Hector?" Brian asked.

"He got pneumonia and was breathing hard. Couldn't move his wheelchair no more. Cat was sleeping with him. Hector said it was his guardian angel come to take him to Heaven. Then he died. I ain't seen the cat since." The man was silent for a moment, and then said, "Maybe it really was his angel."

"How long ago was that?" Brian inquired.

"Some couple days ago. I ain't got no calendar, and I don't want no calendar."

"Thanks. That's a big help," Mark said, pulling a ten-dollar bill from his wallet and setting it on the man's garbage bag of belongings.

The two then walked back to the street and rejoined Kevin and Johnston.

"Good information?" Kevin asked.

"Yeah. Another good lead. A very good lead," Brian nodded.

52

Friday, August 24
10:13 p.m.

Four people overwhelmed the basement apartment, leaving little room to move. Kevin leaned against the refrigerator, crunching on ice cubes from an orange plastic cup imprinted with the logo of the 76ers basketball team. Johnston and Brian slouched on the couch, drinking beer from bottles dripping with condensation. Mark sat on the floor next to the old TV and gulped from a water bottle until it was empty. "Now, a beer please," he panted, tossing the empty toward Kevin.

Kevin caught it and dropped it into the garbage can while simultaneously retrieving a beer from the refrigerator. He opened the bottle, passed it to Mark, then flipped the cap over his shoulder into the garbage.

"Thanks. That was a smooth move," Mark said.

"No problem, but don't try it at home. I'm a trained professional," Kevin said as everybody broke into guffaws. After another moment, Kevin asked, "Is everybody cooled off enough to think?" Brian and Johnston nodded while Mark began sipping from his beer. "Detective Johnston, why don't you start with what we got. Mark, do you mind taking notes?" Kevin said, tossing a note pad and pen into his lap.

"I guess I'll take notes," Mark said after putting down his beer and wiping his condensation-damp hand on the carpet.

Johnston began speaking when Mark was ready. "We handed out twenty-two flyers and interviewed seven people. Four were before we added asking about street people. Only three had seen a stray cat that matched, or loosely matched the description of our perp. All the sightings were about a week old. One was in the green space on Eighth. The other two were on the street, but the exact location was not provided."

"That pretty well sums it up," Kevin said. "I think we had a few cooperative folks that will call if they see the cat. The rest, probably not," Kevin added. He took a swallow of the meltwater in his cup and looked at Brian. "How about you guys?"

"Well, we gave away almost all our flyers, but I didn't count. We talked to about twenty- five people, wouldn't you say?"

Mark looked up. "Something like that. We'll keep score next time," he chuckled.

"Anyway, we got really lucky on a couple. The funniest was these two guys waiting for a taxi. They knew quite a bit about the cat. The first guy was pretty whacked out on something. I don't think he knew what planet he was on. His companion said he tried to feed a yellow cat some milk and tuna but got a good scratch on his hand as thanks."

"An oozing scratch by any chance?" Kevin asked.

"He said it took a while to stop bleeding. I saw it, and I'm guessing it was our cat's handiwork," Brian said, then Mark jumped in.

"The over-medicated guy then told us he'd seen the same cat very recently at the ACME store on South Fifth maybe two days ago." Brian nodded his head and Mark continued, "But given his state, the companion doubted his reliability as a witness."

"His sense of time might be distorted, but I'm willing to bet he saw it," Johnston said.

Kevin nodded and asked, "What about the guy by the hospital?"

"That's the other good one," Brian smiled. "He saw a cat in Starr Gardens Park, just a couple blocks from the ACME. It was hanging around a guy in a wheelchair named Hector. He said he saw it up close. On top of that, Hector died very recently, probably from complications of pneumonia, with no sign of the cat since."

"Solid work," Johnston congratulated them. "I'll see if I can get any information on Hector. Hopefully, his body has been picked up already."

Kevin rummaged through his backpack and pulled out a map of the city. He unfolded it to the appropriate section and laid it on the floor in front of the TV.

"We are here. The ACME is here. There is Starr Gardens Park. Where did you meet the two guys?" Kevin asked.

"On the corner of Tenth and Clinton," Mark said.

"Great. I'm guessing the cat is already working east." Kevin gestured to the right on the map with his finger. "It's still using the same method it did with Mr. Willy. We need to catch up a couple blocks east and south, then press toward the river, one block at a time. We're a couple of days behind it, but we can close the gap next time. Good work, everybody."

"This has been a load of fun, and I can't wait to do it again some time, but if you folks will excuse me," Brian said, "I have to get up early tomorrow. We're parading a ladder truck for the police funeral march in the morning."

"That's right. Thanks again everybody. We'll try again in a few days," Kevin concluded as everybody stood up. Mark led the way to the door, followed by Johnston and Kevin. Brian collected glasses and empties and then said, "Good night," before retreating into the bedroom.

Mark climbed the steps two at a time and turned at the top. "Let me know what's next."

"Will do, Mark," Kevin called up the steps. "Thanks for the help."

Mark retreated down the street to a minivan and drove away as Johnston made her way up the steps. She stopped at the top where

Kevin came up alongside her. The night air was still warm. The sounds of the city were almost quiet. She turned to face Kevin and looked him in the eye. Kevin returned the long look until she glanced down. Looking up again, Johnston placed her hand on Kevin's shoulder and said, "Listen, the funeral procession tomorrow is going to keep me busy, so I may be unavailable for a day or two."

Kevin nodded. "If there's any way I can help, you know where to find me."

"I do," Johnston replied with a soft smile. Turning to leave, she looked over her shoulder and said in a husky tone, "Good night, sailor." Kevin, frozen in place, watched her walk away until she disappeared from sight.

53

K evin hummed while he surveyed the descending elevator's plain stainless-steel interior. On the opposite wall, a distorted reflection of a patient in a wheelchair showed the patient's head, topped with a mop of gray hair, resting on his gowned chest. His hands were folded together in his lap. Kevin's hospital scrubs appeared as a blurry, bright green shape looming behind the patient. In a casual voice, Kevin asked, "Mr. Hayes, are you related to a Patricia Hayes? She's a second-grade teacher. Do you know her?" but there was no response or motion from the patient. When the elevator doors opened, Kevin said, "Right on, good talk. Next stop: X-ray," and rolled Mr. Hayes down the hall and into the radiology department waiting area. Reaching the check-in desk, Kevin handed the clerk a form. Without looking up, the clerk said it would be at least ten minutes. Kevin guided the wheelchair to a parking spot next to a row of chairs, where he set the brakes and took a seat next to Mr. Hayes. Kevin leaned forward toward the television hanging on the opposite wall and scrutinized the image.

On the screen, a reporter described the scene on Lehigh Avenue and the silent caisson march honoring Moses Walker of the

Philadelphia Police. The camera cut from the reporter to the empty street lined on either side with onlookers. The pavement rose gently to a crest that obscured the distant street. People, standing shoulder to shoulder along the sides, strained to see the source of the sound the camera was just beginning to register. The rapid tap tap of snare drums, subtle at first, began echoing through the North Philadelphia neighborhood. The TV camera zoomed to the blurry black and white shapes becoming visible above the pavement's crest. Before long, the indistinguishable forms became men wearing black top hats and mourning coats, riding on a glossy black Victorian hearse drawn by a pair of huge white draft horses. They were flanked by an escort of kilted musicians and a color guard. As the precession drew closer, a massive line of officers in two-tone blue Philadelphia Police uniforms, four abreast, could be seen marching behind the hearse. The camera panned as it passed, revealing two trucks from the Philadelphia Fire Department parked on either side of the street. Their aerial ladders were extended like an arch with a large US flag suspended between them. The firefighters stood straight and tall, saluting the hearse as it passed under the flag. Farther down Lehigh Avenue, the musician's bag pipes honked to life, and began playing sad notes in time with the drums.

The long procession of marching police officers silently marched in unison. They wore white gloves and black bands over their badges. A light rain shower moved over the formation, dampening uniforms and accentuating the stony faces of the marchers. Slowly they filed past the fire trucks and further down the street made a right turn into a church. At the church doors, a drum kept cadence and somewhere inside a bagpiper played until the last marcher disappeared inside. The firefighters lowered their ladders and struck the flag just as the rain shower became heavy, chasing everybody under cover. The reporter stepped back in front of the camera, holding an umbrella, and described the services that would follow over the next two days.

Still leaning in toward the television, Kevin said to Mr. Hayes,

"That's my brother's ladder truck, but I couldn't tell which one was him. My friend Johnston was in that long line of cops, but I didn't see her either. They kinda all look alike in uniform, but I guess that's sort of the point, isn't it." Kevin finally looked from the screen to Mr. Hayes, who remained motionless, except for the slow rise and fall of his breathing. Kevin said, "That's alright Mr. Hayes, you got other things to worry about."

54

K evin maneuvered an empty gurney down a sixth-floor corridor. At a bank of elevators, he pressed the call button and waited. When the car arrived, a plump woman, dressed in green scrubs like Kevin, exited and said, "There you are. You got a phone message at the desk. Miss June said it was the police calling."

"Thanks," Kevin said without emotion.

The woman stopped and asked, "Are you in trouble?"

"No trouble here," Kevin replied as he pushed the gurney into the elevator and stepped in just before the doors closed. Exiting at the basement level, he turned right and rolled the gurney down the corridor, where he left it next to a line of idle medical equipment. Kevin then reversed direction and walked to an office near the other end of the hall. Kevin peeked around the door frame and asked, "Miss June, do you have a message for me?"

A stern-looking, gray-haired woman sat at a desk, glaring at Kevin over small half-frame glasses. In a gruff voice she said, "A certain Detective Johnston called and would like to hear from you. Are you in trouble? I got no room for troublemakers."

"No ma'am. I'm a witness in a case. Innocent bystander."

"Hmm. I seen a lot of witnesses become suspects by the time a trial is done."

"It's not like that. Nothing to worry about."

"Go make your call," she said, and held out two slips of paper, "and here's your next patient when you're done."

Kevin stepped into the room just far enough to grab the slips and then walked farther down the hall to the employee break room. Just inside the door, he picked up the handset and pushed the buttons on a wall-mounted phone. Leaning against the wall, he fidgeted with the phone cord and looked around the empty room while he waited. Finally, he said, "It's Kevin. Where are you? This connection is awful." After a moment, the noise abated and he said, "That's better. It seems like I haven't talked to you in forever. How are you?" Kevin asked and then listened to the quiet murmur from the speaker. "Sure," Kevin responded and then listened some more before adding, "So, Hector was picked up on Tuesday?" Kevin then said, "Interesting. Mark and his brother-in-law Skip came down last night and we made another sweep down by Starr Park. We didn't really find anything new." Just then an older man dressed in green scrubs walked into the room. Kevin listened to the phone and nodded at him as he sat down in a chair. Kevin continued speaking, "Nothing to worry about. Skip's a good guy. Yeah, I'll talk to you later. Bye." When he hung up the phone, he turned to the man, "Mr. Marshall. How's it going?"

"Another day in paradise." He smiled and added, "and I don't have the police calling me at work."

"Right on. I gotta go." Kevin quickly moved to the door and paused. Looking back at Mr. Marshall, he asked, "Does everybody around here know my business?"

"If Miss June knows, then everybody knows."

"Awesome," Kevin said, and walked into the hallway.

55

Kevin stood on the northwest corner of Thirty-Fourth and Market. A full moon hung over the city and there was a lively crowd all around. Kevin leaned on a light pole and watched the people in silence until a plain Chevrolet sedan stopped in front of him. The right front window lowered, and the driver said, "Get in the back." Kevin opened the rear door, dropped his backpack onto the gray vinyl seat and slid in behind it.

"I was expecting Johnston."

"She's busy," the driver replied.

Kevin pulled the door closed. "Since there's no handle, I guess I'm here until you let me out."

"Police cars are like that," the bald man behind the wheel replied without looking back. "By the way I'm Senior Detective Caporaso."

"Nice to meet you. You work with Johnston?" Kevin asked.

"Yeah, you could say that."

Kevin sat back and watched where the car was going. The driver didn't speak for a long time as he steered the car along a wandering path to the north and east. Eventually the reflected glow of red and blue flashing lights could be seen on the buildings several blocks ahead.

The neighborhood was a row house community turned into apartments, with crowded streets intersected by unlit alleys. "When we get there," the driver piped up, "take a look around, but don't touch anything unless I say it's okay. When it's your turn to talk, I'll let you know, and I expect you to keep this to yourself. Got it?"

"Yes, sir," Kevin replied.

Police vehicles and an ambulance came into view, and the car came to a stop a half block away from the scene. Caporaso got out and walked over to the nearest uniformed police officer. They exchanged words, and the uniformed officer spoke into his radio. After a moment he nodded to the detective who then returned to open the rear door.

"Follow me," the senior detective said as Kevin exited the car.

They weaved around parked police cars and cut between two buildings off North Seventeenth Street. Ahead, several dark figures held flashlights at waist level, pointing toward the ground. A voice said, "Over here, sir."

Caporaso crouched down where the speaker's flashlight revealed a human form lying in the weeds. "How about some more light over here," he said to the others. Two uniformed officers shone bright flashlights on the spot indicated by Caporaso. Looking back at Kevin, he said, "What do you think?"

Without speaking, Kevin stepped carefully around the body and knelt down for a closer look. The face was pale and pulled tight over the skull. The skin on the hands was shriveled, revealing the bone structure underneath. Kevin stood up and silently looked at the detective.

"Seen enough?" the detective asked. Kevin nodded. "Okay. I'll be along in a minute."

Kevin made his way back to the car where he leaned against the rear fender and watched the activity. After the body was loaded in the waiting ambulance, Caporaso walked back and casually rested an arm on the roof and looked at Kevin. "Look like the others?"

"Yeah. The tissue is practically mummified, so it doesn't rot and the bugs aren't interested in it. The smell isn't any stronger than the ambient garbage stench. From the weeds grown up around it, and accumulated dirt streaks, I'd guess he's been there awhile. I noticed the alley doesn't really go anywhere and there are no windows overlooking it, so it could have been weeks." Kevin looked down at the cracked concrete and blacktop under his feet and said, "Any idea who it was?"

"He had a Temple University student ID on him. Trevor Flynn. His roommate reported last seeing him out on a bender two weeks ago. He also said Flynn was taking the semester off to go on tour with Phish, so nobody even thought to look for him until a few days ago."

"Any idea what killed him?"

"The medical examiner will let us know."

"If he was hitting the liquor hard, my guess," Kevin exhaled, "he might have choked on his own vomit when he passed out in the alley." The two men were silent for a few moments before Kevin spoke up again. "Why did you have Johnston call me? I mean, what am I here for?"

"Frankly, it's a short cut. We can skip a lot of steps in the investigation by calling in some help." The detective shrugged, "Why beat around the bush when we can just rip it out by the roots. For better or worse, you seem to be the subject-matter expert."

"Great. Am I going to get all the calls for this kind of thing?"

"Just until we get the answers we need. Since your name kept coming up, I might as well meet you in person."

Kevin shook his head and closed his eyes for a moment. When he opened them again, he asked, "How much has Johnston told you about this situation?"

"Enough. We can talk more while I take you back to your apartment."

"Fantastic. Do I get anything for my time and expertise? I mean riding around in a cop car sounds fun and all, but a guy's still got to pay the rent."

"Sure, we can pay you the standard rate. What do you make at the hospital?"

"What's that got to do with it?"

"The department will pay the same hourly rate you make in your regular employment."

"Screw that. Go find another expert in mysterious desiccated death. Besides, I don't want to be obligated to you guys unless there is a real paycheck involved."

The detective laughed at Kevin's reaction. "Johnston said you had a little moxie."

The two men remained silent until Caporaso stopped the unmarked police car in front of Brian's apartment. The senior detective got out and walked around to open the right rear door. "You may hear from me again," he said as Kevin exited.

"Before you go, where does the PD stand on this cat thing?" Kevin asked.

"I'm not sure I understand your question," Caporaso said, shutting the door.

"Is there an official investigation? Are you guys gonna take the ball and run with it? Because I'm happy to let you have it. I didn't want in, and I'm happy to get out."

"There isn't an investigation, and cats are not our business."

"But you have bodies turning up under suspicious circumstances and a transforming cat-man."

"That may be, but so far, the cause of death in each case appears straightforward. The condition of the bodies might be unusual, but that looks environmental, not criminal. When there is obvious evidence of a crime, we'll investigate. Until then, the police will not get involved."

"What about Johnston?"

"As long as it doesn't interfere with official business, what Detective Johnston does on her own time is not our concern," Caporosa said in a flat voice. "But if you screw with one of my people, it will become my business. Clear?"

"Crystal clear."

"I'll see about getting you some kind of compensation. Good

night." The senior detective briskly walked back around the car and climbed in.

Kevin watched the car motor down the street and then turn the corner in the direction of the center of the city. "I guess I'm still the point man," he said to himself. Pivoting toward the front door, Kevin immediately froze at the sight of someone emerging from the apartment's darkened stairwell.

"Hello, sailor," said the soft voice of the shadowy figure.

"You had me there. Another second and this was going to get physical."

"And probably not the kind of physical either of us wants," Johnston said as she emerged into the moonlight. "Sorry about that." After a pause she reached out and touched his hand, guiding him forward again, and said, "How was your ride along?"

"Just another shriveled up dead guy on a Friday night," Kevin replied in a tired voice. "I didn't expect to find you here. Is everything okay? I mean I kind of expected you to take a step back now that you are working again."

"You heard the boss. What I do on my own time is none of his business," Johnston said.

Kevin shrugged and stepped down to the door of the apartment. "Want to come in? There's no entertainment to speak of since Brian's working, but I could stand some company."

"I was hoping you'd ask. It wouldn't be polite to leave a lady standing on the street at midnight."

"That's true, but then, when do ladies emerge from the shadows to ambush working stiffs coming home from a long day at the office?"

"I guess you have a point," Johnston said.

Kevin led the way down the steps and unlocked the door. He flipped on a lamp by the couch and set his backpack on the kitchen counter. "Before you grill me about what just happened, can I get you a beer or something?"

"Yes, thank you," she replied while dropping on to the couch. "Then tell me about your evening with the boss."

"Is he really your boss?"

"Yes."

"Outstanding. I'm glad I didn't get too sassy with him. As far as my evening goes, somebody called in a dead guy who's been missing for a while. The body was in a weed-choked alley up in North Philly. Dried up, just like the others," Kevin described while retrieving a beer bottle from the refrigerator.

"That's pretty far away. I wonder if it's the same cat. Could there be another?" Johnston asked.

"I'm not sure I want to know the answer." He handed her the bottle and sat on the couch. "I don't even want to ask the question," Kevin said while rubbing his temples with his fingers. Johnston took a pull from the bottle and then slid her hand over and caressed Kevin's knee.

"It will all work out. Complex investigations are like that. Just asking the questions is discouraging because you know how much work is required to find the answers."

"Brian talked to an animal control guy. He said feral cats range over about a square mile in the city, but I doubt this is a run-of-the-mill stray. This guy could be a victim of our original subject." Kevin shifted on the couch and put his arm across the back of the cushion behind Johnston. "Or maybe not. It doesn't fit our estimated three-week interval. How do we know?"

"Take it easy. We're getting smarter every day. It just takes time," Johnston said as she leaned her head back against Kevin's arm and took another drink.

"But what happens to all the people that end up mummified in a vacant lot or abandoned house?" Kevin said with a sigh.

"We'll find the answers, but it won't happen tonight. You have to be patient. In the meantime, I think you need to forget about cats for a while." Johnston pulled herself closer to Kevin, and her voice dropped to a whisper. "It'll drive you crazy, if you let it."

"We wouldn't want that," Kevin replied. She caressed his leg and slowly reached for the light switch with her free hand. The lamp clicked off at the same moment the bedroom telephone rang. It rang five times before the answering machine picked up the call. A female voice could be heard coming from the machine. "Sorry. I have to take the call," Kevin said. He untangled himself from Johnston's arms and stumbled in the darkness for the phone. He picked up the handset and said, "Hello?" Kevin listened for a moment and then spoke again. "Sure, I can do it, but next time could you give me a little more notice? Okay. See you then. Good night."

"Who was that? Not competition, I hope," Johnston asked.

"My old boss, Daisy," Kevin said feeling his way back in the dark. Kevin sat back down on the couch and said, "She needs a bartender tomorrow night."

"That's my arm."

"Sorry. She's got some high-dollar private party, but I don't have to be there until four."

"Good. I was just getting comfortable with where this is going."

"Me, too."

56

Saturday, September 1
3:45 p.m.

Kevin pedaled his bicycle east on Spruce Street under the mid-afternoon sun. The street was quiet, and he made quick progress by hopping curbs and crossing against traffic lights. At Fifth Street, the road sloped down toward the river and he was able to coast much of the way. Crossing over Christopher Columbus Boulevard, he wheeled into the Penn's Landing parking lot and cut south. Squeaking to a stop at the gangway of the *Moshulu*, movement in the far corner of the parking lot attracted his attention.

Kevin locked up his bike and started up the gangway. From the higher vantage point he could see a light-colored animal spring from behind the dumpster into a nearby shrub. Kevin remained stationary for a minute, watching for movement, but eventually gave up and continued to the main deck.

"Hey, Daisy," Kevin greeted his former boss, who was hunched over a stack of papers at the bar.

She looked up at the sound of his voice. "I'm so glad you're here. We were wondering how to cover this private party without Mitchell. You're my savior."

"Who's Mitchell?"

"Another in the long line of bartenders," Daisy replied in a declining voice.

"Okay, that explains it. By the way, are you having an animal problem over by the dumpster?" Kevin asked.

"Some cat is hanging around over there. It keeps getting into the trash and making a mess."

"A cat? What does it look like?"

"I guess it's kind of pale orange with stripes. It's always dark when I see it, and it runs away at the first sign of trouble, so I've never seen it up close."

"Is Mitchell keeping everything closed up?"

"No, just like coming to work on time, it was just too much trouble for him to lock the dumpster at closing time."

"You fired him, or did he quit first?"

"I fired his scrawny over-tattooed butt. That's why I called you. I got to have first class help for this party. It's for Mr. Martinelli's daughter. You remember him, right?"

"Sure I do. It's hard to forget a major shareholder in the business you work for."

"Good. Let's get to work. We have a lot to do before the who's who of the single scene drop in on us."

Kevin set up the bar and began marking off items on Daisy's check list. Before long, a large man with dreadlocks and a black T-shirt that read *Sound of Love* came trundling across the main deck. The stranger said in a deep voice, "Yo! Where should I put my gear?"

"Over there, if that works for you," Kevin said, pointing toward the ship's rounded stern. "By the way, I'm Kevin and that's Daisy, if you need anything."

Shaking hands with Kevin he replied, "Cool. I'm Darius."

The DJ disappeared down the gangway and returned with a hand truck loaded with equipment. He set up his loudspeakers and console while Kevin watched the sun set over the city and the last of the regular diners depart for the parking lot. From the top deck of the sailing ship Kevin kept glancing at the dumpster area until it was too dark to see any detail.

57

T he DJ's voice, amplified by loudspeakers, reverberated across the deck of the *Moshulu*, "That's all the love I've got for you right now, but don't be afraid to go out and share your love with each other. Good night, everybody!" The pounding music faded to silence and the last remaining partiers shuffled down the gangway and disappeared into the warm starlit night. While Darius carted off his equipment, Kevin cleared up the bar. Looking around the Bongo Deck, Kevin turned to Daisy, "What else can I do?"

"Kevin, you were super tonight. I forgot how efficient you are behind the bar. Why don't you take out the trash while I lock up. Then we can call it a night."

"That almost sounded like you miss me," Kevin said.

"Don't get carried away," Daisy replied.

At the head of the gangway, he collected two handfuls of plastic garbage bags from a large pile and walked them over to the dumpster on the far side of the parking lot. He dropped them and returned for the remaining bags. Once he had all the trash, he swung the bags up and into the open dumpster. The bags crashed into the large steel container. When the reverberations died away, Kevin heard another sound from inside. "Oh crap, the cat!" he hissed to himself. Kevin quickly secured the lid and ran back to the ship. "Daisy! Do you have a flashlight? I think the cat is in the dumpster."

"In my car," she said. "You have to get it out of there," Daisy pleaded as she led the way to her Honda Civic. Opening the car, she retrieved a large aluminum flashlight and asked, "Will this work?"

Kevin took it from her and hefted it in his hands. He switched it on, cast a bright beam of light into the parking lot, and then switched it off. "It's perfect."

"What are you going to do?"

"I want to confirm it's in there so animal control can come get it tomorrow."

"I didn't know you were an animal lover. Are you sure that's the right thing to do?" Daisy said.

"If it runs off, it will be really hard to catch. A night in the dumpster won't hurt it." Kevin said as he turned back across the parking lot.

Kevin tapped the tail end of the flashlight on the side of the dumpster and heard faint scrambling and hissing sounds from inside. He carefully lifted the lid and held up the flashlight to the slit. Peeking inside, he saw glowing yellow eyes and the pale moon face of a bald man looking back at him from behind the pile of trash. He dropped the hatch shut and said, "Gotcha!" Kevin then found the combination lock hanging on the side of the dumpster and secured the locking bar.

"Was it the cat?" Daisy asked when he came back to the car and handed her the flashlight.

"It's in there. I'll make sure it gets picked up tomorrow," Kevin said.

"Thanks. Good night," she said, getting into her car.

Kevin unlocked the cable securing his bicycle under the gangway and rode back to the dumpster. Taking the cable, he looped it through the pad eye on the lid and pulled the top down tight to the handle on the side before securing it with the lock, making it impossible to open the lid. "Not getting away this time," he said to himself, as he mounted his bike and pedaled into the night.

58

K evin rolled his bike up to the front of the apartment and leaned it against the wall. Jumping down the steps three at a time to the door, he unlocked the deadbolt and pushed the door open. Leaving his keys hanging in the lock, Kevin darted directly to the phone and dialed a number from memory.

"Mark, wake up. Are you awake? Good. The thing is trapped in a dumpster down at the *Moshulu*," Kevin exclaimed. He then listened to the phone for a moment before continuing, "Yeah, I locked it up so it can't get away. How soon can you get there?" Kevin listened again. "Great. See you there." He hung up the phone and dialed again.

"Johnston, it's Kevin." There was a pause before he resumed talking. "The cat is trapped in a dumpster down at the *Moshulu*." He listened and then said, "It's not just any cat. I saw it go in as a cat; and when I looked inside several hours later, it wasn't a cat anymore. I'm certain of it." There was another pause. "I'll see you there as soon as I can."

Kevin made one more phone call. "I need to speak to Brian Maloney. It's an emergency." Kevin listened in silence for a long time before saying, "Sorry to wake you. I just used my bike lock to trap our friend in a dumpster down at the *Moshulu*. This is our best chance." Kevin listened to Brian for a moment. "Okay, I'll be waiting on the corner of Tenth so you don't have to come up the street."

After hanging up the phone, Kevin returned to the front room of the apartment. He picked up his backpack from the corner and dumped out the contents onto the couch. In the dim light he retrieved several items from one of the green sea bags stacked in the corner and stuffed them in his backpack. "No sleep, dehydrated, ears ringing. Can't get more ready than that," he said to himself as he retrieved a Tylenol from a bottle over the sink. He popped it in his mouth and chased it down with an entire bottle of water from the refrigerator. Tossing the empty bottle in the sink, he exited the door, locked up, and walked to the west end of the block. On the corner of Spruce and Tenth, he sat down on the sidewalk, leaned back against a wall, and immediately fell asleep.

59

Sunday, September 2
5:12 a.m.

Kevin's eyes popped open at the sound of an idling car engine. Brian was in his red Jeep Cherokee six feet from where Kevin sat. "You're here," Kevin observed, then got up and walked around to the passenger's door.

"Sorry I'm late. I had to convince the captain that this was an emergency. And I snagged us some supplies," Brian said as he directed his thumb to the fire department gear in the back seat.

"No problem. I needed another minute or two of rest, anyway." Looking at his watch. Kevin said, "It's quarter after five, the others might be there already. I hope they didn't do anything yet."

"I doubt it, Brian replied. "Nobody knows the combination to your bike lock."

"True, but drive fast anyway."

Brian pressed the gas pedal, and the well-worn vehicle made a sputter from the tail pipe and then surged forward. He drove south to Pine Street and turned left, ignoring the red traffic light. "Good thing nobody's up this early on a Sunday," Brian yelled over the roar of the engine as they accelerated east.

The jeep slowed briefly for the lights that were red, just enough to confirm no traffic was crossing, and then roared ahead. At Front Street Brian swung a hard left followed by a hard right on Spruce. Ahead and to the right was the parking area for the waterfront. Kevin pointed to the destination. "The dumpsters are over in the southwest corner of the lot. Go past them to Lombard Street and swing in by the gates."

"You got it," Brian grunted as he twisted the jeep through the required turns. There were several vehicles already parked in the vicinity of the dumpsters, including police cars.

"Johnston must have called in some backup," Kevin said. "I don't know if that's good or bad."

"They got guns and radios. If this goes sideways, the radios could be useful, but something tells me this cat thing doesn't care about guns."

Kevin and Brian exited the jeep and strode across the grass divider between the street and the parking lot. Mark, Johnston, Caporaso, and a pair of uniformed police officers were gathered under a streetlight. Caporaso looked at Kevin and said, "About time you got here. We were trying to decide how to proceed without you."

"Thanks for coming," Kevin replied. Then he and Brian turned to introduce themselves to the uniformed officers. Both brothers extending hands, Kevin said "I'm Kevin Maloney and this is my brother Brian." They all shook hands, and the two cops nodded.

"We've met before. I'm Eric Archer and this is my rookie partner Mike Church."

"Oh, right. The night you knocked on the apartment door," Kevin said.

"That's right," Archer agreed.

"How did you get involved in this?" Brian asked Archer.

"Me and the senior detective go way back. I usually get the call when something may not go exactly as planned."

"Got it," Kevin chuckled. "You might earn your pay this morning, because we have what might be a multi-species intertransfomationist trapped in a locked dumpster surrounded by a squad of Philly's finest. What could go wrong?" Kevin laughed to himself and then turned to the rookie. "Church, are you a religious man or give any credence to the supernatural?"

"As much as the next guy," Church shrugged.

"Well, hold onto your gun belt, because you are about to see some mysterious shit." Kevin then turned to Caparosa, "Okay sir, tell your expert consultant here about the official plan of action."

"We were thinking of trying to incapacitate the cat with tear gas or pepper spray inside the dumpster, before opening the lid," Caparosa said. "Then we thought maybe you could go in with zip cuffs to restrain it."

"I guess that's one way to do it" Kevin said, "but since I'm not a one-man SWAT team, I'm not too excited about it."

"How about this," Brian chimed in. "I brought an animal catch-all pole from the firehouse. We can get a line on it from four feet away. It will be much easier to control, but I do like the idea of calming it first. I was thinking smoke, or a CO2 fire extinguisher. But then again, chemical warfare might just make it mad. How about a Taser?"

"That might work. Anybody know what happens when a cat gets juiced? Caporaso asked. When no one answered, he said, "I guess we'll find out the hard way. Just so you know, it will be hard to hit a small target like a cat." Looking at Officers Archer and Church, he added, "The darts are going to spread out too far after a couple feet."

Archer responded, "Got it, point blank range."

"Once we get it out, what comes next?" Caporaso asked.

"I brought an animal crate," Mark suggested, pointing to his car.

"We'll put the crate in the back seat of the cruiser," Johnston suggested. "Even if it turns back into a human, it can't get out." The two uniformed cops looked at each other in amazement.

Archer spoke up, "What exactly are we talking about here? Is it a cat or a person?"

"We don't know. Maybe both," Kevin answered with a shrug, and Archer's face drooped. Kevin continued, "Lets get this thing going. It will be daylight soon, and we'll start drawing a crowd before you know it. Brian, get the pole. Mark, break out the crate." Kevin held up his hands and said, "Everybody needs gloves and as much protection as they can get. I expect a knock-down, drag-out fight."

The huddle broke and everybody retrieved gear from their cars. Kevin donned leather gloves and a leather jacket. On his head he wore a pair of Marine Corps issue tan dust goggles over his bicycle helmet. Brian put on his turnout coat, gloves and helmet. The officers retrieved tactical vests, and riot helmets with face shields from the cars.

"I feel a little underdressed," Mark said. Kevin laughed, "Just stay back as much as you can. Okay, Brian, let's take a look in the can."

"Right behind you, brother." Kevin and Brian walked up to the front of the dumpster. Kevin dialed in the combination on the lock and clicked it open. Unstringing it from the lid and handles, the lock banged on the metal side. Rustling could be heard among the garbage bags. "I guess it's awake," Brian observed. Next Kevin pointed to the main tamper lock on the dumpster.

"We'll leave that one locked until we know what we're up against. It will let the lid open an inch or so but not enough for it to get us." Addressing Mark and the police, Kevin said, "Brian and I are going to lift the lid a little for a peek and then close it. I want you guys to shine your flashlights in and tell me what you see." Kevin looked around at the group and directed them up close to the dumpster. "Lights on and at the ready," Kevin counted down from three, and they lifted the lid. Beams of light stabbed the dark interior of the dumpster.

"I see it in the back!" Church cried out.

They dropped it shut again. Kevin exhaled, "Okay, that went better than I expected."

The group retreated to the illumination of the streetlight again, looking at each other in silence until Brian asked, "So what's in there, Church?"

"It looked like a naked man to me. A nasty dirty one, with eyes that glowed bright yellow," Officer Church explained.

"That's our guy. Normal human eyes don't reflect light like that," Kevin declared. "Will the pole work on a person?"

"I think so. The manufacturer says it's rated up to a hundred and fifty pounds. The question is, can we get it on him?"

"We'll soon find out. If it tries to switch to a cat, or any other kind of animal, maybe we can keep a grip on its neck," Kevin commented.

Caporaso looked back and forth between the brothers and asked, "Aren't we going to try to communicate? Maybe talk him into coming out on his own?"

"I think you will find this guy isn't conversant in English, let alone cooperative. But you are welcome to try," Mark offered.

"We probably shouldn't talk to it," Kevin countered the suggestion. "We need it as calm as possible before the next step."

Mark nodded and said, "Good call. Remember not to make skin to skin contact. It will wreck your modeling career for sure. Do you think pepper spray might slow it down?"

"I don't think we should spray him," Johnston chimed in. "When it hits him, his hands will come up to cover his face and maybe block the snare. I'm thinking Taser his ass," Johnston suggested. "It will give a clear shot at getting him under control."

"Tell us how you really feel, Detective," Brian laughed. Then he said, "But really, I think the Taser is a good idea. We'll have several seconds to employ the snare, and won't have to deal with spray getting on us."

"Archer and Church, you want to do the honors from either corner?" Johnston suggested.

"I'll electrify him good, ma'am," Church said with a grin.

"Okay team. This will be kinda like the last one, but completely different," Kevin said while looking around at everybody. "I'm going to unlock the bar on the dumpster. Johnston and I will handle the lid," Kevin said while pointing to where they would stand. "Archer and Church with tasers next to us. You should have a good view of the entire dumpster, except right below you, so be careful. Brian will be in the middle with the pole. Caporaso and Mark take the sides with flashlights. Make sure you point them down and in, not in our eyes. Everybody clear on where they stand?" They nodded together.

"Okay, I will count down from three and on the word *open*, the lid will come up about a foot. If the coast is clear and we have good target, Johnston and I will stay back as far as we can to keep clear of any flying limbs. If we can't see it or it is a danger to us, we'll close the lid." Kevin paused and took a breath before saying, "Assuming the lid stays open, the flashlights will shine in and illuminate the target. Stay on the target, in its eyes if possible. Then Church will fire first, with Archer as the back-up. It's important we save the second one for a do-over. Once the critter is stationary, Brian loops the snare over its head and pulls it closer to the side. If it is still subdued enough, Johnston and I will push the lid full open and attempt to zip cuff the hands and feet. This may be like a rodeo for a while, but we just have to let it get tired before we try to move it to the cruiser." Kevin looked around. "Any questions, ideas, or anything I missed?" Nobody said a thing. "Outstanding. The sky is getting lighter quick, and the sun will be up soon. We'll have joggers and passersby before you know it, so let's go about our business as quickly as we can."

Kevin confirmed everybody was in position. The flashlights were switched on and the snare extended out to full size. Archer and Church armed their Tasers, and Kevin removed the lock as quietly as he could. He looked at each person and mouthed, "ready?" They each nodded. Then he whispered "Three, two, one, open!" Kevin and Johnston lifted the lid and peered inside. The flashlights caught the shape of a cat, crouched to pounce.

Church squeezed the trigger on his Taser, firing the wire darts into the transformed cat. The inside of the dumpster was filled with the pop sound of the darts firing, screeching and the snapping of arcing electricity. The cat was frozen in place. "Get it!" yelled Church. The voice snapped Brian into action. He maneuvered the snare over the cat's head and yanked it several times to get it tight.

"Got it!" he declared, while lifting the cat from the bottom of the dumpster. "Get the cage!" Kevin and Johnston pushed the lid all the way open to the stop and ran back to retrieve the cage.

"We should've had it over here already, damn it!" Kevin cursed in the seconds it took to get to the cage. They picked it up and carried it back to Brian. Mark met them and opened the hatch.

"Church, give it one more zap before I swing it out to the cage," Brian commanded.

Church squeezed the trigger to deliver another charge but nothing happened. "The wires must have come loose," he said. The yellow cat writhed as it hung by its neck from the pole.

"Damn the luck," Brian cursed as he looked behind him. "You guys ready?"

"Go," Mark said. Brian swung the pole over the edge of the dumpster and dropped the cat into the waiting animal carrier. He released the snare and Mark shut the hatch.

Brian dropped the snare on the ground and exhaled. Removing his helmet he said, "That thing was getting ready to spring when the lid opened."

"No doubt," Kevin said. "Let's get it in the cruiser before something else happens." He and Johnston picked up the ends of the carrier and started walking toward the car. The cat spun in circles, hissing and clawing at the carrier.

"Looks like the Tasmanian Devil from *Looney Tunes*!" Archer exclaimed.

"So long as it stays in there, it can do whatever it likes," Kevin replied. At the car, Archer opened the door to the back seat. Johnston and Kevin tried to slide the carrier in, but it wouldn't fit in the door. "Oh give me a break! It's gotta fit," Kevin let out an exasperated groan. He turned to Mark, "Tell me your wife didn't get the biggest carrier available to make sure Fluffy had plenty of room?"

"It goes in my car just fine," Mark said, and then offered, "if you open the other side and Johnston pulls from there while you tip it back, it will fit." Mark then pointed at the obstruction. "It's hitting against the plexiglass divider, right there."

Kevin and Johnston set down the carrier, and she went to the opposite side of the car and came in across the back seat. She looked out at them and said, "Don't look now, but the sun's about to come up.

"Another day dawns over the City of Brotherly love," Mark chimed in.

From inside the car, Johnston said, "Okay, I'm ready."

"Here we go," Kevin said as he and Mark lifted the carrier up to the level of the cruiser's back seat. "Mark, rotate toward you."

As they adjusted the carrier to match the opening as closely as they could, the carrier split open. Church, standing back from the loading operation, called out, "It's changing back to a man!" The enlarging body of a naked man spilled from the broken pieces of the plastic and wire animal carrier. "Archer! Get your Taser on it!"

Archer stepped from behind the car door he was holding open and attempted to deploy his Taser, but was blocked by Mark retreating from the transforming figure. Brian, who was removing his gear, stopped to pick up the pole again, but was too far away to get the snare on it before it broke free and stumbled away from the police car. Kevin dropped the wreckage of the carrier and ran after it.

The human form was not moving fast at the start. The limbs were still coming into shape as it scrambled away toward the ship and the river. Kevin wasn't far behind, but it was getting faster. Kevin dove on it and wrapped it up in his arms. It struggled fiercely, rolling over, trying to bite Kevin's arm through his leather jacket. The legs flailed around, hitting the pavement and peeling off chunks of its own flesh. Brian arrived and tried to snare a limb but couldn't get a clear shot. After a moment, the creature stopped its pitching and jerking and fell motionless in the long shadow of the old sailing ship.

Catching up, Archer asked, "Is it dead?"

"I doubt it," Kevin replied. "It's probably playing possum, like last time. Brian, get the loop around its neck. Archer, have your Taser ready." Kevin lifted his head back to make room as Brian fitted the loop over the bald head of the creature. "Let's get some cuffs on it before it decides to start fighting again.

"I'm coming!" Church said, carrying a bundle of zip cuffs.

"I'm going to ease up a bit to make room for you to get to the hands. Then we'll try to get the feet together. Brian, you hold on tight."

"I got him, bro!" Brian replied. Kevin eased his armlock and Church reached in with a zip cuff to get the first hand. Once it was made fast, Kevin backed off a little farther and tried to roll the torso to free the other hand. Just as Church got a grip on the other hand, Brian saw the eyes pop open. "Here we go, it's coming back to life again!"

The creature regained its strength and suddenly shoved itself free of Kevin's slack grip. It began a powerful crawl, dragging Brian and the catch-all pole behind it. It covered three body lengths on all fours before getting upright and surging ahead. Brian slid further down the pole with every jerk and lost his grip just as Kevin and Church gang tackled it. They went down in a pile, with an aluminum pole sticking out. The mass rolled over until Church was on the bottom. The creature gouged at Church, leaving a bloody laceration along his jawline. Church recoiled in pain and slacked his hold.

Once more the creature was crawling on all fours, dragging Kevin across the pavement. It pushed up with its hands and was upright again. Kevin lost his hold at the waist, so when he found his own feet, he ran after it again.

Approaching the waterfront railing, it hesitated in a confused zigzag. Brian ran to one side and Kevin to the other. "Keep it hemmed in!" Brian yelled.

"Got it!" Kevin replied.

The others were catching up and forming a barrier with Archer at the center. As they closed in, the creature rushed at Kevin. Kevin dropped his shoulder to waist height and wrapped his arms around it. He slammed it against the railing, and both of them slowly pitched over the top. Brian yelled, "Oh crap! Kevin! Kevin!" as he watched them fall ten feet into the black water of the Delaware River.

The others ran to the rail, with Caporaso bringing up the rear, talking into his radio. Arriving at the rail, he said, "Fire and rescue are on the way, along with another unit."

Kevin and the creature were under the water for what seemed like minutes, with clouds of bubbles gushing from deep below the surface. Finally, Kevin floated back up to the surface. He was holding the catch-all pole in one hand and paddling with the other. He rolled onto his back and gasped for breath while peeling the goggles from his face.

"Are you alright?" Johnston called down to him. Kevin nodded and continued to tread water. Brian ran a hundred feet to the south and found a paint spattered maintenance raft tied alongside the sailing ship.

"Come this way, we can get you out on the raft!"

"Can you swim that far?" Johnston asked. He nodded and slowly made his way toward his brother.

Kevin paddled to the raft where Brian was kneeling down, reaching for him. With one swift move, Brian caught Kevin's collar and dragged him out of the water. Then Brian said, "We thought we lost you there for a moment." Kevin bobbed his head in agreement and rolled onto his side, trying to catch his breath.

Johnston left her riot gear in the parking lot and dropped onto the raft to help Brian. Caporaso and Archer returned to where Church sat in the parking lot, a hand holding the gash in his face. "Hang in there, Church, we'll get you dressed up as quick as we can," Caporaso said.

"That was the weirdest thing I ever saw, Detective."

"Me, too," Caporaso agreed as he helped Church lay his head down on the pavement until the ambulance arrived.

59

Water streamed from Kevin's soaked clothing and made a puddle on the wooden deck of the maintenance raft. When Kevin was breathing normally again, Johnston pulled off Kevin's googles and unbuckled the helmet. She gently turned his face from side to side. The skin below his cheek bones was pale and tattered like peeling paint. "You look like hell, Mister," she commented. Kevin managed a half grin.

Brian added, "Bro, you probably shouldn't have rubbed your face all over the naked guy. This time it might leave a mark." Kevin tried to laugh but broke into a coughing fit.

"What happened down there?" Johnston asked while Brian gently helped Kevin sit up. Brian peeled back the saturated leather jacket and tugged the sleeves from Kevin's arms.

"I hit it hard," Kevin said. "A good football tackle into the rail, then we went over the top. It took most of the impact and then just went down. It didn't try to swim or anything. It just stopped moving and sank like a rock." Kevin stopped speaking and caught his breath. "Then it began to dissolve."

"Dissolve?" Johnston asked.

"We were sinking deeper and deeper, and it went from a solid human body to something like a sponge. Then kinda exploded into a cloud of bubbles. Next thing I know, there is nothing there and I'm floating back up."

"You're telling me this thing became a human-sized Alka-Seltzer?" Brian asked.

"Yes, exactly. One minute it's there, just as much as you or me, and the next it's dissolving into bubbles in my grip."

"Water-soluble cat people. Why didn't I think of that?" Brian remarked.

"Do you think that's the end of it? I can't imagine there's any coming back from being liquified into the Delaware River," Johnston said.

"I hope so, because I don't care to do that again," Kevin declared.

"Which part? The wrestling or the swimming with a creepy naked dude?" Brian asked.

"Thanks for putting the whole experience into perspective, bro."

"That's what I'm here for," Brian grinned.

The wail of sirens could be heard approaching from the distance. "I think the cavalry is about here. Hopefully, they'll drop a ladder down," Brian said as he examined Kevin's leather jacket. "I think you're going to need a new skin. This one's looking pretty rough." Brian held the jacket out for them to see. "There's rips from the pavement on the back and elbows and teeth marks on the right arm." Kevin looked at his own arm. There was an oval shaped bruise and swelling corresponding to the teeth marks on the jacket.

Caporaso stuck his head over the rail and looked down at the raft. "Are you guys okay down there?"

"Yeah. Just a little wet," Johnston replied.

"Good. I'm going to send Church with the squad. He's got a pretty serious cut on his jaw, and the bleeding isn't slowing down."

"We'll be fine as long as somebody comes to get us," Johnston replied.

"Mark and I will be back as soon as we get him shipped out," Caparosa said before walking back to the parking lot.

"I hope they can get the bleeding stopped," Kevin said.

"It will stop eventually," Brian reassured him, and turned toward the river where the sun was rising above the skyline of Camden, New Jersey. "Man, what a morning this has been."

61

"I'm so glad you're alright," the old priest said, getting up from his desk to greet Kevin as he walked into the little office.

"Me, too," Kevin agreed. The priest stepped closer and examined the flaking skin on Kevin's face.

"Is it painful?" he asked.

Kevin shook his head and said, "I've dealt with worse."

"Your description of the capture sounded quite remarkable."

"It really was. It was crazy" Kevin replied, then Matthew turned and gestured for Kevin to follow. "The bat cave?"

"Yes," Matthew said. Kevin followed along, listening to his uncle as they walked. "My research and inquiries have finally born fruit." They entered the elevator and Kevin pushed the button for the basement. "I believe we'll have a more complete picture after today," the old man whispered as the door closed.

When the elevator came to a stop, they exited into the dim corridor. The door to the classroom where they did their work was open and light spilled out into the hall. "Did you leave the light on Uncle Matthew?" Kevin asked.

"I did. It would be rude to leave a colleague sitting in the dark, don't you think?"

Kevin chuckled at his uncle's comment until he turned the corner and saw a man dressed in a traditional cassock and wearing a heavy gold cross. He had a thick black beard streaked with white and a nearly bald head.

Matthew said, "Kevin, meet Protodeacon Stepan Micevych."

"Hello," Kevin said, extending his hand.

"I'm very happy to shake your hand," the man said in a thick Eastern European accent. "You may call me Stepan if you like. Your uncle told me of your discoveries. He created a very good picture of you," Stepan said with a smile that peeked out from under his mustache. "But I am very sorry about this," he said as raised his hands toward Kevin's cheeks and touched them lightly.

"It's not the first time," Kevin said.

"Stepan came over from Saint Sophia Ukrainian Orthodox Seminary to shed some light on your encounters," Matthew said, and then gestured to the chairs. "Please sit. Make yourselves comfortable."

Kevin pulled out two more folding chairs and set up a triangle. "So, what do you teach at your seminary?" Kevin asked.

"I don't teach so much classes. I am what is called consultant. When a priest or bishop has problem, I make it better."

"Is that job like a fixer?" Kevin asked.

"Fixer, eh? I don't know," Stepan smiled again. "This is a good job to have? Being a fixer?"

"Sometimes yes, sometimes no," Kevin said. "But making problems go away sounds like a fixer to me."

"Okay, among friends I will try calling my job *fixer*. We'll see how it goes. If the archbishop says it's okay, then it's okay." Kevin and Stepan laughed.

"So have you seen this man-cat creature before?" Kevin asked.

"In the old country I was in the Army. Three years and three hundred twenty-five days." Sitting up stiffly and saluting he said, "I was brand new sergeant in a motor rifle company. It was a bad time, the Panjshir Offensive in Afghanistan. Some men live, some die. When sometimes they die, funny things happen. My comrades tell me they see the ghosts walking around at night, but I go look and all I see is cat. I tell them to put away the vodka. I did not know about these things then. I was just twenty years old!"

"How did you go from the army to the church?" Father Matthew asked.

"I was very confused after fighting, so I go to monastery after army. I put myself in time-out!" Stepan laughed. "I read every scripture I can find, in the original language. Greek, Latin, Hebrew. I learned so much. Who knew I was so good at these things! Now I'm a deacon for twenty-three-and-one-half years!"

"So, if you know how to take care of these cat things, I can hand it off to you, right?" Kevin asked.

"I am too old to make a fight with *destructor animarum*. The job of venator is for strong young man like you."

"That's not exactly the answer I was hoping for, Stepan."

"The call comes in interesting ways and it is often not quite what you expect," Stepan explained. "But we are not here to recruit you into the army. You are already there. We must now give you better ways to fight the enemy. Venator must fight with brain and not so much face, eh?"

"You've got a way with words, comrade!" Kevin replied, "So what is a venator, and why do I feel a little hesitant about where this is going?"

"Nothing to worry about," Matthew said in reassurance, "except the disposition of untold numbers of souls that might never reach their destination."

62

Brian and Kevin sat on the couch, with Johnston on the floor, leaning back between Kevin and Brian's legs. Mark made himself comfortable on a green and white beanbag chair. The TV displayed the football season opener between the Eagles and Browns.

"Good call bringing the beanbag. Maybe I'll get one too. Especially since there don't seem to be any gentlemen willing to share the couch," Johnston joked.

Brian laughed in response. "When you get tired of the floor you can come sit on my lap."

"I'd rather jump in the river with a creepy naked dude," Johnston replied. Turning to Kevin, she asked, "By the way, what became of your meeting with Uncle Matthew?"

"I'm not sure I care to talk about it," Kevin said.

"Why not?" Brian asked.

"I was kinda hoping to have a normal day, you know? Watch the game, give each other a hard time, and have a little fun. It's bad enough I still gotta look at this peeling skin in the mirror. I haven't been able to shave properly in a week!"

"Yeah, but inquiring minds want to know," Mark chimed in. "Come on, at least the *Reader's Digest* version."

"Damn it, you're ruining my normal day. Fine," Kevin sighed. "I'll tell you about it, but then no more until at least Wednesday. Got it?" Kevin demanded.

"No questions until Wednesday," Johnston said in a definitive voice.

"Wait, before Kevin tells us about his meeting, how's Officer Church doing?" Brian asked Johnston.

"They gave him a unit of blood when the wound wouldn't quit bleeding, and he's covered in bandages, but they did finally send him home."

"I'm glad to hear it," Mark said. "Looking at Kevin, I can only imagine what his wound is like."

"Thanks man, I love you too," Kevin replied. "Anyway, do you want to hear about this, or not?"

"Yeah, yeah. Go ahead, Mister Touchy," Brian relented.

"So, Uncle Matthew brought in this protodeacon from a Ukrainian Orthodox seminary over in Jersey," Kevin started.

"What's a protodeacon?" Mark interrupted.

"Shush!" Johnston said with a finger to her lips.

"Thanks," Kevin said to Johnston and continued, "So, he's this big bear of a guy from the old country and has a thick accent. But he's funny as hell and he's basically the *fixer* for the Ukrainian Orthodox Church in America. It's like he's a mobster in a cassock!" Everybody laughed and Kevin continued describing the meeting. "It turns out this thing we've been chasing goes way back. Even before Christ. It doesn't really have a name, but Stefan called it *destructor animarum*, whatever that means in Latin."

"Destroyer of souls?" Mark interjected. Kevin looked at him and grinned.

"You were always better in Latin than anybody else. Anyway, a lot of what we figured out was right on. He said it probably takes the soul, or life force, and uses it for energy to live. Like food. Any time it encounters an unattended recently dead body, it sucks the soul out, shriveling up what's left. Then it takes the form of the last body it sucked dry and moves on to find the next corpse. Like we figured, it normally runs two to three weeks at a time. It can be a cat or a human, but get this. The human is basically a clone of the donor corpse. It looks exactly the same as the original, but without any of the aftermarket modifications."

"Like if the deceased had a spray tan, the clone won't have it?" Brian asked.

"That's right. Stuff like piercings, braces on the teeth, surgery, or anything not natural to the body won't be there."

"So all the folks who saw Jerome's clone without earrings were right to be suspicious. It wasn't a ghost, but it wasn't really him either," Mark added. Kevin nodded and Mark asked another question. "What constitutes *recently dead*?"

"Nobody really knows the exact time frame. What you're really asking is how long does the soul remain with the body after the heart stops and the brain has no detectable activity."

"Well, okay, since you put it that way," Mark shrugged.

"Not long. That's why the cat likes to hang around. It's waiting for the right moment to spring into action."

"You're making me reconsider having a cat in the house," Mark groaned.

"The other part we got right, by accident of course," Kevin added with a grin, "was the water. These things don't like water or oil. If you submerge them in either, they get squishy real fast and then dissolve in a cloud of bubbles, never to be seen again."

"As dad said, I'd rather be lucky than good any day! But what about the possum thing?" Brian asked. "The eyes just close and it stops moving, then a couple minutes later, boing! It's up and fighting again."

"It has a couple of known weaknesses, and that's one. Whenever the sun is rising or setting, and passing through the horizon, it just drops off like it's dead. Then it comes right back once the sun is clear of the horizon. The other weakness is subterranean spaces. It can't go underground. When you knocked it down the steps, it blanked out. Just like at sunrise. Stepan said this is probably why many religions require dead bodies to be buried quickly. Once a body is underground, it's safe from the creature."

All three sat in silence as Kevin described what he learned from his meeting. "If you think about it, you'll quickly recognize that there are a countless traditions we do, but forgot why. These things were largely eradicated because of careful attendance to formalities partly or entirely designed to keep them away. Anything involving washing or holy water for example. These critters won't go near it."

"So why did we have one of these cat-man things cruising around the city, if they are supposed to be eradicated?" Mark asked.

"Stepan said it is like vaccinations. The disease is still out there, but nobody gets sick anymore. Then people stop with the vaccines, and the disease comes back. He thinks it showed up here because Americans are losing their old-time religion. The traditions are getting tossed by the wayside because they aren't cool anymore. Things like the anointing of the sick by a priest. Holy oil is like a repellent to these things, but the modern nondenominational folks don't do sacramental stuff. The one he was really baffled by was companionship cats in nursing homes. Just like the proverbial fox in the henhouse."

"So why doesn't anybody know about these cat creatures?" Johnston asked.

"I don't know," Kevin said flatly. "The Roman Catholic Church doesn't seem to have any corporate knowledge, and the Orthodox is only slightly better. I guess it's been a non-issue so long that people quit paying attention."

"Did he tell you if or how they reproduce?" Brian asked.

"That remains a mystery. In fact, that's Stepan's main focus. He said if anybody ever knew, they didn't write it down, or he hasn't found it."

"Well, that kinda sucks," Brian responded.

"Yeah, it does. Especially since he identified a probable second creature in the information Uncle Matthew collected."

"You're kidding me. There's another one?" Johnston asked.

"The Temple University kid was probably a second cat. It was out of sequence with the one we just drowned. He wasn't a hundred percent, but he seemed pretty sure about it. The other bit he was really interested in was the third hand on the train tracks."

"Oh, yeah? What's the theory?" Brian asked.

"These critters aren't fazed by gunshot wounds, getting stabbed, or even general dismemberment. Stepan is certain about that because he's seen them get hit by machine guns and a rocket-propelled grenade and keep going. In our case, the Jerome look-alike probably lost a hand to the train, but it didn't care. It got a fresh meal and switched bodies."

"That's pretty heavy-duty stuff," Mark sighed.

"If Protodeacon Stepan is the expert, will he be hunting down the second cat? I mean, I'm kinda over this thing," Brian declared.

"He's fifty-seven years old, and was quite adamant that he shouldn't be chasing cats down dark alleys."

"He's going to bring in the Orthodox SWAT team, right?" Mark laughed.

"Doubt it," Kevin said. "But this isn't a new problem, and people have been dealing with it, or not dealing with it for years. We aren't going to fix it today, so I propose we turn our attention back to this football game."

"Fair enough," Brian agreed, closing off discussion of the topic. "I got money on this game, so it definitely requires my attention, but Wednesday, we're going to talk some more!"

63

A plain blue Ford sedan splashed through a large puddle and into the circular driveway in front of the hospital. The windshield wipers kept the steady rain at bay but left an arc shaped smear on every pass. Under the long portico at the front door, Johnston brought the car to a stop and watched the trickle of people emerging from a set of automatic doors. She glanced at the dashboard clock. "I'm on time . . . where are you?" she asked herself.

Johnston turned off the engine and then scanned the radio dial, finally settling on a Top 40 country station. A catchy song was already playing, the singer crooning "There's a little bit of devil in her angel eyes . . . " When the song ended, the DJ's voice filled in the silence of the car, "It's ten twenty on a rainy night in Philly and that was last week's number one hit song, Love and Theft's "Angel Eyes". The new number one hit this week comes from Blake Shelton . . ." The radio cut off as she opened the door at the sight of Kevin emerging from the building. They met halfway, and Johnston wrapped him up in her arms and kissed him on the lips.

"Very nice to see you, too," he said after catching his breath. "That's an unusual public display. What's gotten into you?"

"I've been looking forward to a normal date all week, and that must mean something."

"You're saying you like me for more than my sweet bike?" Kevin asked, and got an immediate punch in the shoulder. "What did you do that for? That hurt."

"Really, that hurt?" she asked.

"No, not really, because you punch like a girl." Kevin laughed and got another punch in the same spot. He winced at the second impact. "Okay, that one hurt. You can stop now."

"Get in the car already," she commanded as she pushed off from him and walked to the driver's door. When both were seated in the car, Kevin leaned into the center of the cabin and guided her face toward his for another kiss. "Hey buddy, knock it off. We're in a city vehicle now. No PDA allowed."

"Sorry," Kevin said while raising both hands to shoulder height. "Please don't arrest me officer."

"I should cuff you and toss your butt in the back seat just to teach you a lesson." Johnston dropped the car in gear and smoothly pulled away from the curb and out into the rainy night.

"So, where are you taking me?" Kevin asked.

"Jailhouse or Little Pete's. I haven't really decided, but they are both that way," Johnston pointed with her hand in the general direction the car was traveling.

"Very nice. Two local favorites. Can't go wrong either way," Kevin joked. After she gave him a sideways glance, he sat quietly for a moment and then half turned toward Johnston.

"You look like you have something important to say," Johnston remarked.

"I have something to tell you," Kevin said. "But on second thought, let's get some food first. I'm starving."

64

Wednesday, September 12
10:46 p.m.

A teenage hostess seated them at a tiny table wedged into a corner of Little Peat's Diner and handed them menus. Unable to stop looking at Kevin's pale and peeling face, the hostess squeaked, "Sandy will be with you in just a moment," then hustled away. Kevin and Johnston looked at each other with knowing grins and turned their attention to the menu. After a moment, Kevin glanced at Johnston over the top of the card. She lowered her menu and caught Kevin looking at her.

"What sounds good?" Kevin asked.

"I think something with a touch of sweetness. A Monte Cristo sandwich," Johnston declared and then smiled softly. She set her menu down and took Kevin's hand in hers. "Something big, huh?" Johnston said. Kevin nodded and started to speak but was interrupted by a waitress.

"I'm Tyra. It looks like I'm going to be your waitress tonight." Kevin and Johnston both looked up and smiled. Kevin ordered for both of them, and the waitress disappeared as fast as she had appeared.

"My meeting with Uncle Matthew this morning was kind of life changing," Kevin said. "I mean more than just learning about the thing,"

"I kind of sensed that on Sunday," she observed. "So, what was it about?"

"Matthew and Stepan needed a few days to work out the details. I haven't said yes yet, but they think I should go into the venator business."

"Venator?

"The Latin word for hunter."

"Wait—you'd be chasing these things full time? You can't make a living doing that," Johnston objected.

"They think I can. Like Stepan does his fixer job. He lives in church facilities wherever he travels, and they compensate him as a professor in the seminary," Kevin explained.

"But he's a deacon. That's what deacons do. They live in rectories and monasteries or whatever, and are supported by the church. How's that going to work for you?" Johnston asked. Then her mouth fell open in a gasp. "Oh, wait a minute . . . this is just my luck." Johnston paused a moment and her eyes misted over. "Please tell me you are not about to swear off the opposite sex for the rest of your life!"

"No, absolutely not! No, no, not a chance on earth," Kevin replied just as a tear was breaking loose from the corner of Johnston's eye. "Come on, it's okay. I'm not taking vows or anything like that. If I took the job, it would be much simpler."

"How? How is this supposed to work?" Johnston asked, while taking her napkin and wiping the moisture from the corner of her eye.

"To start, the seminary here would hire me as part of the staff. Probably something like a groundskeeper, and they'd give me one of the empty apartments on the campus. I'd do the job, coming and going as needed."

That's a relief," Johnston sighed, "but how many of these things are out there that they are going to put somebody on the task full time?"

"I don't know. I doubt there are that many, but as Stepan said, the knowledge and skills will be lost if somebody doesn't keep them alive."

"But why you? Can't they send a priest to do it?"

"I don't know how much you know about priests, but there is

a worldwide shortage of them. The church just doesn't have any manpower to spare, and I've already survived the on-the-job training."

"You sound like you've decided what you're going to do."

"I have, but it isn't what you're thinking."

"Then tell me."

"You see, there's this lady cop, and I really like her and respect her opinion. If she endorses the choice, I'll take the job. If she doesn't, well then, there's always the hospital."

"If you promise I still get to see you from time to time."

"Yes," Kevin said in a slow deliberate tone, while looking directly into Johnston's eyes, "I promise."

She looked down for a moment, and then back up at Kevin. The mist was back in her eyes, but now she had a hesitant smile on her lips.

"Then I guess it's official. I'm dating a cat exterminator!"

ACKNOWLEDGMENTS

This work would never have seen the light of day without the support of my extraordinary wife Angela and son Brendan. Also supporting the effort were John Behen, Mike Kirk, Jarod Gray, Eric Baker, my mom Jan, and sister-in-law Joanne. Also important to the effort was Janet Rupert, my cheerleader for the stuff that comes after getting the story on paper.

Language Planning:
Current Issues and Research

Joan Rubin
Roger Shuy
Editors

Georgetown University Press, Washington, D.C. 20007

CONTENTS

INTRODUCTION

JOAN RUBIN

1. Preliminary remarks. It is entirely fitting that the 1972 Georgetown University Round Table which had as its theme: 'Sociolinguistics: Current Trends and Prospects' should have included a discussion session on language planning. As a new and developing discipline, language planning can offer valuable insights into the nature of language. The study of language planning processes allows us to consider language as one more object of human manipulation—not only by language specialists but also by lay persons who may change its basic nature through their attitudes toward language, their myths about language, and their subjective reactions to language. The discipline has already made many contributions to our knowledge and approaches to language use, attitudes and beliefs, language maintenance and change. As language planning is often defined as the conscious, predictive approach to changes in language and language use (Rubin and Jernudd 1971), its proper application requires the right kinds of information about the sociolinguistic habits of the target population and about the social basis for language policy in order to project productive directions of change.

There is a growing interest in studying the actual processes of language policy formation and language development and implementation. Starting with the 1966 Conference on Language Problems (Fishman, Ferguson, and Das Gupta 1968), an increasing interest in the discipline has been demonstrated as courses have been developed and sessions have been scheduled with the language planning title. In 1968-69, four scholars (Fishman, Jernudd, Das Gupta, and Rubin) spent the year at the East-West Center in Hawaii studying various theoretical aspects of this topic. At a meeting in the spring of 1969, scholars discussed problems of language policy and choice and provided a theoretical framework to language planning. The results of this conference are available in Can Language Be Planned? edited by Rubin and Jernudd (1971). From 1969 to 1972, the International Research Project on Language Planning Processes explored one of the major aspects of language planning: lexical elaboration for modernization. Four countries (Israel, Indonesia, Sweden, and India) were sites for this research. A draft of the results of this project appeared in October of 1972.

2. The session. The discussion session at the Round Table was organized to ascertain how much of a common core of theory there was among scholars interested in language planning, to give scholars engaged in language planning research an opportunity to report on their progress, problems and findings, and to try to assess what sorts of research agencies national development and language problems require.

It became clear during the discussion that even the most commonly used concepts would need more consideration and clarification; such often-used terms as codification, standardization, standard language, flexible stability, and even language planning proved to have different meanings for the participants. Such differences have important theoretical and practical implications.[1] In attempting to further elucidate Prague School definitions of standard language terminology, Dr. Garvin kindly offered to translate a passage from the 1932 volume Standard Czech and the Cultivation of Good Language which is included as an appendix in this volume. Throughout the discussion the term 'language planning' was given different meanings ranging from that of individuals who give some thought and perhaps action to language problems (their own and others) to the more normative position which excludes everything but national governmental planned attention to language problems. Full attention to these various uses of the term was not given due to a lack of time, but serious need to do so still remains.

Another question raised in various ways was the role of the language planner and language planning theory in decision making. Some participants pointed to the responsibility of the language planner in helping, where possible, to bring about 'rational' decisions, given particular language problems and a particular socio-cultural setting. However, the definition and elaboration of such 'rational' criteria (both linguistic and socio-political) must be still further developed.

A representative of a private foundation and one from a government agency were invited to discuss the language research priorities of their organizations and gave oral reports (not included in this volume). Dr. Richard Thompson, of the U.S. Office of Education, expressed a basic need for an assessment of existing language resources and personnel and of the utilization of language resources. Mrs. Barbara Finberg, of the Carnegie Foundation, indicated that their focus was upon basic research in child language development and on minority group language problems. Several of the participants expressed regret that this section of the session was so brief, since they had hoped that more concrete statements about research priorities would have resulted from the discussion.

3. The papers. Current discussions of language planning inevitably seem to lead to discussions of language treatment (Neustupný 1970). As defined by Neustupný, language treatment includes the many different kinds of attention which people may give to language problems. Thus, language planning is but one kind of language treatment. The papers in this volume include descriptions of not only the more narrowly defined kind of language treatment but also other kinds of language treatment. At least two of the papers, those of Jernudd and Rubin, point to the need to see language planning as only one kind of language treatment. Both point to the benefits of considering when language planning demands arise and what the appropriate rationales are for a language planning kind of solution to language problems. Jernudd raises the important question of whether the more consciously organized solutions are necessarily typical of nations labeled as 'developed'. In a more recent paper Jernudd (1972) points to the need to separate the concepts of mature speech communities and economically mature communities.

Two of the papers, those of Bar-Adon and Gorman, discuss language treatment activities, which, while not falling into the more normative definition of language planning proposed by Jernudd and Das Gupta (1971), do indicate that local and national treatment of language is a common phenomenon. Of interest are their discussions of the reasons why the particular kind of treatment was chosen or resulted. In the case of the Galilee dialect which Bar-Adon describes, we see the deliberate fostering of a particular variety of Hebrew. This variety was eventually 'selected out' in favor of another variety of Israeli Hebrew. Bar-Adon offers a very rich discussion of the dialect itself and the social factors which promoted and eventually demoted it. Gorman describes how recent language policy statements in East Africa and especially in Kenya regarding language allocation (which Jernudd has here called 'language determination') are a part of a political scheme to regulate the communicative conduct of the members of the bureaucracy or public service. Gorman mentions some recent government statements regarding language use in public functions. As Gorman correctly observes, the policy decisions regarding language determination have not yet been followed by an

organized statement of implementation. However, in the case of
Kenya, there seems to be no reason to assume that the language
allocation policy could not benefit from more conscious organized
planning. Several of the papers speak to the question of the motivation and rationalization behind language policy. Parker discusses
the importance of the continuing misconception of Quechua as a single
language for the recently accelerated efforts in Peru to promote bilingual education. Pool, in an analysis of recent sociolinguistic
questionnaires in Canada, considers similarities and differences in
attitude among English and French speaking citizens. He found that
the greatest polarization of opinions on language policy was to be
found among persons who were geographically farthest removed from
each other. Barnes offers a nice discussion of the philosophical
(Marxist) background to language determination in China. He notes
that the Marxist linguistic axiom requires that the choice of a national
language arise from some extant dialect and that it be not artificially
constructed. Each of these papers speaks to the sociopolitical problems involved in language determination. Bar-Adon points out that
the role of the language hero, Ben-Yehuda, in Israel in promoting
Hebrew was more myth than fact; however, the myth served as an
important symbol of the new role for modern Hebrew.

In the process of language determination[2] Barnes notes that policy
statements not only reflect the political status of particular social
groups but may also serve to enhance their status. The choice of
PTH as the national language is 'tantamount to the recognition of
the linguistic hegemony of North Chinese in contemporary China'.

The two papers by Garvin give us a good idea of the principles of
language development of the Prague School of Linguistics. It is
especially useful to have these ideas available in English since the
Czechs have already spent a long time working out such principles
and have developed a very sophisticated set. Even in the 1930's we
see that the Prague School called for attention to be paid not only to
the linguistic properties of the standard language but also insisted on
giving equal attention to the functions of this language (they did not
see the standard language as being homogeneous but rather differentiated and rationalized as to function) and to the social attitudes which
the speech community gives to linguistic forms. As the Garvin
translation points out, stabilization (a necessary quality of a standard)
should not be allowed to lead to a complete leveling out, i.e. the removal of necessary functional and stylistic diversification of the
standard language. In the paper by Barnes, there is an extensive
discussion of the types of language problems dealt with by the Chinese
in the process of language development.

The area of language implementation is not dealt with in any great
detail in these papers. This is probably because the implementation

of language determination and development has been least studied even though language implementation is probably a common enough activity within language planning processes. Jernudd points out that even such activities as the sale of government-commissioned or printed grammars and dictionaries should be considered part of implementation; however, they are rarely noted or reported on.

The papers in this volume give us (1) further ideas about the processes of language planning through the descriptions of specific language situations in China, Ireland, Canada, and Kenya; (2) a research outline of a cross-national study in language planning processes; and (3) a plea for clarification of terms and the rationale for theory (Jernudd and Rubin).

In general, while there was great enthusiasm at the session, all of the participants felt that more time needs to be given to clarification of the theoretical core. It was clear from the session and from other expressions of interest that the field of language planning has already posed many challenges for sociolinguistic theory and offers potential assistance for the more practical field of language and national development. The discussion of such theoretical problems has only begun; it needs to be supplemented by field studies which seek to validate appropriate theoretical approaches.

Joan Rubin

NOTES

[1]Thanks are due Einar Haugen and Paul Garvin for their efforts in trying to clarify standard language terms during the course of the session.

[2]In what follows, I will use the tripartite division suggested in Jernudd's paper: Language determination, language development, and language implementation.

REFERENCES

Fishman, Joshua A., Charles A. Ferguson, and Jyotirindra Das Gupta, eds. 1968. Language problems of developing nations. New York, Wiley and Sons.

Jernudd, Björn. 1972. Prerequisites for a model of language treatment. In: Language planning processes draft report (unpublished).
_____ and Jyotirindra Das Gupta. 1971. Towards a theory of language planning. In: Rubin and Jernudd, eds.

Neustupný, Jiří V. 1970. Basic types of treatment of language problems. Linguistic Communications. 1.77-98. Australia, Monash University.

Rubin, Joan and Björn H. Jernudd, eds. 1971. Can language be
   planned? Sociolinguistic theory and practice for developing
   nations. Honolulu, East-West Center Press.
_____. 1971. Introduction: Language planning as an element in
   modernization. In: Rubin and Jernudd, eds. xiii-xxiv.

LANGUAGE PLANNING:
DISCUSSION OF SOME CURRENT ISSUES[1]

JOAN RUBIN

Stanford University and Tulane University

1. What are language problems? Many writers would agree that language planning has as its central focus the identification of language problems. Although there are several examples in the literature of short lists of language problems, most focus on the language code--its choice and standardization. There are, however, beginning to be some suggestions that this focus is not broad enough to cover the important range of problems which are somehow related both linguistically and socio-politically. These suggestions seem to indicate that we will understand both the processes of change and the rationales behind the changes better if we broaden our definitions of what constitute language problems.

One suggestion is that made by Neustupný (1968:287) who feels that: "There is a necessity to think of 'language' problems in the broad context of communication problems, and to include in 'language' problems besides language code problems also the problems of speech." Neustupný reminds us that in considering language problems we should not forget a number of important aspects of the problem: (1) the interrelationship between language code and speech, (2) the relation between language code and other social patterns, and (3) the relation between verbal and nonverbal communication. Indeed, he feels that preoccupation with language code problems (problems of orthography, of choice of variants within the same code, of vocabulary) is essentially dangerous. Such preoccupation can lead to the failure of a reform 'because they did not comply with the problems of

1

other communication patterns and were not accompanied by corresponding policies' (Neustupný 1968:287).

A further suggestion toward the identification and understanding of language problems is that made by Jernudd and Das Gupta (1971). They suggest that instead of focusing only on the linguistic phenomenon that the socio-political motivation/rationale behind language problems also be part of the classification and understanding of what the problems are. They offer the following example of the interrelationship between language problems and socio-political motivation. 'Modernization may create demands for language change and demands for standardization, which may also be directed toward language' (Jernudd and Das Gupta 1971:205-06). What is implied here is that perhaps in many cases the more general phenomenon of modernization creates demands which are also made on language. Thus language problems can only be understood when they are related to the more general processes occurring within a society. Jernudd (1971), places considerable importance on seeing the links between the kinds of language problems and the kinds of decision making.

Three proposals for typologies of language problems have thus far been suggested. Each of them attempts to classify different kinds of behavior toward language problems and will no doubt serve as an initial point in talking about language problems; still we can expect more comprehensive sorts of typologies when we include the complexities mentioned: language code/speech, verbal/nonverbal communication, language as part of the social processes of change, etc.

An early typology suggested by Haugen (1966)[2] is displayed in Figure 1. The definition of linguistic form given by Haugen is 'the

FIGURE 1. Language typology (Haugen 1966).

	Initiation	Implementation
Linguistic form	1. Selection of norm	2. Codification of norm
Linguistic function	3. Elaboration of function	4. Acceptance by intended population

linguistic structure in all its ramifications'. The examples of selection of norm (select or modify old norm or create new standard) and of codification (choice of script, orthography, pronunciation, grammatical forms, lexical items) all seem to refer to the language code.

The definition of linguistic function given by Haugen is 'the variety of uses to which that structure is put'. Under elaboration of function, Haugen still seems to be referring to the language code; examples of elaboration refer to the innovation or adaptation of vocabulary into the realms of scientific, imaginative, and emotive experience. If we assume that this typology is meant to imply some sort of evolutionary sequence, then we may note that each of the first three steps-- which seem to address themselves to the language code--involves the fourth which appears to relate largely to the social side of the problem. [3] We should also note that this typology does not explicate all of the kinds of language problems which others would like to see included in language planning.

A second typology is given by Rabin (1971) who divides language planning aims (? problems) into three kinds based on what sort of disciplinary expert should deal with the problem. While I think we might disagree with the actual items which go into any one subdivision, it does seem of use to see some problems as requiring more information/motivation from the socio-political or the linguistic side. These subdivisions might also relate to the different types of treatment (see section 4 for a discussion of this term) which we might expect language problems to receive (see section 6). The three divisions which Rabin offers are the following:

(1) Extra-linguistic aims: concerning the use of a given language block or the relative extent of usage of competing language blocks. For example, change in the area of use (either geographical or communal). These aims seem to concern primarily sociologists and political scientists and educational planners.

(2) Semi-linguistic aims: changes in the writing, spelling, or pronunciation. Rabin feels that although strong sociological and psychological factors seem to be involved, mostly linguists do the research. There are lots of examples in the literature of the difficulties that such an assignment causes. (Cf. too Neustupný's warning when the other patterns of communication are not considered-- mentioned here earlier.)

(3) Linguistic aims: vocabulary enlargement, vocabulary standardization, style. Rabin notes that this is the province of the normative linguist and the literary practitioner. While involving social variables, these problems are more largely linguistic, he feels.

A third typology of language problems is that offered by Neustupný (1970) who suggests that there are two basically different approaches to language problems. The one he calls the policy approach; the other the cultivation approach. The distinction seems largely to be based on whether the focus of attention is the language code (policy) or whether the focus of attention is that greater attention is given to speaking (cultivation). The problems included in the policy approach are: the selection of the national language, standardization, literacy, orthographies, problems of stratification of language (repertoire of code varieties), etc. Problems included in the cultivation approach are: questions of correctness, efficiency, linguistic levels fulfilling specialized functions, problems of style, constraints on communicative competence, etc. While this approach is appealing because it does separate or at least attempts to separate problems which focus on code or speech, it is also incomplete because Neustupný does not follow his own broader outline which includes nonverbal communication problems nor does it seem helpful for a typology which links the socio-cultural rationale and decision-making process with types of language problems.

Neustupný suggests that there may be an evolutionary sequence to the two kinds of approaches: the policy approach is connected with the study of less developed speech communities while the cultivation approach is found in modern industrialized societies. It remains to be seen when more data on language planning are available.[4] Neustupný examined Japanese language treatment and found such a sequence seems appropriate.

2. Why plan language? There seems to be a great deal of scepticism both among lay persons and linguists about the 'planning' of language. If, for instance as Tauli (1968) suggests, the focus of language planning should be the improvement of language as an instrument of communication by making it more economical and regular, it seems that objections to language planning may have some validity. Linguists have pointed out how difficult it is to assess economy of language. Others have pointed out that the definition of economy can never be entirely linguistic--even if it could be measured. Still others might question the contribution toward national development and/or modernization which regularity might make. This question must be considered in the social framework and not in the abstract as normativists such as Tauli seem to prefer. Finally, some persons more humanistically inclined fear that such regulations might lead to the destruction of normal thought processes--a strong fear but one difficult to establish in fact.

If on the other hand, one takes the tack suggested by Jernudd and Das Gupta (1971) that language is to be considered as a resource, then we can proceed to consider when and where it might be useful, necessary, or important to consider language problems. Language development can be understood within the context of societal development, needs, and values and may thus lead to more appropriate policy decisions. Not all language problems would need to receive public attention. It would appear that they might be expected to receive public attention if and when they are seen to relate to the

collective goals of a particular society. It is of course of great
interest to study when language problems are seen to relate to social
problems and then what sorts of decisions re language are made.

3. What does language planning consist of? Most writers would
agree that it begins with the identification of a problem; but what the
nature of that problem is, is open to discussion. One approach common to linguists has been to focus on the language code--its choice
and standardization. Thus, Tauli (1968:27) defines language planning as 'the methodical activity of regulating and improving existing
languages or creating new common regional, national or international
languages'. As Haugen (1971) notes, both Tauli and Ray are in agreement that the heart of any program is the linguistic evaluation of competing language forms. Jernudd and Das Gupta (1971:197) have chal-
lenged this overly normative and narrowly linguistic approach to
language planning because they feel that it falls short of describing
the more general phenomenon: 'Contemporary treatment of language
planning does not seem to be sufficiently sensitized to the complexity
of the social rationale of language planning in practice'. Das Gupta
(1970:224-25) notes that although even those charged with the task of
language development may fall into the false assumption that official
language planning is essentially a technical assignment and thus, may
assume that language politics are to be viewed as a menace to be
eradicated, that in fact language politics should be seen as a political
issue which demands a political solution. Jernudd (1971) feels that
the complex social rationale of language planning must be understood as a basis for any language planning theory. Thus, Jernudd
and Das Gupta (1971:197) emphasize the need for a broader identification of problems and see that a major task of language planning is
to 'identify the concrete areas of society that demand planned action
regarding language resources'. The critical points here are that
language problems are to be seen within the social and political
framework and that language can be seen as one more resource
which an administration may manipulate for its own goals. Of importance too is the focus given by Rubin and Jernudd (1971) who
emphasize the fact that 'change' of language use and language rules
are the objects of language planning. They note that such change
does not take place in vacuo and therefore language planning must
consider the facts of language within the fuller social context.
    Once one sees that language planning is part of the political and
administrative process, it can also be recognized that such decision
making may meet to a lesser or greater degree certain formal requirements of good planning. (Rubin 1971 discusses these requirements as they relate to language planning.) In broad terms, most
would agree that the planning process requires that in finding solutions

to language problems alternate goals, means/strategies, and out-
comes must be considered. Planning is always future-oriented and
in the consideration of several alternatives, a forecast of future
consequences is made to the best knowledge of the planners (Thorburn 1971:254).

In the process of deciding upon a solution to a problem the several
vested interests may come to focus upon language as a means to
achieve their political/social/economic goals. Because language
may serve so many goals, it is impossible to predict and classify
the implications of policy decisions unless we understand the social
rationale and conflicts underlying such decisions. A typology of
language policy decisions will not allow for predictable results unless
accompanied by a close haul analysis of the socio-political background behind these decisions. It might, however, be possible to
consider several typologies of decisions based on:

(1) The relationship between popular attitudes and actions toward
the language problem and the descriptions/knowledge/attention of a
set of experts (who are more likely to go to the heart of the matter).
This is the sort of thing Neustupný talks of in his 'depth' parameter
(see section 6 post). It is a matter for investigation to examine
whether a language problem tends to be more popularly attended to
or more rigorously attended to and how the two groups interact in a
particular society.

(2) The relationship between political goals and the language
problem. Is the language problem a real one or is language just
being used as a shield for other political goals? One might inquire
whether certain issues (for example, code issues of wide generality)
might not more frequently lend themselves to politicization. Alter-
natively, one might ask whether within a particular nation certain
language problems are politicized as a matter of tradition.

(3) Does the degree of politicization relate to the saliency of
popular attitudes and actions toward particular language problems?

4. Is language planning restricted to government bodies? Jernudd
(1971) points out that language problems are found on all levels of
decision making: individual, group, or national. Further, Das Gupta
(1971) points out that both private and semi-governmental bodies may
be concerned in the working out of solutions to language problems of
national relevance. We might therefore expect that some sort of
'treatment' of language may occur at all levels of socio-cultural
integration for the several levels of socio-cultural integration. Of
interest is the relation between the type of treatment (cf. section 6)
and the type of group for whom it is felt to be a problem. According
to Neustupný (1970) at least some language problems receive attention in any community by nonlinguists as well as by linguists. He

feels that patterns of thinking and talking about language problems are easily (possibly regularly) established and frequently strict constraints are imposed in this manner on the identification and understanding of relevant issues.

Neustupný's view of language treatment serves to widen the scope of language planning or at least puts language planning in a larger and perhaps more interesting framework. Language planning is seen as one kind of language treatment. It remains an empirical question as to what extent different levels of society at different moments in their development choose to treat language problems in the more conscious, systematic, future-oriented fashion which the label planning would seem to imply. By restricting the definition of language planning to that kind of treatment which is governmental and close to the planning ideal, we can then fruitfully explore differences in types of treatment--in what ways and why some type of societies/types of problems may closely approximate the planning ideal.

5. Is language planning restricted to developing nations? It would appear that this is not the case, but rather that different kinds of problems or different kinds of treatment might be expected to arise depending on the type of development. Suggestions have already been made that there may be differences between the kinds of problems nations may concern themselves with at different stages in their development. Looking at the evidence from Japan, Neustupný (1971) notes that two distinct approaches (language policy and language cultivation) have been taken. In the period since the Meiji Restoration, language policy was given a great deal of attention; whereas, since World War II more attention has been given to the cultivation approach. Neustupný hypothesizes that the policy approach is connected with the study of less developed speech communities (the less developed seems to refer to socioeconomic factors) while the cultivation approach is found in modern industrial societies. He suggests that there is a relationship between the economic level and the social and linguistic levels. 'It is the less developed modern (or modernizing) societies in which the policy approach prevails. These societies are characterized by a high degree of arbitrary . . . social and linguistic heterogeneity' (Neustupný 1971:10).

A related question has been: what are the differences between language planning in Europe and in developing nations. Fishman (1971) notes that although there is language planning in both Europe and South and Southeast Asia, the differences between them may be explained by the different kinds of nationalism which have developed in the two areas. Thus, Fishman (1971:14) notes the lesser stress on ethnic authenticity in South and Southeast Asian nationalism is reflected in the correspondingly greater roles of both indigenous and imported languages of wider communication (rather than of vernaculars alone) as languages of central government and higher education. Fishman sees the emphasis on English and French and on Hindi, Urdu, Malay, Indonesian, and Filipino as definite signs of the continued supraethnic stress of South and Southeast Asian language planning. However, he predicts a return in South and Southeast Asia to supraethnic authenticity goals.

6. Is there some productive way in which to compare types of treatment of language problems? While this particular question seems central to language planning, it has not yet really been very much discussed. An initial approach has been made by Neustupný (1970) who suggests that there are at least four ways in which the treatment patterns differ:

(1) Systematicity: this refers to the extent to which problems are treated as an ordered system of items (rather than in some ad hoc way).

(2) Theoretical elaborateness: some treatments are more meaningfully based on sociological or linguistic models while others do not seem so based.

(3) Depth: this parameter seems to relate to getting at the true nature of the problem rather than remaining biased by popular prejudices and/or established ways of dealing with a problem. His example comes from the Japanese: a surface treatment of problems would see all language problems in Japan as that of script reform whereas a deeper treatment would recognize problems ranging from stylistic and lexical to phonological elements.

(4) Rationality: this parameter combines a number of features which might better be separated eventually. Within it are included: affective neutrality (opposed to: affectiveness), specificity of goals and solutions (opposed to: diffuse), universalism (opposed to: particularism), emphasis on effectiveness (opposed to: emphasis on quality), long-term goals (opposed to: short-term goals).

As a beginning approximation to the combining of linguistic and socio-political treatments of language problems, these parameters seem very suggestive. One might question, however, how interesting the second parameter--theoretical elaborateness--really is. Perhaps it might be more productive to consider the extent to which people pay attention to and/or try to use such models. The third parameter (depth) seems to combine a number of comparisons: those, namely, of a factual consideration of the actual problem with (1) popular attitudes toward the problem, (2) popular verbalizations of the problem, and (3) popular and/or political uses of the problem. These may need to be sorted out into different types of depth with different kinds of results. The fourth parameter (rationality) is, as indicated, a combination of too many variables.

It would also be extremely helpful if these parameters, when clarified further, could be measured against actual and optimal policy for different levels of society. Questions which might be asked are: What degrees of systematicity have actual policies had? Which groups in society prefer to use which degrees of systematicity? (Cf. Rubin 1971 who indicates that within good planning at any one point in time, it might not be advantageous to be systematic or rational.) What degrees of theoretical elaborateness have been employed? Or, to what extent have people referred to theoretical models in their language treatment patterns? What degree of theoretical elaborateness is optimal for which language problems and social goals? One could question to what extent one could rationalize long-term goals since planners seem to feel that long-term goals lead to many unpredictable variables. These and other questions could be used to evaluate the parameters suggested by Neustupný. Other typologies of language treatment will doubtless appear as we look at the language planning and treatment data.

The questions isolated in this paper illustrate, we feel, the changing and developing focus of language planning. The problem does not seem to be just one of terminological differences but rather suggests there are differences in theoretical frameworks. More recent authors are focusing on the identification of types of processes, types of values, types of communities, types of language problems, types of treatment and the establishment of the relationship between these. Much more empirical data will be required to establish the proper framework for this complex set of variables.

NOTES

[1]My thanks to Björn Jernudd for his comments on this paper.

[2]Some variants of this fourfold typology appear in Haugen 1966a and 1969.

[3]Haugen 1966a assigns 'selection' and 'acceptance' to 'society' and 'codification' and 'elaboration' to 'language'. Whether these four processes are largely language or societal problems would, in fact, appear to be an empirical matter depending on the particular speech community and on how language problems are handled.

[4]Jernudd (1972) suggests that the connection between a technologically modern society and a linguistically mature one may not be an automatic relationship and should be kept distinct in order to examine just what the relationship might be.

REFERENCES

Das Gupta, Jyotirindra. 1970. Language conflict and national development. Berkeley, University of California Press.

Fishman, Joshua A. 1971. The impact of nationalism on language planning: Some comparisons between early twentieth-century Europe and more recent years in South and Southeast Asia. In: Rubin and Jernudd. 3-20.

Haugen, Einar. 1966a. Dialect, language, nation. In: American Anthropologist. 68.6.922-35.

_____. 1966b. Language conflict and language planning. Cambridge, Harvard University Press.

_____. 1969. Language planning, theory and practice. In: Actes du Xe congrès international des linguistes Bucarest, 1967. A. Graur, ed. Bucarest, Éditions de l'Académie de la République Socialiste de Roumanie. 701-11.

_____. 1971. Instrumentalism in language planning. In: Rubin and Jernudd. 281-89.

Jernudd, Björn. 1971. Review of: Language conflict and language planning: The case of modern Norwegian. In: Language. 47.2. 490-93.

_____. 1972. Language planning as a type of treatment. Monograph Series on Languages and Linguistics, No. 25. Ed. by Roger W. Shuy. Washington, D. C., Georgetown University Press.

_____ and Jyotirindra Das Gupta. 1971. Towards a theory of language planning. In: Rubin and Jernudd. 195-215.

Neustupný, Jiří. 1968. Some general aspects of 'language' problems and 'language' policy in developing societies. In: Language problems of developing nations. Ed. by Joshua A. Fishman, Charles A. Ferguson, and Jyotirindra Das Gupta. New York, John Wiley and Sons, Inc. 285-94.

_____. 1970. Basic types of treatment of language problems. In: Linguistic Communications. 1.77-98.

Rabin, Chaim. 1971. A tentative classification of language planning aims. In: Rubin and Jernudd. 277-79.

Rubin, Joan. 1971. Evaluation and language planning. In: Rubin and Jernudd. 217-52.

_____ and Björn Jernudd, eds. 1971. Can language be planned? Honolulu, East-West Center Press.

_____. 1971. Introduction: Language planning as an element in modernization. In: Rubin and Jernudd, eds. xiii-xxiv.

Tauli, Valter. 1968. Introduction to a theory of language planning. In: Acta universitatis Upsaliensis, studia philologiae scandinavicae Upsaliensia, 6. Uppsala, University of Uppsala.

Thorburn, Thomas. 1971. Cost-benefit analysis in language planning. In: Rubin and Jernudd. 253-62.

LANGUAGE PLANNING
AS A TYPE OF LANGUAGE TREATMENT[1]

BJÖRN H. JERNUDD

Monash University

Why and when do language problems appear in speech communities? What language problems justify planning? When do requests for planning of aspects of language appear? Answers to such questions do not depend on our definition of planning--but we will be in a better position to describe and understand the activities subsumed by these questions if we adhere to one particular definition of planning. The following nominal definition has been suggested by Jernudd and Das Gupta (1971:196):

> [We define language planning] as a political and administrative activity for solving language problems . . . In a national community, the role of conscious superordination of the major interdependent social sectors belongs to the political authority. The broadest authorization for planning is obtained from the politicians. A body of experts is then specifically delegated the task of preparing a plan. In preparing this, the experts ideally estimate existing resources and forecast . . . Once targets are agreed upon, a strategy of action is elaborated. These are authorized by the legislature and implemented by the organizational set-up authorized in its turn by the planning executive . . . In these ideal processes a planning agency is charged with the overall guidance. The nature of guidance varies depending on the responsibility given to the agency in each particular case.

The need was felt to further qualify 'language planning' by adding 'on the national level' as a feature of its definition.

This definition is specified in terms of decision-making theory, and provides a model for discussing the many ways (at greater or lesser distance from the model) in which language problems are actually treated in any national political community. Any speech community treats its language system (set of speech varieties) in ways which can be described in terms of decision-making models, yet only some may approximate, or require, planning of (one or some of) its language(s). It should be emphasized that the term 'planning' as used here must not be misunderstood as normative for, or imposable on, a speech community; we use an action-oriented (i. e. decision-making) model in order to provide an evaluation-metric, thus implying that explanatory relationships should be sought. We ask the reader to recognize the possibility of evaluation within the political-social milieu of any speech community.

Any scholar who commits himself to the study of a foreign community may, involuntarily or not, find himself an agent in political causes. Yet, evaluation is made possible by good theory, and the validity of evaluation is controlled by depth and sincerity of study. The use or acceptance of evaluation, however, is subject to political preferences of any group of people who opt to voice an opinion--be it the studied community, or the international scholarly community. Good planning theory, therefore, explicitly recognizes the supremacy of the expressed preference of a defined political community (which we will assume to coincide with a speech community in what follows and which according to our definition of planning is a nation).

It would be possible to select another approach to situations of language treatment, namely to study the use of the term 'planning' (and equivalent terms in other languages) and explore the content of such activities as the term happens to refer to, in each recorded situation. Such a work-procedure seems rather uneconomical, however, given, firstly, a general planning model from which the present nominal definition has been derived, and secondly, the at least equal opportunity to capture uses of the term 'planning' proceeding from this latter nominal model. Naturally, the latter is subject to revision and specification as knowledge accumulates, which removes any doubts as to its validity.

This paper will place language planning in the wider context of a speech community's 'treatment' (Neustupný 1970) of any language issue. But first it will provide some background to present-day study of language planning, particularly the Language Planning Processes Project.

A new topic of study. The planning of language is a new topic in the literature of social planning. Individual linguists may have paid attention to language planning as a discipline worthy of pursuit many years ago; but it would nevertheless be correct to say that today language planning is being systematically introduced into linguistics. There is growing literature on the planning of language; conferences include language planning as a legitimate subsection of sociolinguistics and applied linguistics; and students can take courses on this topic at some universities.

Today's language planning was born within the sociolinguistics of the sixties in reply to mounting evidence of the need for immediate, practical solutions to the language problems of developing countries. Its direction was also influenced by linguists' and social scientists' experience of and familiarity with immigrant and refugee problems, rather than by initial academic interest in the treatment, cultivation, or planning of languages. Yet, there are national traditions of language cultivation in Europe and also elsewhere (for instance, cf. Neustupný 1970 on Japan and Czechoslovakia). Research should not be conducted only in developing nations, nor only in nations where a language choice has recently been made or where language is a burning political issue. Many questions of language planning--indeed, the hypothetical consequences of choice of language in a developing country, i.e. the future content of language development there--could as well concern the developed nations.

If we attempt to develop a 'theory' for this new topic, then it should be formulated to fit both language cultivation of the old world, i.e. traditions of language cultivation in Europe and processes establishing some amount of language conformity in the Anglo-Saxon countries, and developmental work with language in the new nations and recently modernizing nations. Such a theory of 'language treatment' (of which I consider 'language planning' to be a part) should aim at an explanation of the many different ways in which societies treat their languages.

Because of the many interests that converge on the study of language planning, and because there is no unified international/academic tradition, opinion may be divided as to the meaning of, or constraints to be imposed on, the term 'language planning'. I would therefore like to survey the assumptions of the Language Planning Processes Project, and relate some of my post-fieldwork but pre-analysis thoughts to these assumptions. The Language Planning Processes Project is sponsored by the Ford Foundation. It is based at Stanford University. The Project has studied aspects of language planning in India, Indonesia, Israel, Sweden, and the Nation of Bengal.

A terminological problem. Before going on, let me clear up a terminological point. The term 'language planning' as used by the Project conflicts with the definition that Valter Tauli (1968) gives the term. Tauli wants to formulate principles for language change which give to language a balance of beauty, clarity, elasticity, and economy. Even if we assume that there are better and worse languages, and that linguists should seek a more efficient state of language--do we know enough to develop criteria that can separate what is good from what is bad in language and that can tell us what efficient language is? We know very little about the structure and use of language; and we know very little about people's thoughts, likes or dislikes, about language. The conflict between a linguistically based 'ideal' language planning and an empirically based problems-of-speech-communities language planning demonstrates that a linguist's view of language and his vision of the beauty of language constitute but one aspect of social and linguistic reality: people do indeed have different opinions about their own or others' languages. The linguist is, of course, entitled to his point of view. But there is little need to argue these different meanings of the term language planning. And if a community lacks a common language it matters less if the first effort in bridging that gap is linguistically beautiful (in any absolute sense of that desire) or not (cf. Haugen's 1969 review of Tauli in Language).

Background to the Language Planning Processes Project. Language planning had already been very much in the center of discussion in the autumn of 1966 at the Conference on Language Problems of Developing Nations. The Conference materials as published in the book Language Problems of Developing Nations (Fishman, Ferguson, and Das Gupta) show that the papers--sociolinguistically descriptive or practically diagnostic--are dominated by the often politically sensitive and complex questions of language choice in many developing nations and in Europe. Examples were drawn from parts of Africa, from India, Israel, Peru, Papua, Paraguay. Practical questions concerned future official language, language of education, the role of the former colonial language, etc. In this context, linguistic interest was focused on consequences of language choice, particularly when a formerly local language in a technologically innocent country or a language long used for cultural intercourse but without previous use in technical and/or modern-administrative spheres was to be developed into an official or educational language. Vocabulary attracted the main interest: how it could be enlarged and standardized; and how could so-called foreign words be taken care of. To a lesser extent there were remarks on the need for normative grammars and procedures for obtaining them and for fostering style registers. There were also some comments on choice and change of spelling or writing systems. Some examples of evaluation of competing pronunciations (from Haiti and the Philippines) were given. But in general more data were given on language choice and vocabulary than on other problems. Consequences of language choice and the dependency of language choice on the relative degree of development of available languages or treatment routines for language still remained open to exploratory discussion.

At the East-West Center, a meeting in the spring of 1969 emphasized these questions about consequences of language choice. The working papers are now available in the book Can Language Be Planned? (Rubin and Jernudd). This book has four sections:
(1) the motivation and rationalization for language policy,
(2) case studies of language planning,
(3) a general approach to language planning, and
(4) research strategies and a view towards the future.
Although papers in the first section of the book deal primarily with language policy (sentiment and expediency with regard to choice between languages), the other sections give considerable (but not exclusive) attention to language development. The case studies, for instance, include discussions of orthography and spelling reform in Israel, lexicon in Turkey, the development of Indonesian and Bengali, and language choice and language politics in Ireland, East Africa, and the Philippines.

Kinds of language decisions and their implementation. The expectations of the Project with regard to its study of language planning are described in the collection of research proposals entitled Research Outline for Comparative Studies of Language Planning (in Rubin and Jernudd). The proposals are gathered into three groups:
(1) policy formulation (which should perhaps be renamed language 'determination'),
(2) codification and elaboration (for which terms I would now prefer a single one, language 'development', at least for the convenience of not always having to make a choice), and
(3) implementation.
This tripartite division borrowed Haugen's terms (cf. Haugen 1966) but Haugen's initial formulations may have been allowed to undergo changes of content. (We have attempted to discuss Haugen's scheme in Jernudd and Das Gaupta. Briefly, the paper concludes that Haugen's entire scheme necessarily applies to every language decision.)

I do not intend to repeat again the ensemble of research questions as formulated by the Project paper, but it may be useful to give a couple of examples, and to offer some remarks on the meaning of the tri-partite division.

(1) Language determination refers to decisions concerning the functional distribution of language varieties in a community. Language determination also refers to decisions concerning which variety shall be developed for specific functions. Concretely this refers e.g. to government policy in today's Papua, New Guinea concerning the distribution of English, New Guinea Pidgin, Policy Motu, and tribal languages in e.g. schools, mass media, and administration. Also, this refers e.g. to which of several available spoken New Guinea Pidgin dialects shall be regarded as the referent for further development of written New Guinea Pidgin--there is the dialect of Madang (a publication center) now regarded as the most 'pure' or 'beautiful' Pidgin, and there is the dialect of the central administrative town Port Moresby. (There can be policies of determination, development, and implementation alike. However, 'language policy' at present normally means issues of language determination.)

(2) Language development refers to decisions concerning the standardization and unification of language use, by means of grammars, spelling manuals, word lists, etc. (cf. Ferguson 1968).

(3) Implementation refers to (decisions concerning) the (more or less systematic) attempts to influence language use by propagating the results of decisions on language determination and development. Examples are bills of government regulating language use in specified social situations (education, for instance) or, simply, the sale of grammars and dictionaries. Successful implementation implies an understanding of people's attitudes to language, beliefs about language, and language proficiency--briefly, the context of propagation of 'products' of language planning.

The importance of context of implementation is illustrated by the following Swedish example. If a Swedish speaker knows neither Latin, Greek, nor English and says baby [bebi, beibi, bäbi] but [bebisar] (i.e. mixing Swedish and English pronunciation and morphology), or, centrat (in the singular determinate), it would probably be quite difficult to make him say anything else, should this be regarded as desirable. The examples are uninteresting unless in fact people do want to influence change, and they do: cf. Svenska Akademiens Ordlista över Svenska Språket, the articles baby and centrisk; Om teknikens språk 1970:66 on centrum; Ord och Uttryck 1963, section 3:38; and Dunås 1970:102-03 on centrum and pages 25-26 on baby.

The division of language decisions into those constituting determination of language, and those constituting development of language, forms the backbone of a set of empirical hypotheses which imply that decision-making behavior in some ways differs in the two categories. There are interdependencies between issues of determination and development of language: any language development (clearly and perhaps trivially) implies choice of code. For instance, both categories are constrained by possibilities of effecting desired (criterial) impact on language use with available means. Planning necessarily implies implementation: solutions to language problems take into account (im)possibilities of bringing about language change among a group of speakers. If procedures for implementation are not formulated, decisions on issues of determination and development become meaningless. (We argued above that Tauli's efforts are in vain, and partly because of lacking social and political realism.)

A simple graphic representation of the relationships between our three categories is:

determination $\longleftrightarrow$ development
$\updownarrow$ $\updownarrow$
implementation

An immediate empirical problem of language planning would be to find out under what conditions and to what extent decisions regarding determination of language are constrained or alleviated by the varying developmental conditions (stages) of available language varieties and how the context of implementation constrains any language decision.

Planning as one kind of decision making. The Project emphasized one kind of organization of language planning by selecting to study and therefore assuming the importance of agencies that have been established to manage and prepare language development, namely 'language planning agencies' sponsored by government authority. But societies can solve language problems in different ways, with or without planning.

Although developing countries may present language problems of such a magnitude that a centrally guided and meticulously planned effort may be inviting, there is no a priori defense for building a model of conscious language change on such a system of decision making only. (See Das Gupta 1970 for this broader base in model-building.) Also, planning can be defined independently of kind of language problem. Planning is a model against which actually occurring decision-making behavior can be measured. So, neither planning nor any other procedure for solving language problems can be taken for granted--each has to be shown to be present, justifiable, or advantageous.

Briefly, planning means explicit choice between alternative futures. Often this choice is made by an organization that is particularly established for this purpose. In the best of cases this

organization also attempts to register the success of predicted results. In this sense, language planning appears to lack its full
equivalent in any society. On the other hand many countries recognize conscious language change as a kind of treatment of language.
Thus, in Sweden sprakvard is a well-established practical and academic discipline of Scandinavian philology.

A legitimate research aim is therefore to understand when a
society could advantageously plan language change or to understand
why societies in fact differ in their patterns of language treatment
(including the use or not of planning).

Limits of language planning. At any given time, different kinds
of language treatment may coexist, the one kind being more advantageous than the other for some group of decision makers or for
solving some particular kind of language problem, depending on the
social, political, linguistic, etc. context. Individual decision making
can very well dominate some set of language problems, without
societal (collective) disadvantage, whereas governmental authorization and federal financing may be necessary for other language
problems. (It is tempting to suggest that determination problems
require 'higher-order' administrative and political guidance, and
authorization.) A theory of language treatment must attempt to explain the existence, co-occurrence, and potentialities of different
systems of decision making.

Agencies other than governmental or national can obviously concern themselves with language in an orderly fashion, or be described
to do so. Examples are:

(1) National but nongovernmental agencies: associations of
engineers or other professionals who coin or spread terminology;
the Singapore Chamber of Commerce that constructed and issued
language examinations and a style manual for business correspondence in the Malay language.

(2) Non-national and nongovernmental agencies: the Shell Company in Malaysia that provides its own oil terminology when needed,
although often in association with the official language planning
agency (Dewan Bahasa dan Pustaka) or other oil companies. By its
personnel policy and internal language teaching program, Shell pro-
motes Malay: Shell produces its own language materials teaching a
specified kind of Malay. Or by its language officer who advises on
business correspondence in Malay. In all these activities, Shell
contributes towards the national growth of Malay, but is not primarily concerned with decisions for national spread.

(3) A newspaper's proof-reading function, including the issuing
of detailed instructions about hyphenation, spelling, etc.

(4) The individual author, letter-writer, or even after-dinner speaker--are they not 'rigorous' enough oftentimes in reaching their decisions on language use? One may quote the very sincere discussions in letters to columnists asking how to make a speech, how to address such-and-such a person, when to use certain expressions, how to abbreviate, etc.

In the last couple of examples the rigour or explicitness of the decision making may be weak, but the individual intent and wish to find out is clearly very often strong and the discussion sometimes intricate. Another example on the individual level is perhaps better: the decision to learn or not to learn a new language because a future job may demand it. The weighing of factors entering into the choice may not be put on paper, but it can be an example of argued and explicit choice regarding language.

The above examples approach the problem of definition of language planning by a gradual specification of the requirement of width of impact of a language decision and of observable administrative routines surrounding the decision maker. Shall we apply the term language planning when an office manager or manager of a secretarial pool issues a note specifying which words can be used and which not in writing certain kinds of letters? Or when a scientific team jokingly names a new perhaps revolutionary discovery, breaking phonological rules or not? Or take the word ombudsman in Australian English. Is it a problem of language planning to account for how the Australian Broadcasting Commission (ABC) most probably issued an order through its language specialist that the word shall be pronounced ['ɔmbɐdzmæn] whereas many others decided to say [ɔm'bɐdzmæn]. Does it become an act of language planning when the ABC discusses the word, but not when perhaps some students at the university argue about the pronunciation? We have chosen to exclude these acts from the realm of planning, inviting instead study of these kinds of language decision making as instances of language treatment.

Study of terminology exemplifies different treatment patterns. At present a particularly gratifying question would be to explain or initially to discover differences in selection of language problems and decision-making behavior between (some) developing countries and (some) developed countries. The Project selected to comparatively study terminological development because of its prominence in the treatment patterns of many countries. Project questionnaires and other aspects of its research design emphasized the study of language determination issues on a national level, and the immediate consequences thereof as reflected in the development of terminology.

Development of terminology is common to a great many different language planning agencies and countries. The Central Board for

Development of Bengali in former East Bengal produced about ten word-lists in various subjects. The Swedish Centre of Technical Terminology produces word lists, as do the Dewan Bahasa dan Pustaka in Malaysia, the Hebrew Academy in Israel, agencies in India, Tanzania, the Soviet Union, Austria, Finland, etc., etc. In many countries word-lists provide systematized terminologies for the first time in the national language. Without them it may be difficult to agree on textbook standards so that the national language could be used on a broad basis in schools.

The above-mentioned urgency in preparing terminologies is brought out very clearly in the aims of the Malaysian Dewan Bahasa dan Pustaka, and of the Central Board for Development of Bengali. The fourth aim of the Malaysian agency says: 'to standardize the spelling and pronunciation and to coin appropriate terminologies in the national language'. Note the word coin. Section (b) of the aims of the Bengali Board reads: 'to remove the existing deficiencies in Bengali, particularly in the field of Natural and Social Sciences as well as in technologies, in order that it becomes the medium of instruction at the higher level'. Note the emphasis on education.

Word-lists of developing countries usually enumerate a series of terms without definitions. Meanings are given by a parallel list of English corresponding terms. (See Istilah 1968.) Word-lists from technologically advanced countries, on the other hand, may provide very detailed definitions and foreign language equivalents, and emphasize systematicity of terminology (by diagramming or subclassification). (See Produktionsteknisk ordlista 1971.)

The managing director of the Swedish Centre of Technical Terminology, Einar Selander, has summarized the main aims of Swedish terminological work in the following words (my translation):

> . . . the main aims of systematic terminological work will be to create and maintain semantic order in already available terminology and to implement or suggest new terms in relationship thereto. The first task implies above all the systematization of and establishing of relationships between concepts, and the formulation of content of concepts and definitions, so that terms obtain a precise and unified meaning in different spheres of activity. The second task, to suggest new terms, is often perceived as urgent and is in any case the most extrovert one (Selander 1971).

The differing developmental stages of the Malaysian and Bengali languages, on the one hand, and Swedish, on the other hand, create different lexical results and different emphases in aims. Internal functioning and self-perception of the agencies in the three cases will probably be very similar, yet contexts and outputs differ.

A unifying model of language treatment. Neustupný (1970) offers a crude but overarching model of language treatment that both comprises language determination, development, and implementation and allows statements on differential decision-making patterns. He distinguishes between a 'cultivation approach' and a 'policy approach' to language treatment (cf. my attempt to relate some of Neustupný's terms to Haugen's description of the Norwegian case in my 1971 review of Haugen). According to Neustupný, societies can be characterized as employing the one approach or the other. (It should be noted, however, that features characterizing the approaches are not exclusive, so a policy-cultivation scale may therefore be more appropriate. Empirical research could attempt to define a matrix which can be used to determine a society's place on this scale of treatment by the configuration of values assigned to the features defining the matrix.) Developed countries are found to belong to the cultivation type of treatment pattern, developing nations to the policy type. The former type is characterized by such language problems as 'correctness, efficiency, linguistic levels fulfilling specialized functions, problems of style, constraints on communicative capacity, etc.' (Neustupný 1970:4). These language problems fit our development category above. The latter type is characterized by problems of 'selection of the national language, standardization, literacy, orthographies, problems of stratification of language (repertoire of code varieties) etc.' (Neustupný 1970:4). These language problems largely fit our determination category above. Obviously, a major task of research at the present time is to enlarge our understanding of what actually goes on in any one of those countries where people are seen to pay attention to language.

Neustupný (1970:10) says that a developing country displays 'a high degree of arbitrary social and linguistic heterogeneity' and that 'the diversity within the repertoire of varieties is easily recognizable and leads to a clear policy approach . . . ' It would seem to follow that such a country could profitably use the kind of decision making which we call planning. In 'more developed communities . . . inter-variety relationships become less conspicuous, variation is fine . . . and it is now issues like stability and functional differentiation that matter' (Neustupný 1970:11). Cultivation countries, then, would have a great deal of differentiated ('diffracted') decision making. Neustupný (1970:12) suggests that there are advantages to be derived from applying 'the policy approach in communities characterized by a high degree of social development' and the cultivation approach to less developed societies. It will be necessary to connect types of language problems to ways of decision making in order to make these suggestions meaningful, and the primary division into two approaches subject to testing. Then we may be able to account for e.g. Das Gupta's description of the pluralistic, democratic way in which India gradually solves its language determination issues. Also, the Swedish linguist Teleman (1971) describes Sweden in terms of 'cultivation' features: the source of initiative for language treatment is decentralized. Advice on language use rather than ruling dominates language discussion by agencies. Yet, he advocates more central coordination!

It seems to me that one could propose another base for characterization of the language treatment capacities of developing and developed societies. Developing societies have not yet established automatic links between language use and the expressive needs of modern technology, modern politics, etc. Many language problems, therefore, may necessitate wider discussion and raise more related linguistic or social issues than would be the case in a developed society. In the latter, a net of institutions have accumulated experience in treating recurring language problems--routinized treatment. The problems are absorbed more easily. They become problems of each particular sector of language use (such as education, technology, newspaper production, etc.). In both kinds of societies there would seem to be ample opportunity for language planning.

We must, however, disconnect stage of technological development from pattern of treatment and kind of language system. It has not been disproven that a speech community which is not 'modern' (i.e. not industralized, not technologically advanced, not administratively refined, etc.) cannot be linguistically mature (Jernudd forthcoming), display rich (inter- and intra-variety) language differentiation and accompanying ways of treating language.

NOTE

[1]Dr. Joan Rubin and Dr. Mary Slaughter gave me very helpful comments and editorial suggestions.

REFERENCES

Das Gupta, Jyotirindra. 1970. Language conflict and national development. Group politics and national language policy in India. Berkeley, Los Angeles and London, University of California Press.
Dunås, Rolf. 1970. Bättre svenska. Ord och Stil 2. Studentlitteratur, Lund.

Ferguson, Charles A. 1968. Language development. In: Fishman, Ferguson, and Das Gupta. 1968.

Fishman, Joshua A., Charles A. Ferguson, and Jyotirindra Das Gupta, eds. 1968. Language problems of developing nations. New York, Wiley and Sons.

Haugen, Einar. 1966. Language conflict and language planning. The case of Modern Norwegian. Cambridge, Harvard University Press.

_____. 1969. Review of Tauli, 1968. Language. 45.939-49.

Istilah Fizik, Hisab dan Kimia. 1968. Dewan Bahasa dan Pustaka, Kuala Lumpur.

Jernudd, Björn H. 1971. Review of Haugen, 1966. Language. 47.490-93.

_____. Forthcoming. Mature speech communities and language planning.

_____ and Jyotirindra Das Gupta. 1971. Towards a theory of language planning. In: Rubin and Jernudd, eds. 1971.

Neustupný, Jiří V. 1970. Basic types of treatment of language problems. Linguistic Communications. 1.77-98. Monash University.

Produktionsteknisk ordlista jämte arbets-och meritvärderingstermer. 1971. (Glossary of industrial engineering with job evaluation and merit rating terms.) Swedish Centre of Technical Terminology Publication No. 49. Uppsala.

Rubin, Joan and Björn H. Jernudd, eds. 1971. Can language be planned? Sociolinguistic theory and practice for developing nations. Honolulu, East-West Center Press.

Selander, Einar. 1971. Om att uttrycka sig exakt. Svensk Naturvetenskap. 1971. 201-08.

Svenska Akademiens Ordlista över svenska språket. Ninth edition. Stockholm.

Swedish Centre of Technical Terminology. 1963. Ord och uttryck.

_____. 1970. Om teknikens språk. TNC 44.

Tauli, Valter. 1968. Introduction to a theory of language planning. Uppsala.

Teleman, Ulf. 1971. Språkvårdens argument. Språket i blickpunkten, 194-216. Lund.

SOME COMMENTS ON LANGUAGE PLANNING

PAUL L. GARVIN

State University of New York at Buffalo

1. Rubin and Jernudd (1971:xiii) define language planning as 'decision making about language'; they correctly note the large number of variables other than linguistic that have to be taken into account in studying it: economic, social, political, demographic, psychological (xvi). Clearly, one of the key questions is the relation of linguistic to nonlinguistic variables. The notion 'linguistic' is here used in the conventional narrow sense of relating primarily to the structure and occasionally to the use of language. While my own view of linguistics is broader, I shall retain this narrow use of the term for purposes of this paper.

In the case of language planning, this relation seems to be fairly straightforward: the decisions made in language planning affect linguistic variables, but they are motivated by nonlinguistic variables and their successful implementation likewise depends on nonlinguistic variables.

Another, broader, relation between linguistic and nonlinguistic variables is not limited to language planning but has definite bearing on its study. It can be specified as follows: (1) linguistic variables furnish the recognition signals by which socially significant varieties of language are distinguished in a given cultural setting, (2) nonlinguistic variables determine the choice of socially significant linguistic patterns and/or features.

2. Four terms keep recurring throughout discussions of language planning: literacy, standard language, official language, natural language. They must be clarified and related to each other in order for such discussions to make sense.

24

2.1. 'Literacy' is the best known of these notions. It can be used in reference to either individuals or speech communities. One might wish to use the terms 'individual literacy' and 'group literacy' to distinguish these two senses.

Both types of literacy have been talked about in the language planning literature. The discussion of individual literacy is primarily concerned with the problem of increasing the number of literate individuals. The basic question in group literacy concerns the development of writing systems for hitherto unwritten languages. Ferguson (1968:29) has coined the term 'graphization' to refer to this; it is the aspect of literacy most closely related to the other basic notions to be discussed here.

Both types of literacy involve linguistic variables. Both are matters of degree. Just as a given individual can be literate to a varying extent, so the writing system worked out for a hitherto unwritten language can be elaborated with varying degrees of proficiency and attention to detail. Thus, it is not only a question of the alphabetic or other symbols; but there are also matters of punctuation, capitalization, and a host of other graphic conventions on which decisions must be made in order to develop a full-fledged writing system (for an example from my own experience, see Garvin 1954).

A language for which a writing system has been developed will, of course, be called a written language.

2.2. Standard language. Mathiot and I have defined a standard language as 'a codified form of a language, accepted by and serving as a model to, a larger speech community' (Garvin 1960:783). To this I have later added that 'a given language situation can be described as meeting the criteria for a standard language to a given degree, rather than absolutely' (1959:30). These criteria include, in addition to the defining criterion of codification, a set of structural properties, a set of functions, and a set of attitudes. The structural properties can be considered linguistic variables, the functions and attitudes nonlinguistic. They will be discussed further below.

2.3. Official language. Everyone agrees that the defining criterion for an official language is official recognition by some governmental authority. This is clearly a nonlinguistic factor.

2.4. National language. This term is used in two senses.

One of them, an emotionally more neutral one, indicates that a given language serves the entire territory of a nation rather than just some regional or ethnic subdivision. This is the sense in which, for instance, the term 'lengua nacional' is commonly used in Latin

America; it is then often contrasted with 'lengua indígena'. Thus, Spanish is the 'lengua nacional' of Mexico, while Nahuatl is 'just' a 'lengua indígena'.

The second, emotionally more powerful sense of the term indicates that a language functions as a national symbol. This is the sense in which the term is commonly used in emergent countries; it is then often contrasted with the language of the former colonial overlord. The best known and most clear-cut example is Bahasa Indonesia. It is, of course, contrasted with Dutch.

Both senses of the term 'national language' are characterized by nonlinguistic criteria.

It is to be noted that a national language is often also an official language, while the converse is not necessarily the case.

3. On the basis of the criteria noted so far, the four types of language can be divided into two groups. The first includes written language and standard language, the second official language and national language. The two groups differ as follows: both written and standard language can be characterized in terms of linguistic variables and are a matter of degree, while official language and national language can only be characterized in terms of nonlinguistic variables and are matters of yes/no decisions (a given language is or is not selected by the authorities as the official and/or national language).

Two additional considerations are related to this. One is that the development of a standard language, and to a lesser extent of a written language, requires the active cooperation, if not of the entire speech community, then at least of its intellectual elite. By contrast, the acceptance of an official language or national language requires only the passive acquiescence of the speech community (and can not be achieved in the face of serious resistance). The second more parochial consideration is that the potential contribution of linguistics is much greater in the development of written and standard languages than in the selection of official and national languages. Note, finally, that the requirements for standard-language development are far more complex than those for literacy. (For a discussion of the differences, see Garvin 1959:28-29).

In the light of these considerations, it is proposed that a linguistically oriented discussion of language planning should take standard language as a point of reference.

4. Mathiot and I have characterized a standard language by two structural properties, four functions, and three attitudes.

In line with Prague-School thinking, we have opposed the standard language to folk speech (Garvin 1960:783). I can now further specify folk speech as any variety of language that has not been affected by language planning.

The structural properties are flexible stability and intellectualization. The first of these is 'an ideal property: a standard language, in order to function efficiently, must be stabilized by appropriate codification; it must at the same time be flexible enough in its codification to allow for modification in line with culture change' (Garvin 1960:784). Intellectualization is:

> . . . a tendency towards increasingly more definite and accurate expression . . . In the lexicon, intellectualization manifests itself by increased terminological precision achieved by the development of more clearly differentiated terms, as well as an increase in abstract and generic terms. In grammar, intellectualization manifests itself by the development of word formation techniques and of syntactic devices allowing for the construction of elaborate, yet tightly knit, compound sentences, as well as the tendency to eliminate elliptic modes of expression by requiring complete constructions (Garvin 1960:785).

Flexible stability roughly corresponds to Ferguson's (1968:31) 'standardization', intellectualization to his 'modernization' (Ferguson 1968:32).

The functions of a standard language include three symbolic functions and one objective function. The symbolic functions are the unifying, separatist, and prestige functions; it serves to separate it from another language which may be a related one (from which it may have broken off, as Dutch did from German); it bestows prestige upon the speech community that has been able to develop one as well as upon the individual who has been able to acquire mastery of it; finally, the standard language serves as a yardstick for correctness as well as a frame of reference for literary creativity.

Attitudes were summed up by us as follows:

> The functions of a standard language . . . give rise to a set of cultural attitudes towards the standard: the unifying and separatist functions lead to an attitude of language loyalty, the prestige function arouses an attitude of pride, and the frame-of-reference function brings about an attitude of awareness of the norm (Garvin 1960:787).

5. The important question that arises in this connection concerns the extent to which the above-noted characteristics of a standard language apply to other forms of speech as well. While I have not done

any research in depth on this question, it strikes me as significant
enough to deserve some thought. Let me therefore present some of
my present speculations about it.

5.1. Let me first consider this question in regard to folk speech
which Mathiot and I have defined as the opposite of a standard language (see section 3).

It would seem at first blush that folk speech certainly must lack
the two structural properties of the standard language. However,
the situation is far from clearcut. In regard to flexible stability,
the way in which this property manifests itself in folk speech is
different from its manifestation in the standard language where by
definition it is closely linked to codification. [1]

Concerning intellectualization, the situation is equally complex.
Certainly, folk speech is as capable of extending its lexicon as any
more standardized form of language--many cases of lexical elaboration have been reported for both European folk dialects and non-
literate languages, although, of course, the lexical innovations
usually lack stability (for a case study, see Garvin 1948). But it
would be difficult to envision an intellectualized syntax for any form
of folk speech; at least, none has to my knowledge been recorded.

As far as the functions and attitudes are concerned, they seem to
be present at least in those folk speech communities that are not in
a process of dissolution. They will, of course, apply to small
rather than large populations. Clearly, speakers of the same form
of speech consider themselves part of the same group and separate
from other groups (thus manifesting the unifying and separatist functions), although at times the question arises as to whether the group as
defined by the speakers corresponds to a speech community as defined by strictly linguistic criteria. As far as the prestige function
is concerned, it seems to apply primarily to the prestige of the individual who is considered an expert speaker of his language; the fact
of having one's own language is not usually a source of prestige.
Correspondingly, attitudes of language loyalty are often found in
functioning folk speech communities, that is, those that are able to
maintain themselves against outside encroachment--it is evident that
when language loyalty disappears the speech community will begin to
assimilate to a larger (more prestigious, more powerful) outside
speech community. Similarly, pride will be found in functioning folk
speech communities, most often an individual's pride in his ability
to handle his language, but occasionally also a group's pride of
possessing a language capable of forms of expression that are in
some way considered desirable.

5.2. Let me now turn to the forms of speech, other than the standard, that are of interest to language planning--written language, official language, national language.

The first point to be made here is that since I have specified folk speech by the absence of language planning (see section 3), none of these three forms of speech can be considered a variety of folk speech. Rather, they are all in some way opposed to folk speech. The second point is that of the three, only written language by definition has a place on the standardization scale, since the writing conventions clearly constitute a form of codification, although it may be a very low degree. On the other hand, official language and national language are not defined in terms of codification and are therefore not definitionally related to standard language. However, in all cases mentioned in the literature (cf. Fishman et al. 1968, Rubin and Jernudd 1971) such languages either are established standard languages or serious attempts are in progress to make them into full-fledged standard languages. The extent to which these languages have become standardized can then be measured by the extent to which they possess the standard-language properties discussed here. Let me repeat, however, that--unlike the case of written language--I do not consider standardization a logically necessary adjunct to official-language or national-language status, but rather a parallel development arising from cultural necessity.

Just as the functions and attitudes are applicable to folk speech, so all of them seem to apply also to written language, official language and national language without regard to degree of standardization, though not equally to each of them. It seems that the extent to which they are applicable is directly related to written-language, official-language and national-language status.

Written language seems to be characterized above all by the frame-of-reference function and the corresponding attitude of awareness of the norm. Official language seems to be characterized above all by the prestige function and the corresponding attitude of pride, in the sense that, for a native speech community in a developing country, having one's language selected as an official language bestows prestige upon the community and is a source of pride. National language seems to be characterized, in addition to the prestige function, above all by the unifying and separatist functions and the corresponding attitude of language loyalty, provided the national language has arisen 'naturally' or has been chosen judiciously by the authorities.

6. In the light of the discussion so far it can be said that language planning has two basic ingredients: choice of language and language development, where by the latter term I mean a deliberate effort to achieve higher levels of literacy and standardization for a language.

Language development seems to be dependent on language choice.

The factor of deliberate choice is particularly evident in the case of an official language and/or national language. At the same time, as I have noted in the preceding section, both official and national languages have to have a high level of standardization as a matter of cultural necessity. This means primarily that these languages should have the structural properties of a standard language to the highest possible extent, both that of flexible stability and that of intellectualization. It is clear that the degree of language development required will depend on the choice of language.

What about language choice itself?

The literature on language planning is replete with discussions of language choice. Rather than summing up this discussion, let me just raise a few points in the light of the frame of reference of properties, functions, and attitudes proposed here.

It is evident that the most difficult problem of choice arises where the decision has to be made between adopting one of the world languages as an official language or selecting one of the languages of the country as the national and official language--in Kloss's (1968:71) terms, exoglossic versus endoglossic. It seems to me that the basic consideration in such a choice is the purpose for which the language is intended, which in my frame of reference clearly falls within the purview of function. Let me therefore examine the difference between an exoglossic official language and an endoglossic national language in functional terms.

Both types of language will manifest the unifying and frame-of-reference functions, since they will serve to unify the speech community (or at least its intellectual elite) and will serve as a yardstick for correctness and other purposes in education and other aspects of culture. A national language can, as has been said in the preceding section, in addition be characterized by a strong separatist function which is usually absent in an exoglossic official language. This separatist function can be viewed as the linguistic ingredient in the current world-wide tendency to establish a separate cultural (and political) identity.

Both types of language will have an additional function which has not been included in the list of functions stipulated for a standard language. This can be called the participatory function, that is, the function of the language to facilitate participation in world-wide cultural developments. In the case of an exoglossic official language, it may well be assumed that this function will be predominant.

7. Clearly, the separatist and the participatory function are in conflict. This conflict must in some way be resolved in order to

make a judicious choice of language and facilitate subsequent language development.

An important consideration must be kept in mind here. It is that the world-wide cultural developments referred to above include more than one aspect of culture, and that different aspects of culture affect the participatory and separatist functions differently. The most clear-cut difference is that between the technological and the literary realms, both of which require a standardized form of language for their development.[2]

In the technological realm the participatory function predominates: a type of higher education is required for which a world language is most practical in terms of the availability of textbooks, instructional personnel, etc. In the literary realm, on the other hand, the desire to participate in world-wide developments will often be subordinate to the need for cultural self-expression and the search for cultural identity--hence, the separatist function will predominate.

8. One final point deserves mention. It is that the notions presented here are largely based on a theory of language standardization that has its roots in the European experience. While it is true that the European experience has in certain ways been duplicated in many other parts of the world (cf. Garvin and Mathiot on Paraguay), it can certainly not be taken for granted that this necessarily must be true of all parts of the world at all times. A similar problem is presented by the frequent implication in the language-planning literature that speech communities the world over are desirous of 'modernization', which in effect means some form of acculturation to European patterns. This can no more be taken for granted than the universal applicability of European-based notions of language standardization and related processes.

The crucial question here is the extent to which the European and Europeanized experience constitutes a valid precedent for the other cultures of the world. While interesting and important parallels can be drawn between the present situation in many developing countries and the national revival of the 'lesser nationalities' of Europe in the first half of the 19th century, it is also important to note some of the obvious differences. One of these is that the then emergent European nationalities sought their models for language standardization in the then already established European standard-language communities: thus, the Czechs patterned themselves after the Germans, the Finns after the Swedes, etc. Clearly, in spite of the difference in the degree of standardization of their respective languages, there were many significant cultural similarities between the developing nationality and its model. Equally clearly, this is not the case for many of today's emergent nationalities. Another difference is that many of the then emergent European nationalities had historical precedents similar to those of their models and hence the pattern of development set by these models was a natural one for them to follow--a situation which clearly does not apply to many of the emergent nationalities of today.

The question raised here is particularly acute in the case of populations that consider themselves the victims or past victims of exploitation by Europeans or descendants of Europeans. Notions which from a European perspective seem perfectly obvious and/or necessary may be rejected out of hand. Thus, the suggestion has been made that some of the nationalities in the former colonies might not necessarily go through a process of literacy and language standardization, but might pass directly into a 'Macluhanesque' period where oral mass communication in the local traditional style would be made possible by the electronic media.[3] Who is to say that this is not the way it will happen?

NOTES

[1]I am indebted to Einar Haugen for pointing out to me that the property of flexible stability applies to all forms of speech, including folk speech, since all varieties of language are equally capable of change and expansion. Where the standard language differs from folk speech is that, in order for the standard to meet the multiple requirements of a complex society, flexible stability has to apply not only to informal usage but also to formal codification.

[2]I am indebted to Wingrove Dwamina for bringing this aspect of the problem to my attention.

[3]This possibility was pointed out to me by Orlando Taylor.

REFERENCES

Ferguson, Charles A. 1968. Language development. In: Fishman, Ferguson, and Das Gupta. 1968:27-35.

Fishman, Joshua A., Charles A. Ferguson, and Jyotirindra Das Gupta, eds. 1968. Language problems of developing nations. New York, Wiley.

Garvin, Paul L. 1948. Kutenia lexical innovations. Word. 4.120-26.

_____. 1954. Literacy as a problem in language and culture. Georgetown University Monograph Series in Languages and Linguistics. Number 7:117-27. Hugo J. Mueller, ed. Washington, D.C., Georgetown University Press.

_____. 1959. The standard language problem--concepts and methods. Anthropological Linguistics. 1(3).28-31.

Garvin, Paul L. 1960. The urbanization of the Guarani language--
A problem in language and culture. In: Anthony F. C. Wallace,
ed. Men and cultures, Selected Papers of the Fifth International
Congress of Anthropological and Ethnological Sciences.
Philadelphia, September 1-9, 1956, Philadelphia, University of
Pennsylvania Press. 783-90.

Kloss, Heinz. 1968. Notes concerning a language-nation typology.
In: Fishman, Ferguson, and Das Gupta. 1968:69-85.

Rubin, Joan and Björn Jernudd, eds. 1971. Can language be planned?
Honolulu, The University Press of Hawaii.

_____. 1971. Introduction: Language planning as an element in
modernization. In: Rubin and Jernudd. 1971:xiii-xxiv.

LANGUAGE PLANNING
IN MAINLAND CHINA: STANDARDIZATION[1]

DAYLE BARNES

University of Pittsburgh

1. Introduction. Serious and sustained commitment to a program of language standardization is a relatively recent phenomenon in China. Much the same kind of statement could be made, of course, about other facets of mainland Chinese language planning, such as the national language program or PTH [pǔ-tūng-hwà], the adoption of an alphabetic character annotation system [pīn-yīn] for use in schools, and the gradual introduction of simplified characters. Together with standardization [gwēi-fàn-hwà], each of these initiatives became part of national language policy in the 1950s. But unlike language standardization, all of the other reforms represent the resolution of language issues reaching back in some cases before the establishment of the Republic in 1911.

Orthographic reforms such as character simplification are not considered aspects of standardization policy by the mainland government, and therefore do not fall within the scope of this paper. The time dimension is also circumscribed. After nearly a decade of discussion and decision on major language questions in the fifties, the intensity of debate diminished markedly, and in the sixties, as the Cultural Revolution gained momentum, language planning activity came to a virtual halt. This paper concentrates on the early years of deliberation and policy formulation.

It would be misleading, however, to imply that standardization was completely without antecedents in the pre-1949 period. Some of the earliest attempts to cope with the need for normative usage in

34

technical terminologies, especially in the sciences, were produced
in conjunction with the translation activities of the late Ch'ing Dynasty
Interpreters College [Tūng-wén-gwǎn] in Peking (Wright 1950:331).
A typical example was a manual on chemical equivalents in Chinese
issued in 1882 (Yüǎn Hàn-ch'îng 1953:16). Later, in 1898, a government translation office [Yî-shū-jyú] was established, under the
direction of Lyáng Chǐ-chāu, in response to an accelerated demand
for western knowledge in political economy and in the natural sciences
(Meng 1962:67). Thereafter, until the 1930s, conventions for borrowing foreign terminologies do not seem to have been fixed, nor does it
appear that there was any government authority responsible for dealing with the matter.

During the thirties substantial efforts were invested in the compilation of lists of vocabulary equivalents in scientific and technical
fields (Lwó and Lyǔ 1956:20). The Nationalist organization charged
with this responsibility, known then (and now in Taiwan) as the Institute for Compilation and Translation [Gwó-lî byān-yî gwǎn], was
established as a branch of the Ministry of Education (MOE) in 1932
(Byān-yî gwǎn 1969:1). Between its inception and the end of the Chinese civil war, the Institute compiled and published twenty-five volumes
of word lists ranging over a variety of modern scientific disciplines
(Byān-yî gwǎn 1969:5). In addition to lists of terms compiled for
such disciplines as mathematics, physics, chemistry, various
specialties in medicine, and several branches of engineering, the
Institute also compiled five volumes in the social sciences, including
lists for economics, statistics, psychology, and education.

Despite this respectable beginning, standardization was undeniably
a peripheral language concern in the thirties. The reason for this
is not, as some mainland writers would have it, that the language community and its research organizations were derelict in providing solutions for obvious standardization problems (cf. Lwó and Lyǔ 1956:7).
This interpretation distorts reality by implying official indifference
toward standardization questions under conditions in which a national
language program already enjoyed a wide measure of public support.
It omits to note that the government's language program in the thirties lacked such consensus because language imperatives were differently perceived by different groups during this period. It con-
spicuously circumvents mention that one of these groups, the Communist party, was adamantly opposed during the two decades before
1949 to the Nationalist's national language policy. This last observation is of interest because today PTH, the national language
designate of the People's Republic since 1955, and gwó-yǔ, as the
Republic of China's national language is called on Taiwan, in all
important respects differ only in name, and their status is under-
written by the full authority of their respective governments. Given

the inchoate state of thinking on basic language issues, and the political divisions which underlay them, it is not surprising that standardization was not regarded by any major group as a pressing language necessity.

A clear commitment, at least in principle, to the teaching of a national language based on the dialect of Peking was made by the Nationalist Government's MOE in 1932 (Fang Shih-dwo 1965:58). However, a combination of inadequate preparation on the part of the government and political opportunism on the part of its enemies rendered the policy vulnerable to several kinds of criticism. Communists charged that legislated imposition of a national language across dialect boundaries constituted in reality cultural imperialism by north Chinese over dialect speakers in the south (Syīn wén-dž Conference 1931:54-55). Some further insisted that a legislated approach was superfluous because a nationally serviceable form of Chinese would eventually arise as a natural consequence of increased social and economic intercourse among dialect speakers (Chyū Chyōu-bǎi 1931:31). Others maintained flatly that a national language based on the Peking dialect could not succeed in China (Tsǎu Bwó-hǎn 1952: 153).

Another kind of reservation was related to the problem of massive illiteracy. For those convinced that only a dramatic extension of literacy could unify the nation and guarantee modernization, assigning priority to a national language policy appeared misguided and unrealistic (cf. DeFrancis 1943:239). As the first step in the direction of national development and a democratic polity, a program striking at the roots of illiteracy seemed more rational and appealing. And it was only logical that the most direct attack on the problem was to reach illiterates through their own dialects. However, the proposal that separate romanized scripts be created for this purpose left its advocates open to the countercharge that they were initiating centripetal forces which would reverse the thrust of national unification and result in the consolidation of numerous cultural and linguistic satrapies (DeFrancis 1967:131).

The basic charter favoring a language policy based on the primacy of education in dialects and literacy in separate dialect scripts emerged from a 1931 conference in Vladivostok jointly convened by Chinese communist emigres and Russian language workers to promote the acceptance of one such romanized script, Syīn wén-dž, among Chinese illiterates in Russia. Playing skillfully on the literacy question and the sensitivity of dialect speakers, the charter vehemently rejected the imposition of any single dialect as a national language for all Chinese (Syīn wén-dž Conference 1931:54). In retrospect it is hard to avoid the conclusion that the Nationalist language policy all but invited such attacks by failing to clarify its intentions with respect to the future role of the dialects. On the other hand, the Vladivostok statement is avowedly Marxist in its identification of the monopoly of written and spoken gwó-yǔ with the interests of the ruling class which, it warned, hoped to achieve linguistic tyranny over dialect speaking populations. Despite its fragmentation and geographical isolation for most of the ensuing two decades, the Chinese Communist Party's position on language continued to reflect these fundamental theoretical assumptions.

The view of language and society upon which those assumptions rested was abruptly swept away in 1950 by the publication in China of Stalin's <u>Marxism and Problems of Linguistics</u>. The import of this treatise for communist language planners was to negate completely the identification of language with the interests of class. Denying the earlier orthodoxy of the Russian Marxist school that language constituted a component of the superstructure, serving the interests of the dominant economic class, Stalin insisted that language is not the exclusive instrument of any economic group. Rather, he asserted, language is a cumulative product of history, serving all classes irrespective of their economic position (Stalin 1954:14).

Having identified language as a cultural attribute uniquely unrelated to class interests, Stalin was free to endorse a more conventional view of national language development. Elaborating on the implications of this view for the Chinese situation, Chinese writers noted that, although any dialect is acceptable on linguistic grounds as a candidate for the national language, not every dialect has the political, economic, and cultural credentials requisite for this position. Thus, the impersonal forces of history, rather than legislative fiats, govern the ascendancy of one dialect over others to fill the role of a national language (Lwó Chǎng-péi 1952:423). The implications for North Chinese as a national language in China were exactly what they were for Russian in the Soviet Union. Peking, said Wáng Lì, is China's Moscow (Wáng Lì 1954:15). Writing in the thirties, communist Chyū Chyōu-bái argued that the Peking dialect was a poor choice for the national language because it was neither the political, economic, nor cultural center of the nation (Chyū 1931:41). In the fifties, as heterodoxy became orthodoxy, mainland Chinese writers strove not to be the last in proving that he was wrong.

2. The language situation in China, 1949-56. Mainland government publications recognize eight major dialect regions in China (Lwó and Lyǔ 1956:5-6). With the exception of North Chinese, all of them lie geographically in the southeast quadrant of the country below the Yáng-dž River. According to available population estimates only one, the Southern Mín dialect, fails to meet the numerical test proposed by Charles Ferguson for identifying major national languages

within a country, i.e. a language spoken natively by ten million or
more individuals (Ferguson 1962:15). North Chinese is, again using
Ferguson's terminology, the dominant language, claiming 387 million
speakers, or 70 per cent of the total population of China in 1953, the
last year in which a national census was taken. Although these language groups are routinely called dialects in Chinese publications as
well as by many western observers, three prominent native Chinese
linguists--Jàu Ywǎn-rèn (1943:66), Lǐ Fāng-gwèi (1937:62), and
Lù Jr̀-wéi (1956b:106)--have asserted that a high degree of unintelli-
gibility obtains between at least some of these dialect groups.

Further evidence suggests that the actual range of language
diversity is much greater. Dīng Yì-lán, a representative of the
national broadcasting services, reported that in the early fifties it
was necessary for a large number of regional radio stations to
supplement their Peking language broadcasts with programs in local
dialects. Altogether fifteen of the fifty-five regional stations operating in 1956 were transmitting in more than a single dialect, and
some were programming in three. Excluding broadcasts in the dialect of Peking, a total of eighteen other dialects were on the air
(Dīng Yì-lán 1956:142). In the Wēn-jōu area, to cite but one example,
Dīng estimated that no more than 5 per cent of the listening public
could understand programs broadcast only in Peking dialect. At the
subregional level there may be even finer dialect graduations; one
source claims that, for this same period, over two hundred forms
of local drama were attested, each having, presumably, certain
distinctive linguistic characteristics (SCD 1956:233).

3. Standardization and PTH. Two major linguistic events took
place in Peking in October of 1955. The first was a national conference dealing with problems of orthographic reform which also
served as the official vehicle for launching the new national language
policy. The second, a Conference on Standardization of Modern
Chinese [Syàn-dài Hàn-yǔ gwēi-fàn wèn-tí sywé-shù hwèi-yì] brought
together 122 representatives from government, academic, and
communications-related organizations to give shape and definition
to the national language choice (SCD 1956:226). The Conference on
Standardization arrived at a formula characterizing PTH as a speech
form based phonologically on the dialect of Peking, grammatically on
the structure of the North Chinese dialect group, and lexically and
stylistically on the works of certain representative modern Chinese
writers (PTH Chǎng-shr̀ 1957:10). This formulation clearly distinguished PTH as a modern form from the language of Ming and
Ch'ing Dynasty vernacular literature, often referred to as colloquial
(Lwó and Lyǔ 1956:13). Typical examples of written PTH embodying
standard lexical, grammatical, and stylistic features are available,

according to Nǐ Hǎi-shǔ, in the daily editorials of the People's Daily (PTH Chǎng-shr̀ 1957:63). Apart from this, only two individuals have thus far been publicly recognized as exemplifying in their writing the best in modern prose style--Lǔ Syùn and Máu Dzě-dūng (PTH Chǎng-shr̀ 1957:13).

In taking this action, the People's Government endorsed virtually the same national language policy as had its predecessor. It thereby recognized the historical evolution of North Chinese which, according to the writer Jōu Dzǔ-mwó, had by the turn of the century already become the obviously dominant medium of communication over much of China, particularly as a means of interdialectal intercourse (Jōu Dzǔ-mwó 1957:30). The adoption of PTH, therefore, marked the culmination of a long series of efforts dating from the first days of the Republic in 1911 to establish some form of the Peking dialect as China's national language (Lyóu Fù 1925:15).

The ultimate composition of PTH--Peking phonology and North Chinese grammar and lexicon--has been justified by recourse to several kinds of criteria. The geographic and demographic aspects mentioned earlier are frequently cited in support of the government's language policy: some form of North Chinese is spoken natively by 70 per cent of all ethnic Chinese living throughout two-thirds of China's land mass. It is a justifiable inference that the sheer weight of these figures, which became clear for the first time with the national census of 1953, must certainly have had a powerful effect upon the decisions of language planners.

Important as these data must have been, the literature on language planning is always religious in its observance of the underlying historical forces expressed in this language policy. The policy is consonant with the Marxist linguistic axiom that a national language choice must necessarily arise from some extant dialect form, and cannot be artifically constructed. Thus, every living dialect is inherently a national language candidate because it already has a body of speakers and possesses an internal, systematic organization of its grammatical and lexical components. The selection of one national dialect over others as a national language is unapproachably impartial because it is decided on the basis of the political, economic, and cultural dominance of its speakers. Therefore, the choice of PTH is tantamount to the recognition of the linguistic hegemony of North Chinese in contemporary China.

In China, as elsewhere, standardization implies a deliberate plan to influence the shape of the language (cf. Haugen 1966:65). The total body of decisions about language, formal and informal, which comprise standardization policy constitute the difference between pǔ-tūng-hwà, 'common speech', in the discredited sense in which it was used earlier by Chyū Chyōu-bái, i.e. an amorphous and uncodified vernacular, and PTH understood as the evolving common language of all mainland Chinese. The government concedes that a large segment of this population, especially the current generation of older people and dialect speakers, is unlikely ever to use the standardized form. Indeed, it is unrealistic to expect that even many North Chinese speakers will observe all the phonological and other distinctions in Peking speech in the foreseeable future. Jōu Ēn-lái, in an official discussion of the matter, has acknowledged the existence of these limitations by adopting a set of flexible standards for learners: higher standards for prospective teachers of PTH, for radio announcers, and for school-age youth; lower standards for all others, including outright exemptions for some (JMJP 1/13/58). But if, as linguist Wáng Lì pointed out, succeeding generations are to be brought closer together linguistically, then it is imperative that some standard be available which is accepted everywhere as the national norm (Běi-jīng dà-sywé 1957:5).

Haugen has taken the position that language planning is primarily an attempt to influence the formal style of language as expressed in written form (Haugen 1966:55). It is true that in China standardization is concerned with the written form [wén-sywé yǔ-yán] including augmentation of the lexicon in artistic, socio-political, scientific, and technical areas (Twō Mù 1954:7). The importance of normalizing written usage in the basic lexicon and grammar of North Chinese was also emphasized during the Standardization Conference by MOE Head Jāng Syī-rwò. Haugen's view of language planning, however, seems to assume the existence of a language community which is linguistically far more homogeneous than is the case in China. It is important, therefore, not to lose sight of the fact that mainland language policy comprehends not only the standardization (in Haugen's sense) of PTH, but also its introduction into southern populations where it is not spoken natively. Since mainland linguists have repeatedly insisted that dialects differ most noticeably in pronunciation, it is not surprising to find that progress toward greater phonological uniformity in speech is regarded as integral to the overall goal of standardization.

4. The linguistic goals of standardization. The decision to adopt Peking as the phonological standard for PTH was not an entirely unqualified one, and there are differences among language planners as to how rigidly this standard should be construed. Some veteran language workers, such as Ní Hǎi-shǔ, have cautioned that such a choice was unrealistic (cf. SCD 1956:179). He and others have questioned the appropriateness of nationalizing certain Peking dialect phonological features, among them the -er-ized word finals and unstressed finals (neutral tone syllables).

-Er-ization in Chinese transforms dyàn-yǐng 'movie' into dyàn-yǐngr. In the vast majority of cases, -er-ized speech, while not geographically restricted to Peking, is nonetheless generally considered a hallmark of Peking speakers. Many non-Peking speakers, however, react negatively to it, regarding it as an affectation. Lù Jǐ-wéi has claimed that in Peking -er-ized speech was formerly more prevalent among those with little or no formal education, while its usage today among the educated is diminishing. In Lù's opinion, it is unnecessary to retain the nonphonemic, er-ized forms in the standardized national language (Lù Jǐ-wéi 1956a:53-55). In a revised publication for dialect speakers learning PTH, Wǎng Lǐ also recommended that -er finals be dropped in all cases where they were not phonemic (Wǎng Lǐ 1956:10). The view that nonphonemic -er-ization is indeed dialectal and inappropriate for national usage has been informally, but nonetheless authoritatively, incorporated into mainland language policy. Thus, Peking Radio uniformly deletes all -er-ized forms in broadcasts which are political or governmental in content--in other words, in broadcasts whose audience is a national one (Dǐng Yǐ-lán 1956:144).

Opinion was also mixed over the inclusion of final unstressed syllables in polysyllabic lexemes. Like -er-ized finals, unstressed final syllables are occasionally phonemic; but in the large majority of cases they are not. Jàu Ywǎn-rèn observes that this feature is generally absent in most new terms about modern life, particularly recently adopted scientific terminology (Jàu 1968:38). Jàu is also in agreement with mainland linguist Wǎng Lǐ, as well as Ní Hǎi-shǔ and others, in maintaining that lack of stress in Peking speech is a purely lexical feature (SCD 1956:228). Lù Jǐ-wéi felt that, for these reasons, its inclusion as a normative characteristic of the national language was unwarranted (Lù Jǐ-wéi 1956a:56).

Linguistic surveys of other sound features, on the other hand, served to support and confirm the PTH phonological formula. One such survey, conducted in the early fifties by the Linguistic Research Unit of the Chinese Academy of Sciences (CAS), confirmed that 80 per cent of North Chinese speakers observed Peking distinctions in the production of the gingival affricate, palatal, and velar stop consonants. In only a minority of northern districts did speakers fail to palatalize before -(y)i and -yu. Of thirty-four urban centers with populations over 200,000 in 1951, all but three displayed the same pattern. Other studies revealed less regional uniformity in the matter of the initial n-, l-, and the final -n, -ng distinctions which are made by Peking speakers. Finally, these surveys showed that the distinctive retroflex consonant series j(r)-, ch(r)-, sh(r)-, r- is generally not found outside northern speech areas.

Although interdialectal differences do exist at the grammatical level, they are fairly well understood and do not evoke much interest as, for example, phonology or the lexicon. Inversion of the northern indirect object, direct object word order (Ywǎn Jyā-hwǎ 1960:329) and a confusion of the function of some significant grammatical markers (Lù Dzūng-dǎ 1956:70) are typical examples.

Questions concerning lexical standardization can be divided into two kinds. The first involves decisions pertaining to dialect items and elements in the classical written language. The second has to do with procedures for assimilating loan vocabulary. With regard to the first, discussions at the time of the 1955 Standardization Conference seem to have reached agreement on the position that Peking should be accepted as standard for two reasons: (1) Peking is the representative North Chinese dialect, and (2) as a rule, its terms, compared with those of other dialects, are better understood nationally. Thus, as Lǐn Táu suggested, it would be appropriate to adopt nationally the usage of Peking in the matter of pronouns (Lǐn Táu 1957:83). However, Wǎng Lì, a native of Gwǎng-dūng Province who may have been reflecting a southern point of view, expressed concern that a standard lexicon delimited in this way would be too narrow (JMJP 10/12/55). Some writers have urged the adoption of any form provided only that it proved to be the most widely understood throughout the country (Syāu Jāng 1956:215). It is probable, therefore, that condition two takes precedence over condition one in the minds of many, especially among non-native speakers of the Peking dialect. Accordingly, Wǎng Lì, in a republication of a PTH text for southern learners, recommended replacement of some Peking items by nationally better known equivalents, such as dǎ for dzòu 'strike', and bú yàu for the portmanteau béng 'do not need to be' (Wǎng Lì 1956:10). Nǐ Hǎi-shǔ, a native of Shàng-hǎi, stated that the application of this criterion would probably mean substituting the more widely used bǎ 'syntactic marker of goal' for Peking gwǎn in gwǎn X jyàu Y 'X is called Y' (PTH Cháng-shǐ 1957:63).

This knife obviously cuts both ways, and is the principal argument favoring deletion of much vocabulary of dialect origin. Artistic use of dialect lexicon, especially in dialogue, had been defended on the grounds that it lent power and authenticity to literary compositions (SCD 1956:230). However, as one writer demonstrated in a list of Dūng-běi (Manchurian) expressions found in literature, the character combinations based on local dialects are frequently so arcane as to be utterly incomprehensible in written or spoken form to readers in other parts of the country (KMJP 11/19/55). Film releases containing unacceptable levels of local dialect usage have been subjected to criticism for the same reason (SCD 1956:237). It has been pointed out that, in such cases, the gains in power and authenticity may reduce to zero since they are unintelligible to all but a small minority (ChCJP 12/17/55). One of the most influential writers to subscribe to this kind of thinking was Shū Chǐng-chwūn (Lǎu Shè), a playwright whose fame in large part rests on his manifest skill in the use of dialect forms peculiar to the speech of Peking (KMJP 5/30/55).

Standardization policy favors the vernacular over the classical in writing for the same reason that it avoids obscure dialect forms (cf. Wáng Lǐ 1954:19). Writers whose work reflects a strong classical influence are urged to bring their style into closer conformity with the speech of the people by substituting modern forms for classical function words, such as using syàn-dzài for dž 'now'; dàn-shǐ for rán 'but'; rú-gwǒ for rwò 'if' (Jōu Yàu-wén 1956:29); and hé for yú 'with' (KMJP 10/1/54). Similar treatment is advocated for simple lexemes often found abbreviated to monosyllabic form in semi-classical, semi-colloquial prose, such as writing yǐ for yǐ-jǐng 'already', shí for shí-hour 'time', and jì for dàu 'toward' (CSP 12/11/56).

Lexical borrowing into Chinese was early sanctioned and encouraged by Màu Dzé-dūng himself in a 1942 Yán-ān address (Máu Dzé-dūng 1964:838). Consequently, there has been no opposition either to the principle or to the practice of continuing to incorporate loans into the language. On the other hand, the linguistic mechanics by which loans are sinicized have been the focus of considerable discussion.

One technique for sinicizing loans involves trans-syllabification, or sound translation [yīn-yì]. This process can be seen at work both long ago in Buddhist texts (Chinese Ā-mǐ-twō for Amida) and in numerous current expressions, such as à-sž-pī-lǐng 'aspirin', and lwó-ji 'logic' which are more modern [mwó-dēng] (Tsáu Bwó-hán 1954:107). In each case, the original loan is analyzed into syllabic units, and then characters with similar sound values are selected to represent them.

A second widely used method is transliteration, or <u>meaning</u> translation [yì-yì]. In this category can be found such familar lexemes as mǎ-lì 'horse and power > horsepower', and ywán-dž, 'original and particle > atom', (Gāu Míng-kǎi 1958:8). Here each of the hyphenated syllables is represented in writing by a character having as one of its most important meanings that of the English equivalent in the gloss.

Finally, some contemporary expressions are hybrids, resulting from the application of both of these principles, such as pí-jyǒu '(the sound) p'í and liquor > beer' and pí '(the sound) mí and mouse > Mickey Mouse'.

Both of these devices have their disadvantages. Sound translations can become inordinately long when borrowed from languages
whose words tend to be highly polysyllabic, or in which consonant
clusters, alien to Chinese, are common. Sound translations in these
cases easily grow to lengths which are lexically uncanonical and
intuitively disturbing to native speakers (Ching 1966:112). There is,
in addition, the probability that considerable phonological distortion
may be introduced into the loan if it enters the language through a
nonstandard dialect area (SCD 1956:161). On the other hand, the
meaning of a meaning translation may be ambiguous when uttered,
especially if the translation results in a monosyllable. The danger
in these instances is that an increase in the number of single syllable
words increases the likelihood of homophony (KMJP 6/3/57).

Nontechnical loans, whether di-syllabic or tri-syllabic, are not
regarded as significant problems for the general reading public
(Jōu Yǒu-gwāng 1965:25). In the natural sciences, however, loans
constructed by either sound or meaning translation can assume
awkward proportions. In chemistry, for example, the sound translation for hydrochloric acid becomes hā-yǐ-chū-rwò-kè-lwó-lǐ-kè
ā-syǐ-té. Reliance on meaning translation may not be much more
satisfactory: the Chinese meaning equivalent for phenyl-dithio
carbonyl [sic] is itself an unwieldy seven syllable compound (Tsǎu
Bwó-hán 1954:109). Some suggested alternatives to these multi-
syllabic forms involve the assignment of a single character for
technical loans in one of several ways: (1) new characters can be
created, (2) obsolete characters can be endowed with contemporary
meanings, (3) extant characters can be employed by expanding their
referential domains (Tsēng Jàu-lwùn 1953:3). The creation of new
graphs, however, runs counter to the government's attempt to
emulate Japan's success in reducing the number of characters in
common use. Extensive recourse to any of these approaches is
also objectionable because it may contribute to an increased inci-
dence of homophony among monosyllabic words in speech (Tsēng
Jàu-lwùn 1953:4). Lastly, in view of the tendency toward di-
syllabicity in Chinese word formation observed by many writers,
these single syllable forms may have no more canonical justification
than the attenuated giants obtained by resort to sound translation
(Ching 1969:89).

It is probably safe to say that during the fifties both sound translation and meaning translation were simultaneously employed in
technical fields (cf. KMJP 9/16/54). That this issue was a source
of dissatisfaction, however, was reflected in a mid-1953 meeting
sponsored by the language journal Jūng-gwó yǔ-wèn (Chinese
Language) and attended by twenty well-known figures in the language
planning community, including the head of the CAS Terminology

Section, Jèng Dzwò-syīn. Participants invited to discuss the problems of translating technical terminology were unable to reach a consensus on the superiority of any of the commonly used approaches to lexical borrowing (Mǐng-tsź dzwò-tán-hwèi 1953:33). Individuals writing on this question, by contrast, have been almost unanimous in their preference for meaning translations over sound translations (cf. KMJP 2/28/56). Wáng Lǐ thought that sound translations should be attempted only as a last resort in situations where meaning translations proved unsatisfactory (Wáng Lǐ 1954:17). This attitude may owe more to psychology than to linguistics. Jàu Ywán-rèn, for example, has written that Chinese feel more comfortable with loans in which the characters have referential significance, rather than mere sound approximation (Jàu 1968:139). Substantiation for this intuitive feeling can be seen in the case of the recent Chinese loan for mini-skirt [mǐ-nǐ-chyún]. Originally a simple sound translation, the characters now used to write mǐ-nǐ combine with chyún ('skirt') to yield, appropriately, 'the skirt that captivates you'.

5. National goals of standardization. It would be misleading to construe standardization only as a linguistic end in itself. On the contrary, language standardization--indeed, the whole range of innovative language activity on the mainland--is justified ultimately in terms of larger social, economic, and political requirements. This is quite compatible with Marxist linguistics, which regards language as an instrument vital to social and economic activity (Lwó and Lyǔ 1956:4). But language issues in China have a national significance which transcends spare theoretical canons. The value of a national language (PTH) in standardized form is always closely identified with an exuberant nationalism which pictures a victorious revolutionary China casting off the shackles and constraints of the past and rising, phoenix-like, toward new heights of national purpose, unity, and accomplishment. In this titanic struggle, the lack of a national standard language is considered a major inconvenience, restricting the mobility of personnel in government, party, and military jobs, limiting the efficiency of national forms of communication, and prejudicing the success of the educational system (Lwó and Lyǔ 1956:5). Some of the specific targets of standardization policy, such as motion picture studios and writers that place undue reliance on local dialect forms and thereby compromise the intelligibility of their work for national audiences, have already been mentioned. Lexical diversity in printed form became a source of difficulty in schools when textbooks written in one place proved unusable in another (SCD 1956:229). This would have been confusing for students and teachers alike, for as a rule the language of instruction

in classrooms was the same as that of the local dialect (Lwó and Lyǔ 1956:8).

One other consideration has been cited in support of the PTH and standardization policy. It was once maintained that further practical efforts to implement a phonetic orthography to replace characters must wait the emergence of a single language medium available to all. This point cannot be pursued within the limitations of this paper, except to say that there is considerable doubt whether this argument has much force for the foreseeable future (cf. Leslie 1963:324). Today, a decade and a half after its adoption, public, as opposed to educational, applications of the pīn-yīn system remain minimal. Familiarity with it, especially among youth, seems to be negligible. There are strong indications that the government has decided to defer indefinitely further consideration of a phonetic orthography: Premier Jōu Ēn-lái has himself said privately that there will be no government initiatives along these lines for at least another generation (Fujiyama 1971).

6. Agencies responsible for policy implementation. The need for an organization with authority to deal with the myriad lexical problems associated with standardization, including the treatment of dialect and foreign loans, classicisms, and even commercial product designations, was recognized in one of the small group discussions at the 1955 Standardization Conference (SCD 1956:230). In some limited areas standardization instrumentalities have been created to achieve program goals, but it is difficult to learn much about the full scope of their mandate or the effectiveness of their activities.

By reason of its very practical contribution, probably no agency is as valuable to the process of language standardization in China as radio. The acceptance of Peking Radio as the embodiment of PTH has developed informally, but it apparently enjoys unanimous support in the language community. As those who have listened to it are aware, this is partly because Peking Radio does not broadcast with a voice identical with that of native Peking speakers. This in effect gives it a national, rather than a dialectal, appeal.

In addition to acting as a key operational link in the implementation of standardization policy, Peking Radio also performs a quasi-judicial role in conjunction with the CAS Linguistic Research Unit [Jūng-gwó kē-sywé-ywàn yán-jyōu-swò]. Together these two agencies have enunciated the working principle that whatever is spoken sufficiently often soon becomes habitualized and accepted (Dīng Yí-lán 1956:143). One manifestation of this cooperation--the evolution of program policy with regard to -er-ized final syllables--has been mentioned earlier. It is conceivable that a large number of confusing linguistic problems confronted in standardizing modern

Chinese--double and homophonous readings, the mix between dialect and northern forms, and the criteria for admitting classical expressions--have been handled in this essentially ad hoc fashion. Finally, radio programmers frequently exercise their mandate as national broadcasters by editing out lexical matter peculiar to Peking and not likely to be understood elsewhere. The agency has at other times informally assumed the role of national lexicographer in resolving questions of conflicting pronunciations. In many cases it relies, in addition, on listener responses in distinguishing accepted colloquial pronunciations from obsolete citation forms still preserved in dictionaries (Dīng Yî-lán 1956:143).

The relationship between the Linguistic Research Unit and Peking Radio, however, remains an informal one. The Linguistic Research Unit does not carry any specific responsibility for executing standardization objectives. Rather, its activities are almost entirely devoted to research on the Chinese language (KMJP 1/30/57). In 1956, for example, its six-man staff was concentrating chiefly on topics related to Chinese grammar, literature, and dialect surveys. On occasion the Unit also sponsors seminars for members of the language community to facilitate intellectual exchange and discussion of specific subjects (cf. KMJP 5/30/55).

According to the report of the Soviet lexicographer I. M. Oshanin at the 1955 Standardization Conference, after the October Revolution in Russia a special committee was established to codify approved technical terminologies and publish them for national consumption (Oshanin 1956:103). Oshanin noted that such an agency was already at work in China, referring apparently to the Bureau of Compilation and Translation [Jūng-gwó kē-sywé-ywàn yán-jyōu-swŏ], a part of the Chinese Academy of Sciences since its inception in 1949. The bureau, in addition to editing and publishing scientific journals, was charged also with the responsibility for coordinating decisions relating to the usage of scientific terminology in a number of technical fields (Jîng Ywán 1950:923). The work of standardizing technical terms was eventually organized under a separate unit within the bureau, the Terminology Section [Míng-tsź shŕ] (SD 1957:225). The history and effectiveness of this agency before 1956 remains somewhat obscure. One news item refers to a 1954 publication of the Terminology Section giving Russian, English, and Chinese equivalents in chemical engineering, and claims that over four hundred new terms had been created by the agency in the course of adopting foreign loans (KMJP 8/5/64). Work in this area continued throughout the 1950s, producing two additional compilations--one in 1955, and another in 1959--in organic chemical compounds (KMJP 5/29/63).

In June of 1956, prompted perhaps by a heightened interest in the standardization question, the Chinese Academy of Sciences appears to have reorganized this agency as the Committee on Translation and Publications [Jūng-gwó kē-sywé-ywàn byān-yî chū-bǎn wěi-ywǎn-hwèi]. A major function of this reconstituted department involved increasing the availability of significant contributions to the sciences written originally in foreign languages (KMJP 5/20/56). Its authority for establishing terminological conventions was also renewed at that time; but according to Lyóu Dzé-syān, a frequent contributor to the discussion about standardization in the sciences, the importance attached to its mandate in this area now supersedes that of its publishing activities (KMJP 5/29/63).

The subsequent record of the Committee on Translation and Publications, while admittedly fragmentary, nonetheless suggests that its work met with pervasive indifference. It is true that an official bulletin issued just weeks after the Committee's establishment laid claim to prodigious activity over a wide front (PCJP 8/14/57). And it may have met with some success in encouraging editors and publishers of scientific literature to make better use of existing reference aids and to solicit the assistance of those with appropriate expertise when the occasion demanded (KMJP 12/17/57). Part of the motivation for these promising initiatives, however, springs from a continuing sense of frustration with those whose cooperation is not forthcoming. An open letter published at this time by the Committee's Terminology Section is illustrative of the problem. It reveals a demoralized agency whose efforts are ignored by the very professionals and institutions it is supposed to serve (KMJP 1/4/57). The letter complained that opinion surveys instituted on proposed new terminology often went unanswered, while one plan for unifying terminology in chemistry and physics yielded only a half dozen replies in as many months.

It is hard to reconcile the attitude expressed by the Committee with the frequent charges made during this period and into the early 1960s that the work of standardizing scientific terminology had not progressed satisfactorily. It is often difficult to judge how much of the criticism has substance and how much springs from impatience with the unevenness or the tempo of accomplishments. Some of it emanates from individuals in the scientific community who urge the adoption of the national phonetic annotation system [pīn-yīn] for terminology in the sciences, arguing that only by bringing Chinese usage into closer conformity with internationally accepted conventions can this part of the lexicon be put on a rational basis. On the other hand, some dissatisfaction with standardization activity is factual and cannot be casually dismissed. One instance pertains to the two compilations on organic chemical compounds noted earlier. Comparing the terminology in these two volumes published just four years apart, Lyóu Dzé-syān found that only about 22 per cent of the items were the same, while nearly 45 per cent were entirely different (KMJP 5/29/63). Terminological differences of this magnitude, if not uncommon, entail obvious and serious consequences for related activities such as indexing, cataloguing, and information retrieval, not to mention losses in efficiency and overall convenience.

Occasional and isolated sources suggest that the work of standardizing usages may have been shared by other groups. One of these, working on technical terminologies in general Jĕng-wù-ywàn sywé-shù mǐng-tsź tǔng-yī gūng-dzwò wĕi-ywán-hwèi, was reported active in the early 1950s (Lyóu Dzé-syān 1953:19). Still more vague is an ambiguous reference from the same period to a study committee on chemical terminology Hwà-sywé mǐng-tsź yán-jyōu wĕi-ywán-hwèi (Tsău Bwó-hán 1953:7). No other information about either group has been obtained, suggesting that they were perhaps transient organizations or, alternately, synonyms in the writers' minds for the CAS Bureau of Compilation and Translation. Finally, responsibility for standardization in the military was assigned to army schools and training sections (CFCP 11/11/55).

7. Conclusion. Some features of standardization remain much better understood than others. There is quite a lot of discussion in the early and middle 1950s about a variety of specific linguistic problems and alternatives proposed for their solution. The Standardization Conference, convened in 1955, created a platform from which the language community could address themselves to these issues and improve the level of public awareness of the government's policy.

Far less is known about the formal apparatus organized to implement these policies. A rather broad mandate has been given to communications and cultural media, as well as to professional writers, to define and contribute to the shape of the national language. The role assigned to them appears not too different from that which Joos ascribed to the publishing media in this country (Joos 1960:252).

Least well documented are those bodies apparently responsible for insuring the unification of technical terminologies. It is not even obvious whether there is more than one of these and, if more than one, how their authority is distributed. As for the effectiveness of such bodies, it is worth mentioning that difficulties in winning acceptance for standardization products have not been unique to the mainland. There are indications that some of the situations described above have their counterparts in Taiwan, and perhaps for the same reasons. The former Director of the Institute of Compilation and Translation in Taiwan, for example, acknowledged that in some of the word lists prepared by his organization, more than one translation equivalent occurs--a practice which reflects and perpetuates, rather than resolves, competing usages (Lyóu Two 1970). If this early practice was carried over into post-war mainland publications, it could help to explain the persistent criticism that technical terms continue unstandardized. Moreover, there are scholars working in social science disciplines on Taiwan who will concede privately that the voluminous word lists prepared by the Institute go largely unread, primarily because authors and teachers, once familar with the foreign language in which loan terms originate, tend to use the original form rather than the loan. Determining whether these same kinds of problems confront language planners on the mainland and, if so, how they propose to deal with them, are important questions for future study. Once the flow of information and academics improves, the answers to them will not be far away.

REFERENCES

Běi-jǐng dà-sywé. 1957. Běi-jǐng dà-sywé Jūng-gwó yǔ-yán wén-sywé syì yǔ-yán-sywé Hàn-yǔ jyàu-yán-shř. Wén-sywé yǔ-yán wèn-tí tǎu-lwùn-jí (Essays on problems of the written language. Běi-jǐng, Wén-dž gǎi-gé chū-bǎn-shè.

Byān-yì gwǎn. 1969. Gwó-lì byān-yì gwǎn gài-kwàng (Report of the National Institute of Compilation and Translation for 1969). Táipěi, Táiwān.

CFCP. Jyě-fàng jyūn-bàu (The Liberation Army Newspaper).

ChCJP. Cháng-jyāng ř-bàu (Yáng-dž River Daily News).

Ching, Eugene. 1966. Translation or transliteration: A case in cultural borrowing. Chinese Culture. 7(2).107-18.

_____. 1969. Dissyllabicity of modern mandarin. Chinese Culture. 10(4).88-104.

Chyū Chyōu-bái. 1931. Lwó-mǎ-dž de Jūng-gwó-wén hǎi-shř ròu-má-dž Jūng-gwó-wén? (Romanized Chinese or Chinese based on the awkward traditional character script?). In: Ní Hǎi-shǔ, ed., Jūng-gwó yǔ-wén de syīn-shēng (The rebirth of the Chinese language). Shànghǎi, Shř-dài chū-bǎn-shè, 1949, 29-47.

CSP. Jyàu-shr bàu (Teachers' Journal).

DeFrancis, John. 1943. The alphabetization of Chinese. Journal of the American Oriental Society. 63(4).225-40.

Dǐng Yì-lán. 1956. Gwān-yú syàn-dài Hàn-yǔ gwēi-fàn wèn-tí de yì-syē yì-jyàn (Some ideas about problems of standardizing modern Chinese). In: SCD 1956:142-47.

Dzēng Jàu-lwùn. 1953. Kē-sywé míng-tsź jūng de dzàu dž wèn-tí (Problems of creating characters in scientific terminology). Jūng-gwó yǔ-wén. 14.3-4.

Fāng Shř-dwó. 1965. Wǔ-shř nyán lái Jūng-gwó gwó-yǔ yùn-dung
shř (The history of the Chinese national language movement in
the past fifty years). Tái-běi, Gwó-yǔ ř-bàu shè.
Ferguson, Charles A. 1962. The language factor in national
development. Anthropological Linguistics. 4(1).23-27.
Fujiyama, Aiichiro. 1971. Correspondence with the Honorable
Fujiyama Aiichiro, Member of the Diet for Kanagawa Prefecture,
May 7, 1971. Translated by Okagawa Nagao. Fujiyama spoke
with Premier Jōu Ēn-lái during a visit to Peking in April.
Gāu Míng-kǎi and Lyóu Jěng-tán. 1958. Syàn-dài Hàn-yǔ wài-lái
tsź yán-jyōu (Study of borrowings into modern Chinese). Běi-
jīng, Wén-dž gǎi-gé chū-bǎn-shè.
Haugen, Einar. 1966. Linguistics and language planning. In:
William Bright, ed., Sociolinguistics. Proceedings of the UCLA
Sociolinguistics Conference, 1964. The Hague, Mouton and Co.
50-71.
Jāng Syī-rwò. 1956. Dà-lì twéi-gwǎng yǐ Běi-jīng yǔ-yīn wéi byāu-
jwǔn yīn de pǔ-tūng-hwà (Energetically promote the common lan-
guage using the sound system of Peking as the standard phonology).
In: SCD 1956:276-82.
Jàu Ywá-rèn. 1943. Languages and dialects in China. The
Geographical Journal. 102.63-66.
Jīng Ywán. 1950. Jǐ kē-sywé-ywàn kwò-dà ywàn-wù hwèi-yǐ
(Records of the meeting for expanding the activities of the
Chinese Academy of Sciences). Syīn-hwá ywè-bàu. 2(4).923-24.
JMJP. Rén-mín ř-bàu (People's Daily).
Jōu Dzǔ-mwó. 1957. Tsúng wén-sywé yǔ-yán de gǎi-nyàn lwùn
Hàn-yǔ de yǎ-yán, wén-yán, gǔ-wén děng wèn-tí (A discussion of
the archaic language, the classical language, the classical com-
mon language, and other problems from the point of view of the
written language). In: Běi-jīng dà-sywé Jūng-gwó yǔ-yán wén-
sywé syì Hàn-yǔ jyàu-yán-shř, comp. Wén-sywé yǔ-yán wèn-tí
tǎu-lwùn-jí (Essays on problems of the written language).
Běi-jīng, Wén-dž gǎi-gé chū-bǎn-shè.
Jōu Ēn-lái et al. 1958. Dāng-chyán wén-dž gǎi-gé de rèn-we hé
Hàn-yǔ pīn-yīn fāng-àn (The current tasks of reforming the
written language and the draft scheme for a Chinese phonetic
alphabet). Běi-jīng, Wén-dž gǎi-gé chū-bǎn-shè.
Jōu Yǒu-gwāng. 1965. Yǒu-gwān Hàn-dž gǎi-gé de kē-sywé yán-
jyōu (Scientific research on orthographic reform). Jūng-gwó
yǔ-wén. 134.21-27.
Jōu Yàu-wén. 1956. Hàn-yǔ pīn-yīn wén-dž de byāu-jwǔn yīn wèn-tí
(The problem of standard phonology in the Han language phonetic
system). In: Wáng Lì et al. 1956:29-32.

Joos, Martin. 1960. Review of Axel Wijk. Regularized English. Stockholm, Almqvist S. Wiksel, 1949. In: Language. 36.250-62.

KMJP. Gwāng-mǐng r̄-bàu (Kuang-ming Daily News).

Leslie, D. 1963. Review of Paul L.-M. Serruys, Survey of the Chinese language reform and the anti-illiteracy movement in Communist China. Studies in Chinese Communist Terminology, No. 8. Institute of International Studies, University of California. Berkeley, Center for Chinese Studies, 1962. In: Monumenta Serica. 22, Fasc. 1.322-24.

Lǐ Fāng-gwèi. 1937. Languages and dialects. In: The Chinese yearbook. Shanghai, The Commercial Press, Ltd. 59-65.

Lǐn Táu. 1957. Gwān-yú Hàn-yǔ gwēi-fàn-hwà wèn-tí (Problems of standardization). In: Běi-jīng dà-sywé Jūng-gwó yǔ-yán wén-sywé syì Hàn-yǔ jyàu-yán-shř, comp. Wén-sywé yǔ-yán wèn-tí tǎu-lwùn-jì (Essays on problems of the written language). Běi-jīng, Wén-dž gǎi-gé chū-bǎn-shè.

Lù Dzūng-dá. 1956. Gwān-yú yǔ-fǎ gwēi-fàn-hwà de wèn-tí (About problems in standardizing grammar). In: SCD 1956.69-72.

Lù Jř-wéi. 1956a. Gwān-yú Běi-jīng-hwà yǔ-yīn syì-tǔng de yì-syē wèn-tí (Problems in Peking phonology). In: SCD 1956.48-68.

_____. 1956b. Dzài fāng-yán fǔ-dzá de chǐng-sying syà, pīn-yīn wén-dž néng syīng-de-tūng ma? (Can an alphabetic script succeed in a complex dialect situation?). In: Wǎng Lì et al. 1956.106-10.

Lwó Cháng-péi. 1952. Tsúng Sž-dà-lǐn de yǔ-yán sywé-shwō tán Jūng-gwó yǔ-yán-sywé-shàng jǐ-ge wèn-tí (A discussion of some problems in Chinese linguistics in terms of Stalinist linguistics). Kē-sywé tūng-bàu. 421-26.

_____ and Lyǔ Shú-syāng. 1956. Syàn-dài Hàn-yǔ gwēi-fàn wèn-tí (Problems in standardizing modern Chinese). In: SCD 1956.4-22.

Lyóu Dzé-syān. 1953. Tsúng kē-sywé sym̄ mǐngtsź de fǎn-yì kàn Hàn-dž de chywē-dyǎn (Disadvantages of characters from the point of view of translating new terminology in the sciences). In: Jūng-gwó yǔ-wén. 14.9-13.

Lyóu Fù. 1925. Les Mouvements de la Langue Nationale en Chine. Pekin, Presses de L'université nationale de Pékin.

Lyóu Two. 1970. Conversation with Lyou Two, Director of the National Institute for Compilation and Translation, February 3, 1970.

Máu Dzé-dūng. 1964. Fǎn-dwèi dǎng bā-gǔ (Against archaism in the party). In: Máu Dzé-dūng hsǔan-chǐ (Selected works of Mao Tse-tung). Běi-jīng, Rén-mín chū-bǎn-shè.

Meng, S. M. 1962. The Tsungli Yamen: Its organization and functions. Cambridge, Mass., Harvard University Press.

Míng-tsź dzwò-tán-hwèi. 1953. Běn-shè jyǔ-syíng sywé-shù
yǐ-míng wèn-tí dzwò-tán-hwèi (Seminar on problems of adapting
foreign terminologies). Jūng-gwó yǔ-wén. 14.33.
Oshanin, E. M. 1956. Gwān-yú wén-sywé yǔ-yán gwēi-fàn-hwà de
jǐ-ge wèn-tí (Some problems in standardizing the written language). In: SCD 1956.98-105.
PCJP. Běi-jīng r̃-bàu (Peking Daily News).
PTH Cháng-shr̃. 1957. Pǔ-tūng-hwà cháng-shr̃ (What everyone
should know about common speech). Běi-jīng, Wén-dž gǎi-gé
chū-bǎn-shè.
SCD. 1956. Syàn-dài Hàn-yǔ gwēi-fàn wèn-tí sywé-shù hwèi-yì
mì-shū-chǔ, comp. Syàn-dài Hàn-yǔ gwēi-fàn wèn-tí sywé-shù
hwèi-yì wèn-jyàn hwèi-byān (Collected documents of the con-
ference on problems of standardization in modern Chinese).
Běi-jīng, Kē-sywé chū-bǎn-shè.
SD. 1957. Chywán-gwó wén-dž gǎi-gé hwèi-yì mì-shū-chǔ, comp.
Dì-yí-tsż chywán-gwó wén-dž gǎi-gé hwèi-yì wén-jyàn hwèi-byān
(Collected documents of the first national conference on the re-
form of the written language). Běi-jīng, Wén-dž gǎi-gé chū-bǎn-
shè.
Stalin, J. 1954. Marxism and problems of linguistics. Moscow,
Foreign Languages Publishing House.
Syāu Jǎng. 1956. Lywè tán syàn-dài Hàn-yǔ tsź-hwèi gwēi-fàn
wèn-tí (Brief remarks on some problems in standardizing the
Chinese lexicon). In: SCD 1956.211-15.
Syīn Wén-dž. 1931. Jūng-gwó syīn-wén-dž shŕ-sān ywán-dzé
(Thirteen point proposal for the new Chinese writing). In:
Nǐ Hǎi-shǔ, ed., Jūng-gwó yǔ-wén de syīn-shēng (The rebirth
of the Chinese language). Shàng-hǎi, Shŕ-dài chū-bǎn-shè.
Tsáu Bwó-hán. 1952. Jūng-gwó wén-dž de yǎn-byàn (The historical
development of the Chinese written language). Third ed. rev.
Běi-jīng, Sān-lyán shū-jyú.
_____. 1953. Hwà-sywé míng-tsź mén-wài tán (A layman's view
of chemical terminology). Jūng-gwó yǔ-wén. 14.5-8.
_____. 1954. Yǔ-wén wèn-tí píng-lwùn-jí (Critical essays on lan-
guage problems). Shàng-hǎi, Dūng-fāng shū-dyàn.
Twō Mù. 1954. Tsúng yǔ-yì-sywé de gwān-dyǎn lái kàn pīn-yīn
syíng-shēng dž wèn-tí (A critique of the new phonetic compounds
from the point of view of semantics). Jūng-gwó yǔ-wén. 20.3-8.
Wáng Lì. 1954. Lwùn Hàn-dzú byāu-jwǔn-yǔ (On the standard language of the Chinese people). Jūng-gwó yǔ-wén. 24.13-19.
_____. 1956. Gwǎng-dūng-rén dzěn-ma-yàng sywé-syí pǔ-tūng-hwà
(How can those in Kuang-tung Province learn the national language).
Běi-jīng, Wén-hwà jyàu-yù chū-bǎn-shè.

Wáng Lǐ et al. 1956. Hàn-dzú de gùng-túng yǔ hé byāu-jwǔn yīn (Standard phonology and the common language of the Chinese people). Běi-jīng, Jūng-hwá shū-jyú.

Wright, Stanley F. 1950. Hart and the Chinese customs. Belfast, William Mullan and Son Publishers, Ltd.

Ywan Han-ching. 1953. Tsúng hwà-sywé wù-jr̀ de mìng-míng kàn fāng-kwài Hài-dž de chywē-dyǎn (Disadvantages of characters for establishing terminology for chemical substances). In: Jūng-gwó yǔ-wén. 10.16-18.

Ywán Jyā-hwá. 1960. Hàn-yǔ fāng-yán gài-yàu (Outline of Chinese dialects). Běi-jīng, Wén-dž gǎi-gé chū-bǎn-shè.

MASS OPINION ON LANGUAGE POLICY: THE CASE OF CANADA

JONATHAN POOL

State University of New York at Stony Brook

1. Theorists of language planning have recognized the need for popular support if government language policies are to be implemented. This recognition is evident, for example, in the components of language planning enumerated by Einar Haugen (Language, 1966: 18 and Dialect, 1966) and by Joshua A. Fishman et al., (1971:293, 299-302); but, as the latter also caution, 'The entire process of implementation has been least frequently studied in prior investigations of language planning' (Fishman et al. 1971:299).

Mass attitudes can be viewed as playing two crucial roles in the implementation of language planning. First, in all situations, mass attitudes will have an effect on the degree to which policies calling for changes in mass language behavior are implemented, once adopted by governmental authorities. And second, in certain situations, mass opinions will have an effect on the initial official adoption of various language policies. Situations of the latter sort presumably exist whenever two conditions are fulfilled: (1) the country is governed by competitively elected officials and has a tradition of respect for mass opinion, and (2) the issue of language policy is one of the salient political issues discussed by the mass media of the country at the time. Under these conditions there will be mass opinions on language policy, and these opinions will have some significant effect on policy adoption or nonadoption.

2. A good example of a situation fulfilling these conditions is contemporary Canada. Governed at the federal and provincial levels by legislatures constituted in multi-party elections, Canada has no perenially dominant party and by now has a tradition of competition for popular support. Generally considered a country in which economic class is a fairly unimportant political factor, Canada's most serious problem--and an increasingly serious one--from before its confederation in 1867 until the present, has been relations between its two 'founding races' (Alford 1963: Chap. 5 and 9; Underhill 1964: 2 and 47). The quest for a public policy that would resolve hostilities and grievances between English Canadians and French Canadians reached such an intensity in the 1960s that the federal government appointed and richly funded a Royal Commission on Bilingualism and Biculturalism. The mandate and the subsequent recommendations of the Commission both reflected and augmented public concern with an unsatisfactory and ill-defined linguistic regime, as well as a belief that linguistic policies could indeed go far toward ameliorating English-French relations. If anything, the mid-1960s were the high point of preoccupation with linguistic engineering in Canada; for by the end of the decade the issue had escalated and sovereignty for a state of Quebec, not just equality for the French in Canada, was a seriously debated question.

Even if the aforementioned (and now disbanded) Royal Commission's conciliatory recommendations become casualties of the renewed tension between Quebec separatism and English Canadian backlash, the Commission will have performed an undeniable and enormous service by the information and knowledge which it has generated. Considered by some to have been a multi-million dollar pork barrel for the social sciences, the Commission sponsored a total of 146 research projects, including case studies, surveys, and histories, above and beyond its own extensive hearings. [1] Two of the most potentially useful projects were national sample surveys of the Canadian population, one of adults (using interviews) and the other of teenagers (using self-administered questionnaires), conducted in May of 1965.

Unlike any other survey ever conducted in any country of which I am aware, these surveys combined the following characteristics:

(1) they reached large numbers of respondents, thus permitting more refined analysis than the usual simple frequency distributions and uncontrolled cross-tabulations: the adult survey returned 4,071 completed schedules, and the youth survey 1,365;

(2) they oversampled the regional minorities heavily enough to permit controlled analysis for these minorities (English

in Quebec, French elsewhere), not only for the population as a whole;

(3) they collected information about respondents' opinions on a substantial range of language policy issues; and

(4) they collected considerable additional linguistic information about the respondents, including their language backgrounds, experiences, competences, behaviors, and attitudes. In all, the adult survey contains about 260 items of information, and the youth survey about 185, for each respondent.

Many caveats are in order for him who would interpret or rely on these surveys. There are reasons to doubt the veracity of any verbal interview or self-administered questionnaire, in the first place. There is also evidence that unsophisticated respondents are not reliable reporters of their own linguistic competence and behavior. And in addition, there is some reason to believe that the adult survey responses were somewhat distorted in the coding or punching process. [2] But given the current absence of alternatives, I shall not bother you with complaints that the best is not good enough. Rather let us now, with appropriate caution, take one of the topics illuminated by these surveys and see what knowledge they can provide thereon.

3. For argument's sake let us say that there are two ways to explain the opinion of a given individual on a given policy. First, we can subsume this fact (i.e. his opinion) under a generalization to the effect that the same individual will have predictably different opinions about policies which differ in particular ways. And second, we can also explain an opinion on a policy by generalizations that different individuals having particular different characteristics will also differ in a predictable fashion in their opinions on policies of a particular type. The Royal Commission surveys permit us to explore how opinions on language policy differ, both across policies and across individuals.

In a truly bipolarized situation, proposed language policies would be evaluated according to their expected effect on the balance of privileges and burdens between the two groups, and each member of one group would support all policies favoring it and oppose all policies favoring the other group. Such situations have been described as existing in numerous countries (Rabushka and Shepsle forthcoming); but opinions on language policy in Canada, as revealed by the Royal Commission adult survey, definitely did not fit this pattern. Of the proposed or suggested policies enquired about, some were supported overwhelmingly, others received mixed support, and others were largely rejected among those who would presumably stand to lose from these policies if their effect on the English-French balance of forces were the guide.

The most consensual proposed concession among the English Canadians was that of making the federal government accessible to the people in both English and French. This policy, if implemented, would shift the status quo toward greater indulgence for speakers of French; but 81 per cent of the monolingual English-speaking respondents supported it.[3] Close behind in popularity was the proposed policy of teaching French to English-speaking children in Canadian schools, receiving support from 75 per cent of the monolingual English speakers. The same percentage supported the idea that it would be 'good' (no sanctions for noncompliance) if all Canadians spoke both English and French.

Not all concessionary policies were consensually popular among English-speaking monolinguals, however. Although equal access to the federal government was willingly granted, only 53 per cent favored the policy of making English and French the official languages of all the provincial governments. And while three-fourths of the monolingual English speakers were willing to have English-speaking children learn French in school, only 51 per cent agreed that persons working in a company where the majority were French Canadian should themselves learn French if they did not know it already.[4]

Finally, some proposed language policies offered concessions to the speakers of French that only a minority of monolingual English speakers were willing to endorse. Just 26 per cent agreed that English Canadians should speak French when they are in the province of Quebec. And access to service in French in stores, restaurants, and other public accommodations for French Canadians was considered a justified French Canadian want by only 16 per cent of the English monolinguals.

Among the monolingual English-speaking respondents, then, support for concessionary language policies ranged from more than three-fourths to under one-fourth. The obligation to learn French was accepted most readily on behalf of the next generation and least often in situations (such as inter-provincial travel) where the respondents would see themselves disadvantaged. And the right of French speakers to be served in French was accorded by a large majority for the federal government, by about one-half for the provincial governments, and by only one-fourth for privately owned public accommodations.

A similar pattern emerges for monolingual French speakers vis-à-vis policies of concession to English. Given the nature of the status quo, the spirit of the times, and the policy orientations of the Royal Commission, however, there is not a corresponding policy of

FIGURE 1. Opinions of monolinguals on policies of language-
learning using obligation.

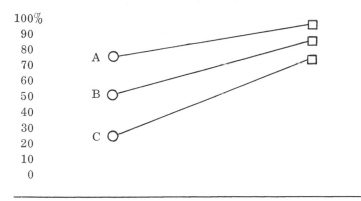

Percentage agreeing that:

A = Your group's children should learn the other language in
    school.
B = Your group's members should learn the other language if
    most speak it at work.
C = Your group's members should use the other language
    when in any province where most speak it.
◯ = English monolinguals   ☐ = French monolinguals

concession to English mentioned for each question about a concession
to French.

The proposals for equal access to the federal government for,
adoption by provincial governments of, and the desirability of all
Canadians being able to speak, both languages were, from the point
of view of French Canadians, no concessions at all, so it is not surprising that these policies were favored by 98 per cent, 97 per cent,
and 99 per cent of the monolingual French-speaking respondents,
respectively. On the other hand, this finding is not trivial either.
Given the legendary devotion of the French Canadian people to
la survivance, are we to suppose that the nearly unanimous belief
in universal Canadian bilingualism reflects an understanding, with
Lieberson, that bilingualism need not lead to assimilation? (Lieberson 1970:Chap. 6-8).

The most willingly accepted concessionary policy among the monolingual French was that French-speaking children should learn English
in school, a proposal supported by 96 per cent. Like their English-
speaking counterparts, fewer approved the principle that employees

not speaking English should learn it if the majority in their company was English Canadian; but the approval rate was still 88 per cent. Fewer, but still 72 per cent, agreed that French Canadians should speak English everywhere in Canada except Quebec.

As might be expected, both language groups, in their frequencies of support, ranked these three proposed policies of language-learning obligation in the same order.[5] But the differences in support for the three policies were much greater among the speakers of English than among the speakers of French. What is most interesting is that a large majority of the French monolinguals were willing to accept every one of the concessionary policies. They exhibited the typical response pattern not of a group in revolt, but of a subservient group: glad to greet any concessions from the dominant group, but also willing to grant it a much more generous definition of justice than it is willing to grant in return.

The policies which were agreed to by large majorities of the English speakers were also agreed to by even larger majorities of those speaking French, but not vice versa. This means that there was substantial English-French consensus on at least some set of policies, including:

(1) that all citizens of Canada should be able to deal with the federal government in either English or French, whichever they choose;
(2) that English-speaking and French-speaking children should be taught French and English, respectively, in school; and
(3) that all Canadians should (ideally) be able to speak both English and French.

Thus the elements of this consensus include forms of both individual bilingualism and state bilingualism.

4. Beyond this consensus, we have also discovered much dissensus--both within each language group and between the two groups. Let us conclude by testing a couple of explanations for the different opinions held by different respondents on the same policies. Much social analysis, of course, does just this, resorting to socioeconomic status, religion, party affiliation, age, sex, and many other characteristics to explain and predict opinions. This brief report, however, will examine (cursorily at that) just two out of the many such questions that might be asked: they deal with language competence and with ethnic environment.

If we define the language repertoire of an individual as the set of all languages and language varieties in which he has any competence, plus the respective competences that he has in them, an analogous concept suggests itself in the realm of language policy. The language policy repertoire of an individual could be defined as the set of all language policies on which he has any opinion, plus the respective opinions which he has on them. The question then arises as to whether the language repertoires and the language policy repertoires of individuals tend to be associated. And the answer to this question is both yes and no.

Neglecting for the present purpose those few Canadians who speak neither English nor French as a principal home language, we can locate every respondent on some point of an English-French linguistic continuum. On one end of this continuum are those speaking English as a principal home language but having no competence in French. On the other end are those with French as a principal home language but having no competence in English. These two extremes are almost the same as the groups earlier referred to as English and French monolinguals, respectively.[6] Half-way between these extremes are those who have both English and French as principal home languages. On either side of this midpoint, arrayed in order of their competence in the second language, are those who speak one of the two as a principal home language and have some, but not native, competence in the other.

If the respondents are ordered on such a continuum, there are some policies receiving close to equal support from all points on it, and other policies for which support varies markedly along the continuum. In general, two fairly consistent patterns emerge.

(1) Those policies which were largely consensual among both groups of monolinguals show only moderate or no variation along the continuum, and the variation which does exist tends to be confined to the half of the continuum where English is the home language.

(2) Those policies on which either or both groups of monolinguals were split, or on which the two groups differed, show strong variation along the continuum, and this variation tends to be monotonic rather than peaked.

For example, both monolingual groups were largely agreed that it would be good if all Canadians were bilingual. On the language continuum, the percentage agreeing with this proposition rises slowly from 74 on the English-only end to 97 in the middle, and then remains at between 97 and 99 all across the French side. A similar pattern exists for the policy of making citizen contact with the federal government possible in either language.

On more divisive issues, however, those in the midpoint of the continuum are also closer to the middle of the support range, rather

FIGURE 2. Language repertoire and language policy repertoire.

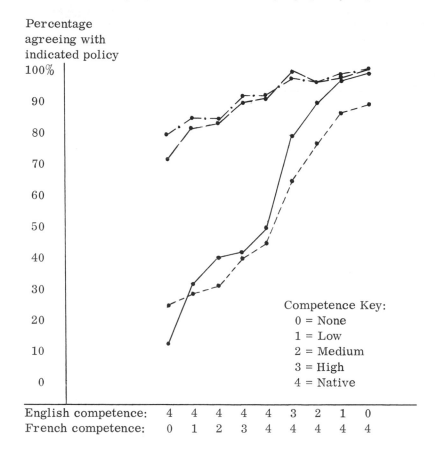

Percentage
agreeing with
indicated policy

| English competence: | 4 | 4 | 4 | 4 | 4 | 3 | 2 | 1 | 0 |
| French competence: | 0 | 1 | 2 | 3 | 4 | 4 | 4 | 4 | 4 |

Competence Key:
    0 = None
    1 = Low
    2 = Medium
    3 = High
    4 = Native

Policy Key:

— · —   Should be possible to deal with federal government in either English or French.

— —   Good if all Canadians could speak English and French.

– – – –   English Canadians should speak French in Quebec.

————   French Canadians should be able to be served in French in stores, etc.

than on the edge of a French opinion plateau. The most divisive issues were over proposed policies that would force English speakers to use (more than to learn) French. The percentage agreeing that English Canadians should speak French when in Quebec rises sharply from 26 per cent on the English extreme, through 46 per cent in the bilingual middle, to 88 per cent on the French end. There is a similar and even steeper incline from 16 per cent through 50 per cent to 97 per cent on the question of whether French Canadians are right in wanting to be served in French in public accommodations.

Of these two patterns, the former is consistent with the findings of earlier research on the same data, namely that while social and economic 'activity' tends to vary more with second-language competence in English among speakers of French than with competence in French among English-speakers, cultural 'attitudes' tend to be associated with competence in exactly the opposite way (Pool 1971). [7] The second pattern, of steep monotonic variation, is significant in that it fails to reveal the presence of a distinct group of bilinguals with separate policy interests. Given the speculation and findings of other scholars about the 'linguistic schizophrenia' and other conditions uniquely characterizing bilingual individuals, and given the fact that the Canadian surveys themselves reveal some other attitudes on which bilinguals tend to respond one way and both English and French monolinguals another way, the monotonic pattern found here on language policy questions was not a foregone result. [8] We find, then, that several language policies, especially those which arouse disagreement between English and French Canadians, evoke considerable differences in support among those with different language repertoires, most consistently among English speakers with different levels of competence in French.

This association between language repertoire and language policy repertoire is of special import given the fact that language repertoire is closely associated with ethnic environment. On the basis of what has been found we must expect that, on an important selection of language-policy issues, those who live amidst members of the other language group are more likely to agree with policies benefiting that group than are those living in comparatively segregated environments, since those surrounded by members of the other language group are more likely to have high competence in the other language. This expectation is confirmed by the data.

If we compare responses in polling districts where one-fourth or less of the names on the electoral lists were French with responses in districts where three-fourths or more of the names were French, we see that for almost every policy a larger proportion of the English speakers favored a pro-French policy in the high-French districts than in the low-French districts. Likewise, French-speaking respondents favored pro-English policies more frequently in high-English districts. The differences are, as one would expect, especially strong for the dissensual policies, such as (for English speakers) whether French Canadians should have a right to service in French in public accommodations.

If familiarity breeds contempt, the Royal Commission surveys do not show it. Even on the question of whether English Canadians should use French when in Quebec, a considerably higher percentage of monolingual English speakers living in Quebec itself supported this principle than of monolingual English speakers outside Quebec-- in spite of the fact that those in Quebec who agreed with this policy could easily be interpreted as declaring themselves personae non gratae.

As opposed to a pattern of polarization in which those who live in closest contact with other groups oppose them the most, the Canadian pattern seems to be one of attitudinal buffering, at least on language policy: those with the most irreconcilable policy opinions are geographically the farthest removed from each other. This distribution of mass opinions is undoubtedly an important asset to those, represented by the Royal Commission, who hope to use creative language planning to salvage coexistence in Canada.

NOTES

[1]See the annotated list of studies in Appendix V of Report of the Royal Commission on Bilingualism and Biculturalism, vol. 1.201-12. The products of this work have been appearing under three serial titles: Report, Studies, and Documents, respectively, of the Royal Commission on Bilingualism and Biculturalism.

[2]See, e.g. Blalock 1970:47-51; Fishman 1969:5-11; Fishman and Terry 1969:636-50; Lieberson 1970:17-20; and Pool 1971:218-19. The latter study is based on the same data but does not consider attitudes toward language policy.

[3]This and subsequent percentages are based on the total of those giving definite answers. The sample has not been reweighted to provide estimates of the responses that an unstratified random sample would have given, for reasons explained in Pool 1971:75-76. By monolingual English speakers I refer to those whose principal home language was English and claimed to speak no French.

[4]An additional 13 per cent agreed to such a principle if it were limited to the province of Quebec.

[5]Such an identical ranking of concession types by the two groups is a barrier, not an aid, to accommodation, because it makes log-rolling more difficult.

[6]Almost, because the two extreme points of the continuum are here defined to include also those claiming two principal home languages, English or French and some other language, a very small group excluded definitionally from either of the 'monolingual' groups. For another type of language continuum, based on performance rather than competence, see Meisel 1970. My continuum, though

intended as a ranker on competence, makes the assumption that those speaking a language regularly at home are more competent in it than others who claim fluency in it: hence the distinction between 'native' and 'high' competence in the continuum.

[7]This difference, in turn, is reasonable in the light of the fact that, in Canada, English is learned more often out of 'instrumental' and French out of 'integrative' motives. This distinction is from Lambert. See Johnstone 1969:83-88.

[8]See, e.g. Lambert 1967:105-08; Gallagher 1968:144-45; and Pool 1971:168. Of course, a question asking whether bilinguals should be paid more might well elicit a peaked response pattern.

REFERENCES

Alford, Robert R. 1963. Party and society: The Anglo-American democracies. Chicago, Rand McNally & Co.

Blalock, Hubert M., Jr. 1970. An introduction to social research. Englewood Cliffs, N. J., Prentice-Hall.

Fishman, Joshua A. 1969. Bilingual attitudes and behaviors. Language Sciences. 5.5-11.

_____ and Charles Terry. 1969. The validity of census data on bilingualism in a Puerto Rican neighborhood. American Sociological Review. 5(34).636-50.

_____ et al. 1971. Research outline for comparative studies of language planning. In: Can language be planned? Ed. by Joan Rubin and Björn H. Jernudd, 293, 299-302. Honolulu, East-West Center Books.

Gallagher, Charles F. 1968. North African problems and prospects: Language and identity. In: Language problems of developing nations. Ed. by Joshua A. Fishman et al., 144-45. New York, John Wiley & Sons, Inc.

Haugen, Einar. 1966a. Dialect, language, nation. American Anthropologist. 4(68).933.

_____. 1966b. Language conflict and language planning: The case of modern Norwegian. Cambridge, Mass., Harvard University Press.

Johnstone, John C. 1969. Young people's images of Canadian society. Ottawa, Queen's Printer.

Lambert, Wallace E. 1967. A social psychology of bilingualism. Journal of Social Issues. 22(2).105-08.

Lieberson, Stanley. 1970. Language and ethnic relations in Canada. New York, John Wiley & Sons, Inc.

Meisel, John. 1970. Language continua and political alignment: The case of French- and English-users in Canada. Paper presented at the 7th World Congress of Sociology, Sept. 15, Varna, Bulgaria.

Pool, Jonathan. 1971. Language and political integration: Canada as a test of some hypotheses. Unpublished Ph. D. dissertation, University of Chicago.

Rabushka, Alvin and Kenneth Shepsle. Forthcoming. The politics of plural societies: A theory of democratic instability. Columbus, Charles E. Merrill.

Report of the Royal Commission on Bilingualism and Biculturalism. 1967. Vol. 1. Ottawa, Queen's Printer.

Underhill, Frank H. 1964. The image of confederation. Toronto, CBC Publications.

NOTES ON THE LINGUISTIC SITUATION
AND LANGUAGE PLANNING IN PERU

GARY J. PARKER

The Ford Foundation

Peru has been traditionally described as comprising three distinct
geographic regions: coast, sierra, and jungle. This division is a
useful starting point for a linguistic characterization of the country.

The coast is a narrow strip of desert interrupted by many fertile
and heavily-populated valleys. It has been entirely Spanish-mono-
lingual for perhaps a century, if we leave out of consideration the
constant stream of immigrants from the sierra (true Quechua-speaking communities do not arise on the coast since the immigrants'
purpose is to be assimilated as quickly as possible into the coastal
or criollo culture; their children who have grown up on the coast have
at most a passive knowledge of Quechua which they try vigorously to
suppress).

The sierra is largely Quechua-speaking, though in the departments
north of Ancash there remain only several small islands of Quechua
speakers. The only other native languages now spoken in the sierra
are Aymara, limited to parts of the departments of Puno, Moquegua,
Tacna, and Arequipa near the border with Bolivia, and its conserva-
tive relative Jaqaru-Kawki, near extinction, in the province of
Yauyos, Lima. The very great diversity which exists within Quechua
is generally still not appreciated beyond the group of linguists who
specialize in this area. This is due both to the lack of published
descriptions of the Quechua spoken in the central departments of
Ancash, Huánuco, Lima, Pasco, and Junín, and to the persistence
of the notion that all present-day dialects are descendants of the

Cuzco dialect of the Incas. This latter hypothesis does not seem tenable; for, if dialect differentiation in Quechua had begun just over five centuries ago, we would now be dealing only with variants of a single language. But the synchronic facts have led quechuanists to reject the hypothesis of Inca origin and even to feel that Quechua was probably a relatively recent arrival in southern Peru. Instead, current theories suggest that the origins of Quechua are in the central area of the highlands where the greatest linguistic diversity is to be found. According to Parker (1969), Quechua is a language family consisting of at least two languages, and at one point in central Peru mutually unintelligible dialects are geographically adjacent. The realization that Quechua is not a single language has major implications for language planning. It would be highly unrealistic to officialize or attempt to standardize any particular form of the Quechua family, since this form would then have to be taught as a second language in most of the country before it could be used in teaching Spanish and in the communications media.

The jungle is extremely complex linguistically, and virtually all our knowledge of it comes from the efforts of the Summer Institute of Linguistics. The total number of speakers of jungle languages (including five areas of Quechua) is estimated to be not much over 100,000; however, these persons speak forty-three languages representing eleven families according to Shell and Wise (1971). The families, all but one of which extend beyond Peru, are Peba-Yagua, Panoan, Tacanan, Záparo, Cahuapana, Quechua, Jívaro, Catuquino-Tucanoan, Simacu, Arawakan, and Tupí-Guaraní.

There have been two Peruvian censuses in this century, in 1940 and 1961; a third will begin in June 1972. In 1961 the counted population of Peru was 9,906,746, and the addition of a small calculated omission brought the total estimated population to about 10.5 million. Questions regarding language distribution took into account only persons five years of age and older, who totaled 8,235,220. The following percentages are of interest: Spanish monolinguals 60 per cent, Indian language monolinguals 19.6 per cent, Indian language-Spanish bilinguals 19.1 per cent, total Indian language speakers 38.7 per cent, Aymara speakers 3.5 per cent, Quechua speakers 35.2 per cent. In using the last of these figures to calculate the total number of Quechua speakers at 2,899,621 we must remember that the census ignored about a million children then in the process of acquiring that language.

From a general knowledge of the Peruvian situation we would predict the following trends: while the absolute number of Indian language speakers has been increasing, the percentage of Indian language monolinguals has been decreasing and the percentages of bilinguals and Spanish monolinguals have been increasing. A comparison of 1940 and 1961 figures bears this out. The percentage of Indian language monolinguals fell from 35 per cent to 19.6 per cent; that of bilinguals rose from 16.6 per cent to 19.1 per cent; that of Spanish monolinguals rose from 46.7 per cent to 60 per cent. When the results of the 1972 census are available we will have a much clearer picture of these trends. The current total population is probably near 15,000,000.

Since 1964, the University of San Marcos with the aid of a Ford Foundation grant has had a project entitled 'Teaching of Modern Languages and Linguistics'. The goals of this project are: to improve the training of Peruvian linguists, to acquire a better knowledge of the country's linguistic situation, and to make recommendations for governmental reforms. Parker is in Peru for two years in part to direct a Quechua dialectology project; Andre Marcel d'Ans is directing a project on the jungle languages.

Through 1971 there had been little evidence of language planning in Peru. The country has always had a uniform educational system, with a single set of textbooks and with Spanish the obligatory language of instruction. Many calls from social scientists and folklorists for the officialization of Quechua and Aymara have been made, but they have failed to arouse any significant popular or governmental interest. The situation is now about to change dramatically. The present government has broken abruptly with tradition and has already instituted major reforms in agrarian, industrial, and other areas. A complete overhauling of the educational system is now in the advanced planning stage, and the first quarter of 1972 has been the scene of events that mark the beginning of real language planning in Peru.

In January the Ministry of Education sponsored the Seminario Nacional de Educación Bilingüe, a full week of talks, committee work sessions, and plenary sessions, to which the country's most prominent social scientists, educators, and language teachers were invited (including foreign experts working in Peru). The final recommendations of the Seminario included the following: Education must be geared to local cultural settings and must be based on careful scientific study of these settings. While Spanish is the only practical candidate for a common language in Peru, it must not be imposed at the expense of native languages. Given the current absence of a common language, all native languages should have official status. Education must begin in the local language, and the schools must be provided with adequate materials. Spanish will be taught as a second language where necessary. Speakers of indigenous languages must be encouraged to cultivate their languages and must be provided with facilities for publication in every form. The universities will place strong emphasis on the study of native languages and will be in charge of the training of teachers and of the preparation of teaching materials for areas where Spanish is not the first language of instruction. There must be an intensive campaign to eliminate all forms of cultural and linguistic discrimination.

In February the government published a preliminary version of the educational reform law for public debate and reaction. At the same time, Peru's leading linguists were invited to confer with the Ministry in refining the definitions of such key terms as 'bilingualism'.

Late in March the final version of the new law was published. It is a lengthy document, dealing with the reorganization of all aspects of education in Peru, and contains four paragraphs of specific linguistic interest. My English paraphrasing of these paragraphs is accompanied by the original text from Ley General de Educación, Decreto Ley No. 19326. (1) Education will take into account the existence of the country's various languages and will encourage their preservation and development. The teaching of Spanish will respect the local cultural settings and will employ the local languages as a medium of instruction (Artículo 12: 'La educación considerará en todas sus acciones la existencia en el país de diversas lenguas que son medios de comunicación y expresión de cultura, y velará por su preservación y desarrollo. La castellanización de toda la población se hará respetando la personalidad cultural de los diversos grupos que conforman la sociedad nacional y utilizando sus lenguas como vínculo de educación'). (2) The learning of indigenous languages will be encouraged, and educational institutions will provide facilities for their study (Artículo 98: ' . . . Se fomentará el aprendizaje de las lenguas vernáculas. Los centros educativos darán facilidades para el conocimiento de dichos idiomas y de su influencia en la lengua y la cultura nacionales'). (3) Wherever necessary the vernacular language will be used in teaching literacy and Spanish and for the conservation of local cultural values (Artículo 246: 'En los casos que sea necesario, se utilizará la respectiva lengua vernácula para facilitar el proceso de alfabetización de los auténticos valores de la cultura local'). (4) Teacher training programs will include the obligatory learning of a vernacular language (Artículo 301: 'Los programas de formación magisterial incluirán obligatoriamente el aprendizaje de una lengua vernácula peruana').

It now remains to be seen exactly how and when these resolutions will be implemented.

REFERENCES

Parker, Gary J. 1969. Comparative Quechua phonology and grammar I: Classification. University of Hawaii, Department of Linguistics, Working Papers in Linguistics 1/1. 65-87.

Republica del Perú, Dirección Nacional de Estadística y Censos. 1966. VI Censo Nacional de Población, tomo III: Idiomas, alfabetismo, asistencia escolar, nivel de educación. Lima.

Republica del Perú, Ministerio de Educación. 1972. Ley General de Educación, Decreto Ley No. 19326. Lima.

Seminario Nacional de Educación Bilingüe. 1972. Comisión No. III: Recomendaciones generales. (Mimeographed.) Lima.

Shell, Olive A. and Mary Ruth Wise. 1971. Grupos idiomáticos del Perú (segunda edición). Lima, Universidad Nacional Mayor de San Marcos; Instituto Lingüístico de Verano.

LANGUAGE ALLOCATION
AND LANGUAGE PLANNING
IN A DEVELOPING NATION

T. P. GORMAN

University of Edinburgh and University of California
at Los Angeles

In this paper I comment upon some developments relating to language policy and, more specifically, language allocation in East Africa with particular reference to Kenya; and to the reaffirmation of the status of Swahili as the national language and its designation as a future primary official language of that state. [1] I also discuss some aspects of policy with reference to a number of recent statements by scholars concerning language planning processes.

I have in mind, in particular, Rubin and Jernudd's remarks in the Introduction to Can Language Be Planned? to the effect that

> We still do not know how language planning actually operates: what are the goals that planners have considered, what motivates their considerations of particular goals and their acceptance of certain goals . . . and what does in fact happen? We do not know in any detail just how well the abstract notions thus far delineated correspond to realities of language planning (Rubin and Jernudd 1971:xxii).

In considering these issues with reference to the situation in Kenya I found it useful to make a distinction between language planning and what I have termed language allocation in discussing language policies adopted in the process of language regulation. By language allocation I mean authoritative decisions to maintain, extend, or restrict the range of uses (functional range) of a language in particular settings. The term language planning is most appropriately used in my view to refer to coordinated measures taken to select, codify and, in some cases, to elaborate orthographic, grammatical, lexical, or semantic features of a language and to disseminate the corpus agreed upon.[2] Decisions on language allocation must normally precede decisions on language planning, so defined.

I adopted these distinctions for a number of reasons; one being that methods of description developed to describe processes associated with language planning (in the more general sense in which the term is frequently used) did not appear to provide a suitable framework for analysis of the processes of language regulation evident in Kenya. I considered in particular the applicability of the schemes elaborated by T. Thorburn and B. Jernudd (in Rubin and Jernudd 1971) in their discussion of cost-benefit models for decision making and an outline (by Jernudd and Das Gupta) of planning processes that might be utilized in the exploitation, as it were, of language as a 'societal resource'. This outline, stated in 'ideal and general terms' lists the following procedures:

> The broadest authorization for planning is obtained from the politicians. A body of experts is then specifically delegated the task of preparing a plan. In preparing this, the experts ideally estimate existing resources and forecast potential utilization of such resources in terms of developmental targets. Once targets are agreed upon, a strategy of action is elaborated. These are authorized by the legislature and are implemented by the organizational set-up, authorized in its turn by the planning executive. The implementation of the tasks may be evaluated periodically by the planners (Jernudd and Das Gupta, 196).

Characteristics of these procedures are a degree of precision in the definition of objectives, realistic appraisal of the possibilities in terms of the resources available and necessary for the attainment of the proposed objectives over a specified period of time, provision for the evaluation or periodic appraisal of the plan and the quantification, when possible, of values for mathematical analysis.

In considering the singular lack of correspondence between these procedures and those associated with language regulation in East Africa, I recalled the observation that Charles Lindblom made some years ago with reference to planning procedures derived from studies of economic planning, operations research, and systems analysis, which is generally applicable to the schemes just mentioned, viz. that they 'remain largely the appropriate techniques of relatively small-scale problem solving where the total number of variables to be considered is small and value problems restricted' (Lindblom 1963:130).

Procedures similar to those itemized by Jernudd and Das Gupta are employed as a matter of course by senior officers of different ministries in the work of central government in the implementation of policies that have been duly authorized; indeed, it could be argued that they are characteristic of the manner in which those with managerial responsibilities in modern bureaucracies develop and implement operational policy.[3] Decisions on national and official language allocation are not generally susceptible to planning of this kind, however, as they frequently involve attempts to alter or regulate in some measure aspects of individual and group behavior and social relationships (in the sense that such policies may serve to affect how people expect other members of the group to behave in certain settings), and because they entail the modification or manipulation of values, beliefs, and sentiments. More particularly, they involve an attempt by political leaders to regulate what might be termed the communicative conduct of the activities of members of the bureaucracy or public service. It is not coincidental that in Kenya, as in Tanzania and Malawi, where decisions on language allocation have been taken, the impetus for the extension of the official functions of an indigenous language has been channelled through the organs of the ruling political party--under whose auspices the initial language policy directives have been issued--rather than through the Ministries concerned and the bureaucratic system, as it were. This fact is relevant to discussion of the nature of the problems involved in language allocation as I have implied above, and to the objectives sought and the techniques used to attain these.

It is no doubt platitudinous to make the point that the organization of a multilingual state requires that explicit or implied policy decisions regarding language allocation are taken continuously at all administrative levels of government. Relatively few such decisions are codified or subject to regulation. The attempt to impose a measure of regulation on the use of 'official' languages, variously defined, has been undertaken in numerous independent states, particularly in South Asia, and these developments have been associated in many cases with the selection of a particular language as the 'national' (or 'state' or 'linking') language.

It has often been observed that such issues have been of less political consequence in the independent sub-Saharan African states than in the South Asian States. The selection of official languages has not generally involved or given rise to interethnic tension or conflict; nor has the selection of national languages in the few areas where these have been designated. Commentators have generally attributed this absence of conflict to such factors as the high degree of linguistic diversity in most African states; and (correspondingly) the small size (relative to India, for example) of most ethnic and language groups within the independent states. The absence of standard languages that might serve as focal points of 'linguistic nationalism'[4] has also been remarked upon. Most significantly, in my view, most African states 'inherited' from the colonial regimes political, economic, social, and in some cases artistic institutions, in which the language of the colonial power was characteristically employed, and have maintained these through the offices of a bureaucracy whose members are trained to work in the second language (Rustow 1967: 154, Emerson 1963, Whiteley 1969:549, Fishman 1968:46).

In recent years, however, issues relating to the selection of national languages and of official languages other than English, have been matters of frequent discussion and debate among intellectuals[5] in Kenya and in other states in Eastern Africa including Uganda, Zambia, and Malawi. One reason for this can be found in the influence of Tanzania where the national language policy is an integral part of a political program whose socialist populist and nationalist elements appeal strongly to many educated East Africans.

The decision taken by members of the ruling party in Kenya to lay emphasis upon the status of Swahili as the national language cannot be accounted for, however, in terms of some form of cultural diffusion.[6] It has been the experience of all the independent states in Africa that as economic and social planning increases the rate of mobilization it also increases the demands made on the Government. The great expansion of educational facilities in Kenya and other independent states has resulted in a corresponding increase in the numbers of citizens educated for much of their school lives in a second language --for many of whom work is not available. In the competition for employment and, more generally, for the allocation of limited resources, ethnic rivalries are exacerbated and the general consciousness of national unity developed during the campaign for independence is dissipated.

In such circumstances one would expect emphasis to be given to those elements of national life and those institutions that attest to the actual or potential socio-cultural unity of members of different ethnic groups. Swahili, which is widely spoken in an attenuated form as a second language by Kenyans, is potentially one such element. In political terms the function of Swahili as a 'neutral' medium of communication is made possible by the fact that its use is not associated with a numerically major ethnic group. But this fact may also serve to explain the absence of any organizations or interest groups with widespread support whose members are willing to devote the resources available to them to support the functional or formal diversification of the language. There was little indication before 1970 of any strong associational pressure or widespread popular demand for a change in policy; but it has to be recognized that many of those who might support the policy change would not make use of the national press, for example, as a means of interest articulation. Nor were any systematic attempts made prior to this time to emphasize the integrative functions of the language. Professor W. H. Whiteley (1971:156) has remarked upon the contrast between Kenya and Uganda in this respect. [7]

In August, however, the Governing Council of KANU, the ruling party, under the chairmanship of the President, passed a resolution to the effect that 'Swahili as our national language shall be encouraged and enforced by all means and at all places in Kenya and that Swahili be used in our National Assembly'. Subsequently, in April 1970, the acting secretary general of the party announced plans for the extension of the use of Swahili as an official language.

The provisions of the 1970 plan called for radical changes in language use by individuals and institutions. [8]

During the first phase of implementation, which commenced at the time of issue, it was required that 'All Kenyans shall speak in Swahili at all times either to fellow Kenyans or non-Kenyans whether officially or non-officially, politically, or socially'.

During phase II, the KANU statement continued,

. . . the official language in all Government duties will be conducted in Swahili. Law Courts and places of higher learning will be exempted during this period. The President, Ministers, and Government officials shall communicate to all people whether Kenyans or foreigners or aliens in Swahili using an interpreter if necessary.

Other significant extracts from the statement are as follows:

All civil servants in all Government, quasi-Government bodies, and in the Diplomatic Service will have to pass oral and written Swahili tests. Promotion, demotion, or even forced retirement will depend and be based mainly on the outcome of these tests.

All future candidates for the National Assembly, County Councils, municipalities, or any of the elected bodies shall be made up of people who can address a group of people in good Swahili for a duration of not less than ten minutes.

'In primary and secondary schools', the statement continued, 'Swahili would be given more prominence in the school syllabus than English'. Either a central institute or regional institutions would be established in which Swahili would be taught. The statement allowed for the use of English in official documents, and in the law courts and places of higher learning during the period of implementation, which extended to 1974.

Judged by criteria derived from a consideration of planning processes of the kind discussed by Professors Jernudd and Das Gupta in Can Language Be Planned?, the scheme would be thought seriously deficient. No mention is made of the financial and human resources that would be required for its implementation nor of the agencies that would be responsible for implementation, evaluation, and revision of the plan, for example.

I hope that what I have said earlier will have served to indicate, however, that the statement of policy should not necessarily be judged according to such criteria. Considered in terms of its objectives the plan should be interpreted as a political act which has the primary objective of conveying to Kenyans, perhaps for the first time, a sense of the importance of the language in the 'life' of the nation. [9] Resolutions of the party have no legal status and the statement was generally interpreted as an exhortation rather than a series of commands and as a warning of future developments.

The immediate effect of the policy statement, as far as this could be observed, was not to affect in any way the extent to which English was used as the medium of 'official' correspondence and communication--this was clearly not the purpose of the statement. It was to discourage the use in face-to-face communication in central government offices of languages exclusively associated with one of the major ethnic communities.

If and when further steps are taken to restrict entry to the public service to those who are able to use 'good' Swahili with a degree of facility, some resistance to the measures on the part of members of the major linguistic communities is to be anticipated; and if it is required that the language be used much more extensively in official documents, opposition to the measures from senior members of the civil service is to be expected. I personally consider that the degree to which any radical changes can be made in matters relating to official language allocation in the near future in Kenya and in the other East African states will depend largely on the extent to which party control over the bureaucracy is effective.

The bureaucracy as 'a central focus around which clusters a whole series of social actions designed to meet systemic goals' (Hoserlitz 1963:171) may be expected to present a degree of resistance to policies that do not accord in some respects with the requirements of

efficient economic planning and development. [10] Additionally, as regards language policies it may be expected that those who have at-
tained official positions partly as a consequence of their knowledge
of the primary language of administration will not in all cases actively
prosecute policies which might serve, in time, to offset the value of
this qualification (cf. Mydral 1968:350, Kearney 1967:24).

The fact that leading politicians are also in many cases ministers
of government does not minimize the differences of approach and
method that are in some respects characteristic of the politicians
and bureaucrats in seeking their different objectives. Political
expediency frequently affects the extent and type of planning that
can be carried out. Mr. A. L. Adu, the distinguished African civil
servant, has observed that

> Ministers are impatient to get on with the programmes they
> have set before them . . . they find in the circumstances that
> the Civil Service machinery is too ponderous for their purpose
> and too deliberate in its procedure for examining and imple-
> menting policies (Adu 1965:230).

Whether one can interpret such differences of objective and method
in terms of a form of conflict between 'authenticity' and 'modernization' naturally depends on the circumstances.

In this paper I have made the point that it is inappropriate to
attempt to interpret or criticize political acts relating to language
allocation in terms of a theory of planning such as that outlined
earlier. I have not, however, attempted to postulate criteria by
which the effectiveness of the statement on language allocation might
be assessed in the light of the political situation in Kenya at the time
the announcement was made. The criteria by which one judges the
efficacy or appropriateness of a political act will be partly determined
by one's own political presuppositions or beliefs. J. V. Neustupný,
for example, suggests four 'general principles (criteria)' that might
be included in a 'full typology of principles (criteria) for "language"
policy viz. Development, Democratization, Unity, and Foreign Relations' (i.e. communication with other specific communities) (in
Fishman, Ferguson, and Das Gupta 1968). Similarly, one's opinions
about kinds of language behavior that might appropriately be subject
to the attention of a planning agency and about the methods that might
legitimately be used to enforce conformity will be affected by such
beliefs. [11] H. C. Kelman (1971:37), for example, admits to a 'general
bias against deliberate attempts by central political authorities to
create a sense of national identity whether by a policy of establishing
a national language or by any other means'.

While I do not question the fact that consideration of these issues is within the academic purview of those concerned with language regulation, within the educational system or otherwise, it is apparent that linguists who are also non-nationals are not ordinarily competent to assess accurately the effects of policy statements such as the one I have been considering. Perhaps, therefore, the most immediate and positive contribution that such scholars can make is by way of continuing to develop a framework of analysis with reference to which forms of language regulation can be systematically described and analyzed both in relation to relevant aspects of social, political, and economic development; and in relation to a more exact and ultimately scientific nomenclature with which related questions can be discussed. The process has scarcely begun.

NOTES

[1]The term 'lugha ya taifa' (lit. language of the nation) is frequently used in discussion of the national language question and it is open to a number of interpretations as is the phrase 'lugha ya serikali' (lit. language of government) which is generally used in discussion of official languages. Political leaders and commentators do not always draw distinctions between the categories of national language, common or 'linking' language and official languages (cf. Das Gupta 1971:37) or between the various interpretations that each of these terms can be given. In this paper I am using the term official language as it is used by discussants in Kenya to refer to the languages used by officials in carrying out their duties in the executive, legislative, or judicial sectors. By primary official language I mean a language in which the legislation of a state is enacted--though it is not clear whether it is the intention that Swahili will in fact be used for this purpose after 1974.

[2]As no such activities are currently being undertaken in Kenya with regard to Swahili I do not intend to discuss the difficulties inherent in such planning.

[3]I am using the term 'bureaucracy' to refer to all civil servants, though it is the civil servants at the upper administrative levels whose views have a direct bearing on policy formulation.

[4]The term is used by S. J. Tambiah with reference to the independence movement in India (Tambiah 1967).

[5]I am using the term 'intellectuals' in the sense Edward Shils used the term viz. 'all persons with an advanced modern education and the intellectual concerns and skills ordinarily associated with it' (Shils 1962:198). Shils' discussion of the socialist and populist elements in the politics of the intellectuals of developing countries,

insofar as these derive from their nationalist preoccupations and aspirations, is illuminating though inevitably oversimplified.

[6]The status of Swahili as the national language had been asserted on a number of occasions prior to 1970. The President's use of the language on formal state occasions had been taken to indicate this. He had also stated that Swahili would eventually be used as a language of debate in the National Assembly; but such motions as were introduced into the Assembly relating to the use of Swahili as an official language had, when passed, been amended to provide for its introduction, alongside English, 'as soon as was practicable'. The amendments were made primarily for reasons relating to what one minister described in 1966 as 'the insurmountable practical difficulties in translating our laws and other legal and quasi-legal documents into Swahili'. The revised Constitution issued in April 1969 reaffirmed that 'the business of the National Assembly shall be conducted in English'. The demands of 'efficiency' were apparently regarded as paramount by those who made this last decision (cf. Gorman 1971).

[7]'Tanzania is, in one sense, no less trifocal than Kenya, but she has chosen to place her emphasis differently; by having Swahili linked with her political ideology, Tanzania makes it possible for the language to act as a continuing force for unity. Kenya, by stressing the importance of the trifocal division of language behaviour has not been able to utilize any one language as a unifying force but must continually reckon with their divisive potentialities. Both countries, however, are faced all the time with the need to reconcile the competing claims of modernity and authenticity. At any given moment, political decisions may appear to favour the one rather than the other; and it is in the light of the need for periodic shifts in emphasis that any policy should be judged' (Whiteley 1971:156).

[8]At the time of the issue of the plan in April 1970 the official language of the National Assembly and of the High Court was English. While there were no regulations governing the use of different languages by civil servants English was also the language in which official correspondence was generally conducted. In the educational system, the introduction of English as the initial medium of instruction in primary schools had been rapidly extended after the attainment of Independence in 1963; and in 1970 the majority of the schools in the country employed the 'English-medium' system. In the government-controlled broadcasting system, programs in English and Swahili were broadcast throughout the day and there were additional programs broadcast on a third channel in fourteen other African languages, in Hindustani and in the Kimvita dialect of Swahili.

[9]Hoselitz (1963) maintains that social institutions can be generally classified as having functions relating to the fostering of what he terms latency, integration goal-gratification, and adaptation. In each of the

countries of East Africa formerly colonized by Britain, the primary role of the party organization might be interpreted as that of serving the integrative needs of consciousness of national identity.

[10]'On almost every level the demands of economic efficiency are sure to conflict at some point with the demands of political expediency . . . ' (Deutsch and Foltz 1963:125).

[11]Questions at issue in the regulation of human behavior are increasingly being discussed in connection with the formulation of 'cultural policy' (UNESCO 1969, 1970a, 1970b:12). Insofar as these discussions serve to direct attention to the ways in which the control and organization of human behavior presents problems which are not encountered in processes associated with the management of material resources, they should be of direct interest to those concerned with language planning.

REFERENCES

Adu, A. L. 1965. The civil service in new African states. New York, Praeger.

Das Gupta, J. 1971. Language conflict and national development. University of California Press.

Deutsch, K. W. 1953. Nationalism and social communication. New York, John Wiley & Sons, Inc.

Emerson, R. 1963. Nation building in Africa. In: Nation building. Ed. by K. W. Deutsch and W. J. Foltz. New York, Atherton Press.

Fishman, J. A., C. A. Ferguson, and J. Das Gupta, eds. 1968. Language problems of developing nations. New York, John Wiley & Sons.

Foltz, W. J. 1963. Building the newest nations. In: Nation building. Ed. by K. W. Deutsch and W. J. Foltz. New York, Atherton Press. 125.

Gorman, T. P. 1970. The national language issue in Kenya. Journal of the Language Association of Eastern Africa. 2(1).

Hoselitz, B. F. 1963. Levels of economic performance and bureaucratic structures. In: Bureaucracy and political development. Ed. by J. LaPalombra. Princeton, N. J., Princeton University Press. 168-98.

Kearney, R. N. 1967. Communication and language in the politics of Ceylon. Duke University Press.

Kelman, H. C. 1971. Language as an aid and barrier to involvement in the national system. In: Rubin and Jernudd. 21-52.

Lindblom, C. E. 1963. The science of 'muddling through'. In: Politics and social life. Ed. by N. W. Potsby, R. A. Dentler, and P. A. Smith. Boston, Houghton Mifflin Co. 339-48.

Mazrui, A. 1967. The Anglo African commonwealth. New York, Pergamon Press.

Myrdal, G. 1968. Asian drama: An enquiry into the poverty of nations. New York.

Rubin, J. and B. Jernudd, eds. 1971. Can language be planned? Sociolinguistic theory and practice for developing nations. Honolulu, University Press of Hawaii.

Rustow, D. 1967. A world of nations. Problems of political modernization. Washington.

Shils, E. 1962. The intellectuals in political development. In: Political change in underdeveloped countries: Nationalism and communism. Ed. by J. N. Kautsky. New York, John Wiley & Sons, Inc. 195-234.

Tambiah, S. J. 1967. The politics of language in India and Ceylon. Modern Asian Studies. 1(3).215-40.

UNESCO. 1969. Cultural policy: A preliminary study. Paris.
_____. 1970a. Cultural rights as human rights. Paris.
_____. 1970b. Some aspects of French cultural policy. Paris.

Whiteley, W. H. 1969. Language policies of independent African states. In: Current trends in linguistics, vol. 7. Ed. by T. Sebeok. The Hague, Mouton.
_____. 1971. Some factors affecting language policies. In: Rubin and Jernudd. 141-58.

THE INTERNATIONAL RESEARCH PROJECT
ON LANGUAGE PLANNING PROCESSES (IRPLPP)

JOSHUA A. FISHMAN

Yeshiva University

1.0 Introduction. The IRPLPP, now coming to an end after three years of operation, represents an attempt to provide comparative data pertaining to the effectiveness of one of the major aspects of language planning: lexical elaboration for modernization. The project has involved five senior researchers acting as coordinators in five research locales (Charles A. Ferguson, administrative coordination, USA; Joshua A. Fishman, research coordination and Israeli data; Joan Rubin, Indonesian data; Jyotirindra Das Gupta, Indian data; Björn Jernudd, originally East Pakistani and ultimately Swedish data), as well as a rather large number of local study directors, associates, consultants, and assistants. The present brief report deals only with the conceptual and methodological organization of the Project. A detailed substantive report should be available, in first draft, within half a year.

2.0 Design. The IRPLPP has focused upon diverse populations in each of the countries in which it has been active. Thus, in each country, the members and senior staff of the Language Planning Agencies have been intensively studied with respect to their language planning views and work routines. Text book writers and educational officers have been similarly subjected to lengthy questionnaires and interviews, as have certain other populations, unique to each country, that are seemingly indicators of particular language planning problems or successes.

2.1. The core design of the IRPLPP may be outlined as follows:
Three countries: India, Indonesia, and Israel.

Three populations: Teachers (at high school and college levels), students (at high school and college levels), and adults (in part parents of the above students, and, in part, a sample of lower white-collar workers).

Three attitudinal-informational criteria of 'successful' language planning: Accurate knowledge and favorable attitudes re the Language Planning Agency/ies, accurate knowledge and favorable attitudes re advocatory agencies generally supporting the work or the goals of the Language Planning Agency/ies, and accurate knowledge and unfavorable attitudes re opposing agencies generally counteracting the work or the goals of the Language Planning Agency/ies.

Three word usage criteria of 'successful' language planning: Naming 'LPA Approved' words in a word-naming task in the humanities (grammar terms), natural sciences (chemistry), and social sciences (civics).

2.2. Thus, the core design of the IRPLPP is a three country by three population by six criteria design which aims at discovering whether there are significant similarities and/or differences between countries and/or between populations with respect to language planning success as reflected by the six criteria utilized.

3.0 Data collection. In connection with the core design two to six hour questionnaires were administered (in Indonesia and in Israel to roughly 250 teachers, 2,000 students, and 500 adults; in India to smaller samples of each population) covering the following topic areas:

Personal background data, particularly in connection with the language repertoire of respondents and their immediate family members.

Attitudes: modernization, national consciousness, and language consciousness.

Word evaluation: attitudes and usage claims with respect to a twenty-five word sample of academy terms in at least one of the three substantive fields for which word naming criterion scores were obtained, as well as attitudes toward indigenousness of vocabulary per se.

4.0 Data analysis. In view of the huge amount of data collected by the IRPLPP the data analysis and interpretation methods selected commonly focus upon quantitative data-reduction and compositing. Thus, e.g. the roughly 1,200 responses per respondent in our teacher study were intercorrelated and factor analyzed. As a result, twelve major factors (representing the twelve largest and maximally different dimensions in our data), as well as from twenty to thirty items dubbed 'nonfactors' (i.e. items that seemed unrelated to any of the foregoing twelve factors) were identified. The items most representative of the major factors (from twelve to sixteen) plus the items most clearly unrelated to any of these factors (from twenty to thirty) have been utilized via cumulative multiple correlation methods to predict each of the six criteria mentioned earlier.

4.1. In addition to the factor analytically derived predictors just mentioned, several a priori predictor scores have also been regularly employed in view of their apparent 'face validity' with respect to our criteria: number of languages respondents claim to speak, number of languages respondents claim to read, number of languages respondent claims father knows, number of languages respondent claims mother knows, and respondent's total preference for indigenousness of vocabulary. In addition, total word naming scores (as measures of total lexical availability) in each substantive field have also been employed, as have all five remaining criterion scores in the cumulative multiple prediction of any particular criterion.

4.2. Although no detailed findings will be reported here it may be said that the above techniques have succeeded in revealing that the factor structures (i.e. the underlying dimensionality) of language planning attitudes, information and usage, are partially similar but largely different from country to country and from population to population. On the other hand, the total variation on our criterion measures has proved to be highly and regularly explainable. Our normal cumulative multiple correlations in connection with the three attitudinal-informational criteria employed are in the 60's and 70's, whereas the normal cumulative multiple correlations obtained in connection with the three word-naming criteria employed are in the 80's and 90's.

5.0. Given the kinds of predictor measures and criterion measures employed by the IRPLPP it would seem to be quite possible to provide rather powerful empirical data in the near future concerning the differential success of language planning activity (pertaining to lexical elaboration) vis-à-vis populations such as those here studied.

The IRPLPP may thus be considered a step ahead in attacking the following general question: Do the explanatory factors related to differential success in language planning tend to be the same or different, and do they tend to be equally powerful or not, across countries, across populations, across usage goals, and across attitudinal-informational goals ?

THE RISE AND DECLINE
OF AN UPPER-GALILEE DIALECT

AARON BAR-ADON

The University of Texas at Austin

The story of the revival of modern Hebrew as a modern living tongue is quite popular. Regretfully, only the popular aspects of that story are usually known, rather than the whole history with its sociolinguistic setting and problems. Sometimes, even scholarly works take those popular accounts for granted. Not too rarely, merely the cliché stories and legends about Ben Yehuda, his family, and the like, are repeated as if there were no other aspects to that rare sociolinguistic phenomenon, which is unquestionably also unique in certain respects, such as the very revival of a classical language after nineteen centuries of dormancy (from about 200 A. D. to the 1880s), the mechanics of language revival, [1] and a few others.

Any serious attempt at thoroughly and properly studying the revival of Hebrew must place it in the proper sociolinguistic perspective and context: in terms of the socio-cultural, socio-political, and socio-economical background, as well as the psychological and demographic aspects of the linguistic revival; in terms of language planning by the Hebrew Language Committee and its successor (since 1953) The Academy of the Hebrew Language, and other institutions, whether official or unofficial; in terms of the inherent problems and extent of realization in real life, and in terms of unplanned developments and even some 'counterplanning' in colloquial Hebrew and in literary Hebrew as well, not excluding the emerging slang, and the like. [2] Several serious attempts along these lines have recently begun.

Some contributions to the study of the related topics of Hebrew child language and the processes of nativization of modern Hebrew by the younger generation and their impact on Israeli Hebrew were made by the present author, [3] but more has to be done in this area too, which is still almost terra incognita.

The topic of this paper is inherently connected with the initial 'planning' and 'counterplanning' in the early formative years in the revival process, including the linguistic and nonlinguistic or extra-linguistic factors. More specifically, it deals with relatively unknown developments in those early stages of the Hebrew revival, concentrating on a deliberate ('planned') and zealously followed attempt at introducing, or 'reviving' (as believed by the initiators), a special Galilean dialect which started close to the turn of the century.

The oral evidence for this research was collected and recorded on tape within the framework of a comprehensive study by this author on the history of the revival of modern Hebrew. [4] It is my conviction that such research should be based not only on written records of various kinds, but also, and perhaps in the first place, on oral evidence from the surviving old-timers, mainly those who had actively participated in the early stages of the revival. [5] It is therefore a pity that this rare opportunity to study first hand a language-in-the-making from its inception and the processes of language revival with all that this entails, has not been fully taken advantage of by linguists, especially sociolinguists and anthropologists. The recent and current work by Chaim Rabin, Joshua Fishman, and a few others in the field is certainly encouraging.

Theoretically, the revival of Hebrew started in the early 1880s, but as we will see later, it was not until twenty years later that it really started becoming a spoken language. The dialect under consideration was initiated within that period in the later 1890s, and it survived in Upper Galilee, as the dialect of the native Galileans, until the early 1920s, when it was overcome by the ambitious 'standard' speech. It is now used only by a small number of survivors, but they are rapidly disappearing from the scene. At this time there are also quite a number of passive witnesses, who did not use it but who still remember it as a reality of the past, as something that had really existed. However, for most of the Israelis it is known (if at all) as part of a legend, or a myth, about some 'strange Galileans', who lived in the isolated pioneering settlements of scenic Upper Galilee at the beginning of the resettlement of Palestine, and who spoke Hebrew 'in a funny manner', which has become an object of mimicry and joking for subsequent generations. Indeed, this ridicule culminated several years ago in a nostalgic play Yamim šel zahav 'Days of Gold' or 'The Golden Days', as we will see below.

In order to fully understand the background, the conditions, and motives, for this sociolinguistic phenomenon and its history to date, one must go back to the dawn of the revival of Hebrew speech in the latter quarter of the 19th century, and to re-evaluate the role of certain trends and individuals in it, including that of Eliezer Ben-Yehuda. A scrutinizing analysis may bring about some revisions in our notions about the period.

In the popular literature about the period, Ben-Yehuda is usually portrayed as the great legendary hero of his time, who brought about the whole revival single-handedly, as it were. He is often called 'The Father of Modern Hebrew' or 'The Father of Spoken Hebrew' in somewhat pathetic statements by some of his contemporaries, [6] and naturally in the writings of the family about him.

Scholarly works on this topic, which are not too numerous, are generally more reserved and critical. However, as one might expect, oral statements by old-timers tend to be more frank, and sometimes even include hints about instances of lip service and politics which were included in certain earlier written records.

We cannot delve here into any elaborate exposition. I do it elsewhere[7] in detail. At this point we can only state that Ben-Yehuda became in the people's mind the symbol of the Hebrew Revival, and as such he will be remembered forever.

Apparently, Ben-Yehuda himself was not able to create a popular movement, and in his later years he was completely absorbed in his enormous Hebrew dictionary, the Thesaurus. At any rate, even in 1904, twenty-three years after his settling in Jerusalem, there were still barely ten Hebrew-speaking families there, [8] and a similar number in the rest of the country. [9]

On the other hand, there is sufficient evidence for a thesis that during the First 'Aliyah, i.e. the First Influx or Wave of Immigration (1882-1903), Hebrew was used almost exclusively by teachers and grade-school students. [10]

Thus the first teachers were actually responsible for the very creating of the revival, for bringing about the actual revival with or without reference to Ben-Yehuda. Their own initiative in the revival of Hebrew at school was part of their raison d'être. With the arrival of the first waves of the Second 'Aliyah, since 1904, the establishment of Hebrew high schools, and later also teachers' seminaries, and the emergence of new 'generations' of youth who had graduated from those early Hebrew grade schools, i.e. of young people who needed a more efficient and richer language than the one for the elementary classroom, Hebrew became the language of communication for growing masses. There does not seem to be a direct impact of Ben-Yehuda on those developments.

How, then, did the revival of Hebrew speech become a reality? And who, then, has done the actual job of revival?

As mentioned above, during the First 'Aliyah--there were the teachers who carried out the revival of Hebrew speech with their grade-school students; during the Second 'Aliyah there was added the factor of the Po'alim--the workers--and the growing youth, who needed a concrete, popular, lively, and efficient language. Through their use of it, Hebrew became the language of the masses as well. At the same time, the teachers expanded their work among the children and the youth, who in turn have had a tremendous impact on the subsequent development of the language, as we show in other studies. [11] We might add that the teachers were instrumental in the creation and manning of the Hebrew Language Committee, too. Since the teachers did play a decisive role in the very revival of Hebrew speech, let us have a closer look at the state of the art at that time.

The truth should be pointed out, that many of the teachers of the time were neither qualified nor efficient. The sad fact is that some of them resorted to teaching for lack of fitness to another job (a somewhat universal problem). Also, there was no centralized system of education at that time, no program and supervision, not even any established guidelines were available to inexperienced teachers. Each individual school did actually set its own policies, and the individual teacher would actually determine his methods of teaching, and the curriculum, and he would even individually decide upon the language of teaching: whether it should be Hebrew, or Yiddish, Ladino, or Arabic, or if mixed--in what combination, and in which of the classes or subjects (secular vs. religious), and the like. Even the decision about the pronunciation (whether Ashkenazi or Sephardi) rested with the individual teacher. It is easy to imagine the situation. [12] Education may not have been as chaotic as it sounds, since it was balanced by the outstanding, conscientious teachers, but it certainly was very unorganized.

Such uncontrolled 'freedom' may lead to anarchy with the wrong teachers, but it may also be conducive to extraordinary creativity with the conscientious, idealistic educators. An idealist could create a popular movement in his own school, even in the entire region, and implement it wherever his popularity would reach, especially if he happened to live in a remote, relatively isolated section of the country, e.g. in Upper Galilee. This indeed was the case of the great teachers Y. Epstein and S. H. Wilkomitz and their associates, who are responsible for the introduction and the development of the dialect under consideration.

Obviously, certain conditions must be present, in order for a special dialect to be successfully introduced, such as 'splendid' isolation of the region, incomplete establishment of the standard

dialect (or nonuniversal recognition thereof), and at the same time
motivated, perhaps also somewhat romantic, initiators supported by
stimulated followers, who would like to have a dialect of their own
that could proudly identify them. In effect, nowhere else could there
be found a more favorable combination of such features than in the
isolated Upper Galilee, at the turn of the century, and with teachers
like Epstein and Wilkomitz as the ideal match, when the emotions
were high concerning the selection of the best possible pronunciation
for the national language, for the contemporary speakers, and for
generations to come. This was meant to be a contribution to the
standardization of the national language, and if not--at least for an
ideal regional dialect, claimed to be a restoration of an old Galilean
tradition, which that wild enchanting region, inhabited by simple-
minded healthy farmers deserved anyway.

Epstein came from Russia in 1886 to be trained as an agricultural
instructor. After a year at Zikhron-Ya'akov in Samaria he went to
Rosh-Pinnah in Upper Galilee. Among his assistants there were
young Sephardi Jews from the nearby city of Zefat. Thus, he had
his first opportunity to get acquainted with their Hebrew pronunciation, which attracted him very much.

In 1891, when he assumed the position of teacher and principal at
the new girls' school in Zefat, he was, naturally, confronted with all
the problems that faced an untrained teacher in a multilingual society,
with the predominant languages of Yiddish, Ladino, and Arabic, while
Hebrew, as the common language, was yet to come. He decided that
Hebrew should be the sole language of teaching and communication at
school. This was a bold decision at that time, when the rest of the
country was still largely undecided as to the introduction of the
'direct' method in teaching Hebrew, ivrit be-'ivrit--'Hebrew through
Hebrew', i.e. by using Hebrew as the sole medium of teaching,
rather than translating into another language.

As Epstein tells us:

Nobody has dreamed of a Hebrew speech. There was no contact between the Hebrew population in Judea and the Upper-
Galilee settlements, either material or spiritual. New
immigrants would constantly flow to the vicinity of Jaffa,
while here, because of the transportation problems, a complete standstill did prevail.

It took about three days to go from there to Jaffa, for instance, using
horses or mules, boats, trains, and stagecoaches. Epstein was com-
pelled to devise his own teaching methods.

He put some emphasis on dictations, wherein he tried to pronounce
all the Hebrew letters (or graphemes). The Ashkenazi or the new

semi-Sephardi pronunciation could not bring out all the distinctions
inherent in the Hebrew alphabet, e.g. ʔ-ʕ, ḥ-x, k-ḵ, t-ṭ, therefore
he adopted the full Sephardi pronunciation, gradually adding even the
'exotic' realization of the emphatic velar stop [q] and the palatalized
stop [ṭ], to those of the ʕAyin as [ʕ] and of Ḥet as [ḥ].

He also acquired the realization of the <u>Bet</u> /b/ as [b] only, i.e.
without allophonic distinction b-v, to avoid the confusion with the <u>Waw</u>
/w/, when realized as [v]. This corresponded to the situation in
Arabic wherein the /b/ has no complementary distribution of b-v,
which led some observers to the conclusion that he, and later his
colleague Wilkomitz, were directly influenced by Arabic. But this
is evidently not the case. My investigations in the area and among
people who were closely connected with both Epstein and Wilkomitz
(including their children) indicate that the pronunciation of the indigenous Sephardim, i.e. the Sephardim of Zefat and all Upper Galilee, was the decisive factor, as we shall see below, although the
original influence on the Sephardim themselves probably came from
Arabic.

Epstein moved to head the school in Metullah, when it was founded
in 1896, and then to Rosh-Pinnah in 1899, and tried to disseminate
his new pronunciation in both. He spent about three years in Rosh-
Pinnah, until his departure for studies in Switzerland in 1902. When
he returned, after World War I, he had evidently abandoned the
'[b] pronunciation', i.e. he reinstated the allophonic distinction b-v,
but solved the problem of phonetic identity of the 'Vet' allophone and
the 'Vav' (<u>Waw</u>) phoneme by adding the realization of the <u>Vav</u> as [w],
as we shall see in a moment.

Epstein did advocate in his writings, in several places, the need
for the realization (or 'restoration') of the 'proper' pronunciation
not only of the pharyngeals (the so-called 'gutturals') <u>ʕayin</u> and <u>ḥet</u>,
in the manner they are pronounced by the Sephardi (Oriental) Jews,
but even that of the palatal and velar emphatics, [ṭ], [k], for /ṭ/,
/q/, respectively. However, he did not write explicitly about the
so-called 'Bet pronunciation'. It is mentioned only in a general way
in a footnote to a later article: 'Evidently, the ancient Hebrew speaker
did not have the fricative allophones of B-K-P; at any rate, he did not
distinguish them so distinctly from the stops, as we do'.[13]

We discuss the whole (historical) problem of spirantization of
/bkp/ and of the entire group of nonemphatic plosives /bgdkpt/ elsewhere.[14] If we concentrate here on the /b/, the spirantization rule
will roughly be as follows:

$$b \rightarrow v/V - \begin{Bmatrix} \# \\ (C)V \end{Bmatrix}$$
condition: $(C) \neq b$

This is part of a general rule (historically and ideally) for all the other nonemphatic plosives in Hebrew which is roughly:

$$
\begin{bmatrix} C_i \\ -\text{ vocalic} \\ -\text{ low} \\ -\text{ nasal} \\ -\text{ continuant} \end{bmatrix} \rightarrow [+ \text{ continuant}]/V - \left\{ \begin{matrix} \# \\ (C_j)V \end{matrix} \right\}
$$

condition: $C_i \neq C_j$

In the current prevailing Israeli Hebrew this rule does not apply to /gd/ and to /t/. Epstein wanted such an exemption to apply to /b/, which is not common in most other Hebrew traditions.

As mentioned above, in his Galilean days, Epstein advocated the de-spirantization of the 'dageshless' (fricative) <u>Bet</u>, or the combining of the two allophones [b~v] of /b/ into one phonetic entity [b], in order to distinguish it from the <u>Vav</u>/<u>Waw</u> which he, as in most traditions, had realized as [v]. However, in his later years he returned to retaining the complementary distribution of [b~v] for /b/, but resolved the resulting identity of the fricative labio-dental allophone [v] of /b/ and of the (common) [v] value for the <u>Vav</u>/<u>Waw</u> by 're-introducing' the realization of the latter as [w], not as [v]. Thus:

In stage I   /b/ →[b]
                    /w/ →[v]

In stage II   /b/ →[b~v]
                    /w/ →[w]

For all practical purposes, his association with the special Galilean dialect terminated with his departure to Switzerland in 1902.

Epstein fathered that special offspring, but Simḥah Ḥayyim Wilkomitz was the one that fostered it and raised it to become an independent Upper-Galilean dialect. Its main features, compared with the prevalent speech, were the realization of the /ḥ/ as the voiceless pharyngeal spirant [ḥ], and of the /ʕ/, which are realized by most Sephardi Jews, and which were recommended for adoption as part of the ideal pronunciation for the revived Hebrew, by most of the early planners of the revival, such as Ben-Yehuda, Yellin, and others. The most conspicuous feature, however, and one that deviated from most traditions, was the realization of the 'dageshless' <u>Bet</u> (or the <u>Vet</u> allophone of /b/) as a plosive [b], rather than fricative [v]. Therefore this dialect was referred to, as mentioned above, as the 'Bet Dialect', although it was not uncommon in several Hebrew traditions, e. g. Iraq, Egypt, Northern Palestine, and Southern Syria and Lebanon.

Unlike Epstein, Wilkomitz came in 1896 as a trained teacher first to Rehovot in Judea, and in 1896 he replaced Epstein in Metullah in Upper Galilee, and when Epstein left in 1902, Wilkomitz replaced him in Rosh-Pinnah, which was the largest modern Jewish settlement there, and had the largest school. Epstein and Wilkomitz were evidently good friends and both were interested in promoting Hebrew education, revival of Hebrew, and the like. Wilkomitz was immediately sold on the idea of a special Galilean dialect and promoted it until his untimely death in 1918. [15]

Wilkomitz was a superb teacher and inspiring educator--but also very firm and resolute. Involved in the overall problem of the national revival, he propagated the idea of both physical and spiritual revival, and of a rural school as a good means for that and for the productivization of the Jewish people. And indeed, before long he turned his school in Rosh-Pinnah into the finest rural school in the country where the teaching of all subjects, academic and applied, was of the highest quality. It became a model school.

This was one of the first schools where all subjects, secular and religious, academic and applied, were taught only in Hebrew, which was most important for the actual revival of the language. Wilkomitz's home became a model Hebrew home (his wife was a Hebrew teacher too), and he insisted on Hebrew not only at school but also in the playground, and persuaded the children to bring the new language to their homes, and teach their siblings, and their parents too. And since he was a very consistent and perseverant man, it goes without saying, that he fought very hard for the dissemination of the Galilean dialect. This task became somewhat easier administratively when he became superintendent in the Upper Galilean schools.

His demands for speaking Hebrew at school and at home and for adopting his recommended pronunciation were evidently accepted not only because he was a revered, inspiring, pedantic, and insisting teacher, colleague, principal, and superintendent, but it also seems to me that there was an important sociological factor added to the linguistic phenomenon: he gave the youngsters of Rosh-Pinnah and the other Galilean villages a sense of pride--pride in their school, in their education, in their occupation as farmers in the remote Galilee, and pride in their unique dialect, which could boast direct connection with and retention of the flavor of the indigenous dialect of the ancient Galileans.

One may also say that there was the following social motivation for the sound change of /b/ → [b] instead of the common /b/ → [b v] (or the despirantization of Vet). The isolated Galilean farmers, who may have been looked down upon by the 'cocky' Judeans, wished to become

'special' and excel in something--so they showed that they were
capable, for instance, of acquiring in full the difficult 'model'
Sephardi pronunciation (in which the Judeans failed), adding to it the
rare pronunciation of the Bet as a sort of 'prestige marker'. [16] This
was enhanced by the above claim of continuing an ancient tradition of
a genuine Galilean dialect maintained by the original Galileans and
their Sephardi descendants.

For the children, that was the 'normal' language (cf. the case of
creolized languages), and although they acquired it at school as a
'second language', through the efforts of their teachers to 'surround'
them with it, it soon became their primary language not only at
school. They brought it home to their siblings and parents, and used
it. Successive dense 'generations' of children (and a 'generation' in
the children's society corresponds, more or less, to a school year!)
soon nativized the language in their own way. [17] In spite of the various
objective advantages of Judea, the actual revival of Hebrew was more
successful in Upper Galilee at the beginning of the Century.

Some of the younger parents joined the circle of Hebrew speakers,
but the major resource of Hebrew speakers was the growing community of young natives, so that by the beginning of World War I there
were already many native young adults, including young parents, who
were brought up on the Galilean dialect.

At that time several events took place which upset the entire
development of the dialect: (1) communication between Upper Galilee and the rest of the country improved, so that Galilee was no
longer so isolated and contacts with speakers of the main 'standard'
language increased, [18] (2) many Judeans were exiled during the war
to Upper Galilee--another exposure to the main speech, (3) the untimely death of Wilkomitz in 1918, which dealt a death blow to the
Galilean dialect, and (4) when mass immigration started after World
War I, with excessive mobility of the population, including the devoted teachers of the Wilkomitz era--there was nothing to hold the
dialect together, and its dissolution started.

But before we describe that phase, let us say a few words about
its struggle in the Teachers' Assemblies and within the Hebrew Language Committee. The Founding Assembly of the Hebrew Teachers'
Association was held in Zikhron-Ya'akov, in 1903. Yellin was
elected President, Wilkomitz, Secretary, and Ben-Yehuda presented
a scholarly lecture about the various pronunciation traditions, suggesting that the Sephardi pronunciation was better. Also, since the
Ashkenazim (Western Jews) had already largely adopted the pronunciation of the Sephardim (Oriental Jews), even in the earlier contacts
between them in Palestine, 'if we come to change the pronunciation,
we will create great confusion and hurt the schools and the development of the Hebrew speech very much'. [19] This was an overstatement,

since neither the Sephardi pronunciation, nor the Ashkenazied version thereof, which became the 'Israeli Hebrew', really prevailed. Yellin doubted its greater 'correctness', but liked its 'charming oriental flavor which is more pleasant to the listener', while Wilkomitz argued for a uniform pronunciation for all schools. The Galilean dialect figured only marginally in that Assembly. [20] Perhaps not many teachers from other parts of the country were as yet fully aware of it, or willing to make a formal issue of it.

However, in the 1904 Assembly in Gedera it figured very prominently. In his major address on 'The Pronunciation and the Spelling in Hebrew', Yellin proposed a 'proper' realization for all the letters (graphemes) of Hebrew, referring to the Galilean dialect only implicitly by rejecting the /b/ → [b] realization in the Sephardi pronunciation 'in several localities'. He attributed it to Arabic influence, and advocated the pronunciation of the Vav/Waw as [w], rather than [v], (like Epstein's Phase II solution). [21]

The Galilean representative, Juda Antebi, himself a zealous genuine native speaker of that dialect, was worried about his dialect and tried to postpone a full debate, proposing the appointment of a 'committee of experts' from Palestine and abroad, which should thoroughly study the problem of changing the pronunciation and submit its conclusions to the next convention--'then we will decide on something for the generations to come'. But others demanded to decide right away about the Galilean pronunciation, particularly of the /b/, 'since it is utterly unpleasant to see that in the Land of Israel, all of which could be considered as one district in any other country, there will be a difference in pronunciation among its citizens . . . This difference stands out especially in the pronunciation of the Bet, which the Galileans always pronounce like the plosive [b]'.

Another factor which turned out to play ten to fifteen years later, a crucial role in the dissolution of the dialect was pointed out: 'Besides, the distance between the North and the South, i.e. between the Galileans and Judeans, is diminishing from day to day by means of the railways which have been spreading in the country'. Mr. Meyuhas pointed out other sociolinguistic factors: 'The Galileans are at a disadvantage for two reasons: (1) because Galileans were already considered even in the Talmud (almost two millenia ago) as people who were not too careful in their pronunciation, (2) because they are the minority'. Then, he accused the 'few Galilean teachers' that 'they are the cause for widening the gap between the future pronunciations in the schools', and demanded: 'Being a small minority they should yield to the large majority, as the teachers from the Diaspora do when they come here'. Antebi tried to save his dialect by arguing that 'we cannot, obviously, decide on the pronunciation of the 'dageshless Bet' (Vet allophone) before we agree upon the pronunciation of the Vav/Waw' which has a bearing on the problem of the students' spelling too.

To make a long story short, [22] the voting was postponed, but the eventual verdict was against the 'secessionist' dialect. Yellin's concluding words may provide insight into that confrontation between the majority 'planning' and the minority 'counterplanning':

> The Galileans . . . are afriad of being outvoted by the majority on the question of the pronunciation of the 'dageshless Bet' (Vet); therefore they wish to postpone it . . . I do not object . . . but I should like to mention . . . that according to my lecture, the Judeans will have to give up more of what they were used to, and change their pronunciation much more than the Galileans. We must realize that we are confronted with a basic . . . problem . . . a ruling for generations, and when the hour of decision comes, all of us will have to give up our speech habits, and accept the pronunciation which we will find proper and true.

In effect, neither one gave up anything. The Judeans never adopted the ideal Sephardi pronunciation 'engineered' by Yellin, and the Galileans went on with their dialect. Evidently the Galilean dialect was doing fine, since a new attack was staged on it as late as 1913 in the Hebrew Language Committee, which consisted of many of the 1904 challengers, with Yellin again as the main speaker. Only Eytan was 'inclined to grant the right of existence to both pronunciations until life itself will determine the winner'. [23]

Life itself determined the winner in its own way. As mentioned above, transportation improved and the isolated Upper Galilee lost its splendid isolation. New immigrants arrived and stronger ties developed with the main administrative, economical, political, and cultural centers in Judea, which increased the exposure to the Judean 'standard' speech. Also, for lack of high schools, etc., there, the Galileans had to go to Judea, where they were exposed to the Judean speech, and to some humorous comments, which had effects too.

For some of the young Galileans, the geographical mobility, for studying or the like, resulted in social mobility, in which case they would try to get rid of the Galilean 'stigma'--the Bet. But such speakers can be detected to this very day not only by 'slips of the tongue', but by hypercorrections in changing legitimate [b]'s into [v]'s, e. g. medaver for medaber 'speaking'. Often, those who returned for good to Upper Galilee demonstrated the greatest loyalty to its dialect. This is an interesting sociolinguistic phenomenon which was observed by Labov in the case of Martha's Vineyard Island. [24]

With the death of Wilkomitz in 1918 and the post-World War I mobility, which brought about migration of many of the pioneering teachers and the original native settlers to other parts of the country, the dialect lost its devoted defenders and main carriers, and there were no new replacements. Thus the middle 1920s may be considered the 'official' end of the dialect. From then on there was no continuity into new generations except for the original speakers who retained it in their own speech, i. e. those that could withstand the pressures of the standard language.

What remained after that is a legend and a rather distorted image in the minds of the contemporaries and several phrases (Shibboleths) for ridicule. A grotesque illustration may be found in a recent play Yamim šel zahav 'Days of Gold' by S. Sheva. It is based on some misconceptions about the dialect and its speakers.

For completeness, I might add that it is also mentioned, with some humor, in novels by S. Zemach, and by S. Y. Agnon, and a whole poem is dedicated to it by Shimꞓoni (see References). Otherwise, the dialect is just about dead and buried.

It is often lamented that we do not have adequate evidence for the date a language or dialect ceased to be spoken. In our case, we had a chance to follow the Galilean dialect from the cradle to the grave, including the 'dramatic event' of its death, and we have even seen the distorted epitaph on the tombstone--an example of planning, counter-planning, and even backplanning on the part of those who later came up with a distorted image of its essence.

NOTES

[1]Cf. Chaim Rabin, 'The Mechanics of the Revival of Hebrew', in Aaron Bar-Adon, ed. (in press).

[2]Some relevant studies, of those that are mentioned in our references, include: Blanc, Bar-Adon, Morag, Rabin, and Sadan. There are also related studies by: Ben-Hayyim, Eisenstadt, Kutscher, Rosén, Sivan, Ullendorff, Weinberg, and a forthcoming one by Fishman, Rabin, and Fellman.

[3]See Bar-Adon 1959, 1963, 1964, 1965, 1966, 1967, 1968, 1971a, 1971b.

[4]It will consist of three volumes: (1) The History of the Revival of Hebrew, (2) Selected Oral Sources, and (3) An Annotated Bibliography. Several studies included in the References are closely related to it.

[5]I have interviewed and recorded in the past decade hundreds of the earliest participators in that revival, including representatives of the first influx of pioneers to Palestine ('The First 'Aliyah'); of associates of Ben-Yehuda; of the first teachers, authors, artists,

political leaders and their lay contemporaries, as well as of the first native speakers of Hebrew in the various sectors and areas in Israel.

[6]In many cases, however, one has the distinct feeling that the pathetic praise is no more than 'lip service'. An example of a popular book on Ben-Yehuda, based on his family sources to a large extent and attributing to him all developments not only in the Hebrew linguistic revival but also in the entire national revival, is Robert St. John's, Tongue of the Prophets, New York: Doubleday, 1952. It is a most delightful novel about Ben-Yehuda, but obviously it cannot be considered as a scholarly study of the revival or even Ben-Yehuda's role in it. Everybody and everything else is dwarfed compared with Ben-Yehuda and his accomplishments.

[7]Especially in Bar-Adon (1970) and (in press a), (1972), and (forthcoming a, b). A long chapter is devoted to him in the study mentioned in note 4.

[8]See Zutta (1929:116).

[9]Cf. Epstein (1947b:17) and Zemach (1967). For more details see The Rise and Decline, footnote 12.

[10]Why only grade-school students? Because there were no high schools until the opening of Gimnasia Herzeliyah in Jaffa (later Tel-Aviv).

[11]Cf. Bar-Adon (1959, 1963, 1965, 1966, 1967, 1968, 1971b, 1972, and forthcoming a).

[12]The literature of the period is full of complaints by concerned educators. I have also interesting oral evidence from some of the first teachers. Details in another study.

[13]See Epstein (1947a:27).

[14]See details in The Rise and Decline, chapters 6-7. They include a discussion of the various Hebrew traditions relative to the realization of /bgdkpt/, and /b/ in particular.

[15]To this day, more than fifty years since his death, he is remembered in Upper Galilee as 'The Teacher' (ha-moreh).

[16]Cf. Labov (1963, 1968:242f).

[17]Cf. Bar-Adon (1967).

[18]Many native speakers told me that they were convinced that theirs was the only 'normal' or 'natural' way of speaking Hebrew, and they were surprised to find a different pronunciation elsewhere, where they 'pronounce the Bet like Vav . . . ' One old-timer could swear that Ben-Yehuda spoke their way, too (which is, of course, wrong).

[19]See Ha-moréh (1959:128).

[20]For details see The Rise and Decline, chapter 11.

[21]See Yellin (1905).

[22]See details in The Rise and Decline, chapter 12.

[23]An interesting document is Zutta's commendation of the Galilean schools 'whose students speak Hebrew in a pure Sephardi pronunciation [disregarding the Bet] . . . while our teachers in Judea are still negligent in this'.

[24]For other points of resemblance, see The Rise and Decline, chapter 18.

REFERENCES

Agnon, S. Y. 1952-1953. [C]Ad hénah, collected works. 2nd ed, vol. 7.
_____. 1969. Recorded interview with him on the revival of Hebrew. January 1969. To appear as an Appendix to Bar-Adon (forthcoming a).
[C]Al ha-rišonim. 1959. Ed. D. Levin. Tel-Aviv, The Teachers' Association Center.
Bachi, R. 1955. A statistical analysis of the revival of Hebrew in Israel. Scripta Hierosolymitana. 179-247.
Bar-Adon, Aaron. 1959. Children's Hebrew in Israel. 2 vols. Jerusalem, mimeo. [In Hebrew with English summary].
_____. 1963. The Hebrew speech of the younger generation in Israel as subject for linguistic research. Hachinuch. 35.21-35. [In Hebrew].
_____. 1964. Analogy and analogic change as reflected in contemporary Hebrew. Proceedings of the Ninth International Congress of Linguists. The Hague, Mouton. 758-64. Reprinted in Bar-Adon and Leopold, eds. 1971:302-06.
_____. 1965. The evolution of modern Hebrew. In: Acculturation and integration. Ed. by J. C. Teller. New York, Histadrut Cultural Exchange Institute. 65-95.
_____. 1966. Shifts in the stress patterns of Israeli Hebrew. Mimeo. Abstract presented at the 1963 Annual Meeting of the Linguistic Society of America.
_____. 1967. Processes of nativization in contemporary Hebrew. Mimeo. To appear in revised form in A. Bar-Adon, ed. (in press b).
_____. 1968. Word order and syntactic structures in children's Hebrew: The initial stages. In: Papers of the Fourth (1965) World Congress of Jewish Studies. Jerusalem. 123-28.
_____. 1970. Studies in the revival of modern Hebrew: The rise and decline of a Galilean dialect. Austin, The University of Texas. Mimeo. To appear in revised form as Bar-Adon (in press a).
_____. 1971a. Primary syntactic structures in Hebrew child language. In: A. Bar-Adon and W. F. Leopold, eds. 1971:433-72.

Bar-Adon, Aaron. 1971b. Child bilingualism in an immigrant society. Preprints of the Chicago Conference on Child Language, 1971:264-318. Quebec, International Centre for Research on Bilingualism, Université Laval.

_____. 1972. S. Y. Agnon and the revival of modern Hebrew. Texas Studies in Language and Literature.

_____. In press a. The rise and decline of a dialect: A study in the revival of modern Hebrew. The Hague, Mouton.

_____, ed. In press b. The revival of modern Hebrew. Proceedings of a Symposium, The University of Texas Press.

_____. Forthcoming a. Shay ^CAgnon u-tehiyyat ha-lašon (S. Y. Agnon and the language revival). Tel-Aviv, Schocken Publishing House. In Hebrew.

_____. Forthcoming b. Studies in the history of the revival of modern Hebrew: The emergence of an Upper Galilee dialect. In Hebrew.

Ben-Yehuda, Eliezer. 1918. Ha-halom ve-šivro (The dream and its solution). An autobiography, first published in Hatoren (New York) 4 (1917-18), in 13 chapters. Reprinted in Ben-Yehuda 1943:i-lxix.

_____. 1943. Collected works, vol. I. Jerusalem. In Hebrew.

Blanc, Haim. 1957. Hebrew in Israel: Trends and problems. The Middle East Journal. 11.397-410.

Epstein, Izhac (Yitzhak). 1947a. Hegyoney lašon. Tel-Aviv.

_____. 1947b. Studies in the psychology of the language and Hebrew education. Jerusalem, Kohelet. In Hebrew.

Ha-moréh. 1959. [In memory of Wilkomitz]. J. Riklis, ed. Jerusalem.

Labov, William. 1963. The social motivation of a sound change. Word. 19.273-306.

_____. 1968. The reflection of social processes in linguistic structures. In: Readings in the Sociology of language. Ed. by J. Fishman. The Hague, Mouton. 240-51.

Morag, Shelomo. 1959. Planned and unplanned developments in modern Hebrew. Lingua. 3.247-63.

_____. 1962. The vocalization systems of Arabic, Hebrew, and Aramaic. The Hague, Mouton.

Rabin, Chaim. 1967. Sociological factors in the history of the Hebrew language. New York, Department of Education and Culture of the Jewish Agency. 13 pp.

_____. 1969. The revival of the Hebrew language. Journal of Tamil Studies. 1.41-60.

_____. 1970. The role of language in forging a nation: The case of Hebrew. The Incorporated Linguist. January 1970.

_____. 1971. The language revival and the changes in the status and character of Hebrew. Orot (Jerusalem). 10.61-77.

THE RISE AND DECLINE OF AN UPPER-GALILEE DIALECT / 101

Rabin, Chaim. In press. The mechanics of the revival of Hebrew. In: A. Bar-Adon, ed. (In press b).

Sadan, Dov. 1970. ^Civrit li-gvurot (Hebrew to its 80th birthday). Hadoar. 40(10).150-52.

Sheva, S. 1965. Yamim šel zahav (Days of gold), a play. In: Teatron (Haifa), vol. 16, June-July 1965.

Sefer ha-yovel šel histadrut ha-morim (The Jubilee book of the Teachers' Association). 1903-1928. Ed. by D. Ḳimḥi. Jerusalem, The Teachers' Association.

Shim^coni, David. 1928. The struggle between Judea and Galilee. An idyl. In Hebrew. In his Writings, vol. 2, Tel-Aviv, Dvir. 33-42.

Tur-Sinai (Torizyner), N. H. 1936. The scholarly work of Eliezer Ben-Yehuda. Ha-'aretz. December 15, 1936. In Hebrew.

Wilkomitz, S. H. 1959. See Ha-morêh.

Yellin, David. 1905. Ha-mivta' ve-ha-ketiv be-^civrit. Jerusalem.

——. 1914. About the 'Hebrew Language Committee' in Jerusalem. In: Histadrut la-safa ve-la-tarbut ha-^civrit be-Berlin. Warsaw. 108-16.

——. 1923. Ben-Yehuda and the revival of the Hebrew language. Journal of Palestine Oriental Society. 3.93-109. A bilingual Hebrew-English article.

Zemach (Zemaḥ). 1956. Pirḥey remiyyah. Reprinted in his Collected writings. Tel-Aviv, Dvir.

——. 1967. Recorded interview. Jerusalem, August, 1967.

Zutta, J. 1929. Bema^caleh ha-har (Uphill). In: Sefer ha-yovel. 112-29.

APPENDIX

GENERAL PRINCIPLES
FOR THE CULTIVATION OF GOOD LANGUAGE

Translated by Paul L. Garvin

Translator's introductory note. This year's Georgetown Round Table on Sociolinguistics happens to fall on the fortieth anniversary of the Prague School's major contribution to language planning, the 1932 radio lecture series and resulting volume on <u>Standard Czech and the Cultivation of Good Language</u>.

At the end of the volume, the Prague School presents another of its sets of theses, this one setting forth its recommendations for the linguist's contribution to the cultivation of good language. These recommendations are remarkably up-to-date and are clearly applicable to many language-planning situations in today's world. Since they have never previously been published in any of the world's major languages, they deserve being reprinted here in English translation as a contribution to the current debate over language planning.

By the cultivation of good language we mean the conscious fostering of the standard language; this can be done by (1) theoretical linguistic work, (2) language education in the schools, and (3) literary practice.

These theses are concerned with the establishment of general principles only for the kind of theoretical linguistic work that actively affects the standard language; this effect can be either favorable or harmful, unless the contribution of the linguist is only for appearances' sake. Theoretical linguistic work can be useful to the standard language only by helping to make sure that the general language meets its

tasks most effectively; this can be accomplished by (1) contributing
to the stability of the standard language, and (2) contributing to its
functional differentiation and its stylistic enrichment; an indispensable
condition for both is the best possible understanding of the current
standard language, that is, of its norm as it exists in fact.

1. At the root of the successful cultivation of the standard language must be the theoretical understanding of the real norm of the
contemporary standard language.

The time span for considering the standard language as contemporary in each case depends on the period when the standard language
became relatively stabilized in its current form. The Czech standard
language became stabilized with respect to the basic features of its
grammatical structure at approximately the time of the national
renascence (particularly through the work of Josef Dobrovský) and in
some other respects not until the end of the 19th century (particularly
through the grammars written by Jan Gebauer); in regard to its vocabulary the Czech standard language in its present form can be considered stabilized only from the 80's of the 19th century on, and in
regard to technical language even later; some aspects of Czech technical terminology are just now becoming stabilized.

The understanding of the norms of the contemporary standard language cannot be based on either a prior norm of the standard or any
form of folk speech, either current or past--contrary to some opinions voiced in [the purist literature]; nor can an understanding of the
norm of the standard be based only on the language used for one particular functional purpose or by one particular literary trend, or in
just one given area of science or of daily life.

It must be based above all on the average literary language practice
over the past fifty years. One should, however, not exclude that portion of the belletristic and technical literature which during the 19th
century served to prepare the current stabilization of the standard
language; in using the older literature (for instance the language of
Palacký, Havlícek, Němcová, Tyl) we must differentiate those elements that have passed into the current standard language from those
that have disappeared from it or have occurred in these works only
as the result of an oscillation between literary and folk elements or
that have maintained themselves only as an echo of the older language.
As far as poetic language is concerned, that is, the language of both
older and contemporary belles lettres, only its nonforegrounded elements can serve as a basis for the norm (and only to the extent that
they are not ossified foregroundings out of the older literary canon);
they must be differentiated from the foregroundings of poetic language
which function as intentional distortions of the norm, and in general
from all possible structural exploitation of various functional, local

and class languages and dialects; one must also take into account the different attitudes that various authors may take towards a standard norm. The foregroundings characteristic of poetic language may, of course, sometimes by a later development pass on into the norm of the standard language, but this usually happens independently of the poet's intention.

Another source of the norms of the current standard language is the linguistic intuition which intellectuals today have for the standard, as well as their oral linguistic practice, but of course excluding any personal local or slangy coloring. Note:

(1) We are here dealing with average literary language practice without any esthetic or factual valuation, not with the language of the average writers.

(2) The above mentioned linguistic intuition and contemporary literary and oral language practice could be called 'the living standard language' or 'standard usage'; the terms 'living language' and 'usage' should, however, not be used as inaccurately as is often done: in using these terms, very often no difference is made between folk language or usage, colloquial language or usage, standard language or usage; very often also 'the living language' is presented as the opposite of the standard language.

(3) We must keep clearly in mind that the standard language does not exist outside of literary and other public texts, be they written or oral; contrary to what [the recent purist literature] might want one to believe.

(4) We must clearly differentiate between, on the one hand, the sources for the technical theoretical understanding of the real contemporary norm of the standard language, and on the other hand, the sources which any user of the standard language can take advantage of to find out about the devices of the language and the various possibilities that the language offers; the sources of an individual utterance may include the language of another period than the present or the language pertaining to another function than that characterizing the utterance.

So far not much has been done in our country in the area of the theoretical understanding of the contemporary standard language. Theoretical understanding and normative codification has been achieved only for the current grammatical structure of standard Czech, particularly its morphology, and all of this only in its gross features and with some definite archaicizing tendencies. The vocabulary of the current standard language is theoretically very poorly known.

The desired understanding of the standard language will require some well coordinated and planned systematic work beginning with some practical manuals and including the monographic treatment of key linguistic details. This work will of course have to be carried out by a strictly synchronic and structural method (that is, it will have to be conducted with constant attention to the interrelationship of the components and their individual relationship to the total system of the language of a given period--in our case, the contemporary period); this method cannot be replaced by a mere statistical method which does no more than mechanically accumulate the material and which, by its assumption that the understanding of the norm requires the prior determination of the usage of all authors and the frequency of use of all speech phenomena by these authors, is more in the way of the work than anything else.

[One-paragraph-long note left out.]

2. It is true that the standard language is not simply stabilized by the dictates of linguistic theory, but its stabilization nevertheless does not occur without normative theoretical interventions. The most powerful interventions by linguistic theory are in the area of orthography, less in the area of the grammatical structure of the language --that is, its phonological, morphological and syntactic structure-- and least in its lexical structure and content.

The following general guidelines can be established for normative theoretical interventions:

(1) These interventions should enhance the stabilization of the standard language and not interfere with it in cases where the language itself has been able to achieve it.

(2) Their aim should not be to historicize and artificially slow down the development of the standard language, but to achieve a stabilization determined by purposiveness (the functional viewpoint), by the taste of the period (the esthetic point of view), and in conformity with the real state of the current standard language (the synchronic point of view).

(3) Such interventions should not artificially deepen the difference in grammatical structure between colloquial speech and the language of the books, unless precisely these differences are to be functionally exploited.

(4) It would be pointless for such theoretical interventions to try to eliminate all oscillation or all grammatical and lexical doublets (grammatical and lexical synonymity) from the standard language. This would be pointless for two reasons: on the one hand, the tendency towards the stabilization of the standard language should not be allowed to lead to a complete leveling out, that is to say to the removal of the necessary functional and stylistic diversification of the standard

language; on the other hand, the standard language would then incur
the danger of depriving itself of the means necessary for the elimination of tedious repetition where such repetition is not intentional--
that is, of the means for stylistic differentiation.

2.1. The codification of the orthography, that is to say of a
stabilized manner of writing, deals on the one hand with an orthographic system, on the other hand with its implementation in detail
(that is, for individual words).

Ideally, a spelling system should represent the phonological
system of a language rather than its phonetic realization, nor should
it forget either the differential morphological exploitation of the
phonology or the visual function of a style of writing and its effect
upon reading. An orthographic system once established should of
course not be changed without good reason; this is why an established system and all proposed changes must be carefully examined
from the point of view of their theoretical validity as well as their
practical usefulness.

The application of the system to individual words must be carefully worked out and as far as possible it should be simple, clear-cut,
and consistent. Here again the phonological structure of the word and
the need for morphological differentiation should be the determining
factors, and not the phonetic structure. The introduction of unusual
spellings for purely historical reasons is to be avoided [example
left out].

[Two paragraphs left out.]

The spelling of foreign words, particularly common ones, should
not follow an orthographic system different from that used for domestic words [examples left out]. On the other hand, it is neither desirable nor useful to adapt international terms to the domestic spelling system and by this change in their written shape introduce a
strange graphic pattern which isolates them from their international
connection (if, for instance, the term joule were to be spelled according to its pronunciation); thus, the original spelling is acceptable for
technical terms in the narrower sense, particularly if they are used
in the technical literature or as trademarks; likewise, proper names
which have not been Bohemianized can clearly be spelled in line with
the original system.

There is a need for the study of recurrent spelling mistakes in
order to differentiate between the traces of older codification and the
inadequacies of current codification or its unnecessary complexity;
when dealing with the orthography one should not forget either the
needs of the schools or those of the broad masses.

Note:

(1) We must differentiate between a theoretical consideration--
concerning either the orthographic system or the details of
its implementation--and the normative intervention itself.

(2) Any intended changes in either the system itself or the details of its implementation should always be announced in
advance, in order to allow for the discussion and criticism
that can only be of benefit to it.

[Two paragraphs left out.]

2.2. The stabilization of standard pronunciation is the job of
orthophony. The standard pronunciation has to be based on the pronunciation of the intellectual circles who speak the standard language
and not the folk pronunciation of any dialect community, not even the
folk pronunciation of important centers such as Prague; nor can it be
based on the folk pronunciation that may be geographically most widespread.

The standard pronunciation requires a highly developed functional
differentiation in terms of the different purposes to which different
utterances are put, and this functional differentiation has to serve as
the basis for the determination of types of pronunciation without the
kind of graded evaluation that is customary in orthoepy ('careful,
careless' pronunciation, etc.). In addition to the normalization of
the correct pronunciation of the standard language attention must
also be given to its esthetic development (euphony . . .).

Particular attention must be given to artistic reading and theatrical
pronunciation, both from the standpoint of its esthetic function in
terms of different poetic and dramatic trends and from the standpoint
of different conditions of performance; we need a professionally sound
theatrical orthoepy. Special conditions of performance may determine
the manner of pronunciation, for instance in broadcasting etc., and
we must study the type of pronunciation suited for these purposes.

2.3. The stabilization of the grammatical structure of the standard
language, which includes its phonological, morphological, and syntactic aspects, is enhanced by linguistic theory on the one hand by
the understanding of the norm as it really exists, on the other hand
by its codification.

The theoretical understanding of the norm has already been talked
about above.

The codification of the properly understood grammatical norm must
pay attention to the fact that even in the case of the standard language
evolution is unavoidable; the codifying effort should not try to arrest

this evolution by artificially and uselessly maintaining or even introducing archaic forms, particularly morphological ones, as the only
correct ones for the standard--as has been done in some cases in the
[purist journals] and the <u>Rules of Czech Orthography</u> [examples left
out]; this would only serve to increase unnecessarily the morphological differences between the literary and the spoken language, as
has already been noted above. The unavoidable development of language brings about the currently existing doublets that have found
their way into the standard language and should not be removed from
it, as has already been noted above in our general guidelines. These
are usually functional doublets (for instance the functional difference
between a genitival and an accusatival construction governed by a
negative verb), but there may also sometimes exist doublets without
a consistent functional difference and they do not do the language any
harm either (for instance infinitives ending in -<u>ti</u> and -<u>t</u>); even such
doublets may at times be exploited functionally or stylistically.
Doublets may also come into the standard language by incorporating
forms from another social dialect and taking advantage of the functional difference [examples left out].

The phonological structure of contemporary standard Czech has
on the whole become quite stabilized and is well known. The few
exceptions are due, as has already been mentioned, to the penetration
of the sound pattern of colloquial Czech into the standard, mainly in
the case of doublets with different shades of meaning and of words of
a certain semantic domain where the corresponding standard forms
do not exist [examples left out].

As far as the morphology is concerned, the current state of
affairs is neither fully known nor satisfactorily codified in all respects. Consistent synchronic description and the analysis of the
real state of affairs will reveal its present structure which has been
masked by the diachronic treatment given to it so far and has been
subject to archaicization, as has already been noted. The codified
norm must therefore reduce the number of obsolete forms that maintain a limited existence in the standard language and mark them ex-
pressly as archaisms [remainder of paragraph left out].

As far as syntax is concerned, one should keep in mind--in addition to the general principles discussed so far, particularly the one
stating that codification should not unnecessarily maintain archaisms--
not to wipe out, in one's desire for stabilization, the functional differentiation made possible by syntactic doublets, as well as not to
impede the development of the special syntactic devices by which the
language of the books differs from colloquial speech; nor should one
forget that the syntactic differences--just as much as the lexical
ones--between the language of the books and colloquial speech are

among the most common devices for the necessary functional differentiation of the standard language.

2.4. The stabilization of the vocabulary in its formal and semantic aspects is least affected by linguistic theory, except for the possibility of linguistic assistance in the creation of technical terminology which will be discussed further below. Theoretical linguistic work here has more of an indirect effect by studying the vocabulary of the standard language and giving a technical description of its current state. In the process of this 'codification', which in essence consists only in recording that which exists, we must keep in mind that it is impossible to determine the meaning of words without regard to their functional differentiation and that we have to pay heed to the different automatizations that arise from different functions; any foregrounding will by definition always be beyond the pale of the norm of the language (unless of course it has been taken over into the norm of the standard language . . .). A precise delimitation of meanings is a necessary requirement for technical terminology but does not apply to the standard vocabulary as a whole.

Since in addition to syntax it is primarily the lexicon that furnishes the means for differentiating the various functions of the standard language, the standard vocabulary must never be reduced to that proper to only one of its functions, nor can it be limited to what the norm has contained so far. New words again must be judged not only in terms of the way they relate to the formal and semantic types of words already in the vocabulary, but also in terms of their functional value, as well as in terms of the needs of the speech community.

2.5. The theoretical understanding of the norm and its codification contributes to the stabilization of the standard language also by allowing the norm to be handed down and understood by others.

Finally, another contribution of linguistic theory to the stabilization of the standard language is to furnish a critique: the language of particular works can be compared to the theoretically established norm and among the differences that have been noted attention can be pointed to dialectal divergences (be they local or social), to archaisms, to barbarisms (that is, the influence of foreign languages), to neologisms, and to divergencies due to faulty theorizing or misunderstanding of theory. Such divergences should not simply be condemned as sloppiness, etc. (as is done by [the purist journals]), unless it is done for educational purposes in the schools or we deal with a case of obvious incompetence in using the language; they may be due to deficiencies of the theoretically established norm from which the linguist shall and can learn his lesson, or they may represent the beginnings of a new development that cannot be held back, or, finally, we may deal

with a deliberate distortion the effectiveness of which has to be re-
spected in spite of our desires for stabilization. As far as poetic
language is concerned, its very essence dictates that any attempt at
fixing the extent of its deviation from the norm is a contradiction in
terms.

3. The theoretical work of the linguist may also contribute to the
functional differentiation and stylistic enrichment of the standard language; for its functional and stylistic differentiation the standard language requires rich and functionally differentiated means of expression, particularly in the lexicon and the syntax, and effective exploitation of these means.

The linguistic contributions will include the following: (a) collabo-
ration in the creation of technical terminology, (b) assistance in the
development of the functional exploitation of the devices of the language and consistent study and development of the stylistic potential
of the language, and (c) critique of particular works of language from
a functional point of view.

3.1. The creation of technical terminology, which is actually an
endless process, can be effectively helped by linguistic theory; in
doing this the linguist should not only see to it that the new term or
the new adaptation of an existing term should be in accord with the
lexical structure of the Czech language, but he should also pay attention to the effectiveness of the terms and their capacity for functional
burdening. He must therefore keep in mind that scientific and legal
terminologies are adversely affected by a close link to expressions
of everyday use because this brings about not only the kind of multi-
plicity of meaning which is ill-suited for theoretical and legal language, but also the kind of emotional coloring of terms which is un-
desirable [example left out].

By contrast, in the terminology of practical and technological
fields this link to words of everyday use and to their meanings and
emotional coloring not only does no harm but often contributes to the
quick introduction and easy spread of the terms [examples left out].
In developing terminologies for administrative and business purposes
one also must keep in mind the need for fixed formulaic expressions.

In choosing terms those words should be given preference which
allow the easy formation of derivatives [examples left out].

Finally, it is not useful unnecessarily to obscure international
origins of technical terminology: coordination with international
usage is achieved not only by the adoption of foreign international
terms but also by maintaining the semantic coincidence of domestic
with foreign terms.

3.2. Linguistic theory can also enhance the development of the functional effectiveness of the devices of the language and point to new stylistic possibilities:

(1) Linguistics can systematically and in detail ascertain the special linguistic means and their exploitation in different functional dialects as used by either individuals or schools of thought, trends, etc.

Note:

(1) It would for instance be useful for Czech philosophic language to have an analysis of the philosophic terminology of Czech Hegelians, Herbartians, positivists, and others.

(2) We need an analysis of journalistic language from the standpoint of its special requirements, with particular regard to things like clichés.

(2) Linguistics points out the possibilities for the functional differentiation and exploitation of the devices of the language, particularly those of the lexicon and the syntax, as well as the evolutionary trends that have bearing on these; it also makes pertinent recommendations, but of course without forcing all functions on all languages.

(3) Linguistics can systematically develop the stylistics of different functional dialects.

3.3. Finally, linguistic theory may also make its contribution by a critique of particular works of language from a functional point of view. Such a critique should not be based on general criteria such as clarity, precision, etc., but rather should evaluate the means of the language and their utilization only in terms of their adequacy to the purpose of the work, but taking into account the author's right to make his individual choices. Thus, precision should be required only if this is the purpose of the work (after all, imprecision may also be functionally justified); the formulaic expressions of the language of business are to be evaluated from the standpoint of their special purpose, etc. Neither in looking at different purposes of individual instances nor in considering the various functions of the standard language should this critique introduce an evaluative hierarchy that might give some function priority over another. If deviations from the norm are found they should be judged from a functional standpoint. Linguistic critique is essentially different from poetic critique; the latter is always linked to esthetic valuation.

REFERENCES

Bohuslav Havránek and Miloš Weingart, eds. 1932. Spisovná
čeština a jazyková kultura (Standard Czech and the cultivation of good language). Prague, Melantrich. 245-58.